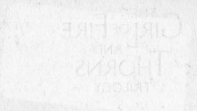

THE BITTER KINGDOM

RAE CARSON

GREENWILLOW BOOKS
An Imprint of HarperCollins *Publishers*

The Bitter Kingdom
Copyright © 2013 by Rae Carson
First published in 2013 in hardcover;
first Greenwillow paperback edition, 2014

The text of this book is set in 11-point Bell.
Book design by Paul Zakris

Library of Congress Cataloging-in-Publication Data
Carson, Rae.
The bitter kingdom / Rae Carson.
"Greenwillow Books."
pages cm
Sequel to: The crown of embers.
Summary: Elisa, a fugitive in her own kingdom, faces great challenges to rescue the man she loves from her enemies, prevent a civil war, and take back her throne but as her magic grows, Elisa discovers the shocking truth about her enemy's ultimate goal.
ISBN 978-0-06-202654-5 (hardback)—ISBN 978-0-06-202656-9 (pbk.)
[1. Kings, queens, rulers, etc.—Fiction. 2. Prophecies—Fiction.
3. Magic—Fiction 4. Love—Fiction.] I. Title.
PZ7.C2423Bit 2013
[Fic]—dc23   2013011912
14 15 16 17 18 LP/RRDH 10 9 8 7 6 5 4 3 2 1
First Edition

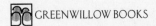 GREENWILLOW BOOKS

FOR MY SISTER, REBEKAH,
WHO WAS THE FIRST TO SAY,
"YOU CAN DO IT."

PART I

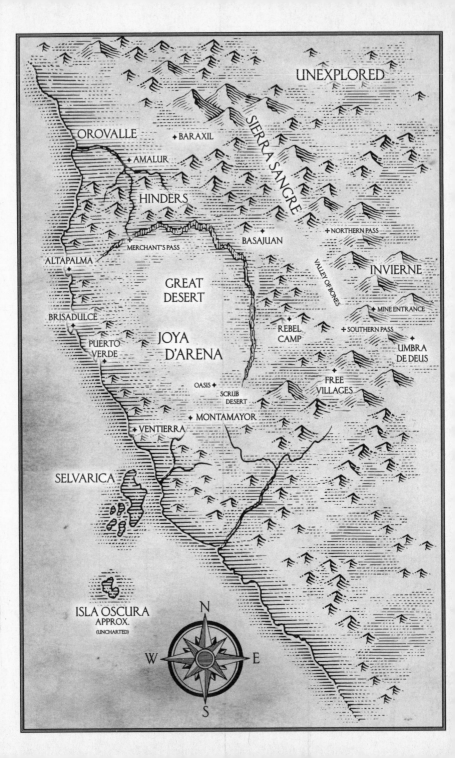

1

WE run.

My heels crunch sandy shale as my legs pound a steady rhythm. With every fourth step, I suck a lungful of dry air. My chest burns, my thighs ache, and the little toe of my left foot stings with the agony of a ripped blister.

Ahead, Belén glances over his shoulder to check on the rest of us. His boots and his tunic and even his leather eye patch are tinged brownish orange with the dust of this desert plateau. We've fallen too far behind, and it's my fault. He checks his stride, but I wave him on.

My companions—an assassin, a lady-in-waiting, and a failed sorcerer—are all more accustomed than I am to hard travel, and I dare not slow us down. We must take advantage of this flat, easy terrain while we can, for we have less than two months to cross the Sierra Sangre, sneak into enemy territory, free Hector, and escape. Otherwise he dies, and the country we've sacrificed so much to save descends into civil war.

I unclench my fists, relax my shoulders so my arms swing

loose, and spring a little harder off of my toes. The burn in my thighs intensifies, but it's only pain, and not nearly the worst I've felt. I'm stronger than I've ever been.

Iron clatters behind me, brittle and sharp. I stop cold and spin, anger bubbling in my chest. But Storm's uncannily beautiful face is so furrowed with frustration that I soften toward him immediately.

His chains have come loose again. They drag in the dust now, streaming from his manacled ankles, each about the length of my forearm. They are magic forged, impossible to remove. The best we can do is wrap them in his leggings so they don't interfere with his stride or, worse, announce our passage.

Mara, my lady-in-waiting, hitches her quiver of arrows higher up onto her shoulder and wipes sweat from her eyes with a filthy sleeve. She sets her bow on the ground and crouches beside Storm's boots. "Maybe if we weave the ties of your boots through the chains . . ."

Storm stretches out an ankle for her. I scowl to see my friend bowed at his feet like a supplicant while he accepts her ministrations with an air of supreme boredom.

"Mara," I say.

She turns a dirt-smeared face to me.

"Storm will be responsible for his own chains from now on."

"Oh, I don't mind!" she says.

"*I* do." Sometimes it's up to me to keep my companions from giving too much of themselves. I wave her off with a mock glare. She rolls her eyes at me, but she grabs her bow and steps away. Storm looks back and forth between us, and I half expect him to protest, but then he shrugs and hunkers down to tend the chains himself.

"We can't go on like this." The low voice in my ear makes me jump. Belén skims the ground like a ghost, even when stealth is unnecessary.

"The next village will have horses that haven't been conscripted," I tell him. "It *has* to."

"And if it doesn't?"

I turn on him. It's bad enough knowing I'll have to mount one of the horrible creatures. But it's worse to consider what I must to do in order to accomplish it. I say, "If the conscription has reached this far east, we'll steal some."

"We're at the very edge of the kingdom!" Mara protests.

Storm straightens and shakes a leg experimentally. The chain stays put. "Conde Eduardo has been planning his rebellion for a long time," he says. "Maybe years. We won't find available transportation until we're in the mountains."

My blood boils, from heat and from anger. Eduardo is one of Joya's most powerful and trusted lords. A member of the Quorum of Five, no less. But he has robbed hundreds, maybe thousands, of their livelihoods to feed his ambition. He has taken their horses and camels, their carriages and food stores, even their young men, for military use. And he has done it so that he can divide my country and crown himself a king.

I grab my water skin from its hook at my waist and take a much deeper draft than I should. I wipe my mouth with the back of my hand and toss the water skin to Mara, who catches it deftly.

"A queen shouldn't have to steal her own horses," Mara says.

"Do you have a better suggestion?" I ask. "Announce our mission, maybe?"

"Stealing will attract attention too."

I nod. "But better than parading in full regalia into the next village and commandeering what I need. With luck, the conde won't hear of the theft for a long time. And if he does, it might not occur to him that it was his queen."

Storm chuckles. "Queen, chosen one, horse thief. Let it never be said that you are not accomplished."

My attempt to glare at him fails when my lips start to twitch.

"In that case . . ." Belén says, a slow grin spreading across his face. "We need a plan."

The sun is low on the horizon, painting the plateau and its toothed outcroppings in fiery shades of coral. The breeze picks up, flinging hair that has loosened from my braids into my eyes and mouth. Though we skirt the great sand desert to the south, the evening wind will kick up enough dust to make travel almost impossible. Not much time left today. "A plan will wait until we've camped for the night," I say.

From habit, I turn to look for Hector, seeking his quiet approval. I don't catch myself until it's too late, until I've lost him all over again.

"Elisa?" Mara says.

I clench my hands into fists. "Let's run," I say. And we do.

2

THE afternoon pours heat onto our backs. The four of us lie on our bellies on a small rocky ridge, peering through the twisting red branches of a manzanita bush to the village below. It's comprised of a smattering of adobe *hutas* and an inn with a stable, all surrounding a cobblestone plaza with its resident well. Date palms rise between buildings, bent eastward from the constant wind. Camels are tethered at the village's southern edge, chewing calmly on a thorn bush. But camels won't take us where we must go. We need horses.

Like all the other villages we've encountered, it's crawling with Eduardo's soldiers. Except this time they wear typical desert garb—linen blouses and sturdy pants, utility belts and long desert cloaks—rather than the red-and-black uniform of Eduardo's countship. Were it not for the red ribbons tied around their arms or pinned to their cloaks, no one would know they were Eduardo's men.

"They've run out of uniforms," Belén whispers. "A good sign."

"Maybe they're short on resources in general," I say hopefully. "Even their weapons look shabby." I peer closer. "Fewer than half carry swords."

"So, what's the plan?" says Mara.

"The horses are stabled behind the inn," says Belén. "That's good. The area isn't visible from the center of the village."

Several men pour from the inn's entrance, laughing and clapping one another on the back. It's an alarming contrast to the regular residents, who scurry from building to building, eyes downcast, trying to look small. "Eduardo's soldiers are using the inn as a temporary barracks," I observe.

"If so, the stable behind it is well guarded," Belén says.

"These are conscripted men," Storm says. "Not regular soldiers. But even if they were trained fighters, they'd likely be as pathetic as the rest of Joya d'Arena's military."

"Our pathetic military defeated yours in a single battle," I snap, before remembering that Storm is probably goading me for personal amusement.

"No, my dear queen, *you* did," he says. "You and your Godstone."

He's right, but I'm not going to give him the satisfaction of conceding. Ignoring him, I reach out and push a branch aside to get a better view.

"Careful, Elisa," Belén says. "We're within sight."

Mindful of his warning, I absorb every detail of the inn below—its awning made of crosshatched branches that cast patterned light on the men beneath it, the small arched windows, the adobe stairway that wraps around the building and leads to a second floor with a dry palapa roof. We are just high enough on our ridge to glimpse the stable behind it. It's very small. No more than eight stalls. There must be direct entry from inside the inn, as well as a larger egress for the horses in back.

"It could catch fire easily," Belén says, too eagerly.

"No!" Two months ago we burned down an inn in Puerto Verde—just to create a distraction. Countless livelihoods were lost. Maybe even a few lives. I promised myself it would never happen again.

"We could take rooms for the night," Mara says. "And sneak out before sunrise with the horses. Belén might have to . . . *dispatch* a guard or two, but it would be better than burning the place down."

"They might recognize their queen," Belén says.

"This far from the capital?"

"Miniatures with my likeness were sent all over the kingdom on the day of my coronation," I say. "Painters copied and recopied it, and . . . wait, maybe you're right." I never did sit for a new portrait—there was no time. Instead, they used an old one from when I was a bored, sedentary princess of Orovalle. And just like with ancient manuscripts, scribed again and again over the years, mistakes invariably creep in until it is nearly impossible to tell which parts are original text. Any likenesses that made it this far are bound to be a confused version of an Elisa who doesn't even exist anymore.

"By reputation, you are portly and unattractive," Storm points out.

"Thank you for the kind reminder," I say.

"But you are neither of those things," he adds, and I whip my head around to stare at him. Did he just pay me a compliment?

Mara pinches off a green manzanita leaf and puts it in her mouth. As she chews, she mumbles, "I could fix your hair in two braids, one on each side like the nomads wear. Smudge your face with dirt."

I'm not sure I need any more dirt on my face than I have already. I scratch at my hairline, where sweat has started to drip tiny mud trails down my face. It itches abominably. Everyone is silent as we consider the thing no one is saying—that Eduardo has commanded his men to kill me on sight.

"They're looking for a group of four travelers," Belén says finally.

"Which means someone must stay behind," I say.

As one, we shift on our stomachs to face Storm. "Yes, yes," he says wearily. "A party of four, one of whom is an Invierno, would mark you as clearly as your Godstone crown."

"We'll find a good rendezvous point for you to wait," I tell him. "I won't leave you behind."

He nods. "I know."

We belly crawl backward, then skid down the graveled hill-side into the narrow arroyo below. As we weave toward our campsite, following the arroyo's meager trickle of water, I wonder at my lack of uneasiness. I should be terrified at the prospect of walking into an enemy barracks, stealing their horses, and riding away into the night. But I feel nothing except raw determination, with a bit of anger for spice.

It's possible I've been through too much, lost too much. War damages different people in different ways; Hector taught me that. King Alejandro became spineless and incapable. His father before him was rash and unpredictable, if I'm to believe court gossip. Perhaps this is my damage. Maybe I am numb to fear because I am broken.

Our campsite lies in a copse of cottonwoods, elevated just enough to stay dry during a flash flood. We retrieve our packs from where we stashed them behind a deadfall. Mara starts putting ingredients together for a soup while Storm leaves to gather firewood. It will be a while yet before we eat; Mara will let the mix soak but won't start a fire until the black of night hides our smoke.

I find an open space and begin the slow, dancelike warm-up exercises of my Royal Guard, exactly the way Hector taught me. It's always difficult at first, because it brings to mind his memory, so vivid and startling that I have to swallow against tears. His callused fingers on my arm, guiding my movement. His breath in my ear as he gives clear, patient instructions. The scents of oiled leather and aloe shaving gel.

But as always, it passes. The movement takes over, the memory fades, my mind clears. When my focus is as sharp as one of Mara's arrowheads, I review everything I observed: the layout of the village around a central plaza, the surrounding ridges and low brush, the young men at the inn who played at soldiering . . .

"Belén." A wicked smile stretches my lips.

He pauses from his sharpening, knife and whetstone

hovering in the air. His one good eye narrows. "I know that look," he says.

"What if we used Storm as a decoy? Convince the village it's under attack by Inviernos? The inn would empty of soldiers. We could take the horses easily. Then, when word reached the conde that our old enemy is attacking again, he'd have to send troops to protect his border. It would thin his resources even further."

His face turns thoughtful. Wind whistles through the scrub brush, and he whisks his knife against the whetstone in sharp counterpoint. At last he says, "Storm's hair. You made him cut it and dye it black. From a distance, they might not recognize him for an Invierno."

"He's tall," I insist. "If he remained cowled and wore his Godstone amulet visibly . . ."

"They'd never believe he was attacking," Mara says from her place at the still-cold fire pit. "Not if he can't throw fire from his amulet."

Mara is right. Storm is not only an enemy defector, he's a failed sorcerer, one of the few Inviernos born with a Godstone. When he was four years old, it detached from his navel, and he began training to become an animagus. But he was never able to call the *zafira*, the living magic that creeps beneath the crust of the world, never learned to bring its fire. So he was exiled in disgrace to my late husband's court as an ambassador.

Odd how being named an ambassador is considered his mark of shame, when the position carries such honor in my own court. There is so much about Invierne and its people that we do not understand.

"I'll stand with Storm," Mara says. "Or hide nearby and shoot arrows from the ridge. There are some piñons in the area; if we find resin, I could coat the arrowheads, light them on fire. Smoke and flames cause a lot of confusion—I know it too well."

Belén gives her an admiring look, and she blushes. He says, "It would be a while before they figured out the fire came from your arrows rather than our fake animagus. Especially if we did it at first light, when the rising sun makes seeing tricky."

"Mara, that's brilliant," I tell her, even as my heart sinks at the thought of setting anything on fire. I hate that I must cut a swath of devastation through my own country in order to save it. Weakly, I ask, "Please promise you'll do as little damage as possible?"

"Of course," she says gently.

"So Belén and I will take a room for the night," I say. "On a prearranged signal—at dawn, so the village can see just enough to identify an Invierno?—Mara and Storm will attack. In the chaos, we'll sneak into the stable and grab four horses. Then circle around for the two of you."

Mara digs into her spice satchel and retrieves a leather pouch. She empties some gray-green flakes into her palm and scatters them into her pot. "You should free the remaining horses," she says without looking up. "Or even kill them. Otherwise, we'll be pursued."

I stare at her. Mara is lovely and lithe, soft-spoken and

unassuming. I often forget how capable and ruthless she can be. She lived a lifetime before becoming my lady-in-waiting, and though she doesn't talk about it much, I know that the scars she bears—the drooping eyelid, the mangled earlobe, the burn mark on her belly—are minor compared to those wounds that no one can see.

"There are so many things that could go wrong with this plan," Belén says.

I purse my lips, thinking hard. Chief among the possibilities, of course, is me. I haven't handled horses since I was twelve years old. My sister, Alodia, always excelled at horsemanship, but I avoided the creatures—at first to prevent yet another unflattering comparison between us, and later because they were so large, and it had just been too long, and somehow in avoiding them I had let myself become frightened of them.

But I'm determined to do it now. For Hector. For my kingdom. Surely there's not much to it? How hard can it be to get on and stay on until we are out of danger?

"I'll scout around tonight," Belén says. "Find a good rendezvous point. We need to convince Storm, then figure out a way to minimize his exposure. They'll start shooting at him as soon as he shows himself."

Storm chooses this moment to push through a wall of bramble and reenter the camp. His arms are full of twisted deadwood, and smears of sweat mar his perfect face. "Convince me of what?"

I take a deep breath and explain the plan.

Storm drops the firewood near Mara's pit and sits beside it, cross-legged. The manacles on his ankles gleam in the failing light of evening.

"In my country," he says, "it is a great crime to impersonate an animagus. Punishable by death."

"But will you do it?" I ask gently.

He hesitates the space of a breath before saying, "Of course. I am your loyal subject."

3

THE inn is a dim, smoky place that reeks of urine, moldy rushes, and week-old stew. Instead of the large sitting cushions and low tables that I've become accustomed to in the western holdings, the room contains a haphazard mix of trestle tables, benches, and stools. Almost every spot is occupied by conscripted soldiers, and they look up when Belén and I enter, then stare unabashedly.

I try to appear relaxed and indifferent, telling myself firmly that this village lies along a trade route, and strangers are not that uncommon.

A burly man approaches, wringing a hand towel. A graying beard curls down to his chest, stopping just before it reaches a once-white apron that has been patched in several places. "No vacancy," he says in a gravelly voice. "But I can serve you up some lamb stew and send you on your way."

Belén and I exchange an alarmed glance. We should have considered this possibility.

"We'll sleep anywhere," I say hastily. "We just need a place out of the wind and dust for once."

He rubs his chin, studying us. "Been a lot like you through here lately," he says. "Fleeing east ahead of the coming war."

Belén nods. "We have family in the free villages."

"Head too far east, and you take your chances with Inviernos," says the bearded man.

"Better them than civil war, when your enemy looks just like your brother," I say.

He peers at me through the dimness, and I expect him to say something like, *You look familiar* or *You're too dark skinned to be from around here.* Instead he shrugs and says, "The loft in the stable is unoccupied. The straw is clean. I'll give it to you for half the price of a regular room."

"Done," Belén says. "And our thanks."

He gestures for us to follow, and we weave through the tables, pass under a wooden stair, and push through a cluttered and busy kitchen. He opens a back door into a small stable that stinks of manure—an improvement on the scent of the common room we just vacated.

The innkeeper indicates a nearby ladder. "Up there," he says. "Four coppers gets you each a bowl of stew. Six coppers gets you stew with meat. Shall I have Sirta bring some for you?"

"Please," I say. "With meat." My expectations for the stew are low, but last time I was in the desert I learned never to turn down a meal.

He leaves, and Belén and I climb into the loft. The ceiling is low and made of dried palm thatch. It's hot up here—a little too hot—and I already miss our camp that is open to the breeze and to the stars. But the innkeeper did not lie; the straw is fresh and clean.

"We got lucky," Belén says. From below comes a soft snort and a hard *thunk* as a horse paws against his stall door.

"Yes, we did." And I can't help but wonder: If luck is a finite thing, to be doled out in increments, have we used it up too quickly? From habit, my fingertips find the Godstone at my navel. *Please, God. Let this work.*

Heat washes through my body as the stone pulses a joyous response. I jerk my hand away.

I've been praying less lately, even though I feel bereft without prayer. Ever since my encounter with the *zafira*, when the magic of the world touched me directly, the Godstone has been too eager, like a tidal wave inside me yearning to rush free.

By the time the girl, Sirta, comes with the stew, it's too dark to discern anything about her. How she maneuvers two bowlfuls up the ladder I cannot guess, but we thank her and eat eagerly. The meat is gamey, and the cook used too much salt, but it's not as bad as I expected.

Normally, I'd use any idle time to practice with my daggers. Belén has taken up where Hector left off, teaching me to defend myself, even to fight a little. But the loft offers little room for exercise, and I don't want to make noise that would draw attention. So after eating, we settle in to wait impatiently. We'll make our move at first light.

I don't realize I've dozed until Belén shakes me. "The sky brightens," he whispers. "Soon, now."

I stretch and blink myself awake, then shoulder my pack and follow him down the ladder.

The back of the stable is open to the outside so that the building resembles an overgrown potting shed. A guard passes the opening at steady intervals. I'm hoping that when Storm and Mara begin their attack, he'll run off on foot instead of pursuing the enemy on horseback.

Seven of the eight stalls are occupied by horses. The eighth is stacked high with hay bales. Most of the tack, however, has been wisely stowed elsewhere. Belén and I poke around quietly and come up with only two saddles, one bridle, two soft halters, and a single blanket.

"Mara and I will go bareback," he whispers. "You can have the horse with a saddle and bridle." I breathe my thanks.

The clang of cast iron and the stomp of footsteps filter through the door from the kitchen. The inn rises early to prepare breakfast. Not much time until someone comes to tend the horses.

"Can we wedge the door shut?" I ask. "It might win us some time." Even the minute or two it would take for the soldiers to realize the door was jammed and run around back would help.

Belén's gaze darts around. "The hay bales! Help me move them."

I open the stall door and wince at the creaking hinges. The bales are too heavy for me to lift, but I'm able to grab a cross-section of twine and drag them backward into place. Belén, on the other hand, stacks them quickly, two wide, two thick, four high, until we've made a solid wall.

"Watch the entrance while I saddle a horse for you," Belén says. "Listen for Mara's signal."

I creep toward the opening, wary of the patrolling guard. The sky is as blue-black as a bruise, and the stars are dimming. As soon as light peeks through the mountain peaks, Mara and Storm will begin their phony assault.

My Godstone cools in my belly, giving me a slight shiver, and I cast my awareness about, alert for danger. If my life were imperiled, the stone would turn to ice, but it is merely chilly. Which means either the danger is distant, or it remains within the realm of possibility. All these nuances now, ever since the *zafira*. It's like I'm living with a whole new Godstone. Or maybe it's always been this way, and I'm only now learning how to interpret its signals.

"You there!" comes a voice out of the fading night.

I whirl to find the silhouette of a man in desert robes bearing down on me. The guard. With a calm that surprises me, I step from the shelter of the stable to intercept his path. Better to keep his eyes on me than allow him to notice Belén preparing the horses.

"Good morning to you!" I call out cheerfully.

"This area is off limits," he says, his hand going to the hilt of his sword.

"It is? We rented space in the loft from the innkeeper. He didn't say anything about that."

"Then you should go back inside."

What to say next? If I don't convince him to walk away soon, Belén will have to kill him.

I sigh loudly. "Please, sir, I won't cause any trouble. It's just that my husband is still in there, snoring up a sandstorm, and I couldn't take it a moment more."

He chuckles, and relief washes through me. The cold of my Godstone begins to ease.

"Promise not to stray from the stable?"

I open my mouth to promise, but Mara's war cry rips the sky. It's high-pitched and eerie, as mournful as death, and knowing it's my friend does not prevent the back of my neck from prickling.

I lurch forward, clutching the guard's robes in what I hope is a decent approximation of panic. "It's an animagus! We're under attack!" The animagi have never announced their attacks thusly, but the guard shoves me away and dashes off.

I turn to find Belén leading two horses my way. The tallest one, a black monster with flaring nostrils, is the one he chose to saddle for me. I shrink a little.

"Don't let her size fool you," he whispers. "She's gentle as a lamb. After you mount her, I'll hand you the reins for this pretty girl too. As you ride, keep enough slack in the reins so she can trot easily beside you."

The second, smaller horse is a bay, maybe a blood bay, though it's too dim to tell, and she prances in place, swishing her tail. Belén grins, patting her neck. "Mara is going to love you," he croons.

I hear distant shouting, another war cry. Storm and Mara only have a moment more before they must dash away to our rendezvous spot.

"The rest of the horses?" I ask.

"I opened the stall doors. I'll set the hay bales on fire as I leave." At my indrawn breath, he says, "The horses will panic. They'll be impossible to catch. Do you have a better idea?"

I feel sick. But no, I don't have a better idea. I can't bring myself to answer Belén, so I place my foot in the stirrup and heave myself up, swinging my leg over the mare's impossible girth. I sway as she adjusts beneath me. She is so huge, and I am so high off of the ground.

Don't think, Elisa. Just do.

Belén hands me the reins to the other horse. I wrap the ends once around the pommel of my saddle and hold tight with my left hand. With my right, I flick the reins of my own horse experimentally, and she steps forward.

"Head east, out of the village. Go slowly until you find your seat. I'll catch up in a moment."

I kick my heels against the mare's sides, and she lurches forward into a lazy walk. We'll have to move a lot faster than this very soon, but I take Belén's advice and concentrate on finding my seat in her swaying rhythm. The mare beside me kicks her knees up a little higher than necessary, and I know she'll be delighted when Mara finally demands that she run.

We skirt the village, keeping to the shadows. I see no one; everyone is hiding, fleeing, or trying to organize a defense. From the corner of my right eye, I catch a smear of brightness as it arcs over the village and plummets to the ground somewhere in the plaza.

Someone screams. The horse beside me *whoofs* as she sniffs

the air, and she dances nervously. Smoke. She smells smoke.

I must get away from the smoke before the horses panic and I lose my already-tenuous control. I kick again, but she takes only a few quick steps before settling back into slow, useless plodding.

More arrows spear the brightening sky. Storm's voice booms across the tiny valley, menacing and curselike. He's intoning something in the Lengua Classica. Then a giggle bubbles from my throat when I realize it's a silly rhyme about poppy fields and drunk sheep.

Panicked shouting, an order for archers to fire, and suddenly the northern sky glows with a nimbus of burnt orange. Buildings block my view, but I know something burns. My eyes sting, with shameful tears and from smoke, as I kick my useless mare again.

Hoofbeats approach from behind, and I twist in the saddle. It's Belén. One fist is clutched in the mane of a tall dapple gray, the other holds the reins of a smaller chestnut. "Elisa, we have to *move!*" he yells.

"I can't!" I say helplessly. "She won't—"

Belén races up to me, leans over, and thwaks my mare on the rump. She jerks into a trot, and suddenly it's all I can do to keep my seat without losing control of my extra mount.

We reach the tethered camels, which are rolling their eyes and tossing their heads in panic. Belén leans down with a knife and cuts them loose, and they gallop off. I watch them go mournfully, wishing I was riding one of them instead. Belén leads us slightly south of the village, and once we're out of sight, we start switching back along a rocky slope, gradually circling north toward our rendezvous point. I lean forward over the mare's neck to keep my seat on the incline.

For the first time since we decided to become horse thieves, real fear stabs my gut—but not for me. What if someone doesn't make it? Mara is used to these hills and gullies; she stands a good chance of disappearing into the scrub and slipping away. But Storm is a stranger here, ill suited to the dry and dusty climate. What if I have sacrificed him? What if we get to the rendezvous point and he is not there?

My heart twists. Storm and I have gone from enemies, to uneasy allies, to grudging friends. I would never tell him so, but I am fond of him. Being queen has taught me that loyal friends are in short supply, and I'm not willing to lose even one of mine.

We reach a narrow gulch, half covered in bramble. Belén brings his horse to a halt, kicks a leg over, and slides off neatly. He grabs my mare's bridle to hold her steady while I dismount. "We lead the horses from here," he whispers. "We must go quietly."

He sets off with his pair, and I follow. The gulch is barely wide enough for two horses, and they bump each other nervously as we travel. I stare at the hindquarters before me, expecting a kick to the face at any moment. But then my mare whuffs into my hair, blasting my neck with moist air, and all I can think is, *Please, please don't bite me.*

The area is a warren of buttes and brambles and gullies. Were it not for Belén I would be hopelessly lost. We take several turns, climb two ridges, circle a giant jutting butte—all the while suffering the onslaught of tumbleweed and manzanita. My cloak protects me from the worst of it, but my cheeks and hands are raw with scratches. A grudging respect for the horses begins to grow inside me. Their skin is so much more delicate than that of camels, but they plod forward, unperturbed.

Belén stops and holds up three fingers—a signal for me to be silent while he scouts ahead. I'm supposed to duck out of sight whenever I'm left alone, but this time there is nowhere to go. Instead, I peer past the horses' rumps to see what has stalled us. Our tiny gulch has become impassable, blocked by creosote and dried yucca stalks and bushes I can't identify. He quietly parts the branches of the thicket and disappears inside, leaving me alone with all four horses.

The sun is high now; we'll have to find cover soon, or a clear path to run. Birds serenade the brightening day, and something rustles in the brush beside me. *A lizard*, I tell myself firmly, even though this is viper country.

Belén materializes out of the thicket. "It's safe," he says. "Mara and Storm are there."

I wilt with relief.

The bramble is too thick for us all to go at once, so he leads the horses through one at a time. When at last it's my turn, he pushes the thicket aside and I squeeze through, my hair and clothes snagging on branches. He follows after, letting the branches swing back, and I find myself in a tiny canyon of sandstone that is barely large enough for four people and their horses.

Mara and Storm sit at the other end in the dry grass. Mara is doing something to his upper arm.

"Are you injured?" I ask him.

He nods. "I was nicked with an arrow. It's quite painful."

Mara rolls her eyes. "It bled a good bit," she says as she wraps a strip of cloth around his arm. "But it's shallow."

"Any trouble getting here?" Belén asks. "Were you followed?"

Mara stands and rolls her shoulders. "I don't think so. But oh, you both should have seen it! Storm was marvelous. And when he started yelling in the Lengua Classica, everyone panicked, and all their shots flew wide—"

"But did you see any trackers among them?" Belén presses. "Anyone we know? We should put as much distance between us and the village as soon as possible, just in case."

Mara scowls at him. "All the best trackers and scouts joined our Malficio, remember? Most of them are with Queen Cosmé now."

He flinches to hear the name of our former traveling companion—and his former betrothed. "It only takes one, Mara."

They all turn to me for the final decision.

"Storm, can you ride injured?" I ask.

"More easily than I can run with these cursed manacles," he says.

"Then we go."

As we're mounting up, Mara leans over and says, "I hit a pigsty. With my arrows. None of the *hutas* burned down, I swear it."

Belén sidles over and adds, "And I did not set the stable on fire. A little banging on the stalls did the trick just fine."

A quick look of understanding passes between the two of them. "Thank you," I whisper. "Thank you so much."

Belén leads us to the east end of the tiny canyon and a narrow opening there. We travel single file through a dry arroyo, then up onto another ridge, where we pick up the pace. Galloping, I learn quickly, is a lot smoother and less frightening than trotting, and my lazy mare grudgingly keeps pace so long as Mara's mount nips at her heels.

I allow myself a secret smile. We did it. We became horse thieves. Now we'll be able to cover twice the distance each day.

We're coming, Hector.

4

HECTOR

WHEN I was fifteen, Alejandro released me from service for a summer, to crew on my older brother's ship. Felix made me learn two dozen sailor's knots. So I know the one binding my wrists is a type of clove hitch, designed to tighten my bonds if I strain against them.

I've tried to keep my wrists relaxed, but the rocking gait of my horse tightens them anyway, leaving my skin bloody and my fingers numb. If by some miracle I escaped, I wouldn't be able to grasp a sword to fight my way free.

Even so, I am not helpless.

The true power of a Royal Guardsman lies in observation, and they have not thought to blindfold me. Overconfident fools.

Our path leads deep into the Sierra Sangre at a steady incline. Sage and juniper have surrendered to taller pines that block out the sun. I like their tart, lemony smell. I close my eyes and breathe deep of that smell—the sharpness cuts through the pain and helps me stay alert, though I'm careful not to reveal it.

The pine trees have other uses too. Every morning, my captors make tea from pine needles. And last night, one of them peeled back the bark, exposing fleshy white pulp that he scraped into the campfire pot to thicken our soup. Now I'll be able to survive in the forest, even if I'm unable to escape with provisions.

We ride single file, with me lodged in the middle. We left Selvarica a full company of fifty men, far too many for me to slip away from. But most of the others have peeled off, called by Conde Eduardo to other tasks. Now only twenty remain. Of those, ten are my countrymen. No, not countrymen. Traitors.

I understand the traitors enough to elude them. I know their training. I can use it against them. But the other ten are a puzzle.

They are Inviernos, though they have unusually dark coloring for Inviernos, with burnished skin and black hair. Spies who have passed as Joyans for many years. But now that I've seen them up close, I'll never mistake them again. They are too beautiful and too forthright to be anything but our ancient enemy.

Nor will I underestimate them.

Franco, the leader of this expedition, rides ahead of me. He carries himself like a warrior, as if barely holding himself in check, ready to explode into movement at a moment's notice. He spied in the palace for more than a year and is as versed in Joyan court politics as he is the art of assassination. He almost succeeded in killing Elisa.

My jaw clenches tight. I'm determined not to think about

her. Sometimes it's a good thing, like when I need a memory to warm myself to sleep, or a reminder of my resolve. But it's too great an indulgence when I'm deliberating, planning, *observing*.

Instead I focus on Franco's neck, imagining my hands wrapped around it, my thumbs crushing the life from his spine and windpipe.

As the sun drops below the tree line, the thin air frosts. Two of my captors help me dismount. They drag me by the armpits to a nearby pine tree and tie me down.

It's the perfect place from which to observe their camp. The traitor Joyans and enemy Inviernos are supposed to be allies on this mission, but they skirt one another with care. Every night the Joyan tents end up clumped together, apart from the others, and their eyes narrow and shoulders stiffen each time they follow one of Franco's orders.

It's an angry, resentful alliance that could burst into conflict at the slightest provocation. I haven't figured out how yet, but I plan to be the provocation.

Once camp is set up, they send a different interrogator to me than usual, but the questions are the same as always.

"Has the queen learned to call God's fire with her stone?" he asks. He's the shortest Invierno I've ever seen, with round, childish features and a wide-eyed gaze. I know better than to believe him harmless.

"I don't know."

"Does the stone speak to her at all?"

"I don't know."

"Has it fallen out? Or does it still live in her belly?"

"I don't know."

I see the blow coming, but my dodge is weak and slow. The Invierno's fist glances across my cheekbone, sending daggers of pain into my eye socket.

"God despises liars," the Invierno says.

I blink to clear tears from that eye. It's going to swell shut, but it's nothing I haven't dealt with before. I say, "Why would the queen share any of that with me? I'm just a guard."

"You must think I'm stupid. You're the second-highest ranking military officer in the kingdom and a Quorum Lord."

I shrug. "The queen is a very private person."

The Invierno raises his fist.

"Hit me all you want," I say. "Pummel me to death, in fact. My answers will not change."

The Invierno steps back, frowning. "You must love her very much," he says, not unkindly.

It's hard to keep my face nonchalant. Because every time someone mentions her, I can't help but consider the wondrous, new possibility that she might love me back.

Be ready, she said. *I'll come for you.*

Oh, I'll be ready. These traitors will be shocked at how ready. And then they'll be dead.

5

BY the time Belén calls a halt, my legs and rear scream in pain. It's as though all the muscle and sinew have been rubbed away, and my entire existence is bone grinding against my granite block of a saddle.

Belén dismounts and reaches up to help me down. I try to lift my right foot from the stirrup, but my body won't obey.

"Elisa?"

I grit my teeth. "Can't . . . move."

He laughs. "Stand up in the stirrups first. Get as high on your toes as possible. It will return some movement to your muscles."

I do exactly as he says, and it seems to help. But just as I'm swinging my leg around, my thighs seize with cramps, and I topple into his arms.

"See?" he says in my ear. "Not so bad."

I whimper.

He helps me straighten up. "Walk around a bit. Maybe

gather firewood. Then we'll practice. Otherwise it will just be worse tomorrow."

Worse? I doubt such a thing is possible, but I nod and start limping away. I should learn how to mind the horse, how to rub her down and maintain the tack. *Tomorrow*, I tell myself. I'll ask someone to teach me tomorrow.

"I didn't realize you were in such pain," Mara says. She has leaped nimbly off her horse, unbothered by the lack of saddle. "You should have said something."

"We can't afford any more delays!"

She sighs. "Oh, Elisa."

"What?"

Mara stares at me, a strange expression on her face. She opens her mouth, closes it.

I raise an eyebrow. "Just say it."

She takes a deep breath. "Once only, and then I'll never bring it up again."

I force my voice to remain calm. "You can say anything to me."

"Here it is, then." Another deep breath. "You're risking a lot. For a man. I know you love Hector. We all do. But he's just one person."

If I hadn't dismissed my nurse, Ximena, she would be right here in Mara's place, saying the exact same thing. One of the hardest things about being queen has been learning when to disagree with the people I love most.

"I'm not doing this for love," I say. "I mean, yes, I love him. But I've loved and lost before. It's awful, but it's a survivable thing." I scuff the toe of my boot through the dirt, uncovering pine needles and half-rotted leaves shed by the cottonwood looming over me. *My* dirt, I think. *My* land.

"I desperately need that marriage alliance with him," I tell her. "It will serve as a bond between our northern and southern regions. But mostly . . ." Here, I pause. The thought is still so nebulous in my mind, but I know it's important. I know it the way I know the sun rises in the east each morning. "I need to see Invierne for myself. I need to learn more about it. Because something is wrong there."

Storm and Belén have been tending the horses, and as one they freeze in their ministrations and turn to stare at me. "What do you mean?" Belén asks.

I start pacing. It hurts, but it feels good too, as if my body craves movement. "They are desperate for something. They sent an army of tens of thousands after me and my Godstone. When that didn't work, they resorted to stealth and manipulation. Animagi martyred themselves to shake my country apart. So much loss of life. So much risk. And for what? Why?"

"It's simple," Storm says. "They believe it is God's will that they have you. They believe he'll restore their power, the kind they had before your people came to this world and changed everything. The animagi could do so much more with living Godstones than with those cold, dead things they carry."

Mara gasps. It's almost like a sob. "They burned down Brisadulce's gate with 'those cold, dead things'! They killed King Alejandro. They . . ." She flattens her palm against her belly. "They burned *me*. You're saying they could do *more*?"

"Yes," Storm says. "Oh, yes."

But I'm shaking my head. "That's not it," I say, and they all stare at me. "I mean, I'm sure that's part of it. But there's more. None of you were there the day the animagus burned himself alive at my birthday parade, but you heard about it, yes? Read the reports?"

They nod.

"He said the Inviernos were more numerous than the stars in the sky. Is that true, Storm?"

He regards me thoughtfully. "There are many more of us than there are of you."

"And that single declaration filled our whole country with panic and rage, because what if Invierne sends another army? Even larger than before? We would not survive another such onslaught. But what did he *not* say?"

"Ah," Belén says. "I see."

"What?" Mara says. "What do you see?"

"The animagus did not say they *would* attack again."

I nod. "Inviernos only speak literal truth. But . . ." I look pointedly at Storm. "I have learned that they frequently deceive through omission."

Belén turns to the Invierno. "Is she right? Does Invierne have no intention of invading again?"

Storm hangs his head. I made him dye his hair black so he wouldn't stand out so much, but now his white-blond roots are growing out in a large skunk stripe along his part. "I don't know," he says wearily. "If my training as an animagus had been successful, I would have been inducted into the ruling council and thus privy to so much more. But I failed."

I stretch my arms high to work out the kinks, somewhat enjoying the burn this produces in my thighs and lower back. "So my next question is: Why not? If they are as numerous as they say, why don't they invade? I think something is preventing them. And I want to find out what it is."

"Maybe they'll invade *after* they have you and your Godstone," Mara says. "Maybe that's why they're using Hector to lure you to them."

"Maybe."

"If they're vulnerable in any way," Belén says, "we should attack. Press our advantage."

Storm turns back to his horse, but not before I catch the flicker of sadness on his face. He is wholly mine now, subject to me in both fealty and friendship. But it can't be easy to hear us discuss the conquest of his homeland.

"I've thought of that," I say softly. But if it's true that they're vulnerable, it means that Invierne is like a desperate mother puma cornered in her den, and thus more dangerous than ever.

We are still too near the village to risk a cooking fire, so we eat a cold meal of dates and jerky. Afterward, Storm sits crosslegged to meditate, and Mara practices a quick draw and pull with her bow and a quiver full of arrows.

Belén and I find an open space to practice, and I learn to block an overhanded strike with a dagger. Belén shows me how to position myself so that my entire body absorbs the blow. We practice until my wrist and shoulder socket ache and my already wobbly legs are as weak as coconut pudding. Exhausted but feeling accomplished, I flip out my bedroll to finally get some rest. No tents—the night is warm enough, and we need to pack up and move out as quickly as possible at first light.

Belén takes the first watch. I don't bother to remove my boots before lying down. I'm asleep in moments.

A chill at my belly drags me from sleep. I wake with a sword pointed at my throat.

I start to roll away, but the sword presses deeper, pricking my flesh as the Godstone shoots ice through my veins. The villagers have found us. We'll be hanged for thieves after all.

But no. The man staring down the blade at me has a complexion as tough as tanned leather. His hair and beard are wild and matted, his clothes ragged and torn, and he reeks of old sweat.

Highwaymen, then. We are being robbed. And murdered, if I don't figure a way out of this.

I move my eyes to place my companions. Mara and Storm are in equally tenuous positions, each trapped beneath a sword held by a ragged man. I can't find Belén. Either he has already fallen, or he is hiding nearby. *Please, God, let Belén be hiding.*

The man looming over me opens his mouth to speak, but I preempt him. "What did you do with the others?" I demand.

He blinks. "Others? What others?"

"Our companions. Five of them. They should have returned from scouting by now. If you have killed them, I'll have your heads." A knife is sheathed in my right boot. I'm not sure how to grab it without being obvious, but I have to try. I bend my knee slightly to bring my foot closer and reach, hoping the bedroll disguises my movements.

"The girl is lying," says the one who has trapped Mara. "They have supplies for four people, no more." His accent is thick and gruff, as if speech comes rarely.

"You're certain? Wouldn't do to have vengeance on our tail," the third says.

My fingertips have reached the top of my boot. "If you let us live, I promise no one will come after you." Just a little farther . . .

"An Invierno!" one yells. "Look at those eyes. Greener than an alpine meadow."

The sword at my neck wavers.

I fling off the bedroll and leap to my feet, drawing my knife. Belén bursts from the bushes, screaming the Malficio war cry.

My would-be captor swings his sword at me. I jump back, and the tip misses my belly by a finger's breadth. We circle each other warily. Someone scuffles behind me, and I want more than anything to turn and make sure my companions are all right, but I don't dare.

"You're a traitor, aren't you, girl?" he says with a wicked grin that displays blackening teeth. "An enemy spy."

If Hector were here, he would tell me to run instead of fight. But maybe I can come up under his guard. Or jam his nose into his brain, or—why is he grinning?

An arm wraps my shoulders and hot, sticky breath coats my neck as a knife pricks the skin just below my ear. "Best to drop your dagger, girl."

Oh, God. He must have dispatched one of my companions to come after me.

I raise my heel and slam it into his instep, like Hector taught me. He screams as bones crunch, his grip releasing. I spin around and thrust my knife with all my strength. He is bent over in pain, so the knife plunges into the hollow of his throat, right above his sternum.

I yank my knife back. Blood sprays, and I blink to clear my eyes as I whirl to face my original attacker.

His eyes are wide with rage and terror, and he leaps at me, raising his sword. The blade flashes in the rising sun, and in this split second, I know I am not fast enough to avoid it.

Then his head whips back, and his body seems to twist in midair. He falls hard to the ground, one leg sprawled unnaturally, an arrow shaft protruding from his bloody eye socket.

I turn around slowly, dazed, breathless. It's a moment before everything makes sense.

Mara stands tall and fierce, bow in hand. Blood oozes from a huge bruise already blossoming on her forehead. "He bashed my head with a rock," she says in a shaky voice. "He thought he killed me."

Behind her, Storm and Belén have wrestled the third man to the ground and are tying his hands. He seems unaware that he's being tied down. He just stares at his fallen companions.

Our bedrolls and supplies are scattered everywhere, covered in dirt and blood. One of my pack's straps is broken, torn from its mooring.

"How did this happen?" I ask. "How did they sneak up on us?"

"It's my fault," Belén says. "I fell asleep on my watch." He runs a hand through his black hair. "I haven't done that since I was ten years old."

His eye patch is askew, and I focus with determination on the bridge of his nose. I say, "Among my Royal Guard, falling asleep on watch is punishable by death." I don't mean it as a threat, and I'm not sure why it comes out of my mouth.

Mara gasps. "Elisa, you can't!"

"No, no, of course not," I say quickly. "It's just . . . this is my fault. I've pushed us too hard. Belén hasn't slept in days. He kept watch last night as *I* slept, and I . . . I'm sorry."

Storm puts up a hand to get my attention and points to the man sitting tied up at his feet. Unkempt hair is bound into a messy queue with a leather tie. He has a wide, flat nose with a large bump at the bridge, like it's been smashed a time or two. His shoulders are like boulders, his forearms veined with muscle. He could break me in two if he wanted, and yet he gawks at me, wide-eyed with terror.

And I realize we've made another mistake. I mentioned my guard. The others said my name.

"You're her," he whispers. "You're Queen Elisa." Even with his hands tied, he manages to prostrate himself, forehead against the ground. "Forgive me, Majesty. I didn't know."

"Murder is not less of a crime when the victim is common born." My knife is still in my hand. I hold it up to the light. "Why did you attack us?"

"For food, Majesty. Supplies. We can't show our faces—"

"You're deserters."

He says nothing.

Conde Eduardo conscripted these men to fight against me, and they refused. From cowardice or loyalty, I'll never know, because now that he has identified me, he must die.

Storm gives me a questioning look, and I nod slightly. In a single fluid motion, he whisks a stiletto knife from somewhere beneath his cloak and plunges it through the base of the man's head, severing his spine. The man topples over and twitches in the dirt.

I'm somehow more horrified by this killing than the other two. So cold, so quick. I take a deep breath. I will not vomit. I will not even flinch. "There are still many things I do not know about you, Storm," I say calmly as the body bucks once more before becoming irrevocably still.

"You have but to ask," Storm says. "I am your loyal subject."

I meet his green-eyed gaze steadily, considering. "Belén," I say. "Storm and I will take the first watch tonight. We have things to discuss."

We don't dare take time to bury the bodies, so we drag them into a thicket of mesquite and cover them with brush and tumbleweed. There's no way to clean the campsite. The best we can do is pour dirt and detritus on the blood puddles and hope no one passes by for a few days.

I scrub at my face and hands with sand, disturbed at how quickly blood goes cold and thick outside the body. My skin still feels sticky with it as we climb onto our horses.

We exit the copse of trees and nose our mounts back onto the trail. The ache in my legs has abated a little, but I'm not sure how I'll make it a whole day on horseback. I think of Hector, and I grit my teeth and spur my mare forward.

Something squeals high above, and I look up to find three vultures circling lazily in the crystal sky.

The sun is not yet high when Mara slumps over her mare's neck and lists to the side.

"Mara?" I call out, but she doesn't answer. "Belén, something is wrong with Mara!"

He whips his horse around—I'm not sure how, since he rides without tack—and gallops toward us. He draws alongside Mara and hooks her armpits just as she topples from her mare's back. As one, they tilt precariously.

I swing my leg around and slide from my mount just in time to grab my lady-in-waiting before Belén loses his grip. He slips off his horse, and together, we leverage her to the ground.

"Storm," I call out. "Will you look around for a campsite?"

I don't bother to see if he complies, for Mara groans loudly, only half conscious.

"It's the blow to her head," I say. "She's concussed." I shouldn't have ordered everyone to set off so soon. I should have taken the time to check everyone's wounds.

Belén slaps her cheek lightly. "Stay awake, Mara."

She groans again, blinking, her eyes unfocused.

"She saved my life," I murmur as Belén palpates the pillowed bruise on Mara's forehead. My heart sinks into my stomach as I realize he's looking for a crack in her skull.

"Mara is a warrior," he says simply, and he gazes at her with such respect and affection that my heart aches a little. "Did she ever tell you how she found your Malficio camp? How she led twelve children through the wilderness to safety after the Inviernos destroyed her village?"

"No," I say.

"Shut up," Mara mumbles.

He reaches out as if to stroke her cheek but stops himself, instead grasping her chin and turning her head to the side to get a better angle. "I don't think anything is broken. But she should rest. She'll probably vomit a lot."

I breathe a sigh of relief.

Storm returns with news of a small clearing nearby, hidden from view but easy to access. No water source in sight, but we always carry extra and should have enough for a day or so.

Belén helps Mara to her feet and hitches her arm over his shoulder. "Elisa, can you lead our horses?"

I control the shudder before it can pass through me. "Of course." *Horses aren't so bad*, I tell myself, and these have been perfectly docile. I grab the reins of my mare and lead her forward, hoping Mara's and Belén's horses will follow. They do.

We've penetrated the foothills enough that sand and shale have ceded to gravely soil and stubborn grass. We make camp in a brown meadow surrounded by juniper bushes and struggling, stunted trees. The Sierra Sangre looms over us, the jagged peaks capped in snow that shines pristine in the sun, but blurs icy blue in the shadows. I can't imagine conquering such a landscape armed with only mountain ponies and determination, but conquer it we must.

Beyond them lies Invierne, Storm's homeland, my enemy, a country no one from Joya d'Arena has been allowed to set foot in for centuries. And yet they have invited me—no, coerced me—to come. To trade my life for Hector's. To offer myself as a living, willing sacrifice toward an end I cannot guess.

They have no idea what is coming.

While Storm ties the horses to the scrub oak, Belén and I help Mara stretch out on her bedroll. "Elisa?" she whispers as I feel her forehead for fever. "My head hurts."

It startles me. So rarely do I hear Mara complain. "I could heal you," I offer. I've healed before with the power of my Godstone. I can only do it for people who are dear to me, and at great physical cost, but I can't bear to see my friend in pain. Worse, our objective cannot bear more delays.

She shakes her head. "No, no, not yet. If one of us has to lose consciousness, it might as well be me." Her head lolls to the side, and her eyes drift closed.

"Mara? Belén says you shouldn't sleep."

"Just . . . resting eyes. Heal me tomorrow. If I'm not . . ."

Belén slaps her awake again.

"I hate you," she says.

"Yes," he agrees solemnly. "For years now."

I clamber to my feet. "I'm going to have a long talk with Storm. Tell me if something changes. Also, you *will* get some rest tonight. Think of it as a royal command."

His lips quirk. "Yes, Majesty."

Storm has tied up the horses, and now he sits against a tree trunk, his long legs sprawled out before him, his eyes closed. He always wears a cowl and cloak, no matter how stifling the desert heat, but for once his hood is tilted back, the ties of the cloak undone and open, showing the thin tunic beneath. It's soft linen, and the hem and seams are embroidered with a border of golden flowers with winding blue stems. It's far too lovely a frock for traveling.

With his face uncovered, his eyes closed and his features relaxed, I'm reminded how beautiful he is. Such a fine cast to chin and cheeks, with slightly tilted eyes and a small, straight nose leading to full lips. He looks like my sister, I realize with a start. She has the same uncanny beauty, the same delicacy that hides a sharp mind and steely focus.

My sister. I haven't seen Alodia in more than a year. I hope she got my message, that she's willing to participate in a parliament with Cosmé and me and will be waiting in Basajuan. I'll need the support of them both if I'm to retake my country.

Storm opens one eye and peers at me. "What do you want?"

I grin. "The pleasure of your charming company, of course."

He grunts, but he shifts aside to give me space against his tree trunk. I settle next to him, stretching out my legs. It feels nice to be in a different position. After being in the saddle so long, it seemed as though my legs would shape themselves to the barrel roundness of my mare's body and never straighten again.

"You want to know about me," he says. "How I killed that man so easily."

I nod. "I've seen three people kill that efficiently, and all of them were highly trained." I count them off on my fingers. "My former nurse, Ximena, who was groomed to be my guardian by the Monastery-at-Amalur. Hector, who is the commander of the most elite military force in Joya d'Arena. And Conde Tristán, who once rescued me and several of my Royal Guard almost singlehandedly. You move like them. So fast, so assured, so . . ." My voice breaks. They're all people I'd give anything to see safe and in good health again—no matter the terms of our parting.

"Yes, I'm like them."

I sigh, frustrated at how he makes me work for every smidge of information. "Why? Are you an assassin like the man who took Hector?"

He snaps, "I'm nothing like Franco."

"In all the ways that matter, no. Storm, just tell me."

He brings his knees to his chest. "I was trained to defend myself and to kill without hesitation because I am a prince of the realm. Everyone with royal blood receives an education in the killing arts."

"Just how close were you to the throne of Invierne?"

He shakes his head. "It doesn't work that way. There is no one king so much as a council of rulers called the Deciregi. Your people would think of them as priest kings."

"The Deciregi," I murmur. "They're animagi, then? Sorcerers?"

"Yes. The ten most powerful in the world. A Deciregus must be of royal blood *and* born with a Godstone. I was groomed to represent my family in the Deciregi from a very young age. But I failed. My stone fell out too early, and I was never able to call upon its magic. So later, when my cousin was born with a Godstone and showed potential, they named him successor instead and exiled me to Joya d'Arena."

"To recoup some of your honor in the role of ambassador."

"I was to bargain for port rights and make inquiries as to the identity of the new bearer."

"But you were forced to go into hiding?"

"Exactly so. Once the Invierne army began to gather, I knew my people had given up on diplomacy. This second failure made my life forfeit."

The Deciregi. The most powerful animagi in the world. Those I've already faced seemed powerful enough, with their firebolts and invisible shields—not to mention their mysterious attraction to my Godstone, which makes it nearly impossible for me to hide from them.

"It's brave of you to return with me," I say, "given the death sentence on your head."

He shrugs. "We'll sneak in and out as quickly and quietly as possible."

I bend my knees and rest my elbows on them, looking over toward Belén, who still leans over Mara's prone form. I smile to myself. Mara hates Belén much less than she lets on.

"Elisa?" Storm says. "That is your plan, is it not?"

I place my fingertips to the Godstone, seeking assurance in its solidness. "Yes. But it won't be as easy as you make it sound. That's why they took Hector, after all—to draw me to

Invierne. They're expecting me. So, if stealth doesn't work, I will make a loud and noisy entrance and wreak as much havoc as possible." I turn to measure his reaction to what I'll say next. "A deception may be in order. If we can't rescue Hector quietly, I want you to pretend I am your prisoner."

His mouth opens. Closes.

"I know lying is difficult for you," I add hastily. "But deception is not. You had no qualms about convincing Eduardo's soldiers you were an animagus."

"I will not have to lie?"

"Not with words, no."

He returns my gaze, and his green eyes dance. "Then, yes, I like this plan. They would not kill me if I brought them the bearer of the only living Godstone. They would welcome me as a hero."

"A prince of the realm."

He leans back against the tree trunk and closes his eyes. "A prince of the realm," he agrees softly.

One way or another, I *will* have Storm reinstated and his honor restored. I haven't told him yet, but he has an important role to play in wresting my kingdom back from Conde Eduardo. And I suppose now is as good a time as any to begin putting that part of my plan into motion.

Carefully I say, "Since going to meet the *zafira*, my Godstone has been more alive inside me than ever. More sensitive to my prayers, more . . . everything."

His eyes turn as hard and glittery as emeralds, with either anger or excitement. "But you *gave up* the power. You brought a whole mountain down on the *zafira*!"

"Yes, I tried to give it up. And I don't buzz with power the way I did when we were on that island. But it's still there. Like a pesky fly that won't be swatted away. I think the *zafira* isn't as done with me as I am with it. So I might as well use it, right?"

"Of course."

"So once we are into the mountains, away from the villages and priests who might sense my Godstone, I'd like to try a few things. I can already heal with it, and when I was connected directly to the *zafira*, I was able to create a protective barrier to fend off the gatekeeper."

"You made things grow too," he adds. A muscle in his jaw twitches, like he's barely keeping his excitement in check. Maybe this is a conversation he has been anticipating. "And you freed me by breaking my chains. Nothing has been able to break them since."

"And I couldn't break them now, without direct access to the *zafira*. But there are some things I could always do just by reaching through the skin of the earth. Something happened to me in that cavern, Storm. And though it's nothing like the feeling I got when the power was swirling all around me, I suspect . . . I hope . . . that I can do more than I used to."

His fingers are fisted in his tunic now. He knows what I'm going to say next.

"So, I'd like to try summoning fire, like your animagi do. And . . . I'd like you to try it too."

He doesn't say anything, doesn't even look at me.

I press on. "I suspect the *zafira* changed you too. You

could sense it as we approached, remember? And it touched you, claimed you for its gatekeeper before I stole you away. So maybe it has awakened your stone a little. Maybe you can do things with it now that you couldn't before."

His hand goes to his chest, where he clutches the amulet that hangs hidden beneath his tunic. I've seen it only once before—a tiny iron cage, black with age, that houses a blue jewel just like the one that lives in my navel.

Except his is powerless. Dead.

"We could train together, you and I." Gently I add, "No one need know about it, save our companions."

He is silent for a long time. One of the horses snorts and tosses her mane. Something rustles in the tumbleweed beside us.

"I will try it," he says at last. "Once we are in the mountains. Near the divide, beyond the free villages, is a weeklong stretch of travel where we will not encounter even a trading post. That will be a good time."

"Yes," I agree, relieved to have convinced him so easily. "A very good time."

6

HECTOR

IF Elisa were here, she could pray warmth into her body with the power of her Godstone. It gives me comfort. She'll never be so cold as I am now.

Wind whistles down the mountain slopes, penetrating even my leather armor, flinging needles of icy rain. The Inviernos greet the cooling weather with laughter and smiles of relief, but we Joyans hunch over our horses for warmth, letting our mounts guide us rather than raising our faces to the wet cold.

In spite of the clove hitch, I stretch my fingers open, then tighten them into fists. Open, close—over and over again, to force warmth and movement. The effort grinds the ties into my wrists, but I keep at it. The air has gotten so cold that icy numbness is a greater danger than injury.

But by the time Franco calls a halt, I know I've miscalculated. I've lost the battle and my palms have cramped, my fingers curled into useless claws. Which means I must now deal with both numbness *and* injury.

One of the Joyans, a stocky man with a chipped front tooth,

comes to help me from the saddle. I know him vaguely. A soldier from the city watch, one of General Luz-Manuel's men. Yet more evidence that our highest-ranking military official has been plotting treason with the conde.

If I don't dismount quickly, I'll be yanked off. My left leg is steady in its stirrup as I swing my right leg over and slide to the ground. I can do it without grabbing the pommel now, though I always pretend to. With a little more practice, I'll turn the dismount into a hard kick to someone's face.

The Joyan with the chipped tooth drags me toward a pine tree, forces me to sit, and ties me up, wrapping my waist three times. He ends with a hasty triple-looped rolling hitch—a knot that is unique to Puerto Verde. Sunny Puerto Verde. I'm not the only one who is a very long way from home.

I say, "It's wrong that the Inviernos drag us into their icy winter without outfitting us properly. It's like they *want* us to suffer."

"Shut up," he says.

He yanks on the rope, testing it. Satisfied, he stands and gazes toward the warm, bright campfire. It's surrounded by laughing Inviernos. He rubs at the thin linen covering his arms.

I have made him notice. That's all I need to do.

Later, Franco himself brings soup in a bowl. It's gamey and thick with pine-bark pulp. I peer over the rim while I slurp it down. I've gotten better at doing everything with my useless hands. When I get back to Brisadulce, I may institute this as a training exercise; all my men should learn how to eat, ride, and use the latrine with their hands tied. "Where are you taking me?" I ask Franco, not expecting a response.

The Invierno smiles, slick and cruel. I'd love to obliterate that smile with my fist, but I tamp the image down. I won't let Franco get under my skin.

"To our capital, to face the Deciregi," he says. "We'll hold you there until your queen comes for you."

The Deciregi. I repeat the word silently so it will stick in my memory. "Then you'll let me go?"

"Don't be an idiot. Once we have your queen, you'll never rest until you get her back. We'll have to kill you."

"But you said—"

"Did we?"

I narrow my eyes. *Come with no thought to returning,* Franco said to Elisa, *for this is pleasing to God. You may bring a small escort, but no soldiers. Otherwise, he dies.*

Only now do I hear what was unspoken. *When you come, he still dies.*

"You are liars," I say. "All of you. You don't lie with words, but your intent is ever to deceive."

Franco grabs the empty bowl from my hands. "It's the highest art form, deceiving without lying. A word is the only thing in the world made more powerful by absence than existence."

The Invierno straightens and peers down a delicate nose, as if sizing me up. When he was a spy in Conde Eduardo's entourage, he shuffled and carried himself with a slight hunch. Now that there is no longer need for pretense, I see how very tall he is—taller even than Storm.

"What do you want?" I ask wearily. "Tending to the prisoner is surely beneath you."

"Your queen. When I allowed her to say good-bye to you, she whispered something. What was it?"

"I'll come for you. Stay alive for me, Hector. And be ready."

"She said to escape if I could, because she can't risk a whole kingdom to rescue one man, not even a Quorum lord."

"You lie."

"With words or without?"

Franco frowns. "I saw the way she looked at you. You are life and breath to her."

He's wrong about that. Elisa loves fiercely, it's true. But she loves with her heart *and* mind. If she comes for me, it will be part of a larger plan to rescue all of Joya.

I don't realize I'm smiling until Franco says, "See? Just thinking about her makes you shine with her fire. Bearers are like that, you know. God always chooses the ones who inspire great loyalty."

I hate that he presumes anything about her. "How would you know? There is only one, and you know nothing of her."

"There are two."

"What?"

Franco gives me that edged grin, then turns his back and ambles toward the campfire.

Two bearers.

I stare after him, shivering in the dark. Maybe I should ask for a blanket, but I don't want to appear weak. Or maybe appearing weak is the better strategy.

I'm about to call out when something jabs the back of my knee. I shift, and the jabbing disappears. Shift again, and it returns, sharper than before.

It feels like an arrowhead. Or a discarded spear point. All I know for sure is that it might be a way free.

My heartbeat deepens, smooth and slow, as if I'm preparing for battle. I glance around to make sure no one is looking. Then quietly, carefully, I reach down with my tied hands and slide my fingers under my leg. I strain so hard that the ropes around my body cut off my breath, but I'm almost there. I snag a sharp edge with the tip of my left middle finger, slide it from under my leg through the dirt, lift it in my cupped hands to the moonlight.

It's a flake of stone, as hard as flint. No, more like glass, shimmering and black. Obsidian. With an edge sharp enough to cut rope.

I wedge it between my thumb and forefinger, and I begin to saw at my bonds.

It's slow going, and the movement cinches the rope, making me breathless with pain. It will take many nights' work. I'll have to hide the stone during the day and hope they don't search me.

When my hands cramp, when blood drips into my palm, when I'm shivering so badly from the cold that the pain is a dull ache, I maneuver the rock into the pocket of my pants.

I lean my head back against the tree trunk and close my eyes to review my conversation with Franco. The Deciregi, he said. *Two* bearers.

Which would be wiser? Escape as soon as possible so Elisa doesn't have to pursue too far into the mountains? Or wait and learn more?

I flex my hands, trying to force warmth into them. But they are cramped from sawing and dangerously numb. If it gets any colder, frostbite will render me useless to her, no matter what. I'm running out of time.

7

ONCE again we are too near the trail for a fire. But we are surrounded by plenty; Belén scrapes the spines from the fleshly leaf of a prickly pear cactus while I dig through piñon pinecones. We dine on fresh greens and nuts, and there are enough nuts left over that I put a handful in Mara's spice satchel, thinking they'll make a nice addition to a soup or stew.

Mara vomits up her dinner.

But her dizziness passes soon after, and finally Belén lets her sleep. I insist he sleep too, as Storm and I take watch.

The sun dips below the horizon. I work through Hector's training exercises. Some of the poses require so much balance and focus that I forget how frustrated I am at being delayed here while he drifts farther away from me.

I'm sheened with sweat by the time I finish, and breathing hard. But I can't sit still. Storm watches, bemused, as I pace our campsite. Maybe I'll pace all night, or practice with my daggers. Belén and Mara could certainly use the sleep.

Clouds pass over the moon. The temperature drops suddenly, and I shiver. My cloak is folded up on my bedroll, but I can hardly see where to go. I step in its general direction, tripping over detritus as I go.

"Storm?" I whisper.

"Yes. A big one," he whispers back.

Lightning cracks the sky to the east, leaving a flash memory to guide me. The toe of my boots finds the bedroll, and I bend over, feeling around for my cloak. There! I swing it around my shoulders and tie it at the neck.

I try to remember: Did we camp in a dry wash? Would a flash flood drown us all? Which direction was the trail, exactly, and could I find it in the utter dark if I needed to?

With Mara injured, and with the temperature dropping so quickly, maybe it's worth the risk to have a fire.

I feel around for my pack, reach inside for the tinderbox. I'm searching for a branch or a dry cone, something to give me a little bit of light so I can find decent firewood, when the first fat drops splat on my cheeks.

Lightning spears the sky again, followed by a crack of thunder. The horses snort and shuffle their hooves.

"We need to find shelter," Storm says. "Immediately."

"A little rain won't hurt us," I say.

"Have you ever seen hail? Sometimes in these mountains, the chunks of ice falling from the sky are as big as my fist."

I gasp. No, never have I seen such a thing. "Belén!" I yell. "Mara! Wake up."

I hear scrambling, a muffled grunt, and a curse.

"Is someone coming?" Belén says. "You shouldn't yell so l—"

"Thunderstorm. There may be hail. We need to find shelter." The drops are falling faster now, in a symphony of varying drum taps as they land on leaf and dirt and rock. A horse whinnies.

"The cottonwood," Mara says. "I sheltered my sheep under a cottonwood when storms came up too quickly to lead them home."

"I'll see to the horses," Belén says. "Get under the tree. Spread out the bedrolls in the branches above you."

The bedrolls won't keep out the rain, not the way it's coming down now. But maybe they'll help protect us from falling ice.

We scramble to follow Belén's suggestion, bumping into one another in the dark. The branches of the tree are low, and we are able—through much swearing and scraping of knuckles against branches—to get the bedrolls spread out above our heads. Belén guides the horses to the other side of the tree and ties them down. No bedrolls for them, but it will have to be enough.

"Times like this," Storm grumbles, "it would be useful for one of us to be able to call fire with a Godstone."

"Nothing would light anyway," I say. "Not in this deluge."

But I can't stop thinking about his words. We shiver together as the rain slaps our bedroll canopy. I pray hard for wisdom and warmth, and as the Godstone sends tendrils of heat through my body, I wonder about calling fire, about what I would have to do.

The animagi almost always use blood to wake the *zafira* and pull it from the ground. And the animagi send fire from stones that are caged in amulets or embedded into staffs. Neither is an option for me. How am I supposed to shoot fire from my belly? Would my clothes burn? What about my skin?

One of the greatest frustrations about being the only chosen one in four generations is that there is no one to tell me what to do. I've only centuries-old scripture to guide me, pored over by learned priests and eager revolutionaries who decide what those scriptures mean based on their own desperate hopes. None of them have felt God's own power rippling through their bodies; none of them really *know.*

It seems to me that when God decided he wanted to communicate with humankind, he could have come up with a much better plan.

The sound of the rain changes from drum taps to shattering glass; the hail has come.

Our bedrolls sag with the weight of water. It drips from my nose, soaks my cloak, and I feel I'll never be dry again. Hail bounces and cracks all around us. One huge chunk rolls up to the toe of my boot, and I pick it up. It's solid ice, half the size of my fist, crusted in dirt.

A horse screams, and I lurch up, hitting my head on a branch.

"Nothing we can do for it now," Belén shouts above the noise.

I bring my knees to my chest and huddle against the tree trunk, pressed in on either side by the shoulders of my friends.

I pray in a furious bid for warmth and comfort. *God, we can't afford to lose a mount. Please keep our horses safe. Keep Hector safe. Make this storm pass soon. Is it your will that I learn to use the stone's destructive power? If so, I could use some guidance. Storm could use your help too. I don't know if you answer the prayers of Inviernos. Actually, I'm not sure you answer mine either, but if you do . . .*

Eventually my head drops onto Mara's shoulder, and I fall asleep praying.

I wake to sunshine flashing on puddled water, to dirty clumps of hail melting in the shadowed lees of boulders, to rock wrens singing like it's the best day of their lives.

Aside from the crick in my neck, I feel refreshed and restored. I'm suddenly grateful for that horrid storm. It forced a rest that I didn't have the wisdom or patience to allow.

Mara's mare has a bloody gash on her neck, but she seems fine. Mara cleans the gash and smothers it with salve—the same salve she uses every day on her burn scars. The mare accepts these ministrations like an attention-starved puppy.

Until recently, I believed all horses were alike. They've been giant, four-footed animals with ugly dispositions and alarmingly large teeth for so long that it's a bit startling to notice how different their personalities are. Mara's mare, for instance, is a blood bay, except for a wide white blaze down her nose that suits her perpetually excited demeanor. My huge, plodding mare has a dark-brown coat that seems black at night, with the most unruly mane I've ever seen. Her shaggy forelock covers her right eye and reaches almost to her mouth. Maybe the reason she moves so slowly is that she can hardly see where to go.

Mara's mare head-butts my lady-in-waiting in the chest. Grinning, Mara plants a kiss between her wide, dumb eyes, then murmurs something.

"Have you named her?" I ask.

"Yes! Her name is Jasmine."

I grimace. "But jasmine is such a sweet, pretty flower."

Mara laughs. "Have you named yours?"

"Her name is Horse."

She rolls her eyes. "If you want to get along with your mount, you have to learn each other's language. That means starting with a good name."

"All right." I pretend to consider. "What about Imbecile? Or Poops A Lot?"

Mara shakes her head.

We lay out our bedrolls in the sun while we down a quick breakfast of pine nuts, jerky, and flatbread. The bedrolls are still wet when we roll them up and attach them to our packs. I should call an early halt and give them time to air out again. Or maybe we'll just sleep directly on the ground tonight. It can't be worse than sleeping hunched beneath a cottonwood during a thunder burst.

Belén shows me how to saddle Horse, and I promise to try it on my own next time. We mount up, Belén leads the way, and moments later we're back on the trail.

The ground turns rocky as we enter a series of steep switch-backs. Our horses' legs are so spindly and fragile, and I fear they will snap like kindling on the jagged outcroppings that mar our path. But the horses clomp along unbothered, and after a while I forget to worry.

We pause for lunch in a small green valley, divided down the middle by a crystal creek. Trout dart under the grassy bank as we approach, and Mara squeals. "We could have fish for lunch!" she says. "I can show you how to catch them with your hands. Trout are the easiest to clean and spit, and then—"

I picture Hector being driven through these mountains, weeks ahead of us. I would bet my Godstone crown he's planning his escape, trying to delay their progress. God, I hope he's being treated well. What if he's injured? Or starving? "We water the horses, and then we move on. We'll rest when we've made camp for the night."

Mara looks away. "All right."

Guilt stabs my chest. I'm pushing too hard again. I don't know what else to do.

As we ride, Storm tells us this trail is usually well traveled, for it's one of only two main trading routes between Joya d'Arena and the free villages that hug the alpine slopes. But in the days since the highwaymen attacked us, we've seen no one.

"It's the coming war," Mara says. "No one will leave the shelter of the mountains to trade. They fear conscription into the conde's army."

"It doesn't surprise me that he would extend his draft into territory that doesn't belong to him," I say. Eduardo comes from a long line of ambitious condes, and over the centuries, several attempts have been made to annex the free villages into the countship of Montamayor. But they are a wily, reclusive, and independent people, and far more trouble to govern than they are worth.

"We should stock up on supplies in the free villages," Storm calls at my back. "Now that we have horses, we can carry more."

Storm has proven adept at assuring his own comfort. I glance back over my shoulder at him and say, "I may send Mara to pick up a few things, but I'm not sure it's safe."

"It's definitely not safe," he says. "But no one there will recognize you. Even *I* can walk through the free villages. It's the one place where your people and mine exist in relative peace."

I rein in Horse and twist in the saddle to face him. "Truly?"

"I always speak truly."

I frown. "My old tutor, Master Geraldo, taught me all about the free villages. He never once mentioned peace with Invierne."

He shrugs. "I wouldn't call it peace with Invierne. I'm sure Invierne would love to annex and control the area just as much as your wayward conde."

I turn back around and spur Horse onward to catch up to Mara and Belén. She takes a few quick steps, then slows to her usual plodding, but I'm thinking too hard to mind.

Master Geraldo said the free villages were a dangerous place, a magnet for black market merchants and army defectors and wanted felons. It makes sense that it would attract the same type of people from Invierne. But it's strange that he never mentioned an Invierno presence.

Or maybe not so strange. Only recently have I realized how

much Master Geraldo kept from me, especially anything pertaining to the Godstone I bear. My old tutor wasn't the only one. My sister, Alodia. My nurse, Ximena. Even my brief and well-meaning husband, Alejandro. All of them conspired to keep the chosen one—me—ignorant. Unsullied by damning knowledge. They believed God had ordained my obliviousness, based on an alternate translation of one of the *Scriptura Sancta*'s more obscure passages.

They were wrong.

Suddenly I want to see the free villages more than anything. I want to see my people and Storm's living side by side. I want to know what a place without king or council looks like, how a society can exist without fealty.

Mostly, though, I want to see it because during the last year I have learned, through much heartbreak, that the things people work hardest to keep me ignorant of are the things most worth pursuing.

8

WE find ourselves on the bald face of a giant granite outcropping. The trail disappears, marked only by piles of stone left by previous travelers to guide the way across the bare mountainside. Without the cover of pine forest, the wind is as loud and steady as a rushing river, the sun bright and fierce.

We take a moment to gaze westward toward the desert and see how far we've come. Below, the foothills spread wide, forested nearby but becoming sparser and sparser until they disappear into a hazy yellow horizon. Looking down at the vast landscape makes me feel strong, like I've accomplished something magnificent.

I imagine the Invierno soldiers who traveled this unforgiving path. There must have been an endless stream over many years to have amassed the enormous army that eventually attacked and nearly destroyed my capital city. I am filled with a sense of grudging admiration for the determination and stubbornness such a venture would take.

We cross the outcropping and drop into a grassy valley.

Storm says the first free village is just ahead, past a copse of spruce. Though no one here is likely to recognize us, Belén has warned us to be alert at all times. I clutch my reins so tight they dig into my palms, because at last we've come to a place where we can ask openly about travelers who have passed through before us.

I momentarily forget all this when I catch first sight of it. Massive stone walls jut from rolling grass, rising four or five times the height of a man before ending in jagged ruins, as if a giant cleaver has lopped off their tops. Chunks of quarry stone lie scattered throughout the meadow, half buried in sod.

I've seen this before—huge granite blocks so tightly fitted that the mortar is either invisible or absent, vegetation scaling the sides, corners rounded and worn smooth from centuries of wind and rain.

It's just like the hidden valley Storm and I discovered on our way to the *zafira*—the valley I destroyed. Perhaps the towers in this mountain village were also built by the ancestors of the Inviernos, long before God brought my own people to this world.

The village has grown up around these ruins, incorporating ancient walls and cornerstones into its own odd architecture. We pass a small cottage that uses one of the towers for its rear wall. Its roof is steep and pointed—never have I seen such a steep roof—and smoke curls lazily from a fat chimney. A stout woman dressed in doeskin leans over a porch railing, beating dust from a large pelt with a club. She studies us as we pass, but seems unconcerned.

Farther in, we encounter a large plaza of paver stone. Market stalls ring the area, and merchants cry their wares to everyone passing through. It's a busier, louder place than the commandeered village where we stole our horses. Looking around, listening to the rhythm of haggling, I could almost forget that a war is coming.

We toss a few coins to a stable boy who promises to feed and rub down our mounts, then Storm leads us toward the inn—a larger building with two gable windows. The setting sun reflects against the panes, and I can't shake the feeling that they're fiery eyes, glaring at us.

We're stepping onto the wood-plank porch when something flashes bright blue in my peripheral vision. I turn, puzzled.

Beside the inn is one of the many merchants' stalls, and it's obvious why this one faces west. In the setting sun, its wares are as bright as candle flames, for the stall is filled with glass. Glass of every color, sculpted into goblets and jewelry and candlestick holders, even blown into delicate sculptures of animals and people.

A mobile hangs from the ceiling, dangling squares that dance and sway in the gentle breeze, throwing prismatic shards against the walls of the hut—and against the face of the tall, supremely beautiful Invierno woman inside.

Storm nudges me forward, but I can't stop staring. She has light-brown eyes shaped like a cat's, an elegant nose and chin, and shining reddish-brown hair. If her coloring were a little darker, if she were not quite so tall, she would look like a Joyan woman.

She returns my stare without flinching, her expression curious. My Godstone flashes warm, and her eyes widen slightly.

I stumble up the stairs, Storm at my back. "I think she sensed your Godstone just now," he whispers. "I'll speak with her later and try to convince her it was mine."

I nod numbly, allowing myself to be led inside.

The interior is dim and hazy, acrid with smoke from both the enormous hearth and the pipes of several bearded man huddled around a table in the corner. Dry rushes line the edges of the room where the wall meets the stone floor. I watch, aghast, as one of the bearded men stands, turns toward the wall, and urinates into the rushes.

As soon as he is done, a little girl no more than eight years old darts over with an armful of fresh rushes that she drops right on top of the old ones. One of the men reaches out and pinches her rear, but she ignores him and scurries away.

I'm about to tell Belén that maybe coming here was a mistake, that replenishing our supplies can wait and I'm not that curious about this place after all. But a tall man in a fur cap and a shop apron places himself between us and the doorway, eyeing us hungrily.

"You are Joyans, yes?" he says. "You have come a long way in a perilous time."

His words are friendly, but cold calculation hardens his roving eyes as he sizes up our bearing, our cloaks, even our desert boots. We outfitted ourselves carefully, choosing nondescript clothing. Perhaps it is not nondescript enough.

Belén's return grin is equally calculating. "My companions

and I hope to do a tidy business where lesser merchants fear to tread," he says.

"Wise! Very wise indeed. You'll be taking rooms, then?"

"Yes," Belén says. "Two, please. And what does your cook have today?"

The man's gaze fixates on Belén's eye patch. "Venison stew. The best in the mountains." He leans forward and says, in a conspiratorial voice, "But for our higher class of customers, those that have the coin for it, we also have a limited amount of lamb shanks braised in garlic sauce, served with fresh flatbread."

My mouth waters.

Belén turns to me for a decision. Reluctantly I say, "The venison stew sounds delicious." We've drawn enough attention to ourselves with our finely woven shirts and thick cloaks.

I think of Mara's spice satchel, hidden in her pack. Once we realized we would make the first leg of our journey on foot, we exchanged most of our coin for spices, which are less cumbersome to carry. Mara's satchel holds marjoram, allspice berries, cardamom, dried ginger, and even some saffron—enough wealth to get us killed if we are foolish.

And Mara isn't the only one with hidden cargo. Shoved down into the bottom of my own pack is a wooden box containing my crown of shattered Godstones. Storm insisted— and rightly so—that I might need it at some point. It's worth more than this entire village, and its discovery would identify me with absolute surety.

"Mula!" the man yells, and the tiny girl who carried the rushes dashes to his side and looks up, wide-eyed. Why would someone name a child a word that means "mule"?

"Venison stew for our guests," the innkeeper bellows. "Four bowls. Quick, or you'll feel the back of my hand."

My Godstone eases warmth into my belly as I peer at her departing figure. It's hard to see in the dim smoke haze, but there's something unusual about the cast of her nose and chin, about the way she moves.

Belén directs us to a table. It's rough-hewn, the planks poorly joined. We sit on stumps to await our meal. I hope the little girl serves us. I want a better look at her.

We don't wait long. She hurries up, balancing four bowls in a miraculous feat, and slides them onto the table. Murky brown stuff slops over the side of one of them. She stares at the slight mess, horrified.

She is so tiny that even though I'm sitting, her head barely reaches my shoulder. Her limbs are scrawny beneath the ragged hem of her shift. Her feet are bare, her toenails crusted with dirt. A large bruise purples her forearm.

She looks up at me with pleading eyes, and I gasp. "Please don't tell that I spilled the stew," she whispers.

Her eyes are lightest brown, almost yellow, like a cat's. And she has the same high cheeks and delicate chin as Storm. But her skin is darker than that of any Invierno I've seen, her short, ragged hair a sooty black. My Godstone pulses warmly, as if greeting an old friend.

"Lady?" she says again, and her voice quivers. "You won't tell, will you?"

"There is nothing to tell," I say gently. "I see no spill."

Her grin is as quick and bright as lightning, and she dashes away.

"Why so interested in the girl?" Belén asks around a mouthful of stew.

"I thought she might be an Invierno child," I say, grabbing my spoon. "But now I'm not so sure."

"She's a mule," Storm says.

I pause, the spoonful of stew halfway to my mouth. "What do you mean?"

He takes a deep breath, as if greatly burdened to instruct me in something so obvious. "She's a mixed child. Part Invierno, part Joyan."

I set my spoon back down. "Oh. Are there . . . many . . . mixed people?"

"Oh, no, they are quite rare. A union between our people rarely produces children, and when it does, they grow up to be infertile, unable to bear children of their own."

"Ah," I say, though my heart is racing. "Mules." This is what Master Geraldo didn't want me to know. But why?

"Just so. This stew is terrible."

"They've watered it down," Mara says, her nose wrinkling. "And the turnips are old. Maybe moldy."

It's obviously no great revelation to my companions, but my mind whirls with ramifications. Mixed people. Why had this possibility never occurred to me before? "Do our people intermarry, then?" I ask.

"Sometimes," Storm says. "In the free villages. Such a marriage would never be sanctioned in Invierne, though."

"In the village we come from," Mara says, with a chin lift indicating Belén, "there was talk of a marriage to an Invierno trader, generations ago, before the border skirmishes got ugly. But I never thought it was true."

"Interesting." I finally take a bite of my stew, and Mara is correct—they've watered it down so much it might as well be soup.

"What are you thinking, Elisa?" Belén asks with a narrowed eye.

"Don't you think it's odd that, in spite of my royal education, no one ever told me about mules?"

He shrugs. "Maybe they didn't want you to know how similar Inviernos actually are to us. Painting the enemy as being as inhuman as possible is a great way to win a war."

I choke down a chunk of potato, hardly tasting it. "Maybe," I say. "But I want to talk to that girl again."

The bearded men at the table across from us eye us warily as we're scraping the last of our stew from our bowls. I'm relieved when Mula returns. "Your rooms are ready," she says. "I will show you."

We follow her through the common room to the back stairs. As she steps up, the bottoms of her bare feet flash bright blue, and I'm so startled I almost stumble.

"Slave mark," Mara whispers.

I frown. Joya d'Arena has not allowed slavery for centuries. My home country of Orovalle never allowed it.

"Here," says the girl. She opens a door to reveal a small room with two cots. A table rests against the wall between them. On it are a clay pitcher and a half-melted candle, lit from above by a single window too high to look out of. "Your other room is across the hall," she adds.

"Thank you," I say, and I hand her a copper coin, which she shoves into her mouth.

I want to ask her some questions, but I'm not sure where to start or what to say, so I'm glad when she lingers, her eyes roving over our packs. "What's in there?" she says around her mouthful of coin.

"Just supplies," I say.

"Orlín says you're traders."

"Orlín?"

"So what are you trading?"

Mara steps forward, eyes narrowed. "Did Orlín put you up to asking?"

The girl's golden eyes shift left, but she nods once, sharply.

My disarming smile is wasted on her, since she will not meet anyone's gaze. "You may tell Orlín that we have some spices," I say. "Just marjoram and sage. But if it trades well, we'll come back with more." The lie sits easy in my mouth. When did I become so comfortable with deception?

She nods and turns to slip out the door, but she pauses, her tiny hand on the frame. "He says you're fine lords and ladies," she says over her shoulder. "He has a very bad want for seeing inside those packs. But don't say I told." And she scurries away in a flash of bright blue.

I sigh after her. "I guess we should all stay in the same room tonight. And rotate watches."

"Our packs should be guarded at all times," Mara adds.

"By your leave," Storm says, "I'd like to find a barber to trim this loathsome black from my hair."

I grin, but my amusement is fleeting. "Will you make some inquiries, too? Find out if—when—Franco's party passed through? And I'd love to know if anyone remembers a prisoner, and . . . and what state he was in."

"Of course, Majesty."

"I'm going to see if I can trade for some tack," Belén says. "Our horses do well enough bareback, but past the timberline, our path is going to be very steep and I'd rather have saddles."

"Thank you, Belén."

"Will you and Mara be all right by yourselves?"

Mara and I exchange a look of mutual longing. "Oh, yes," I say firmly. "Mara and I are going to order baths."

Mara and I sit on the cot, clad only in our spare blouses while our regular clothes are with a laundress. She combs my damp hair, and the slight tug on my scalp is so familiar, so comforting. With my eyes closed, I can almost imagine that Ximena is the one working through my hair, that I didn't have to send her away after all.

I open my eyes. It was an inevitable decision, and it won't do me any good to wallow in regret.

"How is your head?" I ask Mara. The bruise above her brow is no longer swollen, but the color has turned the sickly yellow of urine. I'm hoping it's a good sign.

"Better," she says. "I don't get dizzy anymore."

"Belén was very concerned for you. He didn't leave your side once while you were drifting in and out of consciousness."

She freezes, and I wince as the teeth of the comb dig into my scalp with the weight of her hand. After too long a pause, she says, "Oh?"

I hide a smile. "Yes. The way he looked at you . . . you are dear to him, Mara."

She resumes combing, but her strokes are rhythmic and thoughtless. She combs the same section of hair over and over again. "Maybe . . ." she says. "Maybe I'm dear to him like a sister. We've become friends again."

It's hard not to laugh. "You know how you always tell me I'm pathetically ignorant in matters of love?"

She pulls my hair back and begins to separate it for braiding. "Well, it's true. You were the *last* person to realize Hector was in love with you."

"Yes, well, everyone is ignorant when it comes to their own life and love."

"You think so?"

"I think . . ." I struggle to find the exact words. "I think sometimes when we find love we pretend it away, or ignore it, or tell ourselves we're imagining it. Because it's the most painful kind of hope there is. It can be ripped away so easily. By indifference. By death. By . . . the need for a political marriage. Or maybe that last one is just me."

Her fingers move from habit, and I wish we were back in my suite, sitting in front of the vanity mirror so I could see her face. "You think I'm pretending away my hope?" she says in a small voice. "Because it might hurt too much?"

"I don't know. But that's what I did with Hector. Even though part of me knew I loved him."

She plunks down beside me on the cot and lets her face fall into her hands. "I'm afraid," she whispers into her palms.

"Belén adores you. I'm sure of it."

"Not of that." She raises her face, and I have to remind myself that the rippled scar pushing one eyelid down—a gift from her abusive father—always makes her appear sadder than she is. "I could not bear it, to fall in love again, only to have him die."

"You're thinking of Julio." The boy she was secretly betrothed to, before she fled to the rebel village and met me. She doesn't speak of him often, but over time I've eked bits of the story out of her.

"Don't you ever think of Humberto?" she counters. "Surely losing him so suddenly makes you . . . wary."

"I think of him often," I say softly. "Though less than I used to."

"You loved him." Her voice is almost accusing.

"I did. It was different, though. I loved Alejandro too, in a small way. I seem to have great capacity for it. Alejandro was the most beautiful man I'd ever seen. But Humberto was the kindest, a different kind of beautiful."

"And Hector?"

I take a deep breath, for talking about him is both wondrous and painful. "Hector is my friend. I trust him in everything, always. But when I'm with him, it's like my blood is on fire.

And now that I understand you can love someone in different ways at once, I'll never want less."

She sighs. "Julio was my friend. And Belén was my fire. But now . . ."

"Now Belén is becoming a friend too." I shake my head in mock despair. "A deadly combination."

A little grin sneaks onto her face. "We are doomed, Elisa."

"Indeed, I think we are."

She starts to giggle, and then she's laughing so hard that tears leak from her eyes.

"What, by God's righteous right hand, is so funny?"

"You!" She gasps between breaths. "Giving *me* advice on love!"

And it hardly makes sense, but laughter pours out of me like a stream too long dammed, and then we're hugging on the cot, both of us breathless, until she suddenly sobers and says, "You're the best friend I've ever had, Elisa." But the moment it leaves her mouth, she stiffens and pulls her arms away. "I'm sorry. That's not appropriate. I would never presume—"

"And you're mine," I say truthfully. There's a hole inside me that she fills, something I wouldn't get from being queen or winning a war or even being with Hector.

"You're the sister I never had," she adds.

"And you're the sister I always *wish* I had."

She barks a laugh. "Someday you'll have to tell me all about Princess Alodia and why things are so difficult between you."

I nod, my thoughts suddenly far away. "When I figure it out," I murmur, "you'll be the first to know."

9

I braid Mara's hair for a change, and I have just finished when Storm returns with close-cropped hair the color of corn silk and a new swagger. He stands tall, his head high, the cowl of his cloak thrown back for the first time in weeks. The shorter cut brings out the planes of his face, giving his cheeks and jaw a more chiseled nature. Were he not so preternaturally tall and oddly colored, he would be almost handsome.

He catches Mara and me staring and rubs his hair, frowning. "It will grow back," he assures us. "By the time we reach Invierne, it will be less shameful."

"I'm relieved to hear that your vanity has weathered this egregious trial unscathed."

"Thank y— Oh. Sarcasm again."

"Actually," Mara says, "I was staring because it seems whiter than it used to be. Maybe I got used to the dye."

"You think so?" His eyes spark with hope. "I thought it might be, but I wasn't sure."

Mara and I exchange a perplexed look. "This is a good

thing?" I venture. "To have whiter hair?"

"It's a mark of magic. The oldest, most powerful animagi have the lightest hair. It's the one thing that has given me hope, made me think that maybe I could still learn to call the *zafira*. Because in spite of my continued failure . . ." He lifts his chin. "My hair does bear the mark of one who is learning the art."

I touch my thick sleeping braid. My hair has been as black as night for most of my life—until the sun leached the color from strands around my face, leaving them a washed-out red. But maybe it wasn't the sun. Maybe it was my Godstone. Will my hair be as ghostly pale as Storm's someday?

"I asked about Lord Hector," he says.

Mara and I straighten so fast our shoulders knock.

"What?" I demand. "What did you hear?"

Storm settles on the floor and crosses his long legs. "A group came through. Large, well armed. A mix of Joyans and Inviernos, though the Inviernos were all dark of skin and hair. The barber told me they mistook the Inviernos for mules at first, because of their coloring. Most of them made camp just out of sight. Only a few entered the village to trade for supplies."

"*When?* When did they come through?"

"Less than a week ago."

We are closer than I realized. "And did your barber notice a prisoner among them?"

"He did not."

My shoulders slump.

"But I asked the glass merchant outside the inn, and she

remembers him distinctly. One of the men traveling with Franco is a cousin of hers, so she spent time in their camp, trading information and news for him to take back to their family in Invierne."

"And how . . . ? Is he . . . ?"

Storm gazes at me with uncharacteristic sympathy. "She said he was beaten badly."

"Oh!" I reach out and find Mara's hand. She clasps mine tight.

"She said he is pale and sick. His skin was as white as an Invierno's."

I nod, because the lump in my throat makes it impossible to speak. Hector is strong. I know it well. He will do his best to survive. But when I finally find my voice, it's to say, "I will destroy Franco. Utterly destroy him."

"I anticipate that eagerly," Storm says.

I give him a sharp look. "Oh?" Though he harbors little loyalty to those of his homeland, I've never heard such resentment in his voice before.

"Franco is an unrighteous man," he says firmly. "My uncle, once in line for a position in the Deciregi, was killed under mysterious circumstances. My family has long suspected Franco, though we cannot be sure."

"You sound sure."

He shrugs.

The sun is low enough that Mara lights the candle on the small table. I should try to sleep. We need all the rest we can get. But now that I know Hector is so close, I'm twitchy with the possibility that we could catch him before he reaches Invierne. Maybe we won't need to enter enemy territory after all. It's a long shot. I will have to push us even harder than before.

I'm about to suggest—probably unwisely—that we head downstairs or go for a walk or *anything* that will get me out of this tiny, stifling room, but the sounds of a scuffle filter through the door. Something bangs against the wall, followed by muffled protests.

My hand flies to the dagger at my waist. Storm launches to his feet as Mara grabs her bow from the floor.

A knock sounds. "It's me," calls Belén.

"Enter," I say, but I unsheathe my dagger.

The door creaks open, and Belén thrusts the girl Mula ahead of him. She stumbles to her knees, then curls into a tiny ball on the floor, hands protecting her head. The bright blue slave marks on her heels are very clear now—thick circles, each with a dot in the middle. It's like her feet have eyes, and I shudder.

"I found her snooping in the room across the hall." He tosses a small leather bag onto the floor beside her. "That was in her hand."

Belén's jerky pouch. A harmless thing to steal. But I'm glad we thought to keep our real valuables always within reach.

"I didn't mean to steal!" she says. "It was a black thought, and I tried to make it go away, but it smelled so—"

I reach down for the pouch, and she flinches so hard she knocks the side of her head onto the floorboards.

"I'm not going to hurt you," I say. "Sit up. Look at me."

She does, but her eyes are as wide and her muscles as tense

as a cornered cat's. She scoots back against the cot and huddles there, knees to chest. Her arms and calves are stick thin, and shiny calluses encircle her wrists and ankles. Someone ties her up. Often. Maybe every night.

I reach into the pouch for a piece of jerky and toss it to her. She snatches it midair and shoves into her mouth.

"So I'm curious, Mula . . . is that your real name? Mula?"

She just shrugs, continuing to chew, and her gaze on me does not waver.

"It will do for now. Mula, if you weren't in the room to steal, why were you there?"

Her mouth freezes. She looks to Belén, back to me.

"It's an easy question," I say.

She swallows the jerky and says, "Just curious. About what was in your packs. I wanted to know what marjoram smells like."

"Did Orlín put you up to it?" Mara asks gently.

She hesitates a little too long before saying, "No. I did it my own self." She glares at Mara, as if daring contradiction.

"God despises liars," Storm says, and I shoot him a pained look.

I pace for a moment, worrying my thumbnail with my teeth. The innkeeper's relentless curiosity is a problem. If he discovers what we carry, he might murder us in our sleep. I sigh. So much for a good night's rest in actual beds. "All right, then. Everyone pack up. We're leaving."

"No!" cries the girl. "He'll—"

Belén grabs her by the collar and hauls her to her feet.

"Gently!" Mara says. "She's just a little girl."

He scowls, but he relaxes his grip. "I'm not letting her go until we're packed, with everything accounted for."

We gather our things quickly. My pack feels light, and I remember that Mara and I each have a set of clothes with the laundress. But I'm not willing to wait.

We shoulder our packs and head downstairs. The common room is crowded now, thick with smoke and sour ale and unwashed bodies, noisy with laughter and music. Three men near the hearth strum vihuelas, and their enthusiasm almost makes up for the reed-thin sound of the poorly made instruments.

Orlín the innkeeper weaves through the crowd toward us, carrying two wooden mugs. He sets them on a table nearby, where they are instantly claimed by grubby, weathered hands. Orlín wipes his hands on his apron, shouting, "Some ale for you all? I also have a nice batch of dandelion wine in the cellar."

"We're leaving," I say.

Before I can blink, he swings his huge arm and backhands Mula across the face, sending her crashing into a bench. "What did you do?" he bellows.

Mula clutches for the bench, misses, grabs at it again. She tries to pull herself to her feet, but she reels, her knees buckling.

Orlín takes a step toward the girl, but in a flash, Mara's dagger is at his throat. "Leave her be," she says with deadly calm.

The laughter in the room fades, the music stills. Stools scrape against the wood floor. Somewhere behind me, a sword is whisked from its scabbard. We are surrounded and outnumbered.

Mara, what have you done?

My hand twitches toward my own dagger, but I don't pull it. Not yet. Neither do Storm or Belén, though they both survey the room, sizing up our options. Maybe the situation can still be salvaged.

The knob of Orlín's throat bobs against the point of Mara's dagger. "It's the height of rudeness," he says, his gaze on Mara's fisted grip, "for a guest to draw in a man's own home."

"It's worse," she hisses, "to beat an innocent girl senseless."

"The mule is mine. I can do whatever I wish with it. Do you tell the cook not to slice the turnips? Do you tell the scullery maid to be gentle with her rags?"

Mara's face reddens. The daggers presses deeper. Blood wells at its tip, and a tiny rivulet slips downs the innkeeper's neck and disappears under his collar. The common room is silent except for heavy breathing, the creak of a floorboard, embers popping in the hearth.

We must withdraw at once, but I'm not sure how. I could order Mara to stand down. But her dagger at the innkeeper's throat might be the only thing holding back utter chaos.

Think, Elisa.

Mula whimpers from the floor, and I spare her a quick glance. Her eyes are glazed. Blood streams from a cut on her forehead.

"Mula!" I say. "How much did Orlín pay for you?"

She tries to focus in the direction of my voice, blinking rapidly. "Three . . . three silvers."

So little! The entire worth of a person is little more than my laundress's monthly allowance.

I say, "I'll buy her from you."

Orlín's gaze turns calculating, but I hardly care, because Mara's hand is wavering. I give her an encouraging nod, and slowly, reluctantly, she lowers the blade. But she does not sheath it.

The innkeeper takes a relieved breath. Keeping an eye on Mara, he says, "I bought it when it was young and weak and stupid. I've spent years training it, feeding it, making it strong. I won't let it go for less than eight silvers."

I pretend to consider. "That is more than I expected. I'll have to do some trading to come up with that kind of coin." Which is a lie. How ridiculous we were, to think that trading more than half our coin for spices would lighten our purse to an unremarkable amount. Now that I think about it, buying supplies *has* become less and less expensive as we've moved away from the populated coastal areas. We probably carry more than this man sees in a year. "But if you give me the night to come up with it, I'll give you ten. Eight for the girl, and two more for the inconvenience of our misunderstanding this evening."

His eyes widen. Then his face breaks into a huge grin. "Done!" He spits into his palm and holds it out to me.

Ugh.

But there is no help for it. I spit into my own and clasp his tight, smiling relentlessly in spite of the slickness between our palms.

Everyone relaxes so suddenly it's like a bubble popping. People return to their seats. Mara sheaths her dagger. The din of chatter and music is gradually restored.

"You still plan to leave?" Orlín says, wiping his palm on his stained apron.

I hesitate. Maybe the danger is past, and we can sleep easy. But no, we have just made a very public display of wealth. Best to camp outside the village and eat nothing that hasn't been prepared by our own hands.

"We'll be back in the morning. I'll give you three silvers now to board the girl tonight and ensure her safety, the rest tomorrow when we collect her unharmed."

He nods agreement, and as Belén fishes some coins from a small purse, I look down at my new slave.

Mula is still on the floor, her skinny, bruised legs sprawled out. She clutches the leg of the bench as if her life depends on it, and her eerie, golden gaze is fixed on me. "You bought me," she whispers. "You bought me."

The protest dies on my lips before fully formed. I've no intention of making this girl slave for me, but it would be unwise to say so aloud. I'll explain later, when we're on the road. *Oh, God, what am I going to do with a little girl?*

I turn toward the door, gesturing for the others to follow. We're nearly free of this stifling place, and I prepare to breathe deep of open air and safety when I hear Mula shout, "Did you see *that*? A lady bought me! I'm going to be the slave of a fine lady!"

We collect our horses from the ostler and lead them to the

village outskirts. It's dark and cool, the stars so bright that the sky seems like a tapestry woven of night bloomers. This high in the mountains, the trees are sparse and stunted, but we find a group of pines thriving in the shade of a granite cliff and make camp among them. I eye the cliff gratefully as we flip out our bedrolls. It's one less approach to guard.

Belén tends to the horses, and Storm settles down to pray. No one speaks. Mara's features are set stubbornly, as if she expects a scolding. She deserves one, and I have to give it to her. My stomach roils with the sudden understanding that I cannot be both queen and friend to her in this moment.

"Mara," I say.

She is shifting through her pack for something, and she looks up at me, her eyes narrowed.

"I understand why you intervened on Mula's behalf," I tell her. "But—"

"No," she whispers. "You really don't."

I have scars too, I want to say. *And some are even carved into my flesh.* But I hesitate. Because if Mara told me she knew exactly how I felt, I wouldn't believe her either.

"Fine. I don't understand. But if you endanger our purpose again by being rash and ridiculous, you will walk home to Brisadulce alone."

"He was going to kill her!"

"I doubt it. She's valuable property to him. Even so, it was a bad decision. She is not worth your life to me. Or Belén's or Storm's. She's not worth my whole kingdom." I cringe inwardly at my callousness, but it's not the first time I've had to weigh lives against each other, and it won't be the last.

Mara stretches out on her bedroll. She puts her hands behind her head and gazes up at the night sky. I wait a moment, thinking that she will surely apologize. Or at least thank me for buying the girl. But she says nothing.

Sighing, I sit down on my own bedroll and unlace my boots.

The morning dawns bright, clear, and cold. I spend a few moments breathing, watching with wonder as the air leaves my body and turns to fog.

Storm sniffs, and his face darkens.

"Storm?"

"Winter comes early," he says, staring off in the direction of the white-capped peaks. "Even if we're successful in retrieving the commander, we risk getting trapped in these mountains."

We rush to pack up, and return to the inn to find Mula waiting at the door. When she sees us, her face breaks into a smile, displaying two huge, slightly crooked front teeth.

She is as naked as the day she was born but doesn't bother to cover herself. Her bruised body seems made up entirely of knees and elbows. A welt juts out of her forehead like newly risen dough. Bright purple stretches down from it and hugs her right eye.

"Where are your clothes?" I demand.

Her smile falters. "You didn't buy my clothes," she says. "Just me."

I take a deep, calming breath. I grab the reins to Belén's horse and say to him, "Please go settle our account with Orlín." If I walk in there myself, I'm liable to let Mara gut him after all.

As Belén enters the inn, Mara hands Jasmine's reins to Storm and says, "I'll fetch our laundry. Mula can wear my extra blouse for now."

I nod, and she hurries off. Mula and Storm stare at each other in a mutual sizing-up that for some reason amuses me.

"Are you an animagus?" she says. "You look like an animagus. But your hair is ugly."

His green eyes flare wide. "I am a pri—"

"Storm!"

His mouth slams closed. Then: "I am nobody," he says instead, his eyes downcast. "Nobody important."

I study him thoughtfully. "Storm is my very good friend," I say. "And you must mind him while you are with us."

"Oh, yes," she says. "I will mind perfectly. You are going to be so glad you bought me."

Not likely. I don't dare take her to Invierne with us. I can't be slowed down, and I can't worry about yet another life. Maybe someone in the next village will agree to care for her in exchange for being well paid. I sigh loudly. It will mean flashing coin and drawing attention yet again.

Mula stares as if reading my thoughts. "I can cook," she says. "And clean. I can keep your clothes washed. You don't have to go to a laundress ever again."

"How old are you?" At first glance, I thought her no more

than eight years old. But something about the way she talks, and her piercing golden gaze, makes me wonder if she might be older.

She just shrugs.

"How long were you with Orlín?"

"Four years."

"And before that?"

She gestures toward the merchant booth full of sparkling glass. The Invierno woman's back is to us as she arranges baubles on a table. "I was with *her* for two years. But she had a bad season and had to sell me."

I glare at the Invierno. "And before that?"

"I don't remember. I was too little."

If the girl has six years of memory, she is probably nine or ten.

"Do you have a name besides Mula?"

"Sometimes Orlín calls me Rat," she says. "He used to catch me nibbling on . . ." Her mouth freezes open. "But I don't do that anymore! I swear it!"

"A little girl deserves a proper name," I say.

"Like what?"

I think for a moment, but nothing comes to mind. "How about you name yourself?" I say.

She stares at me agape. "For true?"

"For true."

"Anything?"

"Anything you want."

She looks down at the ground and kicks a clump of grass

with dirty toes. I resist the urge to pull my bedroll from my pack and wrap it around her naked body.

"A name is a grave matter," Storm says.

She looks back and forth between us, her tiny features screwed into a mask of utter seriousness. "I will think hard about this," she says.

"Let me know when you've decided." I suppose Mula will do for now.

Belén barrels out of the inn and high-steps down the stairs, swinging his pack over his shoulder. "Where's Mara?" he asks. "We should leave at once."

"What happened?"

"I'm not sure. Maybe nothing. But Orlín hardly looked at me as our money changed hands. Everything was too quiet. I have a bad feeling."

I trust Belén's instincts more than just about anyone's. I hand him his reins. "Mara is fetching our laundry. Then we'll ride hard until we're well away." Most of the merchants have finished setting up their booths now, and the courtyard fills with people. They eye us warily as they go about their business.

Belén stares down at Mula, frowning. "And the girl?"

"We'll figure something out."

"What happened to your eye?" Mula asks, pointing at his patch.

He is saved having to respond as Mara hurries up, her arms full of neatly folded linens. "She tried to charge me double," she says. "Word is out that we have coin."

Quickly we divvy up the linens and shove them inside our

packs. Mara shakes out her blouse and hands it to Mula. "Put this on."

Mula does, and the hem nearly reaches her knees. The neck-line threatens to hang off one shoulder, but the girl doesn't seem to care. She strokes the linen lovingly. Then she lifts the hem to her cheek and caresses her face with it, revealing all the parts we just took such pains to cover.

"Mara, you're in charge of the girl. She'll ride with you."

"Of course."

Horse lips my braid as I move around her to mount. "Stop that," I mutter, but I pause to give her muzzle a quick scratch.

Mara scoots back in her new saddle to make room. Storm lifts Mula as if she is no heavier than a fallen leaf, and Mara wraps a steadying arm around the girl's waist. Mula clutches the pommel like her life depends on it. "I've never been on a horse before," she breathes.

"They're not so bad," I say, giving Horse a kick. We ride out of the village at a leisurely walk, not wanting to attract attention, but the horses sense our nervousness and step high, flicking their tails. The moment we're out of sight, we break into a hard gallop.

10

HECTOR

THE snow fascinates me.

Though its cold leaches into my bones, I can't help lifting my bound hands to catch the falling flakes. They land, sparkling and light as butterfly wings, only to melt against my skin into something so commonplace as water.

It's a reminder that transformations happen in a second. That my status as a prisoner is a fleeting, ephemeral state, needing only the right circumstance to dissolve it.

We have descended to where trees grow again. It's colder on this side of the mountain, cloudier, stormier. Every time the snow begins to fall, the Inviernos mutter to one another in hushed tones. Franco glowers incessantly. He cuts our rest stops short and orders us into a gallop whenever we reach a flat stretch of trail.

They read something worrisome in the weather, the same way I can sniff the ocean air, gauge the color of the sky, and feel in my marrow that a hurricane is coming. I listen hard to their conversation for clues, pay attention to the chilling breeze on my face, note the way the horses paw through the light layer of snow on the ground to get to the grass underneath. Because whatever it is they are sensing, I want to sense it too.

Anything that worries my captors presents an opportunity for me.

When we stop briefly to graze the horses in a small alpine meadow, I already have my ear turned toward Franco when he says to his men, "Keep to the center of the meadow. Don't let the horses stray toward the mountain laurel."

The Joyan who always rides sentry beside me helps me dismount. His knuckles are huge and his fingers are crooked; he's a brawler who has used his fists too often. "I need to relieve myself," I say.

A few weeks ago, this exact request was met with a shrug and a "Soil yourself for all I care." But I've given him no trouble. They've purposely kept me weak from hunger, and I've made sure they see how my hands have stiffened into useless claws. He grabs me by the collar and pushes me toward the edge of the meadow without a word of protest.

But I have full use of my hands now. My bonds remain stuck to my skin, crusted on by blood and sweat. But if I were to separate my wrists, anyone could see the unraveling mess of hemp created by night upon night of sawing with a now-dull rock.

We near the stunted trees, and my captor gives me a shove. I allow myself to stumble. I hope I'm not overdoing it. But a quick glance over my shoulder assures me the Joyan sentry has already lost interest. He gazes back toward the center of the meadow, where the horses cluster together, chomping on frozen grass.

I won't have much time. I scan the foliage around me, mentally sorting it, eliminating the familiar. Not lupine, not ferns, not paintbrush . . . there! A shrub with long, waxy leaves and dried flowers that might have been pink or red during high summer.

I glance back again. The Joyan is not watching.

I snap off a sprig of mountain laurel, shove it down my shirt. The Joyan still does not look my way, so I grab a huge handful. I pat it down beneath my shirt to even out the lumps.

"What's taking so long?"

I nearly jump. "Almost done," I answer in a bored voice, pretending to tie up my pants. I turn around and say, "Thank you." The laurel scratches the skin of my abdomen. I resist the urge to look down and check for telltale bulges.

He grunts and leads me back toward the horses. I'm not sure what I'll do with the mountain laurel. I just know that a plant worth avoiding is a plant worth having. Elisa taught me that.

I've memorized the rolling hitch knot used to tie me to a tree each night. It's a variation on a knot my brother Felix taught me, easy to tie and untie if one's hands are free. Usually, the traitor Joyan who ties it puts the knot off to the side, just out of my reach. But Franco has been pushing so hard, everyone is exhausted, and I am a model prisoner.

Inevitably, tonight, the Joyan gets careless. The knot isn't quite so tight. Not quite so far off to the side.

My limbs tingle with before-battle anticipation. As every-one stretches out on their bedrolls and the evening fire burns low, I think I might come out of my own skin with readiness.

I consider escaping but reject the notion immediately. Though I'm not as handicapped as I've led my captors to believe, I'm weak from hunger and stiff from lack of exercise. I would need to steal one of the horses to get fast and far, but I could never sneak past the perimeter watch on a horse.

And I keep hearing intriguing bits of conversation. Something about a gate, another *sendara* that leads to a place of power.

So instead of escaping, I'll do what I can to slow us down and give Elisa a chance to catch up. In the meantime, I'll learn all that I can.

Tonight, the chip-toothed Joyan sits cross-legged on the ground before me—a little farther away than usual. I close my eyes, letting my head drop to the left, and feign sleep.

Eventually the breathing of my guard becomes deep and nasal. I open my eyes. The Joyan is definitely asleep.

I survey the camp, seeking movement. Everyone slumbers, though I know the perimeter watch patrols just out of sight. A cloud covers the moon, shrouding everything in darkness. Good. It will be easier to sneak around.

The ropes don't allow much range of motion, and when I bend my elbows, I can barely reach the knot. It's awkward work, and I'm not sure how I'll tie myself back up later. But I am committed to my course.

I shake the ropes loose and step out of them. I pause, breath held, listening for movement.

Tree frogs chirrup nearby, and a slight breeze rustles the pine boughs. The air is crisp and dry, with a citrusy tang. It will snow tonight. I smile into the dark, for I am developing my nose for snow.

But it means I must enact my plan before it falls, lest my footprints betray me in the morning. I creep toward the horses, reaching beneath my shirt for the mountain laurel. It has been chafing my skin all day, leaving tiny, itching welts.

The horses nicker a soft greeting, and I crouch low, for someone is surely on watch nearby. I'm counting on the horses' swishing tails and the way they huddle together for warmth to disguise my movements.

I know exactly which mount goes with which rider. I weave among them until I find the little chestnut with white fetlocks ridden by the brawler who guards me during the day. I offer her a handful of mountain laurel, palm flat to avoid nips. She lips it up eagerly.

I'm sorry. So very sorry. You're a good horse, and you deserve better. I hope it will be just enough to make her sick and no more. But I'm not sure.

I don't have enough to poison all the horses, so I make my selections carefully. Only Joyan horses, and I choose mountain ponies over large war chargers, hoping their smaller bodies will be more susceptible.

I am heartsick as I creep back toward my tree. *"Treat your mounts as brothers-in-arms,"* I always tell my men. *"They are soldiers to your cause and your closest companions."*

The Joyan traitor still sleeps, chin to chest, his left hand twitching in the dirt. I could kill him right now, if I chose. My fingertips itch with the need to wrap around his throat.

Keeping a wary eye on him, I step back into the circle of rope, sit against the tree trunk, and work the rope up around my chest and arms. I yank it as tight as I can, which isn't very tight at all. The triple hitch knot takes me four tries, and I position it too far forward, but I manage it.

I've done the best I can. I press my wrists together, but they've been unbound for days now, and it's only a matter of time before a closer inspection reveals my deception. I close my eyes to await the snow.

11

STORM leads us now as we leave the timberline far behind. For a few days, our path winds through grassy meadows filled with wildflowers, crystal brooks, and herds of tiny deer that lift their long necks to regard us as we pass, flicking ears and tails but otherwise paying us no mind.

The meadows thin, and on Storm's recommendation we dismount and pull grass, stuffing as much as we can into our packs because, as he explains, it might be days before we cross the watershed and find good grazing for the horses again. And sure enough, soon we've ascended so high that nothing grows, save for random patches of lichen and a few stubborn stalks of yellow paintbrush.

The air is too thin, the light too bright and close, and we shiver in the shadows only to sweat in the sunshine. The peaks jut around us, sometimes graveled, sometimes jagged, sheltering year-old snow on their leeward sides. Tiny short-tailed mice scuttle from our path, and raptors circle through the peaks. The world is an immense garden of gray and white, and

I marvel at how like a desert it is, with its varied hues of color and teeming life—but only if you pay attention.

Though we bought Mula a pair of sturdy boots in the last village, they always end up tied over the pommel of Mara's horse. Mula runs back and forth down the path before us, plucking paintbrush blooms, chasing darting mice, collecting oddly shaped rocks, until exhaustion suddenly takes her and she climbs up into Mara's saddle and falls dead asleep to Jasmine's rocking gait, her tiny, blue-tattooed feet swinging miles above the stirrups.

We interviewed a few families in the free villages, hoping to find someone to care for the girl while we traveled to Invierne. But they always eyed our packs greedily, and they sized up Mula like she was a juicy rabbit. One afternoon, after I watched a group of Joyan children spitting on a mixed-blood boy and poking him with sticks, I decided that Mula would stay with us. I expect I'll begin regretting the decision any moment.

Between jagged peaks, we catch glimpses of storm clouds that are blue near to black and crackling with lightning. Storm explains that the Sierra Sangre is a cloud trap, and the other side of the continent is wet and cool. He warns that these peaks will be impassable soon, maybe within weeks, that the snow will be so deep that travelers would drown in it. So we travel fast, starting with the rising sun and falling onto our bedrolls exhausted with the day's last stubborn light.

Now that we are away from the free villages, and near enough to winter that no one but the most desperate and fool-hardy walk this trail, I begin to pray again. And when I do, the *zafira* is like a tidal wave rushing through me, filling me to overflowing with heat and power. I am certain the *zafira* changed my Godstone somehow. Or maybe it changed me.

So, one afternoon, we encounter a small valley that is sheltered enough by the surrounding peaks to harbor a bit of soil and some dry, stubborn grass. We pause to let the horses graze their fill—and to allow Storm and me to practice with our Godstones.

While Belén and Mara stretch out in the grass to rest and Mula explores the valley, Storm and I stand across from each other in awkward silence. The longing in Storm's face is hard to look at, so I focus on the fact that the bright mountain sun has reddened his cheeks and caused the skin on his nose to flake away.

"So . . . er . . . maybe we should have blood?" I say at last. "Whenever I watched an animagus do . . ." I make a vague gesture with my hand. "There was always blood."

Storm rubs his chin, considering. "But you have never needed blood. You healed Hector, moved the Aracely through a hurricane, broke my chains, and never once used it."

I nod. "I tried it a few times, with Father Nicandro in Brisadulce. We used to experiment with my Godstone. But nothing ever . . . No, wait! When we were on the island, I accidentally pricked my finger on the thorn of a sacrament rose. It felt like the whole world shook. I saw lines of power for a moment, coming from all directions toward a central point. So maybe I should try it with blood too."

"Blood?" says a voice at my elbow. "Do you want some?"

Mula thrusts out a scrawny, sun-darkened arm. For the first time, I notice the tiny white scars along her forearm.

Bile rises in my throat. "You've been bled before?" I ask in a faltering voice.

She straightens and says proudly, "I'm a good bleeder. Orlín sold my blood to the animagi all the time. It makes me tired, but it's not so bad." She shrugs. "Better than scrubbing the common-room floor."

I turn to ask Storm if bleeding innocent children is a common practice in Invierne, but he seems just as appalled as I am. "We won't be needing your blood, girl," he says gruffly. "Go play."

She peers up at him. "But you *are* an animagus, aren't you? Even though you said you're nobody."

He avoids her gaze. "I'm not a sorcerer."

"For true?"

"I always speak for true."

"Storm always speaks what he *thinks* is true," I interject. "Now go play, Mula. And thank you for your generous offer, but Storm is right—we will not need your blood."

She starts to meander off, but then she whips around and says, "But you have a sparkle stone, don't you? You both do. I can tell."

"Go play!" we both say at once, and she darts away.

Storm and I face each other again. "Exasperating child," he grumbles.

"Tell me about your training, Storm," I order. "I want to know everything you learned until you gave up."

Storm considers. In the distance, I hear Mula say, "Mara, how come you have that scar on your eye?"

"The trick," Storm says, "is to become one with the world around you." He shrugs sheepishly. "Though, to be honest, I'm not sure what that means. But my tutor had me do this." He pulls his Godstone amulet from beneath his tunic and takes it off; the chain is just large enough to fit around his head. He stands tall, his feet shoulder-width apart. His amulet swings from one hand as he reaches it to the sky.

"My tutor said it's important to ground yourself to the earth," he explains. "Otherwise the power rushing through you can throw you off balance. And you must always aim your amulet or staff away from your body, for when the *zafira* courses through it, it will be too hot to touch."

"I don't have a staff or amulet," I point out. "Just me."

"Indeed, I am very interested in seeing what happens with you. Archivists at the Morning Temple—that's where the training of novices takes place—speculate that someone with a living Godstone would be immune to its more dangerous properties."

I nod, remembering how the animagus who held me captive used magic to freeze everyone around him. But it didn't work on me.

"You think I'm even immune to a Godstone's fire?"

"I doubt it. It becomes a natural thing after it leaves the stone itself, burning and spreading just like any other fire. But you might be immune to your own."

So I follow Storm's example and set my feet shoulder-width

apart. I imagine that my legs are rooted to the earth, conduits for the magic creeping beneath the earth's skin.

"Now what?" I ask.

"This is the part I never mastered," he says with a grimace. "But my tutor said that if I closed my eyes and blocked out everything around me, I should feel a connection to the magic of the earth. Almost like the tug of a string." He lowers his amulet and shrugs. "But I never felt anything. I failed—"

"Try it. I'll try it if you do."

He opens his mouth, closes it. Stares at the amulet dangling from his hand.

"It's just you and me," I add softly. "No one need ever know what transpires here today."

He reaches with a forefinger to hook his hair behind his ears—a nervous, useless gesture, for it is still too short. "All right," he says. "We'll try it without blood first. Ready?"

I close my eyes. I concentrate on the feel of the earth beneath my feet. I imagine a string connecting me to the *zafira.*

Power rushes into me like a flood. My Godstone flashes hotter than desert sunshine, and my limbs tingle with an overwhelming desire to spring into action.

I crack open one eye and peek at Storm. He is panting, his face is flushed, and tiny beads of sweat collect on his upper lip.

"Anything?" I ask.

He opens his eyes, and a huge smile spreads across his face. "Oh, yes," he breathes. "It's like a thread of power connects me to the world." He stares wide-eyed at his caged amulet. A tiny spark pulses at its center. "What about you? Do you feel the thread?"

"It's more like a rushing river. A really *warm* river. I could probably heal someone right now. I'm not sure how to call fire, though." As I relax my focus, though, the power drains out of me as if I'm a sieve.

"You're supposed to direct the line of power through your Godstone somehow. And apparently it helps to think angry, destructive thoughts."

"How pleasant."

He nods. "If by 'pleasant,' you mean the exact opposite of that. Here, I'll try it." He closes his eyes, breathes deeply, holds his amulet out toward the granite outcropping. "Just reach down," he murmurs, "find the thread, direct it toward the stone." His brow furrows, and his breathing quickens. "Then think about something that makes you angry—"

A stream of red-orange fire erupts from his stone and pounds against the cliff, trailing sparks to the ground.

The fire fades quickly, and I stare at the circle of char left behind, mouth agape. "You did it! Storm, you . . ."

I turn to find him knocked to the ground. His long limbs are sprawled at awkward angles, and his amulet smolders beside him in a carpet of dead pine needles. But his smile is huge, and his green eyes blaze with triumph. "With practice," he says, "the fire will get so hot it will turn blue. Then white. A white fire is powered wholly by the *zafira*, and will continue to burn even when it's out of fuel. For years, sometimes."

I think of the charred ring of destruction around my capital city and its unquenchable embers. "It was a white fire that struck Alejandro. And Mara. Mara's burn resisted healing until I healed her myself." I reach my hand down. We grasp forearms, and I help him to his feet.

In his other hand, he dangles his now brightly glowing amulet at a safe distance. "With practice I'll be able to aim better," he says. "Ground myself so I don't fall down."

My lips twitch. "I just hope you don't set the mountainside on fire while you figure it out. And maybe you shouldn't try for a white fire just yet. Not until you have some control."

His eyes narrow. "Your turn," he says in challenge.

I take a deep breath and turn toward the granite face. I imagine myself shooting fire from my belly, which sends me into a fit of giggles.

"This is humorous for you?"

No, I suppose it's not. In answer, I close my eyes and open myself to the *zafira*.

It comes in a rush, eagerly, as powerful as a sandstorm, as gentle as a feather. "Well, hello," I whisper, as if greeting an old friend.

Now to focus it all on my Godstone, the conduit for my power.

But unlike Storm, I feel no single thread. There is nothing to focus on. Instead, my whole body hums with power.

My whole body. That's the difference. A living Godstone is not the conduit.

I am.

"Elisa?"

I lift my right arm and point toward the granite face. "Storm, you might want to step farther away."

And it's as easy as telling it where to go. It blasts out of me, a bolt of blue-hot fire that explodes against the cliff face. Shards of rock fly everywhere. Something stings my cheek.

I fall to my knees, gaping at the smoldering crater in the granite. The rock is glazed over, melted like glass. I feel empty, used up, like I could sleep for days.

Storm's laughing penetrates the haze. I turn to find him doubled over. "You're not supposed to let it all out at once!" he says between gasps. "You're supposed to loose it in controlled bursts. No one else in the world has so much power, and yet you are the clumsiest thing I've ever seen. You are as vulnerable as a babe."

I smile sheepishly. "We both have a lot to learn."

"Yes. But, Elisa?" His uncanny eyes flash with glee. "We're animagi now."

12

HECTOR

ONE of the horses died. Not the tiny mare with the white fetlocks, and I'm not sure why one horse should matter more than any other, but I'm glad.

Four others sickened. Their bellies swelled and they collapsed onto the ground, thrashing their legs. The Inviernos had seen mountain laurel poisoning before, and they assured the Joyans that their horses would most likely be well enough to travel in a day or so. But Franco is out of patience with delays. After an afternoon's debate, he ordered everyone forward, leaving the Joyans without healthy mounts behind.

There are now only sixteen captors from whom I must escape.

Poisoning the horses halted our progress for less than a day, but I sit straighter in the saddle, feeling stronger. Not helpless. Maybe I can do it again. My mind spins with other possibilities. Anything to slow us down and give Elisa a chance to catch us before she's forced too deep into enemy territory.

It's almost like protecting her.

I think hard about it as we navigate the tight, rocky trail of the mountainside. Below us stretches Invierne, a vast land forested with pine trees that, by some trick of light, seem as blue as the deepest part of the sea. Fog sends billowing tendrils through gorges and ravines. It rains or snows several times a day.

After an evening meal of pine nuts and thin soup, the chip-toothed Joyan comes to tie me up for the night. My bonds are so badly frayed now that he is derelict not to notice. If he worked for me, I'd make him scrub chamber pots for a month.

"Marreo," I say, using the name I've heard others use. "A word."

"You have nothing to say that I care to hear."

"It's strange, don't you think?" I say as he works the triple hitch. "That only *our* horses got sick."

"Your horse is fine. So is mine."

"I mean only Joyan horses got sick."

This would normally be met by a smack across the face or a hissed warning to be silent. But Marreo just frowns.

I'm encouraged. "It's convenient that they outnumber us now. I won't be surprised if you're all dead or left behind by the time we reach the capital."

This does earn me a cuff, and my head spins with the impact.

"Trust the Inviernos if you want to," I mutter, blinking rapidly. "But I am not your enemy here."

I am most definitely his enemy, and if he has any sense he knows it. I'm praying that he does not have any sense.

He grunts and walks away. I stare at his back, hoping the

traitor will fall asleep on watch again tonight.

He does, and I'm the only one awake to observe when Franco speaks quietly to one of his men. After a hushed conversation in a language I don't recognize, they clasp forearms, and Franco whispers, "The gate is closing."

"The gate is closing," he responds, as if by rote. They part, and the Invierno unsheathes a long dagger and slips back up the trail.

The traitor Joyans we left behind will not be making it home after all.

I would never send only one man to dispatch four. Franco must have the highest confidence. It's true that these Inviernos might be the most dangerous men I've encountered. They move with predator grace and display a level of fitness I've only seen among the most elite soldiers.

I refuse to let myself feel sorrow for my countrymen. Treason deserves no less.

Even so, there is no sense of triumph that my prediction to Marreo has already proven true. And if the Joyan soldiers don't stand a chance, then neither does Elisa. Though she surprises me at every turn, she is no warrior.

Somehow, I have to even the odds.

13

I can't tell the exact moment we cross the watershed, but one day our path slopes downward more than not, the clouds thicken, the icy mix of rain and snow becomes relentless.

Storm and I practice with our Godstones each night. We create makeshift targets by scratching them into the cliff face, but hitting them feels like trying to thread needles with boulders. We are clumsy, haphazard, imprecise. Our sessions make me glad for the lifeless rocks and constant drizzle. Were we surrounded by forest, we'd likely set it on fire.

Precision seems beyond my reach, until the evening I stumble upon the trick of using my dagger for a focus. By holding something in my hand and pushing my power through the object, I'm able to both direct and stem the tide so that I don't exhaust myself with a single blast. Oddly, my dagger remains unscathed—just like my clothing. I am so giddy with triumph that I hardly sleep all night.

Late the next morning, just as we've descended below the timberline, the breeze brings a strange scent, something both rotten and sugary—like rancid meat.

Ahead, Belén holds up a fist to halt our procession, and we rein in our mounts. He waves with three fingers—the signal for silence—and slides from his horse. He creeps forward and melts into the trees.

Horse whinnies, and I pat her neck to calm her. Mula twists in the saddle to face Mara and loudly whispers, "What's the matter?" Mara shushes her.

Belén returns a moment later, his face grave. "Bodies ahead," he says. "Four men and four horses."

"Invierno or Joyan?" I ask.

"Hard to tell—they've been dead more than a day. But Joyan, I think. Their throats were slit, execution style. No sign of struggle. It happened very fast."

My face drains of warmth as I flash back to the Battle of Brisadulce, when animagi slit the throats of their own people to soak the earth with blood and work their fire magic. "And . . . was there . . . did any of them . . ."

Belén's face softens. "Hector was not among them."

I loose a breath I didn't realize I was holding.

"Who's Hector?" Mula asks.

Storm says, "It's rare for Joyans to cross the divide. Rarer still to do it this late in the year. If they aren't Conde Eduardo's men assigned to escort the commander, I can't imagine who they are."

My heart kicks in my chest. So close. We could intercept them within days. Maybe sooner.

I'm not sure what will happen then. Could we infiltrate their camp and sneak Hector away? What if we are forced to engage in a full-out battle? Though I'm handier with a weapon than I used to be, thanks to Belén's training, I've little close-fighting experience. Maybe we can take them unaware. Maybe . . .

My breath catches. My Godstone. I could *kill* with it now. If I wanted to.

The mounts prance nervously and show the whites of their eyes as we near the place where Belén found the bodies. We see a horse first, a dun-coated creature lying across the path, its belly hugely swollen, flies circling its wide-open eye. We step carefully around it as the others come into view: three more horses off to the side, their bodies flat on the ground save for their necks, which stretch upward, hung from their halters. They died while hitched to a tree.

I don't see any human bodies. Belén must have pulled them out of sight, and I make a mental note to thank him later.

Someone whimpers, and at first I think it's Mara, until I hear her say, "Just don't look, Mula. We'll be past them soon enough."

We travel as fast and as far as we dare, and it is nearly dark before we begin looking for a campsite. I light a fire with my Godstone, hoping it's the last time we'll have a fire for a while. With luck, by this time tomorrow we'll be too near our quarry to risk it.

Which means that Storm and I ought to practice tonight. It might be our last opportunity. Or are we too near the Inviernos? Would they sense our magic?

Mula unloads everyone's packs and flips out bedrolls, though no one tasked her with this. Then she scurries around collecting firewood. While Mara fries up some corn cakes, Mula sits cross-legged near the fire, back straight, and closes her eyes.

"Are you a follower of God's path?" I ask.

She opens one eye and snorts. "God hates me," she says.

I gape at her.

"I never pray anymore," she adds. "I was just thinking."

I swallow my surprise enough to ask, "About what?"

"My name," she says. "You all are fine lords and ladies. And warriors. Your slave needs a good name. A strong name."

Belén looks up from oiling Mara's bow. "What about Little Squirt?" he says. "Or Skinny Girl?"

"Belén!" Mara snaps.

But Mula is grinning. "It's better than Old One-Eye," she says.

"Knob Knees," he says.

"Beak Nose," she throws back.

"Blue Feet!"

"Messy Hair!"

"Those are all terrible names," Storm says, looking perplexed.

Mula stares at him a moment, and then bursts out laughing. Her laugher is high and crisp and utterly unself-conscious, and soon enough we're all laughing with her. Even Storm cracks an uncertain smile.

After we eat, Storm tells me that only an animagus or a priest could sense us at this distance, and it's probably safe to practice. So we send fire bolts against a rocky mountainside, leaving scorch marks and blackened moss. Storm's control is improving too, his bolts becoming smaller but more powerful and better aimed. My fear that we'll set the forest around us on fire is greatly reduced.

It's a relief to the let the fire flow out of me, as if my mostly prayerless journey has kept it too long dammed. I'm dancing a tiny candle flame on the tip of my dagger when I say, "We improve at an alarming rate, Storm. Every day, the *zafira* is easier to call."

He nods. "We will continue to grow stronger as we approach the capital. All the animagi are at their most powerful there."

"Oh? Is it a place of power? Like the island?"

The glowing embers from our last assault on the mountainside give a sharp cast to his nose and cheeks. He radiates dangerously as he says, "There is a source. Not the *zafira*, but . . . a lesser something. I would have learned about it had I completed my training."

I plunk down on the ground and cross my legs, snuffing the flame with a thought. I study the blade; it radiates heat but is otherwise unscathed. "Then why do they need the *zafira*?" I muse. "Why did they send an army after it if they already have a source of power?"

"When your ancestors came to this world," he says, "you forced us to give up our land and retreat across the divide. You changed us with magic from another world. Made us more like you. It was thousands of years ago, but no one has forgotten. The Inviernos are a bitter people, Majesty. They will stop at nothing to reclaim what they believe to be theirs."

I'm not satisfied with this explanation. "But why now? If they've been angry and bitter for several millennia, what has caused them to act only now?"

"I wish I knew."

"Did he call you Majesty?" says a voice at my shoulder. "Storm, why did you call her Majesty?"

Storm's features freeze with dismay.

"It's fine," I tell him. "She was bound to figure it out eventually."

Mula crouches before me and peers into my face, golden eyes narrowed. "Is she a condesa?"

In a resigned voice, Storm says, "You have the privilege of addressing Her Royal Majesty, Queen Lucero-Elisa né Riqueza de Vega."

Mula's eyes grow huge. With a loud whoop, she jumps up into the air, pumping her tiny fists. She tears off across the clearing toward our campfire yelling, "Mara! Belén! I am slave to the *queen!*"

I wince. I must soon have a solemn talk with the girl, wherein I introduce the word "discretion."

14

HECTOR

FIFTEEN captors. I work through several scenarios in my head, and always come to the same conclusion: Fifteen is still too many.

Too many for me to fight. Too many for Elisa to fight, for her party is bound to be small. I must get them to expend their energy fighting one another.

My skin is still welted from its last battle with mountain laurel. I grit my teeth as I shove more down my shirt, into my pockets, even down my boots—enough to poison many horses this time. It's easier to hide my movements now that waist-high ferns bask in the shelter of giant sequoias.

When night comes, I slip the rope and creep over to the picket line. This time I feed the Invierno horses. I contemplate giving Franco's horse an extra helping but decide against it. It's not the horse's fault his rider is a murderer and a spy.

As I'm tying myself back up, snow begins to fall. I still wear only light desert armor; my captors have not bothered to protect me against the cold. A smart strategy. The first fat flakes melt against my skin, and I shiver.

In the vast silence of snowfall, I suddenly feel very alone. I'm usually adept at shielding my mind against thoughts that could weaken me. But my resolve is failing. I miss my men, with their bawdy jokes and boundless energy. I miss the hot sun and the endless desert horizon. I miss sparring each morning with Prince Rosario.

I miss her.

For the first time, I allow myself to consider that she might not come at all. Ximena would try to prevent her, I'm sure of it. Elisa told Franco she loved me. Was it an act to get me quickly away? I wouldn't fault her for it. I should reconsider rescuing myself.

But, no. She whispered that she would come, and nothing changes her mind once her course is set. I fall asleep hoping for it, dreading it, telling myself to be ready if the time comes. Imagining a thousand ways it can go wrong.

Sometime during the night I wrap my arms around my shoulders in a desperate bid for warmth. Which is how, in the morning, my captors discover my severed bonds. I wake to the splitting pain of a boot to my ribs. I can only absorb a few kicks before blackness retakes me.

15

W<small>E</small> don every single item of clothing we brought with us—
extra shirts and tunics, stockings, and underthings. Belén
shows us how to stuff our boots with dry grass—a trick he
learned while scouting for Queen Cosmé. Even Mula ceases to
balk at wearing boots and, instead of scampering ahead down
the trail, stays quietly in the saddle, curled up against Mara's
chest for warmth.

The cold is so overwhelming, so everywhere present, that I
almost don't notice when my Godstone turns icy with warning.

"Belén!" I call out.

He halts his mount and twists to face me.

I drop my voice. "My Godstone! It . . . I think someone is on
the trail ahead of us."

My companions know exactly what my stone's warnings
mean. Without being prompted, everyone moves off the trail
and into the cover of trees. Belén dismounts, pulling his dagger
from its sheath. "Back soon. Stay quiet." He takes off down the
trail at a fast but silent jog.

Mara whispers, "They must be very near for your Godstone to react so, yes?"

"I don't know! Everything is different since the island."

We share a long look. It might be Franco. And Hector.

"Is it the bad men?" Mula whispers.

I nod. "If there is fighting, I want you to hide, understand?"

Mula's eyes are very large.

Mara gives her a squeeze. "If you get scared, just don't think about it. Close your eyes and think of something that makes you happy until one of us finds you."

My first lady-in-waiting, Aneaxi, used to tell me something similar. I thought it was ridiculous, even as a child, because by telling my mind not to ponder something, I was certainly pondering it.

"All right," Mula says, gazing up at her like a trusting lamb. "I will think about my name."

Then again, maybe Mara knows a lot more about children than I do.

The sun curves high, and the near-frozen moisture on the ground steams into the air. The horses paw at the carpet of pine needles. Mula grows fidgety. Finally Belén returns.

His breath frosts in the air. "It's Franco."

Horse dances beneath me, and I realize I'm squeezing her with my knees. "Any sign of Hector?"

"Tied to a tree. Badly beaten." At the look on my face, he adds, "But clearly alive."

Determination hardens like a rock in my gut. "How far up the trail? Can we catch them?"

"All of us, traveling in stealth, could be there by the time the sun is at its zenith. They are stalled. Some of their horses have sickened. As I left, Eduardo's and Franco's men were starting to argue. I wouldn't be surprised if a fight breaks out. If it doesn't, we might be able to provoke something."

"Maybe Mara can shoot an arrow into their midst?"

Belén shrugs. "I was thinking a throwing knife in Franco's neck would do the trick."

"How many men?" Storm asks.

My face warms. It's the first question I should have asked. I've let my concern for Hector override common sense and caution.

"Five Joyans, ten Inviernos. We are vastly outnumbered. But maybe if we take them by surprise—"

"I have a plan," I say with more confidence than I feel. Are Storm's and my abilities too new to put to such a dangerous test? At what point does a bold plan become reckless?

"Elisa?" Mara prompts.

"We'll have to be very quick and very precise, but this is what we're going to do."

We wait until dusk. The wind picks up, masking the sounds of our movement as Mara and I sneak down the slope toward Franco's camp. Mula follows behind at a safe distance, with stern orders to keep out of sight. All our exposed skin— faces, necks, hands—is smeared with mud. Our clothes are turned inside out so the rougher, duller warp shows. I grip a dagger in each hand, and a spare waits in my belt. Mara has an arrow notched in her bowstring.

Voices drift up to us before we spy them through the trees, blurred and dark in the fading light. Everyone is talking at once, and I can only make out a few words—something about poison and horses and freezing to death in the snow. Their talk becomes louder and more heated as we steal down the hillside. Belén was right—they're ready to come to blows.

They just need a little nudge.

By waiting until dusk, we've made it easier to sneak up to the camp unseen, but we've also made it difficult to see. Mara *must* be able to see well enough to distinguish an Invierno from the others.

I mouth "Closer," and Mara nods.

Slowly we weave toward them, using the massive trunks for cover. I'm so much quieter than I used to be, my steps light, my balance assured. Humberto would be proud.

Mara holds up a fist, and I duck behind a tree as she does the same.

"I say we leave," comes a man's low voice. "Now. Take the horses and get away from here. Do you really think the Invierno dogs will take us inside their capital city and then let us live?"

It's the perimeter guard. They've drifted much closer to the camp than they should, no doubt drawn by the arguing. "I don't feel right leaving the commander with them," comes another, gruffer voice.

The din of argument turns to shouting.

"We must decide quick!" says the first man. "They're intent

on their mission. If we move fast, they'll not take the time to pursue."

Mara slips from behind her tree, draws her bow, sights.

"And the commander?"

"We slit his throat. Better that than whatever the dogs have planned for him."

Fear stabs through me, as merciless as a dagger.

The fletching is tight against Mara's cheek as she holds steady, waiting for Belén's signal. She won't shoot the men nearby; instead she will shoot over them, or maybe between them, into the throng below. I peer slowly around my trunk to get the lay of things. The two guards are less than a stone's throw away, but hardly more than black shapes among the trees. Their backs are to us. Beyond them, several others are silhouetted against a glowing campfire.

Belén's signal sounds: the caw of a mountain jay, three times in quick succession.

I hold my breath as Mara's arrow flies. It skims so close to one of the guards that he puts a hand to his ear is if batting away a mosquito.

It impales a tall figure below in the back. He topples face-first into the campfire, scattering embers and sparks. Silently I count. *One.*

"You filthy Joyan animals!" comes Storm's unmistakably Invierno voice. "I knew you'd betray us!"

I freeze, worried that he has overplayed it, but I needn't have, because the camp erupts into chaos.

Steel rings on steel. Someone roars an order to form up.

Another body topples into the campfire. *Two.*

The guards launch down the slope toward the fight, but Mara sends arrows flying, two in quick succession. One guard drops to his knees, an arrow sticking out of his neck—*three*—but Mara's second shot goes too far left and the other man whirls, shield up, and spots her.

He charges. Mara notches another arrow.

My Godstone pulses with energy, and I fill up like a cauldron, ready to boil over with power. My stone *wants* to unleash its fire on the world. And I want to let it. *Not yet, Elisa.* I grip my daggers tighter.

Mara's shot flies a little wide, scraping his arm. He bellows rage.

He reaches the spot where I crouch hidden. I launch at him, right arm raised high. He whirls, whips ups his shield, and blocks it neatly. My shoulder aches from the impact, but already I'm swiping low with my left hand. The blade lays open his right thigh, and he drops to the ground. Mara sends an arrow into his chest.

Four. Only eleven to go.

I take the barest moment to catch my breath before whispering, "I'll find Hector."

"Be safe." She notches another arrow and heads down the slope.

I skirt to the left toward the horses. The sounds of fighting fade. They've figured out that they've been tricked. I just hope they damaged each other sufficiently first. I risk a small prayer. *Please, God, lend strength and speed to my friends.*

A bolt of blue fire sears my vision and smacks a tree near the campfire. Dry pine needles burst bright, then plunge to the ground in a shower of ash and sparks.

If Storm is using his Godstone, it means I've little time.

The horses loom before me, huge black shapes in the growing dark. They toss their heads and snort as I weave through them. Everything is so dark now. Black lumps could be bushes or boulders or people. If only I had more light!

I agreed not to use my Godstone unless things became desperate, to save my strength in case someone needed healing, but surely this is desperate enough. I draw on the *zafira*, and my daggers begin to glow. The light catches on something ahead—rope wrapped around a tree trunk, bright against the bark. I snuff the power inside me, and the world goes dark again as I rush forward.

"Hector?" I whisper.

A gasp. Then . . . "Elisa?"

I drop to my knees and attack the rope with my dagger. The sounds of battle are growing furious. "Are you injured? Can you fight?"

"Am I hallucinating?" Oh, his voice. So achingly familiar—deep and slow and precise. But he's talking from someplace far away.

I smack his shoulder. "I need you in the present moment, Hector. Can you walk, at least?"

He laughs, though it ends in a cough. "Yes, I can walk. I have a broken rib, two broken fingers on my right hand, and a concussion. My shield arm is fine. If you have a spare shield, or even a dagger or short sword—"

"I brought an extra dagger for you. God, this rope! I can't saw—"

"An Invierno, coming this way. A giant with a very long sword. Please tell me you have a bow?"

I leap to my feet and place myself between Hector and the approaching enemy. He rushes at me, and I plant my legs and center myself the way Storm taught me, drawing strength from the earth, becoming one with it.

The *zafira* fills me up. I focus it all on the daggers in my hands. They begin to glow, revealing the desperate face of my attacker and the long line of steel in his right hand.

I swing my right dagger around my head and slingshot a firebolt toward him. He dodges left, and it grazes his shoulder. But he keeps coming.

I sling a smaller dart from my weaker left. It hits him square in the belly, and he bends over, his tunic blackening. Still, he stumbles forward.

The power is draining from me. I don't have time to gather more.

"Watch the sword arm!" Hector yells.

The Invierno raises his blade. Time slows. I know exactly what to do.

I block with my left dagger—just like Belén taught me—while thrusting with my right. I take him deep in the belly as the impact shivers down my forearm and pounds my shoulder socket. I jerk upward with my dagger until the blade lodges in the bone of his sternum. His sword clatters to the ground.

I try to yank my dagger out, but it's stuck. He topples, his hot blood pouring over my hand. I put the flat of my foot against his ruined belly and shove him off. My dagger jerks free, and I stumble backward. *Five.*

The earth sways. I spent too much magic too quickly. Or maybe I'm trembling because I just flayed open a man's belly. I stagger toward Hector and fall to my knees beside him, gasping. "These ropes. Too tough. I can burn them, but need a moment to . . ." My voice trails away as finally, finally, I look at him.

His gaunt face is covered in a curling beard, his left eye is swollen shut, his lips are cracked and peeling. But he stares at me with the same intensity as always, and it feels like coming home. I reach up with a forefinger and gently trace his eyebrow.

"Elisa," he whispers. "I need you in the present moment."

I snap into focus. In the distance, Belén yells something, and Mara shouts in answer. They are still alive. It spurs me to action.

I squeeze Hector's shoulder. "I'm clumsy at this, so when I start burning, do not move."

After he nods, I hurry behind the tree, running my hand along the rope until I feel the frayed spot where I had been sawing. I take a steadying breath, then reach deep into the earth for the *zafira*. It comes more slowly this time, but it comes.

Be controlled, Elisa. Be precise. I let just enough power leak out to dance a tiny flame at the tip of the dagger and no more. The still-damp blood on my blade sizzles, and I swallow against gagging. The *zafira* throbs inside me, begging to burst free, but I hold it tight. My forehead drips sweat. The rope begins to blacken and curl.

"Footsteps," Hector says. "Behind us."

The final coil of rope splits, and Hector launches forward, even as I whirl to see what approaches.

Too late. A sword descends. I roll left, and the sword lands on the end of my braid. He pulls back to stab, and I kick hard, catching his kneecap. He falls on top of me, and before I can squirm free he pins my legs with his knees, grabs my hair, and yanks my head back to expose my throat. I thrust with my daggers, but they glance off his armor.

Hector roars, flying through the dark at my attacker. Together, they crash to the ground, and Hector pounds him with fists, over and over again.

I scramble toward them on all fours. Hector's broken fingers, his broken ribs . . . he can't last long.

My daggers begin to glow again, and I shiver with power. I will send every last drop of it at my enemy. I will burn him to ash.

But I can't get a clear angle. They grapple, rolling in the dirt. The attacker grabs Hector's broken fingers and tugs them backward. Hector yells, but he does not give quarter, jabbing relentlessly with fist and elbows and knees.

They roll again. Hector is pinned. I see an opening and dart forward, swiping the attacker's hamstring. He screams while his skin sizzles. I stumble back, choking on the smell of burning flesh, while Hector throws him off.

Hector springs to his feet. "Knife!" he yells, reaching a hand toward me but never taking his gaze off his enemy, who is bent over, gasping, in the dirt.

My hot daggers would melt his hands. I clamp one between my teeth and fumble my spare knife from its sheath. The injured man struggles to his feet in spite of his useless leg. His wound does not bleed; my blade cauterized it.

"Here!" I toss the knife, and Hector snatches it from the air, flips it around for a better grip, then throws it.

The blade zings through the air so fast that I hardly register it until our attacker topples back, the hilt protruding from his throat. He lies there wide-eyed, twitching and choking on his own blood.

My heart still kicks in my chest; my breath comes fast. He is small. Dark, like me. A Joyan traitor.

I look up to find Hector staring at me. He is bent over slightly, clutching his injured side. The sound of battle is fading around us. "Belén!" I call.

"Here!"

"Mara!"

"Here!"

"Storm!"

No answer.

Hector needs no prompting. He strides over to the fallen Joyan and, wincing, bends over and yanks the dagger from his throat. He wipes it on the Joyan's shirt. "Let's find him," he says.

We weave through the nervous horses toward the campfire. Figures manifest—Mara, without a single arrow left in her quiver; Belén, whose eye patch has come askew. They're both breathing hard. Bodies litter the ground. Mara's bow is drawn with her last arrow as she surveys the bodies around her, watching for movement.

"They're dead, Mara," Belén says. "We got them all."

Their gazes lock. Mara lets her bow drop into the dirt, and they start toward each other as if an invisible force draws them together.

Hector clears his throat.

They whirl on us, startled. Mara's gaze drops to the ground, and she finds it necessary to pick something off the sleeve of her shirt.

"Lord-Commander," Belén says as we approach.

Hector reaches out with his left hand, and Belén clasps it. "Belén. Lady Mara. Thank you for coming."

"Where is Storm?" I demand.

"He ran off after Franco," Mara says. She points southward, where the forest growth is thick and dark. "That way."

"Why?" I murmur, though as soon as the word leaves my lips, I know exactly why. He is done being frightened of that man. But Franco is a trained assassin, and I fear that Storm, heady with new power, has underestimated him.

"Did anyone else get away?"

"No," says Belén. "A few were killed fighting each other, just as we hoped. We got everyone else. But I should have kept better track of Franco. I should have targeted him first."

I wave off his apology. "We accomplished our goal. I just wish Storm hadn't run off."

"Do we pursue?" Hector asks.

I pace in front of the campfire. Glowing embers left over from Storm's magic are scattered throughout the clearing, bathing us all in eerie warmth. How long will they glow?

"We must retrieve Mula before going anywhere," Mara says. "She's still hiding in the trees."

I nod, hating the thought of risking the little girl more than we already have. I turn to Belén. "Can we track them in the dark?"

"Yes, but it will be slow going."

"Hector, can you travel? Or should I heal you first?"

He shakes his head. "You always pass out after a healing. We can't afford the delay. I can ride, but I think"—he holds up his hand to display unnaturally crooked fingers—"I ought to set and splint these first."

I turn my back on my companions and stare into the trees. They seem as dark and impenetrable as night itself. "All right then. We find Mula, set Hector's fingers, and—"

A shape flies out of the dark, barrels into me, taking me to the ground. Agony shoots through my skull as red blotches my vision. Blood fills my mouth. I turn to spit, to breath, but hands wrap around my neck, crushing the life from me.

My mouth opens and closes, as if the motion can suck air into my dying lungs. Blackness narrows my vision to a single point of focus; my attacker's delicate face and chin, his wild, not-quite-Joyan eyes. Franco.

Something knocks him to the side. Air rushes into my lungs so fast I almost choke on it. I clamber to my feet, swaying, my stomach heaving. I fumble for my daggers.

"Mula!" Mara screams.

Franco is pounding brutally at something beneath him. A tiny something.

The *zafira* rushes into me, filling me like rage. I raise my daggers, but Hector gets there first. One hand on the back of Franco's head, one on his chin, and *snap!* Franco topples over.

Mula lies on the ground, unmoving. I rush over to her, drop to my knees. The daggers thunk into the dirt beside me.

"Mula," I whisper.

"Bad . . . man," she manages. Something gurgles in her unnaturally concave chest.

No. No no no no no.

Rosario said something similar once. And thinking a little of Mula, but mostly of the precious little boy I'm helpless to save right now, I place my hands on Mula's crushed chest. "For my love is like perfume poured out," I say, and I send all the power of the earth into her.

Her tiny body arches beneath my palms, and she screams and screams. Am I pouring too much into her? But I can't seem to stop.

When I'm as dry as deep desert, I collapse on top of her.

16

I wake to the warmth of sunshine and the scent of rabbit stew. I'm wrapped in my bedroll, facing a cheery fire. Mara's iron cook pot steams beside it.

"Elisa?" Hector's worried voice.

I sit up, rubbing my eyes. "Where's Mula? Is she . . . ?"

He sits on a log beside me, polishing his new dagger. His broken fingers are splinted and wrapped in linen strips. "She'll be fine. Franco kicked her ribs in. But you'd never know." His voice holds a touch of wonder.

"And Storm?"

"He appeared soon after Franco. I think he's upset with me for killing him."

I slowly get to my feet. My muscles burn, and my neck throbs with the phantom memory of Franco's bruising fingers. I stretch my arms to the sky, trying to loosen everything up, surprised and grateful to have come through a hard fight with no lasting injury.

Hector jumps to his feet when I do, from habit, I suppose,

for it is rude to remain sitting when one's queen stands, but I hate that there is any formality between us. I reach out to take his hand, but he flinches away, and I drop my arm. Hurt wells up in my chest.

I look around the campsite, trying to appear nonchalant. It's a small glen, hugged up against a granite outcropping. Was it Hector who carried me here when I was unconscious?

"Where is everyone?"

His gaze has not left my face. "Belén is hunting. Mara found a stand of blackberries; Mula is with her. Storm left, saying only that he'd be back. Everyone deals with the aftermath of battle in their own way."

Hector's left eye is purple and still nearly swollen shut. His hair is wild and matted, his clothing torn, his nails cracked and crusted with black dirt. I ache to wrap my arms around him.

"How do you feel?" I ask, for lack of anything better to say.

"I'll be fine in a day or two." Then he adds, "Thank you for coming for me."

His words are kind, but his tone is bland and his expression rigid. He is near enough that I could reach out and grab his shoulders, but I have no idea how to close the vast distance between us.

He was angry with me when we parted, and rightly so. I deceived and dishonored him. Never again. *Honesty in all things.*

"We're betrothed," I blurt, at the same moment he says, "There is another bearer."

"What?" we both say.

He runs a hand over his matted beard. Strange how his

cuticles, the shapes of his fingers, the curve of his thumb, are so familiar and dear, even beneath the grime.

"I would never hold you to it," I say in a rush. "It would build up support in the south. I'm hoping the announcement has stalled Eduardo's efforts. But I won't make you. You don't have to . . . marry me."

The log he was sitting on is a giant fallen tree trunk that stretches across the edge of the clearing, half buried in sod and wind trash. One end is jagged and black from lightning. Hector plunks back down onto it and slumps, as if the weight of his shoulders can no longer be borne.

I sit beside him, holding my back straight, careful not to touch, even though I want to, more than anything.

He says, "You wielded those daggers as one born to it. And your magic. It's . . . godlike. You're—you're one of *them* now."

I'm not sure why his words cut so deep, but they do. "No," I whisper. "Not like one of them. I'm much *more* powerful than even 'one of them.' Honesty in all things, right?"

He turns to peer at me closely, his good eye narrowed.

"The truth, Hector, is that it scares me, how powerful I've become. Almost as much as it delights me."

His beard twitches, and he almost, *almost* smiles.

"Daggers aside," I say, "you should also know that I found myself in quite a predicament earlier with a highwayman. I stomped on his foot, just like you taught me. It was very satisfying."

And then he does smile, and my heart swells so huge it hurts. "I hope you broke his foot," he says.

"I'm certain of it." And because I have no patience for dissembling, because knowing something bad is better than not knowing at all, I say, "So, about our betrothal—"

"That was a very romantic proposal."

I suppose teasing is better than a flat-out rejection. "I should have thought to bring flowers on this wretched journey. And a minstrel to compose an ode to your virility."

He turns away, and I stare at his profile, recognizing the fierce mask he wears when he's thinking hard. Just when I've decided I can bear the silence no longer, he reaches out and grabs my hand. "Do you want me for a husband? Or for a political bargaining piece?"

I squeeze his fingers gratefully. It's so much more of him than I had a moment ago. "Both," I tell him truthfully.

He sighs. "May I think about it?"

"Of course." And then I add, "I understand your hesitation."

"You do?"

I twine my fingers with his. "Not just anyone could be married to a sorcerer queen. It would take someone extraordinary. The strongest of men." And even though it's pushing things a little too far, I say, "You may not be up to the task."

"You're manipulating me."

"Is it working?"

He doesn't answer, but his eyes crinkle with a glimmer of a smile.

"For now," I say, "you can tell me what you meant about another bearer."

He nods. "I might as well tell everyone at once." He releases my hand and gets slowly to his feet, favoring his left side. "And I want to know exactly what you and Storm are capable of now. Then we need—"

"It can wait until tomorrow." I love that even broken and bloodied, half starved and exhausted, his only thought is for our next move. "You need rest. Fresh clothes." I wrinkle my nose.

He nods with mock solemnity, and I turn to go find Mula and see for myself that she's all right.

"Elisa."

I freeze, tamping down the hope blossoming in my chest.

"I thought about you every day. And I don't know that I could have managed if not for that. But I . . ." his voice trails off.

I breathe deep through my nose. "Have you eaten anything? By the smell, Mara's stew is about ready."

"I am hungry." His gaze drops to my mouth, and my lips buzz. He says, "And I would like to replace my clothes. I've been wearing these for weeks straight."

"And please shave that . . ." I make a vague gesture toward his face. "It's disconcerting."

"As my queen commands."

Belén goes back to the Invierno camp for the distasteful work of scavenging clothing and supplies, including gloves for everyone.

Mara uses the last of our cornmeal to fry up some cakes, which she sprinkles with pine nuts and dribbles with honey. Hector eats four.

Storm sits cross-legged in front of the fire, gazing off into the darkening sky. Though he clutches his amulet tight, he cannot hide the way his hand shakes.

Mula flips out her own bedroll and tells Hector it's for him. I'm about to correct her, but then I realize Belén will probably return with an extra. Hector falls into it gratefully.

"Are you the commander?" Mula asks, squatting down near his head. He manages a nod as his eyes are drifting closed. "I'm Mula, but that's just my name for now. Did you know that Elisa is the queen? She has a sparkle stone. She healed me because I'm her best slave. Want to see my feet?"

"Mula!" Mara calls. "Firewood, please."

The girl jumps up to help, and Hector shoots Mara a grateful glance before losing consciousness.

In the morning, Hector sorts through the goods Belén brought back and selects two daggers, a short sword, and some new clothes. He hacks off his beard with one of the daggers, resharpens it, then uses Belén's soap to shave. By the time he's done, Mara has a breakfast soup ready. He eats two bowlsful.

"Why are you staring at the commander?" says Mula, and I jump.

"I'm not."

"Yes, you are."

I glare at her, and she slinks away. But she's right. I'm soaking up his presence, worried that I might blink and discover he's not here after all.

After we've eaten and washed up, we sit around the campfire. It feels like the most decadent luxury, to huddle close to the flames in relative warmth instead of hurrying to our mounts and heading down the cold trail.

It hits me all at once. I did it. I rescued Hector. We could turn around right now, beat the approaching winter over the pass, and be in Basajuan a little early.

The thought fills me with warm relief, but it's short-lived. There is something else I must do first.

Mara is the one to open conversation. "Lord Hector, you said something last night about another bearer?"

He pokes at the fire with a stick, crunching embers into ash. "Franco said there are two. I tried to get him to tell me more, but he wouldn't."

I turn to Storm. "Do you know anything about this?"

He shakes his head. "Though, it makes sense that someday, someone would be born with a Godstone that didn't fall out. It hasn't happened for millennia, not since your people came to this world. But I suppose it could."

My limbs tingle with . . . excitement? Dread? An Invierno bearer would be my enemy. And someone who grew up surrounded by sorcery might be formidable indeed. But what sets my hands to trembling, what squeezes my chest so hard it hurts to draw breath, is the simple possibility that there is someone out there like me.

"Did you hear anything else?" I ask. "Anything at all?" I wince at how pathetic and pleading I sound.

"About the other bearer, no," Hector says. "But he mentioned something called the Deciregi."

"The ruling council. Yes, Storm told us about them."

"And I overheard talk of a gate. Another *sendara*."

I sit forward. "Oh?" Ximena and I speculated that there might be two gates, one that leads to life and one that leads to the enemy. The *Scriptura Sancta* alludes to both. If so, I most certainly destroyed the first when I brought a mountaintop down onto the *zafira*.

Hector is nodding. "They called it the *sendara oscura*."

"The gate of darkness," I whisper.

"Franco pushed us hard. I thought it was because of the early winter. But I then I realized our urgency had to do with the gate. They think it's closing. Or maybe dying." Hector frowns. "I'm not sure what that means exactly, but that's what they kept saying. 'The gate closes.' It was like a mantra they passed around, or a war cry."

My mind whirls as facts fall into place like puzzle pieces.

"Have you heard anything like that before?" Mara says to Storm. "Anything about a gate?"

I already know what he's going to say. "Yes. It leads to the source of power animagi draw on in the capital city. I would have been brought to the gate had I completed my training. What lies beyond is a secret, only revealed to full initiates."

Hector regards me steadily. "We're not going back, are we?" he says.

My path is as crystal clear as an alpine brook. "We are not."

The others whip their heads around to stare at me, aghast.

"We're going to Invierne," I explain. "To the capital city."

"Elisa, no." Belén rises to his feet, his fists clenched. "I used to believe you had to go there to fulfill a prophecy, but I was *wrong.* We don't know what that prophecy means. The 'champion' could refer to anyone. Let's leave today. Now. Cross back over the mountains, head north to Basajuan, and be there in time for your council with Cosmé and your sister."

The fire crackles, and a glowing cinder lands near the toe of my boot. As I watch it fade from fiery orange to dead gray, I say, "I'm not doing this because of a prophecy."

"But it says—"

"It says, 'He could not know what awaited at the gate of the enemy, and he was led, like a pig to the slaughter, into the realm of sorcery.' I know it too well, Belén. It's been hanging over my head for more than a year. Am I the champion that will be led like a pig to the slaughter? Am I going to die young or disappear like most of the bearers before me?" I grind the now-dead cinder into the dirt with my boot. "But it doesn't matter. Scripture never makes sense except in hindsight. I must make my choices based on reason and observation. And I choose to go to Invierne."

Hector's face is resigned, and I know he understands, even if the others don't. "Because their source of power is dying."

I nod at him gratefully. "The gate is closing. Maybe we can help it along. Destroy it utterly, the way I destroyed the gate to the *zafira.*"

"We have a civil war brewing!" Mara says. "Going to Invierne would give Conde Eduardo even more time to shore up support. What about the people we left behind? Tristán, Lucio, *Rosario.*"

I wince. She's not wrong. Prolonging our journey is a huge

risk. It will put so many people we love in danger.

"The prince should be safe," Hector says. "He's too valuable."

God, I hope he's right.

Belén adds, "If the gate is dying, why not just let it die? Mara is right. We have a civil war to worry about."

I lock gazes with Storm. "Because if it's dying, Invierne will *have* to attack again before their power source is gone. Right, Storm?"

"Yes. I did not realize it until now, but yes." Storm clutches the amulet beneath his cloak. It has become a reflex for him, the same way my fingertips always seek my Godstone. "The Deciregi have struggled to build support for another onslaught; we lost so many people in the last one. But if the gate is truly dying, our crops will begin to wither soon. Our mothers will become barren. They'll have no trouble raising an army then. It will be even bigger than before."

"So we go now," I say. "And we destroy the gate before they can build another army. And then . . ." It's so preposterous, so huge, so perfect. "We have what Invierne wants—knowledge of another power source. If we succeed, if we *survive*, I will use their ensuing desperation to bargain for peace."

PART II

17

WE crouch on the lip of a high cliff overlooking Umbra de Deus, the capital of Invierne and the largest city I've ever seen. Steep walkways wind through warrens of stone cottages and stepped gardens, spired temples rise from impossible slopes, and stone plazas take advantage of every tiny plateau. The entire city catches the sunlight, sparkling brilliantly, as if it is made of tiny glass shards.

From this distance, the Inviernos look like insects crawling all over the mountainside. The steep, switchbacked highway leading to the front gate routes a steady stream of movement in either direction. It's dizzying to watch. My own capital city could fit inside this one three or four times. Storm was right—the Inviernos outnumber us by a terrifying amount.

Hugging the base of the city on three sides is a twisting whitewater river. The eastern curve steams violently, sending tendrils of mist into the city's lower streets. It steams because high above it and far away—though not far enough to suit me—are two cone-shaped mountains gripped by crooked fingers of glowing orange lava. Storm calls the mountains the Eyes of God, and he assures us they are safe, that they've been sending the earth's fiery blood into the river for millennia.

"Seems like a dangerous place for a nation's capital," I observe.

"It's a place of power," Storm says. "Our ancestors believed the volcanoes gave them better access to the *zafira.*"

"And do they?"

"It's a cause of great debate among the scholars of my people."

Hector frowns. "I don't like this at all. The only way in is through the front gate."

"I have not seen a more perfect defensive architecture," I admit with reluctant admiration. I would hate to lay siege to this place. I suppose they could be starved out over time, but the mountain slopes are too bare to sneak up unseen, too steep and dangerous to navigate at night.

Belén says, "Storm, are you *sure* there is not a secret way inside?"

"If there is, I do not know of it. But it is as I said. I can get help. Just like the citizens of Joya d'Arena, we are a fractured, quarreling people. And my family, once they understand you are on a mission of peace, will jump at the chance to aid you and gain advantage over the other nine houses."

Mara says. "We know nothing of your family. I grew up near the border, and all I know of Inviernos is bloodshed and cruelty and rage and . . ." Her voice trails off as tears fill her eyes.

"And me," Storm says softly. "You know me."

I sigh. We've been arguing about this nonstop for several days. I can't put off making a decision any longer.

Storm continues, "They're expecting Elisa. Waiting for her. They surely sensed the way we called on the *zafira* to deal with Franco's men. Such an outpouring of magic could only come from a bearer."

"You're worried about an assassination attempt," Hector says. "Even if she arrives in an official capacity."

"Exactly so. Let me go alone," he insists, and turns to me. "I'll bring back help. We'll hide you in a cart, smuggle you in. We could paint your skin. Your features do have an Invierno cast, you know, even though you are short and stubby."

I glare at him.

"I can pass for an Invierno," Mula says cheerfully. "I just have to cover my feet." She is lying on her back, chewing on the end of a dry stalk.

Hector says, "I hate to say it, but—"

"It's our only plan," I finish, and he nods grimly.

Storm rises. "I'll be back by sunset," he says. "Stay out of sight."

I reach up and grab his hand. "You're sure they won't kill you on sight? There's a death sentence on your head!"

"I can reach my family compound before I'm recognized. They'll delay turning me in to face my sentence once I claim knowledge of the *zafira*. They *will* help us."

I squeeze his hand, and he shifts uncomfortably. "You are my loyal subject, Storm. Which means if you are not back in a reasonable time, we must figure out a way to come get you. We don't leave our people behind."

He blinks. "I understand."

I release his hand, and he disappears down the slope.

"You have truly come to trust him as one of our own," Hector observes.

"I have."

We stare at each other, and I'm glad to note that after a few days of regular food and rest, he seems less gaunt and ragged, and the bruising around his eye has faded to a muddy yellow. We stare long past the point of awkwardness. His gaze drops to my lips. I'm the first to look away.

I say to no one in particular, "But like Mara, I don't trust Storm's family. So stay alert, everyone."

A light snow is beginning to fall—again—as Belén gets to his feet. "I'll keep an eye on the trail." His disappears in the same direction as Storm.

The rest of us huddle together, cloaks clutched tight. This near to the city, there will be no fire, no praying. It's going to be a long, cold wait.

The molten fingers of the Eyes of God glow bright as a sun against the darkening horizon. Insects flit through pine boughs, their bulging abdomens glowing like night bloomers. Mula has fallen asleep on Mara's shoulder. Hector and I sit side by side, not quite touching. Just like he did during our final weeks together, after I destroyed the gate to the *zafira*, he avoids any physical contact. It seems as though things ought to have changed between us, somehow. But they haven't, and I'm not sure what to do about it.

Footsteps crunch through the underbrush, and we launch to our feet, drawing weapons. Even Mula jolts awake and whips out a dagger, her face fierce in the dying light.

"It's just me," says Storm. He strides toward us, followed by another, whose thick cloak and heavy cowl cannot hide her willowy, feminine shape. Belén brings up the rear. His sword is not yet drawn, but his hand rests on the scabbard.

I peer at the newcomer, expecting to feel the usual jolt of alien wrongness at her appearance. But when she lowers her cowl to reveal long coppery hair and eyes the green of pine boughs, I feel nothing but grudging admiration for her beauty.

Storm says, "I present to you The Frozen Waterfall Mourns Her Raging Youth." And then he adds, "My sister."

I'm not sure why I'm surprised to learn he has a sibling. I say, "Thank you for coming."

I wrack my mind for memories of the Invierno ambassador who visited Papá's court when I was a little girl. Do Inviernos bow? Curtsy? Is there a formal greeting that my father used?

After too long a silence, Storm says, "You may call her Waterfall."

She gives him a sharp look.

Storm explains, "Joyans find Invierno names complicated and incomprehensible."

I glare at him. Storm and I are going to have a conversation about "complicated and incomprehensible" versus "overwrought and inefficient."

But she merely shrugs. "Waterfall will do for now." She speaks the Lengua Plebeya with careful attention, drawing out each syllable as if testing it. "Which one of you is the sorcerer queen? Oh . . ." Her gaze settles on my face. "It is you, of course." To her brother, she says, "You're right. She has the look about her, even though she is stubby."

I open my mouth to ask what she means, but I sense Hector at my shoulder, in his usual guard position, and I have to swallow the lump in my throat. It is *so nice* to have him back.

"My brother says you wish an audience with the Deciregus?"

Taking Storm's cue, I say, "Yes. I have knowledge of something your people have been seeking for thousands of years."

Her eyes narrow. "What kind of knowledge?"

If Storm did not share the nature of our mission, then she must trust him very much to have followed him out here alone. "I know where the *zafira* is," I tell her.

She gasps. But her face hardens immediately, and she says, "You lie. All you Joyans are liars."

"Queen Elisa speaks truthfully," Storm says. "She took me there. I have seen the *zafira* with my own eyes, felt its power course through me."

She taps her lower lip with a forefinger as her eyes rove my face and body. Beside me, Hector's fingers curl around the hilt of his sword. From somewhere high above comes the screech of a raptor.

"I brought some powder to lighten your skin," she says at last. "But I'm not sure it will be enough; you're too short. We also brought a cart. It's on the trail below. You must ride in it, hunched over, so no one can see your true shape." Her gaze shifts to Hector. "You too must ride in the cart. You are too . . . broad. The rest of you will walk beside the cart or ride in on horseback. I will powder your faces and hands, but stay cowled. Except you." She lifts her chin at Mula, who is clinging to Mara's leg, eyes wide. "My brother says you bear the slave mark?"

Mula nods.

"Then you will lead. Walk barefoot. No cowl. With luck, everyone will think my brother and I are bringing in a batch of mule slaves."

I look around at my companions. "This might be it. The gate of the enemy. None of you are required to accompany me. It's your choice."

Belén shrugs. "It's a perfect plan."

"As easy as falling in love," Mara adds.

"Foolproof," Hector agrees.

I don't deserve such friends. I blink against the sting of threatening tears and say, "All you Joyans are filthy liars."

Waterfall's "cart" is a small, two-wheeled fruit wagon, pulled by a single draft horse. Its wooden floor and sides are stained dark and smell faintly of rancid juice. It's barely large enough for Hector and me both. I smile to myself as I settle beside him, squeezing between the wall of the wagon and his hard shoulder.

The powder on my skin tingles. It smells of ash and dust and old flowers, and I fight the urge to sneeze. I study the back of my hand with dismay. It doesn't look light skinned so much as dirty.

Mula and Storm take the lead, Waterfall smacks the draft horse, and we set off, rattling and creaking down the trail. Mara and Belén follow behind on their mounts. We left Horse—along with Hector's mount for company—on long leads in a sheltered glen with plenty of grazing. I crane my neck for one last sight of her, hoping she'll be all right until I get back.

Hector holds his elbows tight to his sides, trying to make himself as small as possible. I barely refrain from rolling my eyes.

But as we bump down the trail, our shoulders occasionally knock, and he flinches each time. Exasperation bubbles over, and I blurt, "You don't have to try so hard to avoid me!"

His face freezes, but then he looks sheepishly off into the distance. "It doesn't seem right to . . . take liberties when I have not given you an answer." He says it quietly, and I have to strain to hear.

"There's an easy solution to that," I point out. "Just say yes."

He turns his head to regard me, and my breath catches. How did I not notice, the moment I met him more than a year ago, how very striking he is?

"I don't want to be a prince consort," he says. "I have little desire to rule, even less to be a figurehead, and that's what a prince consort is, you know. A useless trinket on the arm of his queen. It's not what I ever imagined for myself."

My heart is sinking like a stone, but then he adds, "For you, though, I am considering it."

Mara and Belén ride just out of earshot, but Mara catches my eye and gives me a quick wink. I send her a mock glare.

Hector adds, offhand, "You could order me to marry you. You're my queen, after all." His gaze on me is unwavering as he awaits my response.

"No," I say, shaking my head. "Never."

He arches an eyebrow.

"You once said you couldn't have me just a little, that just a little wouldn't be enough. Remember?"

"Yes," he whispers. I hope he is also remembering the way he kissed me that night, the way he held me close, thinking it was the last time.

"I feel the same. I want *all* of you, Hector. I want the political match you bring, yes. But I would be miserable if I didn't have your heart too."

He lifts a forefinger and traces my bottom lip. My skin soaks up his touch like I am parched desert, desperate for spring rain. I barely manage not to lean into him. "You feel so strongly about me, then?" he says.

"Don't be daft. I *love* you."

He grins. "You've never said."

I blink up at him. "I haven't?"

"Not directly. You told Franco so, but it crossed my mind once or twice that you might be lying, saying what he wanted to hear."

Is that what all this was about? He was worried about how I really feel about him? I work very hard to keep my expression serious. "Well, I do. I love you."

He raises his eyebrow again. "More than you loved Alejandro?"

"I never loved him."

"More than you loved that boy from the desert?"

"His name was Humberto, and now you're just being petty."

He has not stopped grinning like a little boy about to open his Deliverance Day gifts. He leans closer until our lips are a finger's breadth apart. He brushes a strand of hair from my neck, and I shiver. "If we were alone right now," he says, "I would . . ."

"I would let you."

The wagon hits a rut, and our foreheads crack together, which startles a too-loud "Ow!" from me. He raises fingers to his head, wincing.

"Stop!" I say. "You'll rub off the powder."

His hand freezes, then he lowers it, grimacing. "Well, come here, then." Not that there's anywhere to go in this tiny cart, but I duck under the crook of his arm, which he wraps around my shoulder. I'm careful to keep my powdered face away from his cloak as I lean into him. His lips press against the top of my head, and I close my eyes.

"I love you too," he whispers in my ear. "Wholly. Madly."

"Does this mean you'll marry me?"

"I suppose."

I elbow lightly him in the stomach. "Even if it means being a prince consort? And being married to someone so egregiously powerful?"

He sighs. "Even then."

"If it helps, I'd like you to continue on as commander of the Royal Guard and my personal defender. I mean, if *you* want to."

His arm around me tightens. "I'd like that."

"Now all we have to do is live through the next few weeks."

"I confess, I suddenly have an overwhelming desire to survive."

My whole body tingles warmly. I'm very glad I never stopped taking the lady's shroud.

"Hoods up, everyone!" calls Storm. "We're about to turn onto the main highway."

As one, we flip up our cowls, which surely seems suspicious to anyone watching. But as the trails curves around to merge with traffic—hoards of Inviernos on foot, a few carts like ours, one large carriage with a team of four—I see that cowls are the fashion of the day. Or maybe it's a practical necessity in this cold climate.

Our ride smoothes the moment the wheels clunk onto the slight lip of stone paving. I peer over the edge of the cart. Each paver stone fits so perfectly to the next, and the thin lines of mortar sparkle with tiny bits of colored glass. This highway is a work of art. It doesn't seem fair that my enemy should have such a glorious highway when the main thoroughfare leading from my capital city is rife with ruts and half covered in sand. Because of our recent war with these people, I've had no funds for repair.

I know it's small-minded of me even as the thought pours out, but I can't help it: If I ever lay siege to this place, I will turn this offending highway to rubble.

The Inviernos surrounding us are invariably tall, lithe, and lovely. Seeing so many, pressed so close together, I realize how odd my people must seem to them, how graceless and stunted and dark.

"Try not to gape," Hector whispers. "You'll attract attention."

He's right. I curl tighter against him, trying to seem invisible, instead listening hard to the world around me. It's a cacophony of footsteps, cartwheels, and clattering horseshoes, and just below it all, the constant hum of chatter. I catch several words in the Lengua Classica. But there are more words I don't recognize, the syllables stretched out in swinging high and lows, like a song. Storm once told me the Inviernos have been here for thousands of years, that my own people are comparatively recent interlopers on this world. So it makes sense that they would have their own language, something ancient and alien.

I sit straight up as the thought hits.

"Elisa?" Hector says.

"*Why* do so many Inviernos speak the Lengua Classica?" I whisper, fast and low. "If our people brought the language to this world, and the Inviernos were already here as Storm claims, why did they adopt it?"

Storm looks over his shoulder and shoots me a glare. I lean back against Hector, chastised.

"Storm always says what he believes to be true," Hector says. "But maybe he has been misled about this."

"Maybe."

We travel the rest of the way in silence, and as the Godstone cools in my belly, I grow frustrated with my cowl. It blocks too much of my vision. The skin of my neck starts to prickle. Danger could be coming up behind me, even beside me, and I would not know until it was too late.

Our cart jerks to a halt. I start to lift my head to peer around us but think better of it.

"State your business," comes the sibilant voice of an Invierno man.

"Cargo bound for the Deciregus of Crooked Sequoia House," says Storm, and I can't help but admire the way our deception is hidden in the truth of his words.

"Prepare for inspection."

Hector's arm slips from my shoulder and reaches beneath his cloak toward his scabbard. My own hand seeks out the dagger in my belt.

"Are you in the habit of inspecting the merchandise of Deciregi?" asks Waterfall smoothly. "His Eminence would prefer to maintain privacy and discretion in this matter. But just so you have something to mark in your ledger . . . come here, mule girl. Show him your feet."

A long pause. I exchange a quick glance with Mara. She and Belén have affected an air of arrogant disinterest, sitting tall on their mounts, their gazes never deigning to linger on any one thing for more than a moment.

"You may pass," comes the Invierno voice. And then, more formally, "The gate of darkness closes."

"The gate of darkness closes," Waterfall answers. The cart lurches forward.

We pass beneath a massive archway, and I blink against sparks of reflected sunlight, for the whole structure is made up of small glass blocks set in thin lines of mortar. More glass hangs from the top by thin ropes. They are gem shaped and brightly colored, spinning and swaying in the breeze, casting prisms on the surfaces around us.

Our path begins to twist and climb the moment we are inside the city walls. We pass food vendors, a blacksmith, two glassblowing booths, and a small plaza where three young boys are playing a game with sticks and a ball. It all looks so familiar, so normal.

But differences begin to manifest. Everyone's clothing is oddly uniform, with only minor variations on a theme of embroidered tunics beneath thick cloaks with cowls. We pass stocks containing five Inviernos—three men and two women—who are naked and shivering, bruised and beaten, wallowing in their own filth. Two corpses, darkened and withered, swing from ropes attached to a high turret. A vulture perches on the head of one.

No one smiles.

We pull into a carriage house. A segmented door rolls shut behind us, clanging to the ground, leaving us in total darkness.

A rush of footsteps. The whisk of drawn steel. Torchlight sears my vision.

I blink to adjust. We are surrounded by an entire company of Invierno soldiers, their swords drawn. Behind them, a line of archers has drawn their bows.

18

"STEP from the cart, please," someone says. "You two, dismount. Move slowly; keep your hands visible."

Mara and Belén share a slight nod. Hector does not reach for his sword, but his hand hovers near his waist. My companions are prepared to fight and die if I order it.

The wagon wobbles beneath my weight as I get to my feet. I push back my cowl and say, "We will do as you ask. You have nothing to fear from us."

The others follow my lead. Belén and Mara swing off their horses, and Hector stands beside me. Belén offers a hand and helps me step from the wagon.

The soldiers part to make way for another man. He is of average height for an Invierno, with slicked-back golden hair and a severe nose. A tree is embroidered over the left breast of his cloak—a bright evergreen bending under its own weight.

"I am the seneschal of Crooked Sequoia House. Please follow me."

He whirls and strides away, not bothering to see if we follow.

But we do, and even though we are surrounded by soldiers, I'm encouraged by the fact that they have not made us give up our weapons.

He leads us through narrow corridors lit by torches. Everything shimmers—the walls of granite and quartz, the glass shards in the mortar, the silver sconces. We turn a corner and come face-to-face with enormous double doors made of knotty pine. My Godstone turns to ice.

The seneschal swings the doors open to reveal a towering audience hall. A giant sequoia grows right out of the floor, so vast that I cannot gauge its full height. A short stone wall surrounds the massive trunk, and light streams down from clerestory windows, illuminating its high green boughs. The strange insect birds I first discovered on the hidden island flit through the branches. A shimmery layer of detached gossamer wings blankets the base of the tree.

Beyond the tree is a throne, made of the twisting, woven trunks of juniper. On it sits the most frightening and beautiful Invierno I have ever seen. His skin is near translucent and baby smooth, and the hair flowing past his waist is as white as a summer cloud. He clutches the armrests with long, slender fingers. His right hand is bare. But his left is gloved in a shining metal gauntlet with barbed fingertips.

His eyes have no pupils, no irises. Instead, they are as black and liquid as tar.

He is attended by young Inviernos in bare feet and knee-length shifts. They stand near the throne, a handful on each side, and I cannot tell if they are male or female. Each of their shifts displays the same embroidered sequoia as the seneschal's cloak.

My Godstone pounds ice through my veins, but I refuse to let the pain show on my face.

"Kneel before His High Eminence," the seneschal booms. "The Bitterest Cold Cannot Shatter the Mighty Pine, Deciregus of Crooked Sequoia House." Storm and Waterfall drop to their knees before the beautiful Invierno, and everyone follows suit. Except me.

The Deciregus—Pine—lifts his spindly bare hand to the Godstone amulet hanging from his neck and fingers it absently. "You do not kneel like the others?" comes his sibilant voice.

"I am queen of Joya d'Arena and bearer of a *living* Godstone. I kneel to no one."

He grins, displaying teeth filed to points. "Welcome to Crooked Sequoia House, little queen." He turns to Storm, who has prostrated himself forehead to the ground, arms stretched forward. "Rise, He Who Wafts Gently with the Wind Becomes as Mighty as the Thunderstorm."

Storm gets to his feet, but he keeps his gaze downcast as he says, "Hello, Honored Father."

I look at him sharply. He never told me the Deciregus was his father.

"My failed son. You have returned home to face honorable death, yes?"

Storm's head snaps up, and he returns his father's black gaze unflinchingly. "No."

The Deciregus opens his mouth, but I jump in before he can

say anything. "Your son is my official liaison to Invierne and under my protection. Harming him is an act of war." I catch Storm's eye and offer a slight smile. "He is no failure."

The Deciregus hisses. "What do you know of Invierno honor, little queen?"

"I know that your condescension shows little. If we are to negotiate port rights for your people, I insist you address me properly, as Your Majesty."

He taps his bottom lip with a slender forefinger. "We no longer need port rights, if we have you."

"You do *not* have me." My words are clear and strong, but my heart races. Maybe, finally, I will learn why Invierne sent a massive army through the desert after me. Why they stole Hector in a scheme to draw me here.

"You could not keep her against her will," Storm says. "She is too powerful." I hope he is right.

"If you did not come to stay, *Your Majesty*, then why did you come?"

I frown, realizing my companions are still on their knees only because the Deciregus has not yet released them. "Joyans, rise," I command, and everyone stands. Mara shoots me a grateful look. To the Deciregus I say, "I have come for knowledge." A partial truth, but the Inviernos barter in such things.

The Deciregus considers. He studies each of my companions, his gaze lingering a moment on Mula. At last he says, "The Frozen Waterfall Mourns Her Raging Youth, please prepare quarters for our guests."

Storm's sister is the only one still on her knees. Her eyes

shift to avoid his gaze, and her voice shakes as she stands, saying, "Yes, Honored Father," and then sweeps from the room. I stare after her, wondering if I have read her terror correctly.

I've been in this situation before, and I expect to be placed under house arrest. I listen for the sounds of drawn weapons and marching feet. But no one makes a move. The Deciregus says, "What knowledge, exactly, do you seek?"

I don't hesitate. "I want to know why you have pursued me so doggedly. I want to know where the gate of darkness leads. And I want to meet the other bearer."

If he is surprised that I know even that much, he does not show it. "And what do you offer in return for this knowledge?"

"Knowledge for knowledge, of course. And . . ." I wave a hand nonchalantly. "A few other minor concessions. If you tell me what I want to know, I will reveal the location of the *zafira*." The fact that it lies buried beneath a mountain of rubble will have to wait for another time.

His Godstone flashes bright blue as he launches to his feet. "How do I know you speak the truth? All Joyans are liars."

"So everyone keeps telling us," Hector mutters under his breath.

"I have seen it with my own eyes," Storm says. "I passed beyond the gate and tasted its power for myself. This is why my sister agreed to lead us here to speak with you—she sensed the growing power inside me. And Queen Elisa would be dismayed to discover that harm had come to someone who aided her."

Is that why he sent Waterfall away? To be punished or killed?

But upon hearing Storm's words, something in the Deciregus's face changes. He steps down the dais, arms outstretched. Hector shifts into a defensive stance beside me, but the sorcerer has eyes only for Storm. "My son," he says, and they clasp arms. "The only Invierno in thousands of years to pass the gate that leads to life. If the *zafira* let you live, then you are truly an animagus now."

I eye him warily. His change of heart seems too sudden, and his smile does not reach his eyes.

The Deciregus turns to me. "All three of your questions lead to the same place. Rest. Eat. Tonight, while the city sleeps, I will take you to the Temple of Morning, where you shall have your answers."

The seneschal signals, and a gaggle of barefoot Inviernos surrounds us and herds us away with the press of their frail bodies. We leave the audience hall and its massive sequoia behind for a dank tunnel that smells of algae and rat urine. After a few turns and a single flight of steep stairs, we come to a doorway that opens into a small stone chamber. There are several windows, but they are high up, making it impossible to see in or out. Tapestries covering the walls and rich rugs the colors of sunset can't keep the place from feeling tight and cold.

"I apologize for the accommodation, Your Majesty," the seneschal says. "But it's the best we can do for now. We dare not put you somewhere prominent. Crooked Sequoia House has many enemies, and I would not place bets on your survival should it become known that we have offered you hospitality."

"Thank you," I say. "The room is fine."

"I suggest that you and your party refrain from doing any magic. Every animagus in the city would sense you, if they have not already."

"We have no intention of using magic while enjoying the hospitality of Crooked Sequoia House. Except to defend ourselves, of course."

"Of course. I'll have refreshments sent. The door will remain unlocked—you are not prisoners here. But my strong recommendation is that you stay out of sight." The seneschal bows and departs, swinging the heavy door closed behind him.

"Well," says Mara, staring at the door. "That went better than expected."

"It went *too* well," Storm mutters. He runs his fingers through his near-white hair and stares off into the distance. "I knew my father would jump at the chance to help us, but . . ." Doubt lines his beautiful features.

"Waterfall was sure he would too," I remind him. "You must have had good reason."

He nods. "He is one of only two Deciregi who believe that making war against your people is a shameful waste of resources and an evil in the sight of God. And allying with Joya's queen and bearer would be a great coup against his enemies. Still . . ."

"I did not like him," Mula says. "I did not like his eyes."

"We will be wary," I promise.

"Are you sure it's a good idea to tell them where the *zafira* is?" Mara asks. She and Belén sit side by side on a narrow cot, their shoulders a finger's breadth apart.

I let out a breath of frustration. "No," I admit. "I'm not sure. But if what they believe is true, that our people *stole* it from them thousands of years ago, along with their land and liveli-hoods, then it's the right thing to do."

"Also, it's buried under a mountain of rubble," Hector adds. "It would take time and considerable resources to mine through to it."

I can't help the grin that spreads across my face. "Exactly. I like the idea of the Inviernos being thus occupied for many generations. I have a navy. They don't. If they misbehave, we'll simply cut them off from the island."

Hector regards me with open admiration, and my face flushes. The moment passes too quickly. "We should be pre-pared for an ambush tonight," he says.

"When they come for us," Storm says, "they'll divide us. They'll insist that only animagi enter the Temple of Morning."

"I will insist otherwise."

"They'll be quite firm," Storm says. "They *might* allow you a personal attendant."

"Belén will accompany me."

Belén nods, but Hector says, "No. I'll go."

"Your ribs! Your broken—"

"Belén only has one eye."

I glower at him. Hector is a better man than that.

He grabs my hand, and even though everyone is watching, he pulls me toward him and brings my fingers to his lips. His gaze on me is fierce. "Don't make me watch them take you away."

I swallow hard, realizing I don't want to let him out of my sight either. "All right."

Dusk is turning to night, and the high stained-glass windows cast jewel-like shadows across the walls. Oil lamps are set in alcoves around the room, and Mula takes it upon herself to light them all. Waterfall brings a tray with food and drink—an aromatic bread filled with pine nuts, hard-boiled duck eggs seasoned with basil and sage, and a large steaming pot of tea. I give a quick thought to poison, but Storm falls upon the food without hesitation, and I follow his lead. Everything is too dry for my taste, and savory rather than sweet, but still satisfying. Mula mewls like a kitten when she tastes the duck eggs and promptly shoves two more into her mouth.

Waterfall leans over to gather everything back onto her tray. Her breath catches, and her hand flies to her side.

Storm grabs her forearm. "How many?" he asks in a near whisper.

Waterfall wrenches her arm away. "He was merciful. Only five lashes." She grabs the tray and sweeps from the room without looking back.

I stare after her, my skin crawling.

"You think my father treats her unfairly," Storm observes.

"Are all Inviernos so harsh with their own?"

"Oh, no. My father is considered lenient and softhearted."

I gape at him.

"We uphold discipline and loyalty to the house above all things," he explains. "My sister agreed to help us without consulting the house prince. She should have gone to him first."

Mara says, "Then why didn't she?"

Storm shakes his head. "She could not have gained audience until this evening. She would have delayed action, increasing the risk that you would be discovered. Or worse, giving another house a chance to make a move. If she had spoken to him without acting, she would have received at least thirty lashes." At our horrified looks, Storm shrugs. "We have a saying. My people call it 'choosing the path of fewest lashes.'"

"That's terrible," I murmur, half to myself.

"You mistake 'terrible' for 'different,'" he says. "You have a similar saying, do you not? 'The lesser of two evils'? How many times have you found it necessary to choose between bad and worse? Many, I think, in just the short time I've known you."

It's different, somehow, to be physically punished for such a thing. I'm not sure how to explain, so I just nod. But my heart is sinking, for we have such a long way to go toward understanding each other.

Dusk turns to night, and still no one comes. The others stand aside to give me room to pace, accustomed to the habit by now.

I've been in this situation before. Was it a year ago—less?—when Conde Treviño used the auspices of hospitality to place us under house arrest? When his soldiers came for us, Humberto was the one to accompany me, only to be brutally murdered moments later.

I sense Hector watching me as I pace. I turn to face him, to soak up his presence, to memorize his features. Unbidden, the image flashes in my mind—a knife sliding across Humberto's precious throat, his life blood spilling out onto my hands.

His gaze turns quizzical. "What is it?"

I stride toward him, fling my arms around his waist, rest my forehead against his chest. His arms wrap my shoulders. "I don't want anything to happen to you," I whisper.

"Ah. I see."

I wait for the ensuing platitude. Ximena would have offered one. *Everything will be fine, my sky.* The back of my throat suddenly stings to think of her. Sometimes, maybe, she is just what I need.

But that's not Hector's way. I look up to find his gaze as intent as always—with love, I see now. And honesty.

"It's my duty to ensure something happens to me instead of to you," he says. "It's an eventuality you must be prepared for. And if it does, I want you to fight through it. Promise me, if something happens to me, you will stay the course."

And sometimes what I need is for my fear to be addressed forthrightly. I nod up at him, feeling a little stronger. "I promise."

A knock sounds at the door.

Everyone jumps to their feet, hands to weapons. I glance around and see readiness in the eyes of my companions. "Enter!" I call out.

The seneschal opens the door. "Your Majesty," he says with a slight incline of his head that would never suffice as proper deference in Joya d'Arena. "His Eminence the Deciregus requests your company and that of his son. He bids you come quickly and with all possible quietude."

"Of course." I gesture for Hector to follow.

The seneschal raises a hand to stop me. His fingers are long and spidery and as pale as the moonrise. "Only animagi may pass through to the Temple of Morning."

I almost roll my eyes at the sheer predictability. Before I can respond, Storm says, "But each animagus may bring a personal attendant. It is the law, and you must allow it."

The seneschal's blue eyes narrow. "Attendants are slaves. They come only to serve."

Hector glares him down. "I am my queen's to command. In everything."

They size each other up for a moment, and finally the seneschal shrugs. "As you wish." He turns to Storm. "Will you bring an attendant as well?"

Storm looks to me, and I consider. It would be nice to have Belén's blade with us. But I mentally divide our strength and realize I dare not leave Mara with only a little girl to fight at her back. "Mula will accompany Storm," I say.

Mula steps forward quickly, her golden eyes bright.

As the four of us follow the seneschal out the door, I glance back, expecting a final good-bye or a wish for luck. Mara gives me an encouraging nod, but she can't hide the concern in her face. Belén snakes a hand over to grab hers, and she squeezes back fiercely.

The seneschal leads us deep into Crooked Sequoia House, through narrow corridors dimly lit by torches. We reach a door made of pine so old it is dry and cracking. He pulls a large brass key from his pocket and inserts it into the lock.

The door opens to a small, windowless room. Its gray stone walls and floor are completely bare—save for the large tapestry hanging on the opposite wall. The seneschal shifts his torch, and the light reveals the tapestry to be a woven masterwork in stunning colors. An animagus stands atop a high promontory, overlooking a green valley. He is different than the Inviernos I've encountered—taller, as thin and wispy as a stalk of grass, with blue eyes so large they seem to engulf his face. He has only three fingers on each hand, and I cannot tell if the differences are the result of a primitive style of art or if they represent an accurate depiction.

The animagus raises his staff to the sky, and blue lightning streams from the tip, colliding in a shower of sparks with a giant insectlike creature the size of a small building. The creature's gossamer wings are stretched wide, and its gaping black mouth screams its death throes.

The door slams shut behind us, and I jump. "That tapestry is ancient," the seneschal offers. He speaks softly, but his voice echoes. "It illustrates a great victory, the details of which are lost, alas. But we keep tapestries like this in good repair, hoping we'll someday know more."

"Does such a creature exist?" I ask, reaching up to reverently trace a spidery black leg.

"Not anymore, though we have found their remnants. When your people came to this world, they destroyed or changed everything they considered a threat. Now only Inviernos remain, along with some lesser cousins of this great bug." His voice turns wistful. "We are all shadows of what we once were."

I open my mouth to ask more, but he pushes the tapestry aside to reveal a low, dark tunnel. I give Storm a questioning look.

"I knew there was a secret entrance," he explains, "though I didn't know where. The ruling houses are arrayed in a crescent around the Temple of Morning. I'm sure each house has an entrance of its own." He stoops low to follow the seneschal inside. "I believe it is safe, Majesty," he says over his shoulder.

Mula steps in after him with no hesitation, but Hector peers inside and says, "There is little quarter for sword work."

"An enemy would share the disadvantage," I point out.

He nods and gestures for me to go first. But he adds, "Have your daggers ready."

19

THE tunnel is so small that we go single file. Mula walks upright; the rest of us duck to avoid the low ceiling. Only the seneschal carries a torch, and once the tapestry swings back into place, I can't see where I'm placing my feet. It's the perfect place for an ambush, and we all step quietly, ears pricked.

Since coming to the city of Umbra de Deus, my Godstone has been riotous with activity—cool one moment, hot as a fire the next. All the things my stone responds to are gathered in once place—close friends, enemies, other Godstones. The Deciregi aside, who knows how many animagi inhabit this place, each with a stone of his own? So I have been ignoring it, knowing there is no way to parse its message, to determine which proximate thing it responds to at any given moment.

But as we proceed down the tight, dark corridor, everything changes. The flashes of hot and cold are replaced by a soothing vibration, an almost melodic sensation that, if it were a sound, might be a song. It fills my limbs with buzzing, joyous warmth, as if I'm about to greet the sunrise. "Storm?" I say.

"I feel it too," he says, but there is no surprise in his voice.

The torch ahead winks and flashes with the seneschal's steps. The light snags on a gouge in the wall, a curving darkness set off by lighter gray.

"Stop!" I say, and everyone halts. I brush past Mula and put a finger to the gouges. Not gouges—scripted letters. I've seen them before.

The gate that leads to life is narrow and small so that few find it.

"Just like in the tunnel beneath . . . leading to the *zafira,*" Storm says.

"Yes." What he didn't say, what he didn't want the seneschal to hear, is that these same words are also carved into a tunnel beneath the catacombs of my own capital city.

"I'm beginning to wonder if they mark a place of importance," he says. "Maybe a place of power."

"It's worth investigating," Hector says casually. "When we have the time for such curiosities."

When we get back home, he means. Assuming there's a home to go back to.

"His High Honor the Deciregus is waiting," the seneschal says in a biting tone, and he proceeds down the tunnel without bothering to see that we follow.

The ground slopes upward, so gradually that I don't realize it until my breath comes harder and the muscles in my legs warm. The hum of my Godstone grows stronger. And even though I have not called it, the *zafira* slithers from the earth into my limbs, filling me with power. Our path brightens.

The seneschal pushes something aside, and cooler air hits my face. We exit the tunnel into a colossal stone chamber shaped like a perfect half moon. The curved wall stretches the height of several men, and is covered floor to ceiling with lines of black runes in a language I've never seen before. Large tapestries are arrayed at regular intervals, though they seem tiny against the massive wall. I presume that each one hides a tunnel leading to one of the ruling houses. Ten tunnels means ten approaches. We could be surrounded in the time it takes to blink.

Opposite our tunnel, the flat part of this huge half moon, is a wall of stained glass panes set in iron cross work like a port-cullis. Each pane is a different color, with shades of blue and green dominating. Wavering torches, set in sconces around the wall, give depth and shine so that the glass seems molten.

Wind whistles against cracks in a few of the glass tiles, and beneath that, barely within my range of hearing, is the sound of rushing water. Or maybe it's just my Godstone, humming so violently now that surely everyone else must sense it too.

Before us stand two Inviernos in white robes. One is Storm's father, Pine. The other is a woman with straight crystal-white hair that reaches her knees. Her pale, perfect skin is stretched too tight over tiny features. I could not say how old she is, and I can't begin to read her oily black eyes, but her carriage speaks of veteran poise.

"Your Majesty," Storm's father says. "I present Her Eminence The Low Earth Is Friend to Even the Soaring Hawk. She is the Deciregus of Tinkling Fountain House."

She inclines her head. "Your Majesty," she says, drawing out the address so that it sounds like a hiss.

"Your High Eminence. I am pleased to meet you." And I am. I've never seen a female animagus before. But she stares at me with such haughty disdain—eyes narrowed, chin high—and I know there is no possibility of kinship between us.

"Tell us of the *zafira*," she commands.

"My agreement was with the Deciregus of Crooked Sequoia House," I say. "You, I neither know nor trust."

Her eyebrows raise, and I barely hold my smile in check. I could never get away with being so impolitic in Joya d'Arena, but lofty contempt seems to be the right tack in Invierne.

Storm steps forward. "We count Tinkling Fountain House among our greatest allies," he says to me. "Like my father, they believe the war between us has gone on too long and at too great a cost. The Low Earth . . . *Hawk* will be eager to come to an agreement."

"Tell us the location of the *zafira*, and then you will have your answers," Hawk says.

Not a chance. "I want my answers first."

Hawk exchanges a look with Storm's father. Then she says, "We believe you should go first, as a demonstration of the righteous honesty that is in accordance with God's will."

That is exactly the wrong thing to say to me. I practically spit the words. "Do not *dare* tell me about God's will. I have the conduit of his power living inside my body, and even *I* do not presume to know God's will. As far as going first . . ." I look around at my companions: a former enemy who risks his status and reputation for my cause, a slave girl who defended me with her own life, and the man who has promised to give up everything for me.

I speak softly but clearly, and my voice echoes through the vast chamber. "We have come a very long way at tremendous cost to be here. I believe that counts as going first."

Storm's father regards me steadily, but his unnatural black eyes make it impossible to read his expression. He leans over and whispers something to Hawk, and she nods in response. He straightens and says, "Very well. This way."

He gestures us all toward the glass wall. Hector's hand goes to his scabbard, and I check my belt for my daggers.

As we approach, a section of the wall begins to appear a little different from the rest. Were I to look askance, it would seem exactly the same—a patchwork of colorful leaded glass. But straight on, up close, the colors are muted, and the glass ripples like a desert mirage.

"Is that it?" I ask no one in particular. "Is that the gate?"

"Indeed," Storm's father says. "Only those who command the magic of the world can sense the Wall of Morning, much less pass through it. It's the final test required for an initiate to become an animagus."

I step a little closer. "So I just walk through?"

"If you can," Hawk says, and I am absolutely certain she is smirking. "Beyond it are the answers you seek."

"Your Majesty," Hector says. "As your attendant, I would be remiss if I did not observe that this appears to be a trap."

He's right. Something surely waits for me beyond the wall of glass. I know it the way I know the sun rises in the east.

"May I take an attendant with me? Or must I pass through alone?"

"You may try," Pine says with a shrug.

I step closer to get a better look.

"Elisa, stop!"

I whirl to face Storm.

His eyes are huge, and his breath comes too fast. "The initiates, the ones in my class. Half of them never returned." He eyes his father, then lowers his head in shame. His betrayal of his family is complete.

Pine growls low in his throat, and he strides toward his son, metal-clawed hand raised as if to strike his face.

"No!" I cry, reaching for the *zafira*. I surround Storm with a shimmering miasma of power. Pine's claws collide with the barrier, showering blue sparks, and his hand recoils wildly. He stumbles back, clutching his wrist.

"You're not supposed to be able to do that," he hisses. "You're supposed to be untrained."

I give him an edged smile. It was an accident, mostly. I haven't been able to create a barrier since I was on the island, in direct contact with the *zafira*. But what I say is, "You have no idea what I'm capable of."

He straightens, tucks his hair behind one ear with the metal claw of his forefinger, and regards me steadily as if nothing has happened. "In that case, show us you are capable of passing through the gate."

"You agreed to go first," Hector says.

"Very well." And he turns and walks straight into the shimmering wall that is not a wall. It parts like water and swallows him whole.

"My turn," Hawk says with a coy smile, and she follows Pine through the gate.

I stare at the exact spot where they disappeared. Except for a slight shimmer and blurring of color, it seems solid.

"What are you going to do?" Hector asks. "I fear an ambush awaits you on the other side." His voice echoes in the vast chamber, and it should make me feel like we're alone, that our hosts have deserted us. But my neck prickles.

Storm adds, "And there is the small matter of whether or not that gate will kill us, your recent demonstration notwithstanding."

Mula says nothing, but she hitches closer to Storm and grabs a fistful of his cloak.

"Their power source is on the other side. I can feel it," I murmur. How else could I create that barrier so easily? Why else would my Godstone persist in this manic humming? It's the very thing I've been looking for. So close at hand.

I approach the wall as close as I dare. My nose almost touches it. Then I shift to the side until the shimmer fades and the colors brighten. I reach up and rest my forefinger against a vivid blue pane. It's cool to the touch. Ordinary. Laughter bubbles in my throat, and I cover my mouth to control it.

"Elisa?" Hector says.

"Get back, all of you. Against the wall. No, better yet, get into the tunnel behind the tapestry."

Hector's eyes dance in the torchlight. "I don't believe our hosts will be pleased with this turn of events."

I grin. "Indeed, they will not."

Once everyone is safely behind the tapestry, I back as far away from the glass as I can—until my rear hits the stone wall. It's a pity, really. The wall is so ancient and beautiful. Probably a national treasure. I pull a dagger from my belt.

The *zafira* rushes into me the moment I call it. I hold it inside myself for a bit, savoring this feeling of vitality, of power. After too long a pause, I allow some of it to trickle into my dagger.

The blade is a part of me, an extension of my hand, as I point it toward the wall. *Control, Elisa. Use just enough.*

I release the *zafira*, and a bolt of blue fire streaks toward the wall. The glass shatters, and a sudden wind blows my hair back. Broken panes crash to the ground, followed by a wash of tiny shards that float glitteringly like falling snow.

My companions peek from behind the tapestry and gradually creep out. Hector's gaze roves my body, searching for injury, as Mula and Storm survey the destruction.

Glass covers the floor. Beyond the shattered wall is a huge stone balcony, open to the night sky. Pine and Hawk stare at me, mouths agape. A shining stream of blood, black in the meager light, pours from a cut on Hawk's cheek.

Behind the Inviernos is a massive stone slab—no, an altar— shadowed against the night sky and the glowing mountains beyond. The sound of rushing is too loud now, a cacophony of wind and water and something else, something just beneath my range of hearing. The *zafira*, maybe. The air is crisp with predawn chill, and I wrap my arms around myself, against whatever comes next.

Pine shakes with rage, and his metal-clad fingers twitch as licks of blue flame dance between them. He is barely holding the *zafira* in check. "Do you realize what you've done?" he says.

"I believe I just succeeded in using magic to pass your gate," I say. "Doesn't that make me an animagus?"

He continues to gape as Hawk absently wipes at her cheek with the sleeve of her cloak, smearing blood. Hector shifts beside me, and I hear the light *whisk* of drawn daggers.

Pine breathes deep through his nose. The fire licking his metal fingers winks out. "Very well, then," he says. "Come and find the answers you seek." He whirls and steps toward the black altar.

"Too easy," Hector mutters.

"Storm?" I whisper. "Anything you haven't told me? Any idea what your father is planning?"

"I know nothing," he says in an equally low voice. His hand comes up to clutch the amulet beneath his robe. "But we should be wary."

"If you betray us," Hector says, "I'll kill you."

Storm bristles. "I was Her Majesty's loyal subject even before she saved my life."

"I'm glad to have you *both* with me right now," I say firmly. "Mula, do you want to go back inside the tunnel and wait there?"

Her eyes are huge. "No," she whispers.

I realize I'm delaying. "All right then."

Hector takes the lead, and glass crunches beneath our feet as we cross the threshold of the ruined wall and move toward the balcony. Hawk and Pine step aside to give a clear path to the altar. Harsh wind hits my face as the altar comes into focus.

Pine does something with his Godstone amulet, and torches spring to life one by one until the altar is ringed in fire. The torch flames illuminate smooth, round river stones, bulging in places, leveled by wind and ice and time in others. The top is perfectly flat and little more than shoulder high. I stand on my tiptoes to peer at it.

Something is up there, something that moves. I step closer.

It's a living thing, a hairless creature with skin as weathered as deer jerky. It lies on its back, its flaccid, jellylike limbs manacled to the rock. When it turns its head to regard me with despairing brown eyes, with *human* eyes, my breath catches in a sob.

"You have come to take my place?" it says in a painful rasp.

"What?" I peer closer. He lies spread-eagle across the altar. His fingers are bloodless, meaty stumps—as if they've been chewed. Lumpy skin swells over the wrist manacles. I follow the line of thin, slack limbs to a shapeless body fully bared to the elements. A bright blue Godstone winks from a naked belly.

I gasp. This creature is one of many bearers throughout history who was never identified—or who simply disappeared mysteriously.

"Behold," Pine intones. "Our living sacrifice."

Red spots dance in my vision, and I'm so angry I can hardly breathe. "This is what you plan for me? This, this . . ." Tears spring to my eyes. "This is barbaric."

"Indeed," Pine agrees. "It's our greatest shame that we are often forced to contend with an unwilling sacrifice. But it is no more barbaric that what your people did to ours. They were afraid of us, of our power. You made us less than we were, with your otherworldly machines."

I'm not sure what compels me, but I reach out toward the creature on the altar and gently brush his cheek with my forefinger. His skin feels like leather. He gazes at me with such hope from browless, lashless eyes.

I whirl to face Pine. "Why?" I demand. "Why torture him this way?"

Pine's face remains implacable. "They made us *human*." He spits out the word like it's a sour piece of fruit. "Too much humanity in our blood made it impossible to bear our Godstones beyond childhood. They started to die in our bodies. After a few generations, only a handful remained who were even born with them."

Pine looks across the balcony, toward the glowing mountains. "But even that wasn't enough to calm their fear," he continues. "They forced us to flee from our source of life and power. The hidden *zafira* was once ours; surely you know that? But away from it, we began to sicken and die. We had to do something just to survive."

He turns to regard me, his gaze fierce. I suddenly feel like a tiny jerboa facing down a hungry jaguar. "We discovered early on that we could draw power through a living Godstone. It's not the same as being near a *zafira* wellspring, but it is enough to keep us from dying out. We used our own children for this at first—the little ones who had the misfortune to be born with a stone. It was a dark time in our history. But then we discovered that your people had not only changed us—they had changed themselves as well. They mingled the blood of our two people, you see, so they could survive better on this world. Some of them, a very few, were born with Godstones."

"Once every hundred years," I whisper.

He nods. "And those Godstones didn't fall out. How could such a thing be? That our enemy could bear the stones that we could not?" He shakes his head. "So we captured a bearer, a girl like you. The *zafira* sustains our living sacrifices. We don't feed them or take care of them in any way. They exist perpetually at the point of death. And it's important that they do. Otherwise they could resist and refuse us their power."

"But this one is truly dying," Storm says.

"Yes. Eventually death takes them all. Some scholars posit that they pray themselves dead. This one"—Pine's voice is thick with contempt—"only lasted a century."

A century. I know who this creature is. The bearer before me.

"Lucero," I whisper.

He smiles, an ancient, toothless smile, and says, "You know my name."

I'm shaking so hard, and I can't stop. This is what they want for me. A century or more of lying on hard granite, exposed to sun and ice, my fingers eaten by vultures.

Hector's hand is on his scabbard, and his gaze darts around, sizing up the area. Our eyes meet. I know what he's thinking. But surely now that I have promised to tell the Deciregi of the *zafira*, their plan for me has changed?

"What about a 'willing sacrifice'?" Hector asks after too long a moment. "Franco said it would be better if Her Majesty came willingly. What does that mean?" He edges toward me. His question is merely a stall for time; he wants to get me away from this place, and fast.

"Exactly twice in our history we've had a bearer come willingly," Pine says. "A willing bearer is permitted free reign of the city. He is waited on as if he were the High Deciregus, his every need attended to. In return, he agrees to willingly let us siphon the world's power through his stone. Both times we had willing bearers, Invierne experienced a golden age. We bore more children, we lived longer. Apparently the *zafira* is richer and more accessible if the bearer does not resist."

I stare at the lump of flesh on the altar before me. Lucero was a poor village boy. Illiterate. Surely the prospect of being treated like a king would have made him a willing participant. Why did he resist?

Hector says, "What aren't you telling us? If being a willing sacrifice is a position of such honor and luxury, surely you would have convinced more than two."

Pine hesitates. He exchanges another glance with Hawk, who nods. Finally he says, "Having power forcefully pulled through a living stone is somewhat . . . uncomfortable, as I understand. But yes, a willing sacrifice enjoys many benefits to compensate."

The Deciregus is too glib. Never have I met an Invierno so willing to part with information. Even Storm, my ally and friend, causes me no end of frustration with his reticence.

Storm must sense something amiss as well, for he says, "We'll no longer need a sacrifice if we have direct access to the *zafira*."

No one responds. Wind whistles across the balcony. Beyond the altar, the silhouettes of the mountains are edged with morning light. One of the volcanoes spews a bit of lava. From this distance, it looks like fiery pudding, the way it sticks together midair and plops onto the side of the mountain.

"Please," comes a whispered voice.

I turn toward the creature on the altar, forcing myself not to flinch at the sight.

"Kill me," he says.

I step closer. His eyes swim with longing. With pain.

"I came to destroy their power source," I admit, softly enough that only he can hear. "But I didn't know it would be a person. Maybe I could take you away from here. I could heal you—"

"No," he says, sharply enough that it startles me. "Everyone is dead. Gavín, Jedro, Melita . . . All gone. My life, my friends. I lived for the blink of an eye. But I've been dying for a very long time."

I'm surprised by his clarity of thought. His sanity. I don't know that I would fare so well.

I lean toward his ear and whisper, "If you want me to kill you, I will. But I'm not sure it's necessary. I'm bargaining for peace. Invierne will never need a living sacrifice again."

Lucero blinks at me with lashless lids, as if trying to focus. Is he blind? He says, "I think that is not a good place for you to stand."

"What?"

The earth drops out from under my feet. My stomach leaps into my throat as I freefall into darkness.

"Elisa!" Hector yells.

I crash onto hard ground. My right leg snaps, a rib, a collarbone, as I crumple like weak kindling. Pain explodes everywhere, and I open my mouth to scream, but I can only convulse.

My lungs are empty of air. Blood fills my mouth. It will choke me if I don't swallow or spit, but I can't. Something closes in around me, something so much darker than the mere absence of light.

20

HECTOR

I'M only two strides away when the trapdoor opens and swallows Elisa.

I leap forward, bellowing for her to hold on, though there is nothing for her to hold on to. The tips of my fingers just brush her braid as she drops out of sight. I crouch at the opening to jump in after her.

My limbs turn to stone.

Sweat pours from my forehead. My breath comes in gasps. I've felt the magical paralysis of an animagus before. I've fought through it and won. But this is no mere animagus, and within moments I know this is a battle I will lose.

A stone slab slides across the dark hole Elisa disappeared into and thuds closed. I can hardly take it in, that I've lost her again. That they stole her right from under my nose.

"What did you do?" someone screams, giving voice to my own rage, and suddenly my body is released and air rushes into my lungs. I topple forward, barely catching myself with my hands.

I spring to my feet, drawing my sword. I lunge toward Pine, but pull up short because Mula has gotten there first. She pounds him with tiny fists, still screaming, "What did you do? What did you do? Bring her back!"

Pine regards Mula with puzzled annoyance, as one would a pesky gnat, but her distraction was enough to free me from the Deciregus's grip.

"Mula, step away now," I order, expecting to be frozen again at any moment. The girl ceases her assault at once and backs away.

It might be best not to launch at the sorcerer after all. I watched my best friend burn in the fiery, unavoidable grasp of an animagus. I switch my grip to a throwing position. I haven't practiced throwing with a sword this size and weight, but maybe I'll get lucky. Or maybe I'll lose my best weapon.

"Take me to the queen at once." I'm in no position to demand anything; I'm just stalling until I can form a better plan.

Pine raises his chin in amusement. Beside him, Hawk chuckles.

I try a different tack. "If you don't take me to her, you'll never learn the location of the *zafira*." I sheathe the sword, sending it home with a decisive *snick*. A weapon won't help me now.

"They don't care about the *zafira*," Storm says, his voice a near whisper. He stares at his father, his expression unreadable. Was he part of the plan the whole time? I should have forced Elisa to be more cautious with the Invierno. "They just wanted *her*," Storm continues. "The other Deciregi would destroy a nation for the *zafira*, but not my father and his allies. They just want peace for another century."

In that case, I'll find the other Deciregi. Tell them that if they free the queen, they can have access to a power source even more vast. But it will only work if I can get us off this balcony.

Hawk and Pine want Elisa for their living sacrifice, so they'll keep her alive. But badly injured. Like the boy on the altar, they want her at the point of death. So she can't resist.

My stomach knots, even as my jaw hardens and my teeth clench. In order to help her, I must leave her. Then I can bargain for her release. If that fails, I'll tear the city apart stone by stone.

Pine and Hawk share a look of triumph. Gently, Pine raises his hand—the bare one—and strokes her cheek. "We did it," she says, smiling up at him.

Pine turns to me. "We will present the new sacrifice to the Deciregi in two days, at the height of our annual Commemoration." His voice rings with triumph. "It will be a great coup for our houses. I will present you and the queen's other companions as well, for my daughter says that you all hold great status in your kingdom."

I glare at Storm, who gazes blandly into the distance, betraying nothing of his thoughts.

"I cannot guarantee your safety at that point," Pine continues. "The others will contend that if you return with news of the queen's fate, your country will declare war on ours and invade. It might be better if you all just . . . disappeared. You'll never be allowed to return home. But in honor of the queen making my son into an animagus and bringing him home to me, I'll try to convince them to spare your lives."

Pine pauses expectantly. Does he presume gratitude? Obeisance? He'll get neither.

Eventually the Deciregus shrugs. To Storm, he says, "You must choose. Will you be escorted back with the others? Or will you retake your place as my heir?"

A muscle in Storm's jaw twitches. Then he says, clear and strong, "My first loyalty has always been to Crooked Sequoia House."

I clench my hands into fists to keep them from drawing my sword and running the Invierno through. My nails bite into my palms—a welcome pain. As soon as I get the chance, Storm is a dead man.

Hawk and Pine move to escort us away. Mula looks up at me for direction, and I nod assurance. Once we're reunited with Mara and Belén, we'll figure out what to do next.

As we crunch across the shattered glass, back toward the tapestry and the tunnel leading to Crooked Sequoia House, Storm is too cowardly to meet my eye. I imagine myself throttling his too-elegant neck. But a glimpse of his chest gives me pause. Through his thin linen shift comes the glimmer of Storm's Godstone, raging bright with power.

He leads us back to our holding room. The door squeals behind me, and I turn just in time to catch a final glimpse of Storm's unfazed countenance before it slams shut and a deadbolt thuds into place.

"Hector! Where is she?" Mara demands.

I swallow hard. "They've taken her. There was a trapdoor, and—"

Grief slams me, so hot and hard that I double over. *Elisa.* How many times have I awakened in the dead of night, gasping, pouring sweat, from the nightmare of losing her?

A hand grips my shoulder. "We'll get her back," Belén says. "I swear it. Now . . ." He pushes me toward the cot and forces me to sit. "Tell us everything that happened," he orders.

Get control of yourself, Hector. I take a deep breath and say, "First, you should know that Storm has betrayed us."

Mara gasps. "I don't believe it."

Mula climbs up into her lap and wraps scrawny arms around Mara's neck. "The commander speaks for true," she says.

I tell them everything. Mara cries a little as Mula strokes her hair. Belén hits the wall with a fist.

Then we make a plan. Then we wait.

If Elisa were here, waiting along with us, she would pace. She would bite at her thumbnail and go back and forth until everyone was dizzy from watching her. In her absence, I pace instead. It's better than doing nothing. And something about the physical movement frees my mind to move more quickly, unhindered.

Hours pass. The sun is high, our tiny room bright, when I hear footsteps, followed by the scrape of the bolt being lifted.

We rush to get in position—Belén and I to either side of the door, Mula in clear view of the opening as she pretends to sleep on the cot, Mara slightly off to the side with her bow drawn.

I shift to the balls of my feet, unsheathing a dagger. This is it.

The door creaks open.

No one moves. No one breathes.

Just a little wider, I pray. Just a little farther.

Something rolls through the cracked opening, and Belén dodges to avoid it. It clunks against the leg of Mula's cot. A water skin. Two more items follow—bulging leather bags.

The door slams shut; the bar thuds into place.

I utter the foulest oath I know.

Mara opens the bags. "Jerky," she says. "And a loaf of bread. At least they don't plan to starve us."

I'm about to resume pacing, but Belén grabs my arm. "It was worth a try," he says. "But next time, we force the door open and fight our way out."

I nod. We agreed to try to capture someone as a hostage and keep casualties to a minimum. If we're to parlay with the Deciregi, we shouldn't start off by killing their people. But I won't hesitate if it's the only way out of this room.

Mula uses Mara's tinderbox to light all the oil lamps in the room. She is holding the largest in her hand when she startles, almost dropping it. Hesitantly, almost shyly, she looks from the lamp in her hand to the door and then back again.

I have a guess about what she's thinking. I've come to admire the little girl. She is as pesky as a mosquito and as full of energy as a spring colt. But she can be calculating. Determined. She's a little bit like Elisa.

"Skinny Girl," I say, using Belén's name for her. I can't bring myself to call her a mule.

When she looks up at me, panic flits across her odd features as quickly and naturally as if from long habit, but she channels it into a glare. "What?"

"It's a good idea."

She looks down at her lamp. Back up at me. Straightens. "I'm going to try it."

"We should break the window first," I say. "Give the smoke a place to go."

Mara and Belén exchange a glance. They've been sitting side by side on the cot, their shoulders brushing, but they separate to look around for something to throw.

"Maybe I could shoot through it?" Mara says.

Belén reaches for her bow, propped up against the wall, and hands it to her.

Mara draws an arrow from her quiver and taps it against her cheek as she sizes up the window. She draws, holds, releases.

The arrow zings through the air, cracks against the window, glances off, and whirls end over end to the ground.

Mara frowns. "Bad angle," she mutters. "I need a more direct hit."

I step forward. "Can you shoot from my shoulders?"

She brightens. "That might work! You'd have to stand firm to give me an accurate shot."

She climbs from the cot onto my shoulders. The heel of her boot digs into the crook of my neck, and I sway beneath her weight. I plant my feet, one leg in front of the other, to find a new center of balance. Belén hands the bow and an arrow up to Mara.

Her weight shifts as she notches the bow and draws. I'm as

still as a statue lest I throw off her aim. The bow twangs; the window explodes. Shards of glass fall like water and crash onto the floor.

Belén steadies Mara as she climbs down from my shoulders.

Mula holds the oil lamp aloft, a question in her eyes.

"Try it," I say.

She pulls the still-burning wick from the clay base, then upends the contents onto the thick wooden door. Sassafras scent fills the room as slick oil drips down the wood grain. The drips never reach the floor; the thirsty wood soaks it up.

Mula steps back as far as her reach will allow. Turning her face away, she touches the burning wick to the oil slick on the door.

I hold my breath.

Nothing happens, and I reach for another lamp sitting in a nearby alcove—maybe we need more oil. But all of a sudden it does catch, in a great *whoosh* of air and heat.

Mula jumps up into the air. "Did you *see* that?" she asks, grinning wildly.

The flames licking at the door are near invisible, as wavering and insubstantial as a desert mirage, save for the occasional flame tip of orange or blue. The heat singes my face. I order everyone against the far wall. We raise our cloaks to cover our noses, and together we watch the door burn.

The fire weakens and dies.

It leaves a shiny black crater, but it's shallow and small. I glance around the room, refusing to give up. Three oil lamps left. In my barracks, anyone caught with four oil lamps in a single room would have served double watches for excess and recklessness. Now I'd give my best sword for ten more.

Mula grabs the nearest and repeats the process of removing the wick, pouring out the contents, and lighting it.

Again, we step back to watch, growing chilly now that the window is open to the winter air. Again, the fire dies.

Mula's shoulders slump.

I finally realize what's taking so long. "We need to scrape off the char," I say.

"Aaah," says Mara. "Because the fire has nowhere to go."

I nod. "We need to reveal fresh wood. Quietly."

Belén steps forward, knife in hand. The blackened area is huge, and it shimmers like cold embers. He scrapes at it with the blade; huge chunks of black fall away, accompanied by finer ash that chokes the air.

"Quieter!" Mara whispers.

"I'm trying!" he answers. But he pauses every few scrapes to listen for footsteps.

When he has revealed a section of gray-brown wood, Mula steps forward and pours more oil into the crater. It's concave enough that she has to fling it forward to coat the wood.

This time when she lights it, the room flashes as bright as day and the door burns just a little longer before fading.

"Should we test it?" comes Belén's voice.

But I'm already there, my short sword drawn. I put the tip of the blade to the deepest part of the crater.

"Careful!" Mara says. "It might be hot."

Mindful of her warning, I press the blade into the wood. Nothing happens.

I switch my grip, and using the cross guard for leverage, I lean my weight into it and push with all my might. I worry about the blade snapping, but all of a sudden something gives, the blade bursts through, my footing slips, and my shoulder slams into the door.

"Quiet!" everyone whispers at once.

I listen for footsteps, a cry of alarm. But there is nothing.

Warm air and weak torchlight sneak in through the hole we created. We need to widen it. I bend closer.

The torchlight reveals another crack. If I can pry it . . .

"I need my gloves," I mutter, and a moment later they are in my hand. "Thank you, Mula," I say, slipping them on. I pry at the crack with my sword until it's wide enough for my hand. Then I slip my fingers through, grip as best I can, and yank. When that doesn't work, I try pushing, then twisting side to side until something budges. Moments later, I triumphantly hold up a piece of shattered, blackened wood, as sharp as a spear at both ends.

I wipe sweat from my forehead with the back of my gloved hand and reach in for another try. "It would be faster," I grumble, "if we could just pound it."

"Also noisier," Mara points out.

I pry out another chunk. The wood is old and dry, and the charred area widens with relative ease, but not enough for me to reach around and lift the latch.

Belén says, "It might be wide enough for a skinny girl."

"*I'm* skinny!" says Mula. I step aside, and she pokes her head through the hole to size up the corridor. Then squeezes an arm through, a leg, and disappears.

I wince at the echoing scrape of the latch being lifted, but then the door swings open and Mula stands there, backlit by torchlight.

I charge outside, glance up and down the corridor, then beckon Mara and Belén to follow. Odd that no one guards our door. They must be very confident that we could never escape the city.

"Anyone remember which way we came?" Mara says.

"This way," I say, and I hurry them north, toward the tunnel that will take us to the Temple of Morning.

We move quietly, but not quietly enough. I'm not outfitted for stealth, and the joints of my leather armor creak with each step. I should remove it. As we creep along the corridor, I peer into crevices, behind statues, hoping for a place to stash it where it won't be noticed.

Something tickles at my consciousness, and I hold up a fist to halt everyone. Did I just hear footsteps? If so, they were faint. Slippers instead of boots. Maybe the swish of a cloak.

It sounds again—soft footfalls that barely echo.

"Back!" I whisper. "The other way. Quickly!"

We scurry back in the direction we came. Mula breaks into a panicked sprint, and I almost holler at her to stop, that running blindly down the corridor is a very bad idea, but yelling would be even worse. She disappears around the corner.

More footsteps—boots this time. They step in time, like my

own men on watch. This corridor is guarded after all.

An exclamation of surprise. Mula has collided with someone.

"What are you doing here, slave girl?" comes a male voice. "This area is off limits."

"I . . . I got lost."

The voices are coming closer. We're trapped. Mara swings her bow from her shoulder as Belén grabs a dagger.

Four Inviernos with soldiers' braids and rawhide armor appear around the corner. They keep formation even as they back Mula toward us. I whisk my sword from its scabbard as the soldiers' eyes go wide.

"Joyans!" one shouts. As one, they draw their weapons.

"Run, fight, or surrender?" Belén asks under his breath. "Your call."

If we surrender, we might not get to Elisa in time. If we run, we'll probably have to fight anyway. And if we fight, we're likely to sustain injury. Maybe even a loss. Probably that loss would be Mula.

My hand tightens around my sword grip. "We fight."

Tears fill Mara's eyes, even as she nods once, sharply.

The soldiers advance. One raises his sword toward Mula's cowering form.

"I'll take it from here," says someone behind us. Without turning, I know it's Storm, his voice as full of arrogant conde-scension as always.

I grit my teeth. I don't care which enemy I kill, so long as I get to Elisa. But maybe the Invierno turncoat will buy us some time.

"Your Honor, these are Joyans," says one of the soldiers.

"Yes. Which is why my father will be most eager to handle them himself."

"But they could be—"

Something washes the corridor in soft blue light and makes the soldier's eyes fly wide with terror.

"You will release these prisoners into my custody," Storm says in a soft but lethal voice. "You will not speak of them to anyone, not even your commander, until His Eminence the Deciregus has examined them himself. You will return to your rounds as if nothing has happened."

"Yes, Your Honor," they mutter, bowing and backing away. Mula runs to Mara's side and clutches at her sleeve.

After the soldiers disappear around the corner, Storm says, "Elisa is this way. Quickly; we don't have much time. She has been trying to escape. I can sense it. And if I can sense it, the others can too. We need rope. There should be some in—"

"Wait." I whirl and clamp the Invierno's thin shoulder. My thumb digs in below his collarbone, hard enough to cause pain, but Storm is as impassive as ever. "You said your first loyalty is to Crooked Sequoia House," I say. "I heard you. Are you leading us into another trap?"

The Godstone swinging from his amulet still glows from whatever magic he used to intimidate the soldiers, but Storm makes no effort to call on it. Neither does he try to break away from my grip. Instead his lips turn up into a sad, slanted smile, and he says, "I lied."

We stare at him.

"You always speak for true," Mula whispers. "Always."

"Not this time."

I'm about to protest, but Storm cuts me off.

"Lord-Commander, I won't pretend to love her the way you do. But I do owe her my life and my honor. I am Joyan now. And we are, all of us, filthy liars."

"Well, if he wasn't lying then," Mara says, "he's lying now. Which means he's telling the truth. So let's go!"

I'm not sure that makes sense, but I release my grip and order, "Take us to her."

Storm heads down the corridor at a fast jog. It's a relief to run freely, knowing Storm can talk or intimidate our way out of any encounters.

We're coming, Elisa.

21

MY consciousness explodes into a world of pain.

I'm dying. I know it with certainty. Blood pours from my mouth, and I choke, then cough, which sends more knifelike pain into my side. My rib has punctured a lung. I will drown in my own blood.

I lie on my back in total darkness. My right leg is cricked beneath me in a way it shouldn't be. My left shoulder sits oddly, and I make a tiny attempt to move it, but fire shoots up my neck and into my spine.

I take a deep breath to calm myself, bringing another fit of choking. Tears leak from my eyes. I don't have much time.

My skull seems intact, and I cling to the thought. If I have my mind, I have everything I need. And just maybe, I can heal myself.

Doctor Enzo thinks I've healed myself instinctively, though more slowly than I've healed others. But I'm not sure what to do. I can't heal my leg in its current position. I would just have to rebreak it later.

Maybe healing is like all the other powers drawn from the *zafira*. Maybe it can be focused. Deliberate.

I'll start with my rib, since that is what's killing me. If it works, I'll probably pass out again. And once I wake up, I'll have to straighten my leg and shoulder before healing them. It will be awful. Maybe the most awful thing I've ever done.

Coughs spasm through my chest, and I turn my head to the side to let more blood pour out.

Don't think, Elisa. Just do.

I close my eyes and open myself to the *zafira*. It rushes in like a flood, filling me with warmth and light. I imagine that I sense Lucero holding the floodgates wide for me. I imagine his toothless smile, his voice whispering "I will help."

How close to death must I be, to hallucinate so?

I think hard about my broken rib. I make the pain in my side my whole existence, embracing it, understanding it. I imagine the bone moving back into place, the tissue inside knitting together.

But it's too much—too much effort, too much sensation. The world spins, and unconsciousness creeps up—too soon.

Let go and let me.

"Lucero?" I whisper.

Promise me. If I do this, you will kill me.

I hesitate.

We don't have much time. I can only draw the zafira *when no one else is using me.*

"I promise."

Pain reaches its fingers inside me and pries me open. My back arches off the ground, and I scream.

Coughing, choking, gagging . . . I wake, and turn over just fast enough to vomit all over the ground. I spit to clear my mouth. Cough a few more times. Spit again.

And I take a deep, glorious breath. My lungs are clear.

I clamber to my feet, trying my best in the dark to avoid the mess I just made. I stretch out my right leg and test it by flexing my foot back and forth. Perfect. A bit of stiffness, but no pain. Lucero must have straightened my leg before healing me, though I've no idea how he accomplished such a thing. I roll my shoulder. It twinges a little; I'll have to be careful with it for a while.

But I'm alive. And healthy. Thanks to the man who is determined to die.

I reach out with my awareness for him, the same way I would reach for the Godstone's power: *Lucero?* But there is nothing. It's like shouting into an empty cave, my only response a faint mental echo.

I call the *zafira* and form tiny candle flames at my fingertips. It's effortless now, either from practice or from being in a place of power. I use the light to explore my surroundings.

The walls are round and made of impenetrable stone. The floor is different—not dirt, exactly, and not stone. Bedrock, maybe. A pile of bloody vomit shimmers off to the side, and I move my glowing hand away to avoid looking. There are no windows. No doors. Just rounded walls that stretch up into darkness. I fell a very long way.

It's a pit.

The walls are too smooth to climb. I kick at the floor—too hard to dig. There must be a way out. If they want me for their living sacrifice, then they must have a means of retrieving me. Maybe with a rope, lowered from the trapdoor above.

If they want me alive, that means they have to feed me, give me water to drink. It means . . .

No, it doesn't mean anything. What was it Pine said? Something about the living sacrifice existing perpetually at the point of death?

I sink onto the ground, my flames winking out. They will starve me until I can no longer defy them. No, I'll be mad with dehydration long before that. Or suffocation, if this pit is airtight. Already the air feels thin and damp from my own exhaled breath. Or do I imagine it?

I hug my knees to my chest and rest my forehead on them, determined to think, think, think, until I've figured out how to escape. I don't lift my head from my knees until I've thought of several possibilities.

The trapdoor I fell through is too high for the light of my meager candle flames to reach. But maybe it's made of wood. If so, I can burn through it.

I unsheathe my daggers, glad for their reassuring weight in my hands. Odd that they never bothered to disarm us. Or maybe not so odd. The weapons of Joya d'Arena are little use in a place of magic.

Unless, like me, one uses them to *do* magic.

I draw in the *zafira* until I buzz with power, until my whole body glows. I spin in place, using the momentum to swing a fireball upward with my dagger. It flies high, explodes against the ceiling, rains golden sparks onto my hair and shoulders.

I wilt with disappointment. I caught only the merest glimpse, but it was enough to see that the ceiling is made of pure stone. There is a slight indention marking the trapdoor, but neither is it made of wood. It's a marvel of engineering, really, to have a door of solid stone that slides so smoothly.

I let myself rest before trying my next idea, knowing things will be easier if I use the *zafira*'s power in strategic increments. I will not exhaust myself. I will not allow myself to be brought to the point of death. So I sit on the ground and close my eyes. I take slow, deep breaths, as if I were going through the warm-up exercises of the Royal Guard.

Nothing will stop Hector from trying to get to me. And if I can't figure a way out of this pit for myself, I need to think of a way to make it easier for him to find me—like he did when I was searching for him.

When calm has again settled over my body, I rise, summoning flames to the fingertips of my left hand, and begin a thorough inspection of the walls and floor. It seems too much to hope that there is a hidden door somewhere, but I look for one just the same.

The walls are made of huge stone blocks. If they are as thick as they are wide and tall, then no dagger will pry them loose, and it is unlikely that any cry for help will filter through. But I do not give up until every block, every mortar-filled crease, has suffered the scrutiny of my probing fingers.

The wall is impenetrable, all the way around.

One section, though, feels a little cooler than the rest. And when I'm done inspecting the pit's entire girth, I return to it and lay my ear against it.

Definitely cold. And I hear something, even through the thick stone. A hum, as unceasing and relentless as rushing water.

Maybe it *is* water. The balcony where the altar stood looked out over a great cliff and the river below. I fell a very long way. I am probably halfway to the river. Maybe closer. And the cold part of the wall is undoubtedly the part that is exposed to wind and water, on the very outskirts of the city.

I begin to pace, worrying my thumbnail with my teeth. The first time I trained with Storm, I blew a small crater into the granite cliff. My firebolt was so powerful that the rock melted, like fired glass. I was exhausted afterward. Storm teased me for being so clumsy.

But could I blow a hole through this stone wall? Nothing for it except to try.

I back away from the cold section, as far as the pit will allow. The last time I did this, shards flew in every direction, drawing blood. A risk I'll have to take.

Once again, I draw on the *zafira*. It fills me slowly this time—I have not rested long enough—but it comes. I draw in as much as I can take, until my skin itches and my fingers shudder with the need to release it.

No careful control, this time. No strategic rationing of power. I grasp hold of every vestige of energy within me and fling it forward in a bolt of ice-blue fire. It crashes into the wall, sprays sparks and slivers of stone in all directions. Pain slices into my left cheek, and warm liquid slips down to my jaw.

The place where my firebolt impacted the wall shimmers slightly, as if molten, but not enough to illuminate the wall. I step forward to get a closer look, but my legs quiver with sudden exhaustion, so I work my way around the pit instead, using the curved wall for support. My breath comes too fast; my heart kicks in my chest.

The wall beneath my fingers warms as I approach, but the area already darkens, the embers winking out, and I can no longer see. I call on the *zafira* to light my fingertips, but nothing comes. I am an empty vessel.

I lean against the wall, panting. *Please, God. I just need to see. Then I can rest.*

Power trickles into me, just enough to light one finger flame. I hold it up to the wall.

Where the stone block used to be, there is now a glassy indention. Only two knuckles deep, but at least it's something.

I'll need every bit of strength I have for the next one, as much power as I can muster. A small water skin is attached to my belt. Next to it is a pouch with a bit of meal made of jerky, cheese, and grain. I can last a few days if I have to.

Finally I allow myself to slide to the ground and close my eyes. Sleep takes me instantly.

My stomach aches with hunger and thirst when I wake. I

take a pinch of meal from my belt and wash it down with a single swig of lukewarm water. It is not nearly enough, and my stomach rumbles angrily.

I don't even know how long I've been asleep. Minutes? Hours? When I first awakened in this pit, my body broken and bloodied, the air was winter chilled. It is much warmer now, and moist, as if filled with my own hot breath.

My bones ache as I clamber to my feet; however long I slept, it was not long enough. My eyes are bleary, my breath ragged, as I back up against the wall, draw in the *zafira*, loose a blinding bolt of blue fire against the stone.

It's weaker this time, the light winks out faster, and I crumple onto the ground with despair. I squeeze my eyes tight. *Think, Elisa!*

I need more power. Maybe I could figure out how to call upon Lucero. Maybe I could channel the power of nearby animagi.

Nearby animagi. Surely they can sense my efforts. Maybe I'll break free only to find them waiting for me.

The thought of escape suddenly feels so ludicrous I almost laugh at myself.

"Hector," I whisper aloud. "This time, I might need *you* to come save *me*."

I wake from another attempt because of the light streaming across my face. Hope surges. Maybe I broke through and didn't realize it!

But no, it's the trapdoor above. I blink against the onslaught of brightness, trying to make sense of it. Do I imagine the shape of a head, framed by the light?

"Will you consent to be our willing sacrifice?" booms a male voice. "Will you make Umbra de Deus your home and never leave, knowing that your noble sacrifice brings prosperity and happiness to the great nation of Invierne?"

"No! Of course not. I'm—"

The trapdoor slams closed, shrouding me again in darkness.

I stare at it, willing whoever it was to return. Maybe I could bargain my way out. Maybe I could lie, say I was willing . . .

I sigh. Maybe I need to blow a hole in the wall and get myself out of here.

The *zafira* comes unwillingly this time. It's like wrestling with sludge to get it to fill up my limbs enough to fling another firebolt.

It's even weaker than the last. My head swims and my bones ache with exhaustion.

An awful possibility looms: What if I'm playing into their hands? Maybe they don't starve bearers to the point of death in this pit. Maybe the bearers bring on their own demise with repeated attempts at escape.

This time, I allow myself a little more food and water. And next time I wake, I'll pray for a while. Eat and drink more. Renew my strength. Because a volley of puny firebolts will not get me out of this pit. But a few monstrous ones might.

Next time I will produce white fire, something that will continue to burn even after I've passed out.

⁙ ⁙ ⁙

My final white fireball explodes through the stone wall.

Icy wind whips my face, bringing the faint scents of sulfur and pine. Even though my legs tremble with fatigue, I rush toward the opening, gulping at the fresh air, afraid to hope.

The top of the opening, where my bolt landed a direct hit, glows like molten glass. Wary of touching it, I peer into the cold night. Umbra de Deus is as brightly lit as any large city. Its radiance filters down the stone ramparts and glistens against the rushing water below.

Only two body lengths separate me from the river, and my hole is right above the temple's foundations, which are ancient, cracked, and crooked—and therefore climbable. But the rapids and the mist rising from the water's surface will make for slippery handholds.

Should I dare the whitewater? I've always been a decent swimmer. But I could just as easily be pounded to death as drown in the current. And if I survived, there's no telling where the river would take me.

I crane my neck to view the wall above me. Except for a lump of moss here and there, the way is too smooth to have any decent handholds. And near the top, the balcony hangs over the edge. I would have to climb underneath it, hanging like a spider.

The only possible route lies sideways along the foundation. Small, dark openings are set at regular intervals. Trash chutes? Gutters? Maybe I could climb up one of them.

I groan. It seems I am destined to spend a lot of time in sewers.

There's no knowing when the Inviernos will return for me. Surely they have sensed my use of magic. I should go now. But after the last firebolt, I'm too weak. I would fall to my death.

I will rest just long enough to get some strength back. I close my eyes and pray. *Please, God, I just need a little blessing from you. Send me strength. Or if you'd rather not, could you please hold my captors at bay while I rest?*

I keep my eyes closed, waiting, hoping. But of course nothing happens. It's not that I expected strength and energy to suddenly fill my limbs, but it would have been nice.

I scoot back into the pit and lean against the wall, wondering whether or not God will do as I ask. If he does, I'll never know whether it's him or dumb luck. Which makes me wonder, somewhat guiltily, why God never answers the obvious prayers, prayers that I can *see* being answered.

Having my body suddenly awash in strength—now that would be something.

I don't realize I've drifted off to sleep until something crashes to the ground beside me. Black shapes roughly the size of my foot pour from a shattered wooden crate. I see eyes, hundreds of them, as round and shiny as marbles, as oily black as a Deciregus's. Tiny claws skitter across the bedrock as they swarm toward me.

Rats.

I scurry backward toward the hole, pulling food from my pouch as I go, scattering it before me. The rats pile on top of one another to get at it, and I almost sob with relief. I've bought myself precious seconds.

Wind whips at my loosening hair as I swing out over the hole. I grasp the bottom edges and let myself hang, seeking toeholds. I can do this. I've climbed before.

But how long until the rats pour out of the hole looking for more food? Whoever threw the crate into my pit had to have noticed how bright it had become, maybe even saw the hole itself. I'll be lucky if I am only pursued by rats.

I creep to the side, limbs splayed like a spider's. The wall is not quite sheer, and as my grasping fingers slip and my arm swings wildly into the air, I realize the slight slope is the only thing keeping me from falling to my death.

My shoulders burn. My knuckles are already scraped, and each time the breeze picks up, I feel like a tiny grass blade, barely rooted, swaying in the wind. The dark sewer entrance is so far off.

Despair almost takes me. I can't go back. But I'm too weak to dare a plunge into the rushing river.

Something skitters above me, and I look up to find noses twitching in the morning sunshine. One bold rat takes a step over the edge. He slips, and his high squeal echoes like a raptor's as his round black body bounces along the wall. The churning river does not even acknowledge his entrance with a splash.

To my left is a stone block that juts out from the others. It might jut out far enough that I can straddle it. I climb toward it, one careful handhold at a time. If I do it in strategic increments, pausing to rest when I can, maybe I'll have a chance.

Sounds carry out through the hole. Footsteps. Yelling. A ringing sword.

I've been discovered. Tears fill my eyes, because I don't know what to do. I can't climb any faster. Maybe I should let them take me, look for another opportunity to escape.

But there won't be another opportunity. Next time they take me, it will be for keeps.

The river. Rapids aside, I won't last long in alpine snowmelt water. And I have no idea where it leads. But it's my only option.

Hard to believe that after everything, after so much worry and dread about my destiny, that my death will be so simple. So without fanfare.

I take a deep breath, steeling myself to let go.

"Elisa?"

I'm so startled by Hector's voice that my feet slip and I swing from my arms, banging into the side of the wall. My shoulders burn like they're pulling out of their sockets, and skin sloughs from my fingers as my hands slip from their holds.

22

"HOLD on! I'm coming," Hector calls.

My right foot finds a toehold. It's not much, but it takes some pressure off my burning shoulders. I just need to be still, to hold on.

Hurry, Hector.

Pebbles clatter around me as Hector descends. I look up to see if he's close and get an eyeful of grit. I blink hard as tears stream down my face.

He exclaims in surprise, and several furry black bodies tumble past me. My fingers are going numb. I might be slipping again, but I'm not sure.

"Hector?" My voice shakes.

"Almost there!"

Suddenly my left hand is grasping at air, and my weight is too much. I'm sliding, sliding down the wall. . . .

Hector swings into place behind me; his arm wraps my waist. "Got you," he whispers in my ear. He's hanging by one hand, holding us both. How is such a thing even possible?

His feet find purchase, and he is rock steady at my back. The relief breaks something inside me. "I'm sorry!" I blurt. "I couldn't stay. I was too weak to fight them off if they came back." I can't seem to stanch the flow of words. "I tried to get to the sewer, but blowing a hole through the wall made me even weaker, and I have no food left, and the rats came, and—"

"Stop." His arm around me tightens. That's when I realize that his arms tremble slightly, that his breath comes too fast. He is as exhausted as I am.

He begins to push us both upward. Between breaths, he says, "You know, it's all right for *me* to rescue *you* every now and then."

"You haven't rescued me yet," I point out.

He grunts, trying to pull us over a lip of stone. His forearms are corded with effort. "Elisa, if you could help, even a little . . ."

I reach up with bloody fingers and find a handhold, then another. Slowly, together, we crawl back up the wall and pull ourselves into the hole I made.

My knees are buckling, but he pulls me to my feet and wraps me in a hug. I hug back, my face smashed against his chest. "Thank you," I murmur.

He pulls away and grabs at a rope dangling from the trap-door's opening. Worried, familiar, dear faces peer down at us.

"I'll make a loop for you to stand in," Hector says. "The others will pull you up. We have to hurry."

He loops the rope and ties an elaborate sailor's knot, then helps me step into it. He fails to hide his grin as he lifts me by the waist and says, "Hold tight. Stand straight and stiff. You'll be easier to pull up."

"You're very pleased with yourself, aren't you?"

"Oh, yes."

Now that I've stepped into his loop, we are eye level. He cups the back of my neck and plants a quick kiss on my lips. "See you at the top." Then he looks up and calls, "Now!"

The rope jerks, and I swing wildly, but I make myself as stiff as a plank of wood.

As I near the top, hands reach for me, and I'm pulled over the edge. I roll onto my back, gasping with relief.

"Are you hurt?" says Mara. She seizes my hands, turns them over to reveal the scraped mess and says, "We'll need to clean and bandage your fingers." She grabs my chin and turns my face to the side, then the other.

"Mara, stop. I'm fine." I sit up and climb slowly to my feet. Then I fling my arms around my lady-in-waiting and hug her tight. Smaller arms wrap us both, and I reach down to tousle Mula's hair.

I extricate myself from them and look around at my companions. Everyone is breathless and wide-eyed from the effort of pulling me out of the pit. Off to the side lies an Invierno acolyte, blood staining his robes. The bringer of the rats, I presume. "Thank you," I say.

"Lucero told us how to open the trapdoor," Storm points out.

I look to the altar and find Lucero's lashless eyes fixed on me. He is smiling. "You promised," he whispers.

My heart thuds into my belly. "I did," I whisper back.

"We must go," Belén says, as Hector pulls himself over the edge and gains his feet. "Our escape has certainly been noticed."

Hector says, "Be alert."

I grab his hand. "Wait. I promised Lucero I would . . . kill him. If he healed me."

No one speaks for a moment. Then Storm says, "You *did* come to destroy the power source."

I stare at Lucero. "I didn't know it was going to be a person."

"I can do it for you," Hector says.

"Or me," Belén says.

"I can put an arrow in his heart," Mara says. "It would be very fast. Almost painless."

"I hate blood," Storm says. "It stains." But he pulls his dagger.

It's tempting to let one of them take this burden from me, but it wouldn't feel right. "Thank you. But I will do it."

I'm sorry, God. I know the murder of innocents is against your will, but so is breaking an oath. And surely this living death is worse in your eyes?

I call on the *zafira*. It comes slowly, for I am both exhausted and reluctant.

Lucero never fulfilled his destiny as God's chosen. The *Blasphemy* was not intended to be his final act of service, for his stone still lives inside him. And now I will take the possibility away from him forever.

I'm startled to hear his quiet voice in my head: *But maybe you will fulfill yours. And I will have helped.*

"Please," he whispers aloud.

He showed me the way, when my body was broken and he healed me. I know exactly what to do. I reach inside his still form to stop his heart.

But something changes. A subtle shift. With growing horror, I realize the power of the *zafira* is no longer being channeled by me. It's being channeled *through* me. "Lucero, what are you doing?"

The power becomes a torrent. My belly turns to fire.

They must die. All of them.

Our essences collide, Lucero's and mine. He weaves them together until they are a single entity, a power so massive that we could crack open the world. Which is exactly what he plans to do. Now that we are one, I see his vision: the Eyes of God, exploding in fiery fury, burying Umbra de Deus in lava and ash.

"No!" I shriek.

I fight, but it's no use. Lucero forces the scalding power through my veins, and I am helpless against it, laid bare and burning. I open my mouth to sob from pain and rage, but even that release is denied me. This is what it means to be an unwilling sacrifice.

Lucero drags me into the depths of the earth, where lava pulses like lifeblood. He reaches as if with giant, invisible fingers into cracks and fissures, prying them open, relentless. The world groans.

Please, Lucero. Don't do this.

They deserve it!

The ground heaves, and I drop to my knees.

"Elisa, what's happening?" Mara's voice, as if from far away. I see her in blurred relief against the distant mountain. Her bow is drawn.

"He's done something to her!" Hector yells. "Shoot him."

A massive boom rocks the balcony, and I snap back to myself, gasping with relief. For a moment I imagine I am light as air and soaring, for I am free, and my power is my own.

I glance around, not quite taking everything in because all I can think is: *How did I not understand, all these years, how precious and glorious it is to belong to myself?*

Then I notice the arrow protruding from Lucero's chest. Blood snakes from the corner of his mouth. His chest rises and falls with short, shallow breaths.

Beyond him are the twin mountains. One has exploded, its top blown clean off. A pillar of bilious gray the diameter of a city rises into the sky. The glowing fingers of lava clutching the mountainside have thickened. Steam sizzles from the river below, and I choke on air tinged with ash and a scent like that of rotten eggs.

Even so, it seems as though wind has carried most of the blast away, and I dare to hope that we might be safe. But the ground beneath my feet quakes again, and I realize the other mountain, the nearer one, is about to follow its brother.

Hector swears. Belén mutters a prayer.

"There is no escaping that," Storm says softly, gazing at the mountain about to devour us all. Mula steps up beside him, and he drapes an arm across her slight shoulders. "I guess it ends here, after all," he says.

No. I plunge my awareness back into the guts of the earth, and I drag the remaining spark of Lucero's life with me.

This time, I'm the one in control. I brutally yank the *zafira* through both my stone and his, weaving our power together, until it feels just as thick and unremitting as the pillar of ash spewing into the sky. Such power, with two living conduits working in tandem. Too much. I could do anything with it.

I feel twisted and dark and *wrong* as I shove it down, down, down the gullet of the mountain, bringing rock and debris with it, choking it dead.

The earth stills to a gentle rumble. I wipe ash from my eyes even as I release Lucero back to himself.

The farthest mountain still sends clouds billowing into the sky. It is bald of forest and snow. The horizon beyond darkens with ash. Night will come early today.

But the nearest mountain has caved in on itself and is now half its former height. Boulders tumble down the side as it continues to settle.

The creature on the altar moans.

"Lucero?" The fletching of the arrow in his chest flutters in the breeze. Blood seeps from the wound. I wait for a reaction, some indication that his life leaves him. But the line between death and living death is too fine. One moment, he is staring up into the sky, and the next he is still staring, but with a little less light in his eyes. Or maybe I imagine it.

The difference is in me. For the first time since arriving in Umbra de Deus, my Godstone quiets. It flashes neither hot nor cold but resumes its usual mild pulsing. In spite of everything, I am calmer than I've been in days. I place my fingertips to my navel and send up a quick prayer of guilty thanks.

"What just happened?" Mara demands.

"He tricked me," I say. "Drew me in so he could channel my power and destroy the whole city."

Storm's face has a sickly pallor. He can't look away from Lucero's limp body. "How long has he been plotting his revenge?"

"Probably a century."

We stare aghast as Lucero's corpse shrivels and grays, then deflates into dust before our eyes. The wind whisks away the top layer, revealing a sparkling Godstone winking at us from the ashy pile.

Storm and I exchange a look. We saw the same thing happen on Isla Oscura to the strange sorcerer there. Storm looks down at his feet, and I wonder if he's thinking of the manacles around his ankles, hidden by his boots, formed when the *zafira* tried to claim him as its gatekeeper when the first one turned to dust.

At the sound of footsteps we whirl, drawing weapons as Invierno guards pour onto the balcony.

Mula stands closest to the altar. I whisper to her. "Grab that stone!"

Her tiny arm darts out, plucks Lucero's Godstone from his dusty remains, and shoves it in a pocket just as Hawk and Pine follow the guards onto the balcony.

"I can't outrun them right now," I mutter to Hector.

"Then we fight. We can handle three-to-one odds. Just stay clear of that pit."

They won't capture me again, for fear that even a Deciregis is no match for a living bearer. The hidden pit was what gave them the advantage.

Pine looks at the dead boy on the altar, then focuses his oily black gaze on me. Fury flows from him in waves. "You have killed us all," he says. "Without a source of power—"

"I have *saved* you all, you colossal idiot." I regret the words as soon as they're out of my mouth. Not the best way to bargain for peace.

"What are you talking about?" Pine demands, but the earth still rumbles, and even before he finishes the sentence his gaze drifts up toward the smoking mountains. "Oh," he breathes. "I felt the earth move, felt an explosion of power, but I thought it was the *zafira* being ripped away from us."

"Your unwilling sacrifice triggered the volcanoes," Storm says. "Her Majesty stopped the eruption."

Pine whirls on his son. "You! You are ash in my mouth. A dung heap that steams in winter winds. The oily scum that covers—"

"Enough!" I yell as the earth continues to rumble and ash drifts down around us like sickly snow. "He is a prince of the realm," I remind him. And then, coldly, "If you want to know the location of the gate that leads to life, you will reinstate him as your heir." My limbs buzz with excitement, with power, and it has nothing to do with magic. This could work after all—if they would just see beyond their rage to what I'm offering.

"He lied to us," Hawk says. "He said his first loyalty was to Crooked Sequoia House."

Storm lied for me? I'm careful to keep the smile from my face. "I'm sure Storm is doing what he thinks is best for the house."

"For all of Invierne," Storm says. "Take us before the Deciregi. Her Majesty will repeat her offer to everyone. Even though the sacrifice is dead, our nation need not perish."

Pine seems to coil in on himself, while Hawk gazes sadly toward the broken, ash-choked mountains. After a long moment of silence, Pine says, "I'm afraid that's impossible."

I take him to mean an agreement between us is impossible, but then he adds, "They're gone. Every single one." He looks down at Hawk, and his metal-gloved hand reaches up to stroke her hair. It's the tiniest gesture, but I twinge with discomfort, as if I'm witness to a very private moment. Pine whispers, "We are the only two left."

"What are you talking about?" Storm demands. "Where did they go?"

Pine looks at me, dead-on. "We were betrayed. Months ago, we agreed as a council to lure you here. To capture you and make you our living sacrifice. But the others conspired in secret. *Their* plan was to lure you here as a distraction."

"Oh, no." My stomach churns, and my heart begins to beat erratically.

"Yes. The other eight Deciregi remain bent on avenging our people. The moment we reported that we had captured you, they left for Basajuan. They took their sworn animagi with them, even their acolytes. They will conquer Basajuan easily without you there to interfere. I wouldn't be surprised if they razed it to the ground."

Mara gasp echoes my own horror. *Cosmé. Jacián. All our friends.*

My sister might be there by now too. Alodia will have brought a diplomatic escort, not a military one. Cosmé has been building her garrison since becoming queen, but it is not yet at full strength. Even if it was, no army could hold back all the animagi of Umbra de Deus, led by the most powerful sorcerers in the world. And once Basajuan falls, Orovalle and Joya d'Arena will quickly follow.

A hand settles on my shoulder, and Hector says, "Elisa, we must go *now.*"

I nod, but to Pine I say, "Will you let us leave? On the understanding that I will do what I can to save your people and bring you to the *zafira?*"

He winces. "Yes."

"Your Eminence, do know that if I make it back to Basajuan in time to save it, I may destroy the Deciregi. You two might be the only ones left. And if that happens—"

Pine and Hawk are already nodding. "Yes, yes," Pine says. "We will discuss terms. You leave us no choice."

"I plan to offer full access and safe passage through my country in exchange for a cessation of hostilities, utter compliance with the laws of my land while in it, reinstitution of Storm as your heir, and . . ." The idea hits, and I almost gasp at its pure simplicity. "And a marriage union between a prince or princess of Invierne and the match of my choosing."

A slow smile breaks over Pine's face, revealing pointed teeth and deep self-satisfaction. "I'm sure my son will be delighted to do his duty and marry whomever you choose."

My return smile is just as smug. He thinks he has trapped me by offering up someone he views as expendable, but he has played right into my hands. "I accept! I promise to make a good marriage for him."

Storm is staring at me, his green eyes wide with horror.

"Will you guarantee us safe passage out of Umbra de Deus?" Hector asks.

Hawk shrugs with seeming nonchalance and says, "We probably could not stop you. We are no match for one whom even the Eyes of God obey. And without our living sacrifice, our own power is a shadow of what it was."

I study her, trying to parse what she's not saying. "I'll repeat the Lord-Commander's question. Will you guarantee us safe passage out of Umbra de Deus? A yes or no will suffice."

Pine frowns. "Yes."

"And will you promise not to pursue us as we travel to Basajuan?"

"I promise."

"You promise what?"

"I promise that I will not pursue you as you travel to Basajuan."

"Will you pursue any of my companions or anything that we carry?"

"No."

"Will you send someone else to pursue us on your behalf?

Or will you inform someone so that they can pursue on their own behalf?"

"No."

"And will you stop anyone who tries to pursue us?"

"N—Yes. Yes, I will."

As we grab torches and enter the tunnel leading to Crooked Sequoia House, Storm sidles up to me and says, "You have learned to bargain like an Invierno."

"Storm, about that marriage agreement—"

"I am your loyal subject."

23

WE leave the city escorted by Pine's own guards. We are not disguised this time, and everyone stares as we pass on the road. They give us a wide berth and whisper to one another as our carriage rattles along, not just because we are foreign, but because of the dangerous speed at which we travel their winding, narrow highway. Or maybe because of the ash still floating down from the sky. It mixes with light rain and turns to thick sludge, collecting on every street and rooftop.

Storm's sister, Waterfall, accompanies us. At the last moment, the Deciregus decided he wanted an additional representative in our party—on "the unlikely possibility" that we are successful in saving Basajuan and will indeed be able to parlay.

He wants a spy, and I'm perfectly happy to comply. Waterfall will know exactly what I want her to know.

Pine provided us with fresh packs and supplies, and Hawk gave us warm, supple cloaks against the biting winter air. Near the edge of the city, we bought fur-lined gloves, a new pair of boots for Mula, and head scarves made of wolverine hair, which the vendor assured us would shed frost in any temperature. It's surprisingly familiar; preparing for extreme cold is not so different from preparing for desert windstorms.

The other Deciregi have more than a day's start, but Hector agrees that it is not an insurmountable lead. We might encounter them on the way. We might even arrive in Basajuan ahead of them. We will plan for both possibilities.

The ashy rain becomes snow as we turn off the highway and onto the mountain trail. The clouds are so low and dirty that they threaten to choke the tops of the pines. The icy air feels like tiny knife blades as I draw it into my lungs.

The thickening blanket of ash and snow makes the world unrecognizable, but Waterfall is able to guide us to the exact spot where she first encountered us. We climb the slippery slope and find the glade where we left our mounts. Two dark horses peppered with white shy away as we approach.

"It's me, Horse," I say in a soothing tone. "I told you I'd be back."

At the sound of my voice, Horse whinnies and tosses her head. She trots forward eagerly, shoves her nose into my chest, and roots around for a treat. I laugh, running my fingers through her long forelock, surprised at how relieved I am to find her unharmed.

We saddle our horses and prepare to mount up. I haven't needed help mounting Horse in a long time, but Hector insists on lifting me into the saddle, and I decide it's all right to let him. Once I'm settled, his hand slides from my waist to linger on my thigh. I reach down to give it a squeeze.

With his free hand, he rubs at a nonexistent spot on my saddle and says in a muted voice, "I'm sorry I deliberated, even for a moment, about whether I should marry you. When you dropped into that pit, I . . ."

"Well, we'll have no more of such foolishness," I say harshly, to cover the wavering in my voice. "We're getting married, and that's that."

He flashes me a quick grin, squeezes my knee, and steps away to mount his own horse. I stare after him, at his broad shoulders and the curling hair that has grown long enough to peek around his winter cowl. If I could skip the upcoming journey, the inevitable battle, even the wedding, just to get to the marriage part, I would do it. I never want to say good-bye to him again.

We ride against the wind, seven of us now, heads bowed over the necks of our sturdy mountain horses. Soon the snow is deep enough to cover our horses' fetlocks. The ash clouds cause night to fall early, and we are forced to stop too soon.

We make camp at the base of a cliff, so that the wall traps the warmth of our campfire and reflects it back. It is nearly impossible to hammer our tent pegs into the frozen ground, but we do it. Fortunately, the tents are steeply pitched, and snow only collects a little before sliding off and tumbling to the ground in great puffs.

Mara makes a bland but hot soup of softened jerky, dried onions, and pine bark, but I haven't slept or even rested since escaping the pit, and I have no appetite. I eat less than half the bowl before giving the rest to Mula, who slurps it down eagerly.

I drag myself into my tent and slip into my bedroll. It's freezing, and my teeth chatter. I know my bedroll will eventually warm to my body, but I don't feel like waiting.

Thank you, God, for sparing the lives of all my companions while we were at the enemy's door. I hope it's not asking too much, but if you could just help us get to Basajuan before the Deciregi do, I would appreciate it.

The truth is, I'm not sure if God looked out for us, or if we won the day ourselves. I'm not sure of anything about him anymore. The stone inside me bears his name, but it turns out that Godstones existed here long before my people brought the knowledge of God to this place.

Even so, my Godstone spreads warmth throughout my body, and I fall asleep praying.

Mara shakes me awake in the morning. I blink bleariness from my eyes and struggle to my feet. I stretch stiff limbs and shake the snow from my braid, which never quite made it inside the tent with the rest of me.

Everyone else is ready to go; the horses are saddled, the tents are packed up, the fire stomped out. "We let you sleep as long as possible," Mara says, handing me a fried corn cake that has gone so cold the honey she dribbled on it has crystallized.

"Thank you," I say around my mouthful of breakfast, but unease fills me. I don't want to be the one holding us back. "Don't let me sleep late tomorrow."

She rolls her eyes at me, then she and Hector pack my tent while I finish eating.

More snow fell during the night. Away from our trampled-down campsite, it is almost knee-deep. Pine boughs sag under its weight. The trees nearest our campfire drip icicles.

"We need to hurry," Belén says. "Another snowfall like that and we'll lose the trail."

"The ash has made everything worse," Waterfall says. "The last time the volcano erupted—in my grandfather's time—the world experienced the worst winter in known history."

"I traveled this path several times during the years when I was an ambassador," Storm says. "Volcano aside, more snow will make traveling impossible higher up unless we cross the divide soon."

"At least the Deciregi will face the same delays we do," I say.

Hector guides his horse beside mine and says, "I've been thinking about that."

"Oh?"

"They can't have missed the eruption. And Pine sensed when the sacrifice was killed. He felt a lessening of power."

"Oh." I frown as understanding dawns.

Hector nods. "They know you're coming for them. Either they will travel as quickly as possible, or—"

"Or they will wait to ambush me." I sigh. Will there ever be a time in my life when someone isn't seeking to murder me? Will I ever feel safe again? "I'll send Belén on scouting forays. Which means you must ride point so he can stay as rested as possible."

"I can scout," comes a high, little-girl voice.

I twist in my saddle to find Mula staring at me eagerly. She rides a horse of her own finally—a dapple gray gelding with a fuzzy winter coat.

"Belén is teaching me. I'm very quiet. Orlín said I had the softest feet he ever knew. That's why I was the one who snuck into the rooms and . . . But I don't do *that* anymore!"

Hector and I exchange an amused glance.

"If Belén says you can go with him, I won't stop you," I say. "But only if he says. And you're not going alone."

She grins triumphantly. "Yes, my lady."

At some point we'll have to tutor her in proper address. Not to mention the fine art of eating with utensils instead of one's hands, or the fact that a little girl ought not expose herself by raising the hem of her shirt to wipe her nose. And one of us should teach her to read and write. If we ever get back home safely, I'll find a good tutor or buy her an apprenticeship.

I'm not sure when I decided that she would come home with us, but now I wouldn't consider any other alternative. Mara would be furious if we left her in anyone else's care. Maybe even Belén.

I let thoughts of the girl continue to occupy me all day as we wind up the snowy mountain. It's better than dreading an ambush.

We make camp in a clearing. Mara gets a fire started, and Hector and I set up tents while the horses paw through the snow to reach the frozen grass beneath. After a cold meal of what Mula calls "tasty balls"—nuts, ground meat, and cake crumbs rolled together with olive oil and sheep fat, I send Belén to scout. He does not agree to take Mula with him, so I allow her to stand the first watch with me.

As everyone else turns in, she retrieves Lucero's Godstone from her pocket and hands it to me. "I kept it safe for you," she says solemnly.

I pluck it from her fingers and shove it in my own pocket, thinking to stow it in the box beside my Godstone crown when I get a chance. "Thank you, Mula."

Moments later, it begins to snow again.

Belén returns in the morning. "No sign of an ambush ahead," he says, shaking snow from his cloak. "But last night's storm makes tracking difficult. I did find a few footprints from a large party traveling ahead of us, but they were old and already mostly snowed in. If we move fast, I might be able to catch them in a day or two on a scouting foray. We'd have to get really close, though. I just can't cover as much ground in the snow."

I shake my head. "I need you sharp, Belén. I won't make the same mistake I made before and exhaust you."

"I can sleep in the saddle with Hector at point."

Hector sits on a nearby boulder, scraping one of his daggers with a whetstone. "And Mara will take up the rear—she's handy with her bow. Storm has the next best distance advantage, with that Godstone of his. I want him beside Elisa. And I want Waterfall where someone can see her at all times."

"You can trust her," Storm says from the side of his mount. He buckles a saddlebag and gives the cinch a final tug.

"You really can," Waterfall echoes in her soft, syrupy voice.

"I have no use for any of you Joyans, and I would just as soon murder you all in your sleep, but my brother is now heir to Crooked Sequoia House and I am bound by oath to obey him."

Storm leans toward her and says in a teaching voice, "Joyans consider it is rude to express one's true opinion unless it is unequivocally flattering."

Her brow furrows. "Then how do they express anything at all?"

I roll my eyes at both of them and walk over to mount Horse. She cranes her neck to give me a side-eyed gaze. I stroke her neck. "Good morning, stupid girl. Ready to ride?" I grab the reins and lead her toward the trail. A head toss sends her ridiculous mane flying, and she steps high through the snow.

We travel in silence. There is an odd, expectant hush over the world, as if the thick snow and rolling clouds demand quiet, and everything is helpless but to obey. Even the footsteps of our horses are muted. I marvel at how like a desert this place is, with nuances of light and color that gradually separate themselves from a seemingly uniform and barren landscape.

It is almost time for our afternoon meal and rest break when Storm clicks to his mount and pulls even with me and Horse. "I smell a storm," he says.

"Well, obviously," I say, reaching out with a gloved hand to catch snow in the palm of my hand.

"No, I mean it's going to get worse."

I wipe my hand on my pants. "Any more will block our trail."

He nods. "We are still at least a day away from the divide.

We should take shelter at the nearest way station."

"The Deciregi may have crossed out of the rain shadow already. If we stop, it could put them days ahead of us!"

Storm leans over, grabs Horse's reins from my pommel, and yanks us to a stop. I glare at him, but all my anger fades when he says, "If we don't stop, we'll die."

"That bad?" I say in a small voice.

"I know little about your desert. I could not survive on my own there. I have needed help and guidance to make my journeys as an ambassador. But I do know the mountains. Here, you need *my* help and guidance. And I say we stop."

I know what Hector would think; he'd worry that Storm is betraying us, that he stalls us on purpose.

As if my thoughts have summoned him, Hector calls a halt at the front of the line and turns his horse around. "Elisa!" he calls. "I feel a storm coming. A bad one."

When two people I trust say the same thing, I must consider it a majority opinion. "Storm, can you guide us to the next way station?"

"It's still a ways off. We must hurry."

"Take point, then."

He and Hector trade places, and we set off again. The trail is narrow enough that my leg occasionally brushes Hector's, but neither of us moves to a single-file position.

"Do you have any rope?" he says after a while.

"A little. We all do. Why?"

"The storm could make it too difficult to see one another. I don't want anyone getting lost."

"Just like a sandstorm."

"Just like a sandstorm. If it comes to that, we'll attach ourselves to a rope line."

Moments ago, I would never have imagined such a thing as the delicate fluff of snow whirling so thick and hard that it could separate us. But the wind is picking up, turning the falling snow to needles on my face, and I blink rapidly, as if focusing my eyes harder will suddenly make my way clear.

Lightning splits the sky right above us. Thunder booms immediately after, followed by a great crack that echoes like a drumbeat. To our right, a massive sequoia topples over. It crashes through the trees around it, shedding snow and trailing sparks, barely missing our path. The sharp tang of burned resin fills the air.

The horses mill frantically, and it's a moment before we have them under control again.

"A thunder snow," Storm calls out. "Quickly!" He kicks his horse into as fast a gallop as the snow will allow. We follow after, and even Horse picks up her pace with little urging.

"Turnoff ahead!" Storm shouts through the rising wind. "So stay close."

Hector kicks his horse and pulls even with Storm. They speak for a moment, then Hector pulls a coil of rope from his saddlebag. Starting with Storm and working backward, he loops the rope through everyone's left stirrup, leaving enough space between horses to maneuver, but not much more. When he gets to Waterfall, he ties off and starts over with a new section of rope.

Once we are lined up, we fork off from the trail onto a path that is completely invisible to me. Our way is narrow and rocky. It's also steeper, with dangerous switchbacks, and I lean over Horse's back to keep my seat as she climbs. It would be easy to lose footing in this snow and slip over the edge.

Lightning flashes again, and the sky is so bright for a moment that a picture of the world around us—the tight slope hugged by snow-laden pines, backlit by a greenish sky—is seared into my mind. Thunder booms, and Horse rears up a little, but I pat her neck and she settles.

Ahead, Belén leans precariously in his saddle, and at first I think he's falling, but then he reaches down and scoops up a large fallen branch. He regains his seat nimbly, then cracks the smaller, forking branches off it as we travel, tossing them into the snow. He's left with a thick pole that's almost as tall as he is. I watch in awe as he balances the heavy pole along his left thigh and rides with it.

The wind whips through the trees, across the ground, sending flurries everywhere. Belén and his horse become a blurry outline of darkness, choked out by relentless white. Someone up ahead yells something, but I've no idea what.

And then a wind blows through, so monstrous that it nearly knocks me from my saddle. I grasp at the pommel, taking comfort in the fact that the others are near, for the rope connecting us remains taut. But I can neither see nor hear them. I am alone in a darkness of pure white.

Horse plows forward resolutely, head down against the wind. "That's a good girl," I mutter, even though I know she can't hear my voice. "The best girl."

My feet and hands are becoming numb, dangerously numb, and my teeth chatter. I pray warmth into my limbs. *Please, God, help us get through this. You've seen us through worse, so I know it's possible. I'm not sure how Storm will find the way station in this mess, but with you to guide him . . .*

Warmth races through my blood in response to my prayer. I've never known if the Godstone's warmth is a true warmth. I've considered that it's illusory only, a mental manifestation that comes from communion with God. I suppose that if I get to the way station and discover frostbite, I'll know. I just wish in the meantime that I could pray warmth into my companions as well.

I don't know how long we travel. I slump over the horse as the wind batters me. I am limp and useless, with a jaw that aches from clenching so hard and a forehead with perspiration gone icy.

"We're here, Elisa," someone says. "We made it." Hands pull me from the saddle, and I don't protest. "Can you stand?"

I'm wobbly, but yes, I can. I look into Hector's worried face and nod. He wraps me in his arms, and we are both so bundled up it's like two pillows hugging. I squeeze back as best I can.

24

WE'VE reached a cave, its opening almost completely covered in deadfall and snowdrifts. Without a word, we attack the entrance, dragging dead branches out of the way and scooping at snow with gloved hands. It's a race against the weather, for every bit of snow we shovel away is half returned to us by relentless wind.

My fingers are numb and my back aches, but I don't stop until we've cleared enough of an opening for the horses to pass through. Hector draws his sword and disappears inside. He returns a moment later. "All clear!" he yells.

The cave's opening is low and crooked and dark, and Horse balks. I give her a kiss on the nose and say in soothing tones, "Are you the stupidest horse who ever lived? Yes, you are!" Her hears perk forward, her nostrils flare, and she follows me inside.

The entrance opens into a wide chamber barely large enough for all of us. In the center is an old fire pit, but with the snow so heavy, blocking any vents, we'll have to be careful. Indentions in the far wall are used for shelves. They hold a small iron pot, some broken cutlery, two chipped wooden cups, and a bundle of kindling.

We lead the horses toward the back, where the cavern curves around a lip of stone and opens into another small chamber. This one is just high enough for the horses to stand comfortably. A small pile of moldy hay lies against one wall. Between that and the little grain we have left, we might have enough to feed them for a day or two.

Mara sets herself the task of getting a fire going, and soon the cave is bathed in cheery warmth. The ceiling is too low, the cavern too crowded, and we might be running out of food. Still, we exchange smiles of shared relief as we unsling our packs and array our bedrolls around the fire pit.

Belén stations himself near the entrance, armed with the long branch he dragged along, and now I finally understand why. Already, a snowdrift re-forms. We'll be blocked in by nightfall.

"We must watch the entrance in shifts," he says. "Keep a hole open for smoke. Otherwise we'll suffocate."

We skipped lunch, so none of us has the patience for a hot meal. But Mara insists on putting something warm inside us before we go to sleep. So as we dine on dried figs, bread, and cheese, she sets water to boiling to make pine-needle tea.

I'm feeling satiated and warm when Hector stands and stretches. "I need to check the horses," he says. He turns to me. "Want to learn how to polish tack?"

It's suddenly hard to breathe, because I know exactly what he's thinking. "All right," I manage.

From the corner of my eye, I catch Mara smiling as I get to my feet and follow Hector to the back of the cave and around the small lip of stone.

His arm hooks my waist, and he pulls me into the dark.

I melt against him. His mouth crashes down on mine, and he kisses me desperately, furiously. I respond by pouring out weeks of frustration and worry into our embrace, running my hands up his arms, over his shoulders. My fingers tangle in his hair as I assure myself that he's here, that he's mine.

His hand slips under my shirt, splays against the skin of my back. I break off our kiss to trail my lips along his jaw toward his ear, where I whisper, "I'm still taking the lady's shroud."

His breath hitches, and he buries his face in my neck and rests there a moment. His heartbeat is as ragged as my own.

Finally he says, "Are you *sure*, Elisa?"

It's baffling and amazing to me how, after everything, he can remain the least bit uncertain of my feelings. "It's one of the few things I'm sure of."

He lifts his head and considers me thoughtfully. Then he tips up my chin with his thumb and kisses me again—a sweeter, gentler kiss that feels like sun breaking through the clouds.

The pit of my stomach buzzes as I press my forehead into his chest, saying, "I *told* you that you would kiss me again."

He laughs. "It's the 'and more' part I remember most vividly." He gently pushes me away, putting a safe cushion of distance between us. He grabs my hands and lifts them to his lips. "When we reach Basajuan, maybe I can get you to myself for a while."

The earth tilts a little.

"In the meantime," he adds, "I really should teach you how to care for tack. I find myself in need of a distraction."

I grin. "Good idea."

The storm rages all night and into the morning. After a breakfast of bean mash and hard biscuits dipped in tea, we gather at the fire to take stock of our situation.

"How much food do we have left?" Hector asks as he polishes one of his daggers. It seems he is always doing something toward the upkeep of his weapons. Maybe I should learn from his example.

"One bag of dried corn, two of grain—we should save that for the horses," says Mara. "Some dates. A round of cheese. Dried meat for one day. I can stretch the meat farther with a stew. I'm out of flour for thickening."

"You can use pine bark pulp instead of flour," Hector says.

"We could eat one of the horses," Belén points out.

My stomach turns at the thought, but I say, "We're nearly out of grain and can't feed them anyway."

"Anything we slaughter will keep for days in this temperature," Mara says.

"I've eaten horse before," Mula says. "Tastes like dog."

"Maybe there's some grass or underbrush buried in the snow outside," Hector says. "But no one ventures farther than that until it clears. And if you do go out, you must be tied to a rope. No exceptions."

We all nod agreement.

"Elisa?" Storm says. "What *if* the weather clears? What then?"

His sister is nodding as he speaks. "The pass is snowed in by now," she adds. "There is no way through."

I turn on her. "Then we'll blow our way through," I snap. "Storm and I. With our Godstones."

She opens her mouth to say something but changes her mind.

"I'm not sure that will work," Hector says.

"Why not?"

"Anything you melt will just refreeze in this temperature. Not even our mountain horses can handle an ice trail. Especially not at an incline."

The walls close in around me, and darkness boils in my center. I can't give up. I refuse to believe that after everything I've gone through, everything I've put my friends through, I'll be foiled by mere weather. Or maybe not "mere weather." The rare cold, the poor visibility, the thunder snow, it's all thanks to Lucero and his volcanoes. "There has to be a way. There *has* to."

"The Deciregi might be stuck too," Belén says. "Or better yet, maybe they're dead."

Storm stares at him. "Do you really mean that? Or are you speaking falsehood to comfort Elisa? I can never tell." To me he says, "The Deciregi were at least a day ahead of us. The storm came at us from behind, so I'm sure they crossed into Joya d'Arena before the heavy snow hit. They're probably headed north toward Basajuan even now."

Everyone ponders for a moment. One of the horses snorts, and the fire pops, sending an ember flitting to the ground near the toe of my boot, where it flares and dies.

"Maybe we'll get lucky," Mara says. "Maybe the storm will blow itself out soon and the weather will break warm."

"Maybe," Belén says, but his voice is tinged with doubt.

I pull my knees to my chest and rest my forehead on them. I mutter, "If the Deciregi reach Basajuan before we do, they'll raze it to the ground and use the area to mount another offensive, even more massive than the first, against Orovalle and Joya d'Arena. We will lose everything." And every*one*.

"We may have to look to our own survival," Hector says. I usually love this about him, that he can be practical and frank in the most dire circumstance. But right now I can't help my twinge of annoyance.

"I want ideas, Hector. Solutions."

"Your safety is my highest priority," he says, just as sternly. "And I won't let you starve in this cave or freeze to death on the trail. If the mountains remain impassable, we must consider retreating back to Umbra de Deus as soon as the weather clears."

I lift my head to glare at him. "What good does it do to protect a queen if there is nothing to be queen of?"

Firelight shadows the planes of his face and gives a shimmer of red to his black hair, making him look fiercer than ever. Softly, he says, "Do you really think I obsess over your safety just because you are my queen? Surely you know better by now."

Vaguely, I'm aware of everyone else shifting uncomfortably, of the storm sending a gust of wind inside that makes our fire dance crazily. But I can't tear my gaze from his face. I know what he's thinking. I could give it all up. I could wait out the winter and then retire to a hidden location, somewhere remote, and live out my days. All I have to do to survive is remove myself from danger. And Hector would be with me.

I've been prepared to give my life for my land and people. But only if it accomplishes something. I've never believed in senseless death. At what point does our situation become so perilous and impossible that continuing the fight is senseless?

God, what should I do?

"I have an idea," Waterfall says.

As one, we turn to stare at her.

"The mines," she says.

Storm frowns at his sister. "Are your orders to get us all killed? Even if it means sacrificing yourself?"

"No! Of course not. I don't deny that the mines are deadly. But they'd offer protection from weather and cold. We could travel halfway to Basajuan through the tunnels. The storm will have cleared by the time we come out."

"Storm," Hector says in a voice more like a growl. "Tell us about these mines. Tell us everything you know. Do not leave out a single detail."

Storm looks to me, and I raise an eyebrow at him. He's going to have to get used to taking orders from Hector.

He sighs. "You may have noticed," he says, "that places of power tend to be underground—or at least near a conduit to the inner earth, like the volcanoes. It's a long-held belief among Inviernos that the deeper one goes into the earth, the closer one gets to the *zafira*."

I nod. "Go on."

"Thousands of years ago, when your people fell from the sky and began remaking this world with their machine magic, my ancestors fled here, to the mountains. But we were cut off from our places of power. After a few generations, we were weakening. Dying out. One of our great leaders, Ugly Twisted Brambles Shelter Bountiful Springs, convinced the nation to dig. As far and deep as we could. He believed—we all did— that if we dug deep enough, we could reach the *zafira*. Create our own place of power."

"So you tunneled into the mountains," Hector says.

"Yes. For generations. It was a national obsession. We used natural caverns as starting places and dug and dug. Inevitably, tunnels collapsed. Many flooded. Some hit bedrock. When that happened, we simply branched out and tried somewhere else.

"But too many people died, some in the collapses, some by breathing poison gas, getting lost, falling to their deaths. Others were caught in the fire of animagi as they brought their Godstones to bear. The project lost support. It was too costly, too deadly. When we discovered that once every hundred years a Joyan was born who never shed his Godstone, who could be used as a conduit to the *zafira*, it ceased entirely.

"The tunnels remained open for another century; they became ordinary mines for a while. We found gold, silver, gem-stones. But the mountains were showing signs of being mined out when strange rumors began. Miners entered and were never heard from again. There were reports of odd noises, strange lights. And when a massive cave-in killed forty miners, the tunnels were closed for good."

The wind stills. The fire leaps high, its flames suddenly straight and strong. The shadows on the wall waver less because gusts no longer push through the entrance. I raise my head, thinking maybe the storm has stopped, but no. The snow has blocked us in.

Belén springs to his feet, grabs his pole, and pokes it through the top. Snow pours in on top of him, but he keeps working until wind whips over our heads again and the flames jerk and twist.

I turn back to Storm. "But the tunnels are still accessible?" I say. "We could travel through them?"

"No," he says, even as Waterfall says, "Yes."

They glare at each other.

"It's not safe," Storm says. "They are too old. Any wooden supports are rotted by now. Many of the tunnels are flooded. And there's something down there. One of the ancient creatures, if I were to guess, from before your people came to this world."

Waterfall is shaking her head. "I've been inside," she insists.

"When?" he says.

"While you were being tutored and pampered, the other Crooked Sequoia children were left to ourselves. We took turns daring one another to go inside. I was the boldest of all of us. I explored for hours. Once I spent a whole day wandering the mines. It's dangerous, yes. But the only things down there are animals. I've seen bats. A few rodents. Even signs of bear."

"Do you know the way?" I ask. "Can you get us to Basajuan?"

"I think so. Once I started going regularly, I learned everything I could about them. I found maps in the Crooked Sequoia archive."

Storm is regarding her thoughtfully. "I would have gone with you," he says softly. "I would have skipped my lessons to explore the mines with you."

A hint of a smile graces her face. "I'm sure you believe that," she says.

My heart twists a little with recognition. Waterfall is like me, the younger sister who yearned for the approval of her older sibling and never got it.

"Do you have these maps memorized?" I ask.

"Almost. The tunnels themselves are named and marked. Many of those markings remain. Some indicate distance and direction. Between the markings and my memory of the maps, I think I can get us through."

"How long will it take us?" Hector asks.

"Several days."

Hector turns to me. "We don't have enough food. No way to feed the horses."

I glance toward the back of the cave, where our mounts take advantage of the rest and warmth, blissfully dozing on their feet. "Then we start slaughtering them for food." My voice is as firm as my resolve.

"How far to the nearest entrance?" Belén asks.

"Half a day's journey. More in deep snow."

Everyone looks to me for a decision.

"What do you think, Storm?" I say. "Can your sister get us through?"

He shrugs. "My sister is a scout of some renown, and deservedly so. If she says she can do it, she can."

Waterfall blinks rapidly at the compliment, and a flush of pink colors her perfect skin.

I say, "Then we go as soon as the weather clears. In the meantime, we'll make our food stretch as far as possible. Hunting and foraging will be everyone's responsibility as we travel."

Everyone nods, but Mara frowns darkly beside me. I remember the night she accompanied us into the catacombs beneath my city. Her eyes were as large as dinner plates while we explored, and when she was given leave to go, she fled, practically sprinting back up the stairs. I reach out and squeeze her hand. She squeezes back.

"Anything I'm not considering?" I ask. "Anyone else have anything to say?"

Silence. Then, tentatively, Mula says, "I do."

We watch as she stands and approaches the fire. She clasps her hands behind her back, shifts from one foot to the other.

"What is it, Skinny Girl?" Belén asks.

She gives him a shy smile. "I have decided on a name."

I sit forward. "Oh?"

"My name," she says with a lift of her chin, "is Red Sparkle Stone."

No one makes a sound. There is only the popping of the fire, the rush of wind, the pawing of a horse.

Finally I manage, "Well. That is indeed a strong and . . . unique name."

Mula's—no, Red Sparkle Stone's—face lights up. "I knew you'd like it! Red is my favorite color. And sparkle stones are strong. The strongest thing there is. I was thinking you should call me Red, the same way Storm's whole name is too important to say all the time."

Oh, thank God. "Red it is, then," I say, and I look around at our companions, daring contradiction. Mara looks stunned. Storm and Waterfall are wholly indifferent. Hector and Belén are trying very hard not to laugh.

25

WE prepare as best we can while the storm rages outside. Mara ties a rope around her waist and heads out into the blizzard. When she returns, she brings a layer of snow and several large strips of pine bark. She shucks gloves and boots and holds her hands and feet near the fire. Her limbs turn bright red as they warm, and her face twists in agony.

Once she can flex fingers and toes without pain, she gets to work scraping thin sheets of inner bark onto a nearby rock to dry by the fire. Then she grinds it with her mortar and pestle and puts the resulting dirty-white pulp in her empty flour bag.

She sends Belén out for another batch, then Storm, and repeats the process all day until her bag is full.

We decide to leave the horses behind. We need the grain we'd feed them for ourselves, and Waterfall insists that they won't fit through some of the mine's narrower passages. Belén assures me that an experienced mountain horse is better suited to winter foraging than its human companions, that if we leave them in the cave's shelter, they'll step out when they're ready to find food, maybe even make their way to the nearest village.

Hector leads Mula's—no, Red's—sweet mare outside into the cold and slaughters her. I'm not sure how he can see to do the deed in the raging storm, but he insists the scent of blood will panic the others if he does it inside. I think he does it to spare me the sight.

He returns with strips of raw meat that he roasts over the fire. At first my stomach turns. But as the scent of sizzling meat fills the cavern, my mouth waters in spite of myself.

He collects fat from the dead horse and gives it to Mara, who boils it down and mixes it with some of the meat, a bit of grain, a few dollops of honey, and a small handful of pine bark pulp. She rolls the resulting doughy mass into balls and gives each of us a few for our food pouches.

I find myself drifting toward the back of the cave, where the other horses are blissfully chewing on our last supply of hay. Horse greets me with a head toss and snuffles around my blouse, looking for a treat. I wrap my arms around her and press my cheek into her warm neck. She lips at my hair.

In the afternoon, Storm suggests we make snowshoes. We've never heard of such a thing, and we ask him to demonstrate, but he scoffs, saying, "I was a prince of the realm. I bought snowshoes—I didn't *make* them."

He describes them as best he can. Belén says they don't sound any harder than making rabbit traps, and he experiments with some low-hanging pine branches that he finds nearby and chops off with an ax. The smaller branches are very flexible, and he's able to weave and twist them into something vaguely resembling Storm's description. He attaches them to his boots by wrapping them with twine, then heads out into the storm. Mara and I giggle at the way he walks—splayed and jerky—but when he returns to the cave, he smiles with triumph and gets to work making more.

I sit beside him to help. I'm clumsy, and the pine branches are stubborn, but it's better than pacing our tiny cavern, worrying about the Deciregi reaching Cosmé and my sister before I can, or the civil war brewing in my own country, or the fact that I've promised a little prince that I'll do everything I can to return to him.

After a while, Waterfall sits beside me. Without saying a word, she grabs a few pine branches and gets to work.

The storm weakens as night falls, and I breathe a prayer of thanks and relief. This time, when we array our bedrolls around the campfire, I flip mine out beside Hector's.

I glance around surreptitiously, feeling daring, my face warm. But no one seems to notice or care, except Hector, who tries and fails to hide a smile.

As we lie down to sleep, he pulls me against him so that I am cradled by his body. I don't know how I'll sleep with his arms wrapped around me, his body pressed against mine, his warm breath on my neck. But I do. And when I wake, the sun is shining.

We fill our packs with as much as we can possibly carry, leaving everything else behind for the next traveler who shelters here. We tie on our snowshoes and hobble out into the hazy sunshine.

The world is blinding, sparkling gray. Pine boughs are so laden with ashy snow that they droop almost parallel to their trunks, and the bottommost are buried in snow near the ground. The snowshoes keep us from sinking too far, but Storm observes that they are nowhere near as effective as good Invierne-made snowshoes. The top layer of snow has already melted and iced over, so we crack through the surface with each step and sink a little before taking the next.

Waterfall leads the way, and we have not gone far before my shins and calves burn with effort. We find the place where we left the path to go to the way station; it's now buried in snow and unidentifiable to me as a trail, but both Waterfall and Storm recognize some landmarks and point us in the right direction.

We double back the way we came as the sun climbs—it's blurry and leached of color, and it remains low on the horizon, even at midday. When we reach a giant sequoia, dead and hollowed out by lightning, we depart from the trail again and hug the base of a steep mountain slope. For once I'm glad for the snow, for the slope is so steep that the snow gives us purchase we wouldn't otherwise have.

Something rumbles in the distance, and Waterfall goes very still.

"What—?"

"Silence!" she snaps. Her bright green eyes turn inward as she listens. More rumbling echoes. Far away, then closer. She puts a finger to her lips and says softly, "We go quickly and quietly. Do not make a sound. The Eyes of God continue to shake the ground, and now there is too much snow. So much that even the mountains cannot contain it."

The rest of us exchange alarmed glances. We follow after single file, pushing through the snow as fast as our awkward gaits will allow.

We dip into a small, pine-choked ravine. The trees are smaller here, and so tightly packed that it's hard to squeeze through. My right snowshoe snags on a trunk, and it rips off. My heart sinks as the entire shoe unravels beside me in the snow.

Experimentally, I take a step without it, and my leg sinks well past my knee.

Strong hands grip my armpits and lift me up. "Hold on," Hector whispers in my ear. "I'll try to fix it." He props me against a tree and bends to retrieve the snowshoe.

Waterfall turns around to see what has caused our delay, and when she sees the broken shoe, fear sparks in her eyes. She gazes up the side of the mountain, her mouth pressed into a thin line.

Hector curves the outside branch of my snowshoe back into place, but his gloved hands struggle to tie it down. He yanks off his gloves with his teeth and tries again, looping twine to secure the branch to the haphazard weaving that makes up the bottom of the shoe.

"Try it," he whispers. I put my foot into place, and he wraps the remaining twine around my boot to hold it. "This won't last long. Go carefully."

We catch up to the others—slowly, so as not to knock my

shoe off again. Waterfall watches us approach with unveiled impatience. She keeps glancing upward, like she's a small rodent expecting a hungry raptor to swoop down at any moment.

The ravine breaks into a clearing. Everything is so choked with snow that it's hard to know for certain, but I suspect we have been traveling a frozen creek bed and now stand upon a small pond. "Just ahead," Waterfall says, pointing. "Into the trees and to the right is a—"

A great crack rends the air, followed by the smack of branches and a muffled crash. I nearly jump out of my skin, and then I realize it's probably just a tree, bent to breaking under the weight of snow.

But Waterfall says, "Run for your lives," and she takes off across the clearing in a wide, rounded gait that could never outrun anything.

We follow as fast as we can. A rumble sounds above our heads, and the earth trembles in response. Red freezes and stares up the mountainside, horrified. Belén sweeps her up and hobble-runs with the little girl tucked under one arm. The extra weight is almost too much, and the snow sucks at each of his steps, threatening to pull him down, down, down.

My breath comes in gasps and my lower legs burn as I tear after them. Hector is right beside me, and I know he could go faster if he wanted to. "Go," I say between breaths. "Don't wait . . ."

My voice is lost in a miasma of rushing and crunching.

Wind lifts the hair from my neck, and I look up expecting a flash flood, but it's a wall of white coming down on us. When it hits the trees, they bow before it a split second before being overwhelmed. Powder geysers into the sky.

I run blindly, legs pumping as fast as I can make them go. My snowshoes tangle, and I crash to the ground. I try to get up, but the snow sucks at my clothes. Bruising fingers clutch my arms and yank me to my feet. Together, Hector and I wade forward. We're not fast enough. I take a deep breath, preparing to be buried alive.

But I'm not. The crunch of snow at our backs is deafening at first but is followed by a silence as deep as death. We stare at each other in awe, both of us covered in powder and white as ghosts. Somehow, we've escaped the path of the avalanche.

Hector wipes snow from his eyes. I'm hip-deep in the stuff, for I've lost my snowshoes after all. I look down, and sure enough, Hector's legs are sunken too.

Our companions are just ahead, looking back at us wide-eyed and breathless.

Except Waterfall. "It's not far," she calls from the tree line calmly, as if we are out having a casual stroll. "I'll lead. Everyone walk in my tracks. It will pack the snow a little and make it easier for the queen and the commander to walk without snowshoes." To me she hollers, "Yell if you get stuck."

Something about her nonchalance gives me strength, and I press forward, refusing to think about how close we just came to death.

We weave through a stand of young pines, over a lip of what I think is granite but might just be a large snowdrift, and come face-to-face with a mound that's too perfect and round to be natural.

We pause to catch our breath. "The entrance is snowed in," Waterfall says. "We'll have to dig."

Mara groans. "Of course we will."

26

WE fall to our knees and shovel at the snow. It's much softer here, and our gloved hands do the trick. Suddenly a chunk of snow breaks free and falls away, opening up a dark hole. We scramble back from the edge.

Waterfall says. "The snow is so deep that we're at the top of the entrance."

We work at the edges, opening up the hole and packing the snow down until Red is able to scramble up and over. After a moment her head pokes up over the edge. "It's dark and smelly," she says with a wrinkled nose.

Mara pulls her tinderbox and one of her precious candles from her pack, lights the candle, and hands it over the edge to Red. The rest of us climb inside and spread out, taking stock.

The tunnel is roughly arched, with an uneven floor that slopes gradually downward. Beams brace the walls at regular intervals, though some have toppled into the center. They are in various stages of decay, and shimmery with cobwebs.

"We'll collect wood and resin for torches and firewood," I say. "As much as we can carry. Storm and I can use our Godstones for light if necessary, but I'd rather save our strength for emergencies."

"There's plenty of wood along the way," Waterfall says. Her sharp features seem nearly skeletal in the shadows cast by our single flame of light. "These beams burn well, and torches are stashed throughout. Some are very old, but they'll be better than nothing. When we encounter the stashes, though, I suggest we take several, because a few stretches of our journey will take us through tunnels that were never well used."

In demonstration, she bends over the shadow of what might be a wooden crate and pulls out a torch that is black and dry with age. She holds it toward Red, who lights the end with her candle. It catches instantly, washing the icy tunnel entrance in shades of orange. "Ready?" she says.

I grab Mara's hand and say, "Will you be all right?"

She breathes deep through her nose and says, "I have to be, don't I?" Then she pulls her hand away and steps resolutely forward.

"Be alert," Storm says. "We'll be going farther and deeper than my sister has ever been. I know that in Joya d'Arena, rumors are something to scoff at, due to the prevaricating, deceiving nature of your people. But in Invierne, rumors of danger should be taken seriously."

"Hopefully, it is less dangerous than volcanoes and

avalanches and freezing temperatures," I say, but Storm just shrugs.

Belén grabs a few more torches from the crate, we tighten the waist straps of our packs, and together we turn our backs on the entrance and follow Mara into the belly of the earth.

PART III

27

AFTER being on the open road for so long, it feels deeply wrong to be closed in, to see only as far as the torch's meager splash of light will allow. We will be in these tunnels for days, according to Waterfall. But we can only see as far as the next few steps.

We walk in silence, ears pricked to detect what our eyes cannot see. So far there is only the scuffing of our feet against fallen gravel, our heavy breathing, and distantly, an echoing *plink-plink* of water. I dread the moment I hear anything else.

These tunnels were not created for comfort. Their sole purpose, at least at first, was to penetrate the mountains as quickly and deeply as possible in search of the *zafira*. So our path twists and curves to take advantage of natural caverns and fissures. The floor is rough, and we step carefully, wary of a twisted ankle. When the tunnels narrows to a crevice, we remove our packs to squeeze through sideways, one by one. Even the packs don't fit—we are forced to unload them, hand the larger items through, and repack them on the other side.

I'm one of the last to go, and I squeeze through, back and breasts scraping rock, worrying what will happen if we encounter a place too tight to get through.

When I reach the other side, I find Mara crouched over, hands on knees, breathing heavily. I start toward her, thinking to offer comfort, but Belén gets there first. He grabs her hand and pulls her against him, wraps his arms around her, and whispers something.

I back away, feeling like an intruder.

Twice we encounter branched corridors that appear as gaping black holes to the left. We stop so Waterfall can study them. Runes, like the ones we saw in the Temple of Morning, are carved into the wall beside them. Both times, Waterfall makes the decision to pass by.

It's impossible to mark the time here. I've no idea how long we've traveled or how far we've come when I consider calling a halt for the day. Maybe it's too early. And we have a lot of ground to make up after being stuck in the storm. But my legs tremble and my lower back aches from the weight of my pack.

It is Belén who decides for me. He stumbles, ramming his shoulder into an outcropping. He doesn't cry out, but I've so rarely seen Belén be clumsy that it stops me cold. Thinking of the night he fell asleep on watch, I give the order. "Let's camp."

"Oh, thank God," Mara says.

We drop our packs and plop to the ground. Mara starts pulling cooking utensils out of her pack, but I put a hand on her forearm. "No need, Mara. We can eat cold food tonight. Just rest."

"Please, Elisa? I need to . . . do something."

"Oh. I see. In that case, I would love some tea."

She smiles gratefully.

Red drags a toppled wood beam toward the center of our tight camp. She and Mara attack it with ax and handsaw. It falls apart a little too easily. They get a fire going, and the light is so much brighter than that of a mere torch that we all breathe a collective sigh of relief.

We don't need a fire for warmth—though the tunnel is chilly, it is considerably warmer than the outside wintry air— but I decide that so long as we can find wood, we should have a fire every night. Just to force a little normalcy on this strange journey.

Hector settles beside me. "Only two approaches to guard," he says, pulling a whetstone and oilcloth from his pack. "We'll only need one person on watch at a time." He starts to whisk the dagger against the whetstone, and I lean my head back against the wall and close my eyes to absorb the familiar sound. For the rest of my life, however long that might be, hearing blades being sharpened will remind me of Hector and Belén.

"No watch tonight," I tell him. "I know it's risky, but we're desperate for rest. I need everyone sharp."

"We're just trading one risk for another," he says. "But in this case, I think it's a good trade."

Red squeals, and we both jump in our seats. Hector is on his feet in an instant, with me not far behind. Her form is barely visible in the shadowy blackness just outside the range of our firelight. She crouches down, staring at something.

"Skinny Girl?" Belén says. "What is it? Are you all right?"

She turns to glare at him. "My name is Red Sparkle Stone."

"Of course. Apologies."

She picks up something off the ground. "I found this. It crawled across my food. I stomped it. At first it was glowing, but not anymore."

She hands it to Belén, who nearly drops it. He holds it away from himself, as if it might bite him. It's the size of my fist. Even in the gloom I can make out segmented legs. Lots of them.

"A deathstalker," Hector says. "Larger relative of the common cave scorpion. They glow when frightened. Their sting is painful and mildly poisonous but not usually serious. The problem is when they swarm. Multiple stings can be lethal."

"Ugh," I say.

"Yes. I agree they are ugh," Storm says.

"Let's hope we never see more than one at a time," I say.

"I'm going to have nightmares," Mara says.

"Too bad we don't have a small cage," Hector says, and we all look at him in puzzlement. "We could trap them. Use them for light."

Warm affection wells up inside me, and I feel a silly grin spread across my face.

"What?" he says.

"It's just . . . I like how practical you are. Willing to use any tool at your disposal."

He studies me a moment. "I'm like you," he says.

We're still staring at each other when Belén clears his

throat. "I suggest we keep our packs closed and our bedrolls tied tight whenever they're not in use."

The thought of slipping into my bedroll and finding a death-stalker by accident gives me a shiver. "Agreed."

"My cousin got stung by a deathstalker," Waterfall says as she flips out her bedroll. As she slips inside, she adds, "He died." She closes her eyes to sleep.

28

THE next day—or maybe only a short time later—I wake to utter darkness. I can't see my hand in front of my face, and I have a moment's breathless panic, but then a spark sears the blackness, followed by a softer, wider light that fills our campsite.

Mara is hunched over the fire, blowing onto the small flame. Her tinderbox is on the ground beside her.

"I'm so glad you can do that in the dark," I say with a yawn as the others stir around me.

"Me too," she says. "But we're going to have this problem a lot. The wood is too dry to bank properly. Whoever stands watch will have to keep an eye on it. We should always have wood within arm's length, just in case."

I nod agreement. "If necessary, Storm and I can make our Godstones glow, though we couldn't keep it up indefinitely."

But I warm myself with the thought. *So long as I have the Godstone, I have light.*

After a quick meal of smoked horse meat and pine-needle

tea, we shoulder our packs and set off. Our path grows steep, so steep that at times we skid our way downward into the belly of the mountain. It seems so wrong that we should go down when every instinct in me screams to go up, toward light and air. Waterfall insists we're on the right path.

When the tunnel curves to the right and then levels off, I'm delighted to give my calves and shins a break.

A crack sounds, then an echoing clatter that ends in a splintering crash.

"My sister!" Storm cries out, rushing forward.

I can't see over everyone's heads, so I push forward, elbowing them out of my way.

Waterfall is crumpled to the ground. Her left leg has broken through the floor. The resulting hole is jagged with splintered wood. She pulls on the leg, but it's clearly stuck. "A false floor," she says, her eyes wide with pain. "You should all step away."

Now that she mentions it, my steps sound hollow, and the ground beneath me has a slight give. We edge backward, testing each step before putting full weight on it. "We'll get you out of there," I assure her. But I don't stop backing away until my heel meets with a slight lip, followed by solid ground. We were walking across ancient planks of wood, I realize with a pounding heart. Disguised by centuries of dust and gravel.

"I'm bleeding," she says matter-of-factly. "I can feel it going down my leg."

Oh, God. I hope she hasn't nicked an artery.

"I'll throw you a rope," Hector says. "Try to get both arms through the loop. Once we have you secured, we'll send someone to start widening that hole."

He pulls the large coil from his pack and starts to loop and knot, his fingers sure. I put a hand on his forearm. "We can't lose her," I say quietly. "She's our only way through this place."

His return gaze is solemn. "I know."

He finishes his knot. "Ready?"

She nods, and he tosses it her way. She grabs the end, manages to get one arm through . . . when the floor cracks again and she sinks deeper. She grunts in pain.

"We've got a good hold on the rope," Hector says, and I see that it's true. Behind him, Belén and Mara are holding tight to it; Belén has it wrapped twice around his forearm. "We won't let you fall."

Slowly, gingerly, she wriggles her other arm through so that the rope curves under her armpits and around her back. "I'm secure," she calls back.

"Now we send someone to break her out of that hole," Hector says to me, "tied to Belén's rope. I'd go, but I think the strongest of us should stay behind as anchors."

I nod, and even as my gut screams *no*, my mouth says, "I'll go."

"I should go," Red says. "I'm the littlest."

I open my mouth to protest, but I know she's right. She's the safest choice. "All right. Thank you, Red."

"I'll hold the torch," Storm says.

Hector makes sure Mara and Belén have a tight grip on the rope holding Waterfall, and then he rummages through Belén's pack and pulls out a second rope. He wraps it between Red's legs and around her waist, then ties it off with a thick sailor's knot. "Go carefully," he says, his voice dark. "Test each step before putting your full weight on it. When you get there, don't try to dislodge Waterfall's leg. Just try to open up the hole so she can move it herself." He hands her Belén's ax.

She nods up at him, swallowing hard, then she screws her face into a mask of determination and sets off. Hector and I grip her rope tight, bracing ourselves in wide stances.

My heart pounds in my throat as I watch her tiny form work its way across the planking, testing each step and letting the floor gradually assume her weight. When she reaches Waterfall, she gets on her belly and splays herself, spreading her weight out as much as possible.

"Smart girl," I mutter.

She attacks the wood around the hole with the ax. Lying on her belly gives her little range of motion for the task, but the wood is weak and dry, and it cracks easily and falls away. I count *one-two-three-four* before hearing a faint crash as the pieces splinter on impact far, far below.

"Big chunk here I think I can get rid of," Red says. "Hold tight to that rope." Her high little-girl voice rings with authority, and Waterfall nods wordlessly and grabs the rope with both hands.

Red slams the floor with the ax. Something breaks away, Waterfall sinks, the rope goes taut. Mara and Belén strain to hold it in place. "Can you move your leg?" Red asks.

Waterfall closes her eyes. Sweat beads on her now-bloodless forehead as she yells through gritted teeth and pulls her leg away from the jagged wood.

"Got it," she says breathlessly. "But it's bleeding badly." She lets go of the rope to grasp at the planking. Red backs up a little to give her some space, but she stretches out a hand to help. Waterfall reaches for it.

The floor collapses, and Waterfall drops away while Red scrambles backward. Mara and Belén are pulled forward a few steps, but they find their footing and hold fast.

"Don't let go!" I yell.

As soon as Red reaches solid ground, Hector and I drop her rope and rush to Waterfall's. Slowly, muscles straining, we pull it back.

Storm has moved to the edge of the false floor. "Can you hear me?" he says. "Are you all right?"

"This rope . . ." comes the labored voice. "Can't breathe . . ."

A white hand peeks over the edge, then a forearm. Storm steps out to help her.

"Storm, no!" I call out, but he ignores me. He lowers himself to his knees and bends toward the hole. The floor creaks.

He grabs his sister's wrist, then her arm. The rest of us keep hauling on the rope. And suddenly, Storm has her. The floor cracks. He leaps backward toward solid ground. His heels slip out from under him, and he lands flat on his back with his sister atop him.

Waterfall rolls away. I drop the rope and run forward. "Storm? Are you all right?" I fall to my knees beside him.

His mouth opens and closes, like a beached fish. He blinks. I check him for injury but see nothing. What if it's his back? What if he can't move?

Air rushes back into him, and he groans like a dying animal. "My back!" he says. "My head! I don't like pain."

I exhale relief, that he is well enough to complain so.

He sits straight up, looking around. "Waterfall?"

"Here," Hector says. "She has a chunk of wood lodged in her thigh. We'll have to cut it out."

Storm drags himself to Waterfall's side. She puts a hand to his cheek. "Thank you for saving me."

I have to roll my eyes at that, because we all saved her. Every single one of us.

"Mara, can you get a fire going?" Hector says. "I need to heat up my dagger."

Storm rises, grabs my arm, and pulls me aside. "Will you heal her? It could get infected. She could still—"

"I doubt it."

"Why not?"

I frown. "It only seems to work on people I care deeply about. But maybe you could heal her? You're the one who loves her."

"I don't know how to heal."

"What you mean is you're afraid to try."

His face turns thoughtful. "Yes, that is exactly what I mean. Forgive me for not speaking more precisely. I fear hurting her.

She is . . ." He looks down. "She is dear to me."

"Let Hector do what he can. If she needs healing afterward, I'll show you what to do."

"All right." He puts his hands to his face, then runs them through hair that now reaches the nape of his neck. "All right."

I've learned to face death and injury when I must, but it's never easy. I step away from the others, into the darkness, telling myself our tunnel is too narrow and small for everyone to be an onlooker.

A tiny hand creeps into mine.

I look down at the girl and squeeze gently. "Thank you for what you did, Red Sparkle Stone."

"You're welcome," she says gravely.

She has been with us for such a short time, yet she was willing to risk her life for our cause. "Weren't you scared?" I ask.

"Yes. But it was a good scared."

"There's a good kind?"

"Oh, yes." Her voice drops so low I have to strain to hear. "Orlín made me scared all the time. Scared I would starve. Scared I would get too cold. Scared he would hurt me again or get so mad that he'd throw me to one of the men. That was nasty bad scared." She pauses, scuffing her boots against the floor. "But you never hit me, even though I'm your slave."

"You're not my—"

"You always feed me. You call me a true name. Now when I'm scared, it's not because of meanness. And today I chose my own scared. It's always a good scared, when you get to pick it your own self."

I squeeze her hand again, whispering, "I think I know exactly what you mean."

In the months since becoming queen, there has been a nebulous thought wavering in my mind, just beyond the clarity of consciousness—that if I wanted to, I could give it all up. I don't *have* to fight for my kingdom. I could abdicate. Hand it over to Conde Eduardo, who wants it so badly. Let him fight it out with Invierne. I could go back to Orovalle, to Papá and Alodia. I would be a failed queen, a failed bearer, yes. But I would be safe. My life would be easy.

I know I'll never do it, even though my current path means danger and maybe even death. It's terrifying. But it's a manageable terror. Because I've chosen it.

I wince at Waterfall's muffled scream. "Got it!" Hector says.

Mara sacrifices some of her precious burn ointment for disinfecting purposes, then Hector stitches her up. I call a halt for the day—if indeed it is day—to give Waterfall a chance to rest and ascertain the true extent of her injury. We'll see if she can walk tomorrow.

But I gaze down the tunnel into the dark, knowing it's too late to turn back, racking my brain for an idea on how to get across the false floor.

After breakfast I tell everyone the plan I came up with while we rested. I'm greeted by silence. "Or," I add, "we can turn around and go back. Take our chances in the snow."

"This is our best option," Hector says.

"I agree," says Belén.

Mara closes her eyes and takes a deep breath, but she nods.

We set up quickly. Hector shows Red how to tie a rolling hitch knot and has her practice several times. We loop one end of the rope around a rocky outcropping, the other around Red's waist.

Traveling this tunnel has been made even more difficult by the fact that it is rough-hewn and jagged, for the goal of the original miners was to tunnel as quickly as possible. But now I'm grateful. There are plenty of places to tie a rope down. It might be what saves us.

We hold tight to Red's rope as she sets off. She holds her cloak out in front of her, and she uses it to brush years of dust away from the floor to expose the rotting wood. We hope that by being able to see the floor, we can avoid the more obviously rotted parts as we cross.

She takes a step on the floor. It creaks. She waits a moment, then takes another step. On the third step, her foot breaks through and she jerks left to retain her balance, clutching at the wall. I brace myself and grip the rope so tightly my palms ache, but she doesn't fall through. She doesn't look back, and she doesn't hesitate. She pulls her foot from the hole and keeps going.

The moment her feet touch solid ground, she jumps into the air with a whoop. "I did it!" she says, whirling to show us her grinning face. "I did it!"

"Good work, Red," I call out. "Now can you tie the rope to something?"

She removes the rope from her waist and looks around. She spots a promising outcropping of rock, then loops the rope around twice and ties it off the way Hector showed her.

"Your turn, Waterfall," Hector says.

She limps forward and grips the now-taut rope that stretches across the hidden chasm.

"Hold on with both hands," Hector instructs. "And try to keep to the path Red used."

I hold my breath as she starts forward. Ideally, we'd tie another rope to her waist. But this one will have to be cut when we all reach the other side, and we dare not risk losing another. I make a mental note that if I survive this and have the misfortune of embarking on another long journey, I will take lots of rope. A mountain of rope.

Waterfall reaches the other side safely. Then me, then Mara, then Storm and Belén. Hector goes last. He insisted on it, saying he is the heaviest and thus most likely to weaken the floor for everyone else.

My heart is in my throat as he sets out. The floor groans beneath his weight. He has only gone two steps when something snaps. The entire floor falls away, and Hector with it.

"No!" I yell, rushing toward the edge. Hands grab at my elbows, trying to hold me back, but I push them away.

The dust clears. The rope sags into the pit, but it is not broken. Hector hangs from it with both hands. He swings one leg up and hooks the rope with his ankle, then does the same with the other. With slow, jerky movements, he executes an upside-down crawl along the length of the rope toward us.

"Hurry, Commander," Storm says. "The rope is fraying."

I whip my head up. Sure enough, the rope is unraveling where it rubs up against the opposite edge. We'll be lucky if it holds much longer.

One of Hector's ankles slips, and the rope sways wildly, scraping hard at the edge of the pit. He swings his leg back into place and keeps going, hand over hand, dragging himself along as the rope unravels, and I can't stop muttering, "Please, God, please, please, please."

He reaches the edge. The rope snaps.

Hector's head drops out of sight as Belén and I lunge forward to grab him, and miss. My chest feels like it's turning inside out, until I see Hector's fingertips, gripping the edge so tight they've gone white.

We grab his wrists, then his arms. My fingers dig into his flesh, and my shoulder sockets burn as I pull with all my might. He gets an arm over the edge, then a leg. I grab the back of his pants and help him to solid ground.

He lays there panting, staring at the ceiling. "That was close," he says.

I stick a finger in his chest. "Don't ever scare me like that again."

Before I can blink he grabs me, pulls me atop him, and right in front of everyone, kisses me soundly. "It's hard, isn't it?" he says, his lips still against mine. "To watch someone you love almost die?"

I rest my forehead against his. "Once this is all over, I say we stop doing that to each other."

He grins. "Agreed."

I get to my feet, pulling him with me. "Can you travel?"

"Like the wind."

I turn to find everyone else staring at us without bothering to disguise their amusement. Except Red, who wrinkles her nose at me. "That was gross," she says.

29

THREE or four days later, we reach a crossroads. Waterfall crouches to read the runes and says, "This way." And we follow her into a different tunnel, even narrower than the last, with a ceiling so low that everyone save Red and me must stoop to pass.

When instinct says it's time to halt for the day, I decide to keep going, for the tunnel is so narrow that we would have to lay out our bedrolls single file to camp. No one complains. We push on and on, until we reach a spot where the ceiling is so low we must get on our hands and knees and crawl through. The walls press tight around us. The rock above me feels heavier than ever. Surely it will give way any moment, tumbling around us, crushing us to death. In this tight space, it would be impossible to run from danger.

In front of me, Mara whimpers. I reach up and squeeze her leg.

At last the tunnel opens into a wide natural cavern, with a high ceiling thick with stalactites that sparkle like icicles, and we tumble into it as fast as we can. It's such a relief to stand up straight, to stretch our arms high. Waterfall stands in the center and holds out her torch, revealing water-smoothed rock and a sandy floor. Dark blots of shadow mar the walls, indicating branching tunnels.

"This place floods regularly," Hector observes, bending down. He grabs a handful of sand and rubs it around in his palm. "No moisture. It's been dry for a while."

"Maybe in the spring?" Belén says.

"Or when winter comes early, after the first thaw," Waterfall says.

Oh, God. What if the sun is shining outside? What if it's melting all that snow?

"Maybe we shouldn't camp here," I say. "Maybe we should keep going." But my legs quiver. If I were to guess, I'd say we've been walking or crawling for a day and a half.

"Rest for a bit," Waterfall says, with uncharacteristic softness in her voice. "Sleep if you can. I need time to figure out which of these tunnels to take anyway."

It's as good a plan as any. We unshoulder our packs and look for a place to lie down. Hector finds a flat bit of rock and stretches out on his side. I stretch out behind him, wrapping my arm around his chest and burying my nose in his back. His hand comes up to trap my arm.

I should savor this moment, with my body pressed against his, breathing in the familiar scents of leather oil and the soap he uses to shave. But suddenly all I can think about is Waterfall. I hope we were right to trust her. We've come so far, taken so many turns, that without her, we would be lost down here forever.

Scritch-scritch-scritch. Something echoes in the dark. I blink to clear fuzzy vision and shake off sleep, wishing for the thousandth time that we could manage more light in this awful place. I roll away from Hector as it sounds again. *Scritch-scritch-scritch.*

I shake him awake, and he lurches to a sitting position. I put a finger to my lips. "Listen," I whisper.

The others breathe softly around us. Waterfall is nowhere to be seen. One of the branching tunnels glows. She must have taken a torch to investigate it.

Scritch-scritch-scritch.

"An animal," Hector says. "Something small. With claws."

"Small is good," I say in a weak voice. My mind tumbles through its brief catalog of small animals with claws that might live deep in a cave. Rats, maybe. Or bats. Do bat wings sound like claws?

The tunnel brightens. The light is steady and sure, blue-white rather than orange.

"Hector? That—"

"Get the others up," he says. "Now!"

We run around shouting, shaking everyone awake. Storm's bleary eyes turn sharp almost at once. "Where is my sister?" he demands.

"We don't know. Be ready. Something is coming down that tunnel toward us."

The scratching is steadier now, louder. It doesn't sound like a small creature with claws anymore. It sounds like thousands of them.

Storm pulls his amulet from beneath his shift. Mara strings her bow, her fingers flying. Belén and I draw our daggers, Hector his short sword. Red grabs a burning piece of wood from the fire and stands beside Mara.

The walls of the tunnels pulse with light. Something scuttles over the lip of the tunnel entrance toward us. Fist sized, glowing. A deathstalker.

Then others pour out after it, a whole flood of them. Red screams as our cavern fills with soft light.

"Get ready to stomp!" Hector yells. He grabs another chunk of wood from the fire. Sparks fly as he flings it at the deathstalkers. It lands near the entrance to the tunnel, and the scorpions part to make way for it, like water rushing around a boulder. "They're afraid of fire!"

The nearest have reached us. Mara and Belén stomp furiously, knees kicking high. Several crawl up Mara's legs, up her back, into her hair.

I anchor myself to the ground, call the *zafira*, and spring up a barrier between us and the tunnel. They pile up against it, scrambling over one another's bodies in a frenzy.

It slows the onslaught, but too many are already upon us. My barrier wavers as I shoot fire into their swarming midst, bolt after bolt. When the fire hits, they turn brown and shrivel, but it's not enough, and I can't maintain both fire and barrier much longer.

Red screams and stomps; Hector hacks uselessly with his

sword. Then more bolts join mine as Storm enters the fray.

Mara is covered in scorpions now, but she grabs her pack, rummages inside, and comes up with a bottle of lamp oil. She flings it into the thickest part of the swarm. I aim a bolt where the bottle landed. Fire whooshes to life, and wind plasters my clothes against my body. Scorpions die by the hundreds.

Do I imagine that the trickle coming from the tunnel is thinning? But so is my barrier. A few deathstalkers scuttle through. Then a hundred. Something pierces my ankle; the sting shoots up my leg. I cry out, dropping the barrier entirely.

"Mara, drop to the ground and roll!" Belén bellows. I wince at the crunch of carapaces, even as I continue to fling fire toward the tunnel.

I'm sure of it now; the onslaught *is* thinning! I almost laugh aloud. But then something else comes down the tunnel—I hear it before I see it, the way it clackety-clacks against the stone. Storm continues to send his own bolts, but they're weaker now. Not as weak as mine, though. I stop, saving my energy for whatever comes next.

It's another scorpion. The mother of all scorpions. Bigger than a tavern building, glowing like a moon. Its pincers snap as its segmented tail curls over its back. A drop of venom collects at the tip.

Hector whips his sword to the ready position. "Belén!" he calls. "I need my forearm shield."

Belén tosses it to him, and Hector catches it deftly. Then the commander of my guard advances on the scorpion.

It reaches out with pincers as if to snap him in half. Hector dodges and arcs his sword down, but he's not quite fast enough, and the scorpion dances away.

Hector darts in, slashing, and nicks one of the legs. The scorpion stumbles but thrusts its tail forward to spear him. Hector ducks, and the tails misses him by a hand's breadth.

The creature skitters sideways, pulling its tail back for another try. Beside Hector, something sizzles. It's venom, shaken from the scorpion's tail when it attacked, now burning through the rock like acid.

"Watch the venom!" I yell. "It burns."

Hector circles the scorpion, keeping an eye on the tail as another drop of venom coalesces at its tip. "It's too fast," he hollers. "Can you weaken it for me?"

But I'm already focusing the *zafira* into a white-hot point of power. I scream, thrusting it from me. My white firebolt plunges into its side. The scorpion screeches, a metal-scraping-metal sound that pierces my head like a knife. But it works— the tail's next shot misses, and its body smokes with char.

It's a little slower now, wobblier, as it rounds on Hector once again. Hector attacks in a flurry of movement, slashing so fast I can hardly track him. The tail whips down again, but Hector dodges and rolls out of reach. A drop of venom sizzles on one of his gauntlets, and he backs away to give himself a few precious seconds to unbuckle it and toss it to the ground.

The scorpion advances. Its tail spears forward over and over again, desperately. Finally it overcommits, stumbles. Hector dodges right, leaps, plunges the blade into the creature's head with a sickening crunch.

It shudders for a moment, then collapses, legs twitching, sword jutting from its carapace. The glow gradually fades.

I look around, collecting my breath, trying not to pass out from emptying myself of the *zafira* so quickly. The other scorpions are gone, burned or scuttled away. The cavern reeks of burned hair.

Mara lies on the ground, her head in Belén's lap. Purple welts are rising up all over her hands and face. They must be all over her body, beneath her clothes. Her breath comes in gasps. Her lips are turning blue. I drop to my knees beside them. *Not Mara, God, please, not her.*

"Heal her," Belén says. His one good eye brims with tears. "Please?"

I bury my face in my hands. "I can't. I've got nothing left. I'm barely—"

"Try!"

The world sways; my vision blurs. "All right," I hear myself saying. "I'll try." I reach down and take Mara's hands. They feel odd, like puffy pillows.

A shape kneels beside me. "Let me," says Storm. "I didn't use everything up the way you did. I might have something left."

"But healing only works for people you—"

"Tell me what to do."

I'm so dizzy, so tired. But I have to stay awake. "It's creation magic, so think about growing and cleansing and . . . I always imagine the power going through my hands into the other person. But I have a living stone. So maybe put your amulet in Mara's hands?"

He wraps her hands around his amulet, holding them there with his own. Mara's eyelids flutter, but they stay closed. I want to tell Storm to hurry, that there might not be much time, but I don't want to ruin his focus.

He closes his eyes. My own Godstone flutters in response as he draws on the *zafira* and focuses all the power on his amulet. Their clasped hands begin to glow.

Mara's back arches, and her sightless eyes fly open—but only for the briefest moment. She crashes back to Belén's lap, and Storm topples over on top of her. "Not enough," he mutters. "I didn't have enough after all."

Do I imagine that some of Mara's welts have turned sickly yellow? That the swelling in her face has subsided? A partial healing, maybe. *Dear God, please let it be enough to save her life.*

I sway to the side, barely noting how Hector catches me before I join Mara and Storm in oblivion.

30

MY first thought upon waking is for Mara. I scramble over and put my hand to her cheek. Not feverish. And her breathing is definitely easier.

"Hector says she might live," Belén says. His voice is ragged, his face bereft. I'd bet my Godstone crown he hasn't left her side.

"You love her," I say gently.

He nods. "But she won't marry me. Says she may never marry. That her first priority is to be your lady-in-waiting, and she's finally doing something she's proud of, and she won't . . . I'm babbling."

I put a hand on his arm and squeeze.

Footsteps draw my attention away, beyond the scorpion's giant carcass to the tunnel it came from. It's Hector and Red, carrying something long and heavy between them.

"No," I whisper. "No, no, no, no."

They lay Waterfall beside the fire. Her once-beautiful features are unrecognizable, her face a lumpy mask of hives. But unlike Mara's, hers are pale and bloodless. And unlike Mara, she doesn't breathe.

Red hurries away as soon as she releases Waterfall's legs. She sits, her back toward the rest of us, and hugs her knees to her chest, head down.

"I knew something must have scared them," Hector says softly. "They only glow when frightened. I think she went off exploring by herself, to make sure we were going the right way."

I glance over at Storm's peacefully sleeping form, dreading the moment when he wakes and learns what has happened. My heart aches for him.

"We'll have to go back," I say. "We might be able to find our way. We can figure out how to get back over that fissure, and . . ." I let my face fall into my hands. There is no getting to Basajuan in time now. The city will burn, my friends and my sister with it.

"Maybe not," Hector says. "She had this." He hands me a scrap of parchment. It's faded, the charcoal smeared, but the lines of a map are still visible. "She was scribbling notes when we found her. She started writing as soon as she knew she was dying, and she didn't stop until she had to."

"You found her alive?"

"Barely. We rushed to get her here. I thought maybe you or Storm could heal her. But she died on the way. She talked the whole time. Telling us . . . she . . ." Hector's jaw clenches, and he blinks rapidly.

Tears fill my eyes. People are always so much braver, so

much nobler, then I ever imagine. "What did she tell you?" Though I think I know.

"Everything she knows about these tunnels. See here?" He points to a hash mark on the parchment. "This marks a water source. And this here? This part of the route is merely a good guess, and she says we should be extremely cautious. And this . . ." His fingertip moves toward a small crescent, its top edge blurred from too much handling. "This is our exit. She said it would bring us to within a day's walk of the northern pass."

I push away the hope sparking inside me. It's too soon to be glad.

Storm stirs. He stretches then sits up, rolling his shoulders.

I see the exact moment he notices his sister's body. He stares, his eyes glassy with shock. Then his fist curls near his mouth as it opens in a silent scream.

I scramble toward him, wrap his slender body in my arms, and bring his head down to my shoulder. We rock back and forth together. Then he starts to keen, a high-pitched nasal sound that sends shivers into my core.

Mara wakes soon after. Her voice is thick and cracked, her movements slow, but she has enough spark to snap at Belén to stop hovering. She makes herself hot tea to help her aching throat and sits beside the fire sipping, staring over the edge of her mug at Waterfall's body. We have laid it out on a rock and covered it with her cloak, which is not quite long enough to cover the toes of her boots.

I come up behind her and reach down to grip her shoulder. "Not much farther," I assure her. "Hector thinks we're only two days' journey from the surface."

She nods, staring off into the darkness. "Two more days," she whispers. "I can do this for two more days."

I bend over and put my arms around her neck, my cheek to hers. "Thank you for not dying."

She grabs my forearm with one hand and squeezes, but says nothing.

Inviernos don't bury their dead; they burn them. We gather as much fallen timber as we can find and built a small pyre. It won't be enough. The wood will burn too fast, and Waterfall's half-melted corpse will be open to scavenge. But Storm insists, and none of us has the heart to deny him this small thing.

We light the pyre. Storm mutters something in the Inviernos' most ancient language, and then we turn our backs and head into the same tunnel where Hector and Red found Waterfall. We move quickly, but we cannot outpace the scent of burning flesh.

We soon reach a larger chamber, and this must be where Waterfall spooked the scorpions, for it is covered in dry moltings. Thousands of empty carapaces crunch beneath our boots as we walk through. One wall is covered in tiny pearlescent orbs that pulse and heave as we pass. Eggs.

We stay as far from the wall of eggs as possible. None of us speak. We are listening hard for the sound of another swarm.

A different tunnel leads us away, and we follow Hector into it eagerly, desperate to leave behind the scorpions' lair. This tunnel is less jagged than the others. Our torchlight catches on a thick vein of sparkling quartz, and I am not too sad and weary to find it beautiful.

We pause at an intersection. Hector tells Red to hold the torch for him so he can study the map. "This way," he says, indicating right again. This time our path slopes upward, and in spite of the burn in my thighs, my steps quicken. The others do the same, for it is the first time in days our path has inclined.

It seems that we travel forever. My awareness of time becomes a palpable, tortuous thing, each step marking a moment, each step coming too slow. I miss arching sun, the changing shadows, rising and falling temperatures. Here in the belly of the mountains, nothing changes. No matter how long we walk, it is still dark, still rocky, still cold and damp, with no end to our journey in sight.

When we pause to eat and rest, Belén frowns at the dried horsemeat in his hand and says something about wishing it was salted and spiced. Mara snaps that he should feel lucky he has anything to eat at all, that it's not her fault they didn't have time to prepare proper food. When Red insists that all the food we eat is delicious, they both turn on her and glare.

Even Hector steps away from the group for a while, and I consider following, but if he's as exasperated and irritable as everyone else, he might want some space to himself.

Storm has said little since leaving his sister behind. He is like the old Storm—taciturn and cold, his face as pleasant and bland as a stone statue. I hope I am not losing him too. Grief does strange things to people—I know it well.

Hector returns from the shadows, holding Waterfall's map. Belén says, "I hope you know what you're doing with that thing," and his voice is snappish and accusatory.

The two men glare at each other.

We need to get out of these tunnels as soon as possible. Or we'll tear ourselves apart in frustration.

I lurch to my feet, dusting off crumbs. "Break is over. Let's go."

Our path turns into a series of uneven steps that wind upward. Water trickles down the steps and into the depths. "Step carefully," Hector warms. "It may be slippery."

"Water is a good sign, right?" Mara says to me. "It's probably not groundwater. It must be coming from outside."

I have no idea if this is true, but I say, "Yes, a very good sign."

We take a left and then a right. I'm studying the wood beams—they are more plentiful here, and the ceiling is a little higher—when Red exclaims, "Light! I see light!"

Sure enough, the shroud of shadows beyond our puddle of torchlight seems a little less black. In spite of Hector's warnings, we step faster, and gradually the walls of the tunnel ahead come into focus—the gray rock, the drip stains from rainwater, the remnants of wood beams.

The tunnel curves around to the left, and we reach a dead end.

"No!" Mara whimpers.

A rockfall blocks our path. Faint light seeps through small

cracks near the top. The air here is fresh and cool, and as we stare in dismay at the blocked tunnel, a breeze whistles through the cracks, bringing the tangy, fresh scent of pine forest.

"What do we do?" Mara says, panic edging her voice.

"Can we move some of the rocks?" Belén asks.

"Maybe," Hector says. "But we might bring the mountain down on top of us."

I say, "I can do it."

Hector raises an eyebrow. "I know you can. But we still have the problem of instability. While you're blowing through it with your Godstone, what's to keep us from getting crushed?"

Storm steps forward. "*I* can do it." His skin is gray in the gloom, like that of a corpse.

"You want me to create a barrier," I say.

He nods.

"It takes a lot of energy to blow through a rock wall," I say. "It took me several tries. I passed out a lot."

He shrugs. "This isn't solid granite like in the Temple of Morning. It has weak points. There and there." He points near the top, where light is leaking through. "I'll concentrate my firebolts there."

"Can you do it?" Hector says to me. "Can you hold the whole mountain up if necessary?"

The last barrier I created collapsed far too soon. But this time, I won't be shooting firebolts at the same time.

"I think so," I say finally. "I'm not sure, but . . . what are our chances of finding a way around the blockage?"

Hector rubs at the stubble along his jaw. "Not good. Not before we run out of food."

"Maybe scorpions are edible," Belén says, and we all shoot him a collective glare.

"I don't want to go back," Mara says. "I'd rather take my chances with a cave-in. And it's not just because I despise caves with all the rage of a hurricane. I'm not convinced it's any safer down there."

"I agree with Mara," Belén says. "We've already encountered a false floor, a swarm of deadly scorpions, and a rockfall. Who knows what else is waiting for us?"

These are the kinds of decisions I hate. It seems my choices too often are reduced to a single question: How would I rather die? Starvation? Scorpion venom? Falling to my death?

Getting crushed to death would at least be quick, so I say, "Let's try it. Storm, are you ready now, or do you need to rest?"

"I'm ready. Let's go easy and slow at first. Small firebolts, small barrier."

I breathe deep through my nose, spread my feet shoulder-width apart, and ground myself to the earth. "Everyone else should probably get back," I say as Storm pulls his amulet from beneath his cloak.

I close my eyes and draw in the *zafira*. Along with the power comes confidence. I feel competent, strong. I hold tight to the power, preparing to exert my will. My Godstone hums joyously.

The barrier is easier this time. I imagine Hector's forearm shield, thinning and stretching, making a canopy over our heads. I sense matter bonding together in the space above me, and I know it looks like magic to everyone else—wavery like leaded glass or a desert mirage—but to me it feels like a natural extension of the world itself.

"Ready," I say.

Storm looses a firebolt. It spears forward, bright orange in the gloom, and collides against the rockfall in a shower of sparks. Gravel rains down around us, bouncing harmlessly off my barrier.

The dust clears. The opening is a little larger, but not much.

"I missed," Storm grumbles. "Meant for it to go a little more to the right."

"Try again. A little more power this time."

I brace myself as he raises his amulet. His next firebolt is as yellow as the sun and blinding fast. The crash echoes through the tunnel. Something groans in the rock above us, but the roof holds.

"Almost!" comes Red's excited voice. "I can almost crawl through! Try again, Storm, try again."

She's right. The uppermost hole is wide enough that I think I see stars.

"I'm good for two or three more at that strength level," he says, but he's panting from effort.

It might only take one more, aimed just right. I brace myself, send a little more power into my barrier, and say, "Do it."

The next firebolt blows the hole wide open. Rock and gravel spew everywhere. A chunk flies backward, knocking my cheekbone, and I stumble. My barrier disintegrates.

The mountain shakes. Pebbles and dust rain down. I snap the barrier back into place, cursing myself for stupidity.

"Elisa?" Hector's worried voice.

"Go!" I yell. The weight of rock strains against my barrier. It's the only thing keeping the tunnel from collapsing around us. "Go, go, go! All of you. That's a command!"

They rush forward and climb up toward the hole. Red disappears first. Her muffled, high-pitched screams reach us from the other side, and Belén darts forward after her. But then comes her voice: "I made it! I'm outside!" she cries, followed by more whooping and screaming.

The weight of this mountain is going to crush me. My shoulders feel like boulders, and all I want to do is sink, sink, sink into the welcoming earth. "Hurry!" I say through gritted teeth. "Go!"

One by one, Mara pushes all our packs through the hole to Red, then she disappears herself, followed by Belén and Storm. Hector turns to me, "Promise me you'll be right behind me."

I nod and wave him on, unable to draw breath to speak.

He scales the rockfall and pushes through the hole, feet first. His shoulders get stuck, and I have a moment of panic, but then he shifts, putting his hands above his head, and is able to squeeze through.

I'm alone, with nothing but a sputtering torch on the ground for company.

My barrier has become so heavy, like a millstone about my neck. Strangling an erupting volcano was easier than this, but there is no living sacrifice to help me now. I push one foot in front of the other; it's like wading through knee-deep sand.

I begin my climb up the rockfall. The mountain roars. Rocks pound the earth behind me where my barrier and I once stood, but I dare not look behind. I find a handhold and drag myself upward, then another. I'm weakening fast. I whisper, "Just a little farther."

My hand finds empty air. Then another, stronger hand wraps my wrist and pulls. The rocks scrape tracks in my skin as someone drags me through the hole, but I dare not give it much notice lest I lose control of my barrier.

And then a breeze hits my face, and I tumble out into a nighttime that feels as bright as day.

Hector clasps me to him, but I push him away. "We need to get clear," I say.

We grab our packs and sprint into the trees, crunching through snow. Behind us, the earth rumbles. We turn around in time to see a cloud of dust puff up into the air. Silence follows, and I'm almost disappointed. The cave-in looks like any other mountain slope.

An owl hoots. Pine boughs rustle in the breeze. Snow blankets the ground, but only up to our ankles. It's crusted over with ice, so the last snow must have fallen a day or so ago.

Red lets out a whoop of triumph, and all of a sudden we're hugging and patting one another on the back and laughing. Even Storm allows himself a small smile.

I launch myself into Hector's arms, and he stumbles backward, laughing. He presses his cheek to the side of my head and strokes my braid. "Waterfall was right," he says. "This area is far enough north that the blizzard missed it entirely."

I give him one last squeeze and extricate myself with reluctance. "We'll set up camp here," I say to everyone. "No watch tonight. I doubt anyone knows where we are, and I'd rather we all got as much sleep as possible. Tomorrow, we travel hard and fast for Basajuan."

31

MORNING light reveals a faint trail leading away from the collapsed mine entrance. We follow it until we find a wider track leading north. The sun rises bright and warm, and the snow continues to melt, revealing horseshoe scuffs and piles of old manure along our path. We hope it will eventually lead to the trading road and the northern pass.

The world is so much more beautiful than I remember, full of color and light and sound. We push ourselves hard, jogging when our trail allows, and each night we collapse into our bedrolls exhausted. But never once do I forget to look around and appreciate the magic of being aboveground.

On the third day out of the mines, we encounter a free village—this one populated with more Inviernos than Joyans—and trade some marjoram, fennel, and a few coppers for fresh food and mounts.

I give a worried thought to Horse as I climb into the saddle of my new mare—a dull dun creature who would disappear against a sand dune. I hope Horse is all right. I hope she found her way back to Umbra de Deus and a softhearted person with lots of treats.

The northern pass is icy but clear, and we join a steady stream of traders, trappers, and even a few herders, all desperate to get through before the first big storm hits. The news buzzes all around us—winter came early, and the southern route is already impassable. Not that anyone would want to travel the southern route, they say. For Joya d'Arena is in an uproar. There is a new challenger to the throne, a powerful conde who has declared Queen Elisa a traitor and blasphemer. He has taken over the capital city and prepares to launch a major assault on the northern holdings.

But there is no news of Basajuan, and we are hesitant to inquire too directly lest we draw attention. So we ride as fast as we can, resting only when we must.

The air changes as we cross the divide. One day we are shadowed by clouds and chilled to the bone; the next we greet warm sunshine and snowmelt. Within a day we have descended below the tree line. Another day takes us within view of Queen Cosmé's capital.

We look down from a high granite cliff over the dry, ridged foothills to the more lush valley beyond. The adobe buildings of Basajuan are barely visible, hazy with sunshine and distance and . . . smoke?

Hector pulls his mount beside mine. "Basajuan burns," he says.

"We're still a day's ride away." I want to hit something.

He shades his eyes with one hand and says, "It's just the

farmland around the city that burns, not the city itself. Not yet. The Deciregi have no army backing them this time. They will go cautiously. Strategically."

"And we must go faster." I kick my mare into a gallop, and the others follow. We pound down the trail, not caring that other travelers dodge out of our way and glare as we pass.

I pray feverishly as we ride. *Please, God, protect them all.*

The countryside is in chaos. Fields of maize, dry and ready for harvesting, send sooty smoke into the sky. Farmers work hard to quench the fires, tossing buckets of water down lines of workers from creeks and irrigation canals to the base of the flames. We pass the charred remains of a chicken house and a blackened field where a single bleating lamb weaves through small corpses as lumpy and dark as coal.

We face a steady stream of oncoming traffic—hastily packed wagons, mothers carrying infants, and even a few shepherds driving small herds of sheep and goats—all fleeing the coming destruction. The masses of humanity and livestock force us to slow down, and I grit my teeth with frustration.

"Any sign of the Deciregi?" I ask Hector as we maneuver around a cartful of cages containing noisy, panicked chickens.

"Just their handiwork," Hector says. "My guess is they will do an entire circuit of the city, close enough to cause panic, but far enough away to avoid the city archers."

Which means they might be on the opposite side of the city by now. This is our chance to get inside unseen. "Basajuan's wall is not defensively optimal," I observe. "It's low, with just a few watchtowers around the outskirts."

"We should prepare to be stopped and questioned, though," he says. "Especially with an Invierno traveling with us."

I glance back at Storm. I grew accustomed to having him travel openly, for he caused little notice in the free villages. But once we crossed the divide, his passing was greeted with suspicious stares. So he flipped up his cowl and now he rides hunched over, trying to look inconspicuous. I'm suddenly grateful for the chill in the air. It gives him an excuse to wear that cloak.

But if we're stopped at a guard tower, he is sure to be recognized as our ancient enemy.

I call up ahead. "Belén."

He and Mara ride side by side. At my voice, they rein in their mounts and twist in the saddle.

When I catch up, I ask, "Do you know a way into the city from scouting for Cosmé?"

He grins. "Definitely."

"Please tell me it doesn't involve a cave or a sewer," Mara says.

"No," he says, and she breathes relief. "If we play it right, we can walk right through the front door of Cosmé's palace."

"That would be ideal," I say.

"Several of your rebel Malficios joined Cosmé's guard after you left," Belén says. "I'll ride ahead—a lone rider can get through this crowd a lot easier than all of us traveling together—and scout the towers, find someone who will recognize you on sight. Then we'll send for Captain Jacián."

Jacián! He helped steal me away from King Alejandro, then

stayed by my side as I led the rebel Malficio. Another dear friend I have not seen in too long. I almost send up a prayer of gratitude, but I stop myself. The Deciregi are near and likely to sense whenever my Godstone is active.

"Do it," I say. "And quickly."

Belén spurs his horse on. We snack on late-harvest apples as we wait for him. Beyond the smoke and charred remains of the countryside, the city of Basajuan is beautiful, with rolling adobe buildings painted in bright pastels. It's a lot like my home in Brisadulce, but its nestled location in the crook of two meeting mountain ranges makes it a little cooler, a little wetter, and the result is lush and colorful by comparison.

Hector has checked and rechecked his weapons. Now he fiddles with the saddlebag, taking items out, putting them back in again.

"You're as bad at waiting as I am," I observe.

He freezes in the midst of inspecting a water skin. "You're right," he says. "I'm accomplishing nothing. I don't know how *you* manage it, though. Waiting on a horse. Unable to pace and bite your thumbnail."

I shoot him a mock glare, but he doesn't notice because his face has turned distant and grave. "This situation has the potential to go very badly."

"Yes."

"Not just for us," he explains. "For the world. The Deciregi could not have known it when they planned their conquest of this city, but you, Crown Princess Alodia, and Queen Cosmé are going to be in the same place at the same time. They could eliminate you all in one stroke."

I sigh, pulling back on my horse to make way for a woman and three barefoot children who are walking along the side of the road to avoid manure. "When I requested this meeting, it didn't occur to me that I was creating a dangerous situation." It was a rushed and painful moment. Franco had stolen Hector away, and I had just learned that Conde Eduardo was engineering a civil war. "But maybe it provides us with an opportunity too."

"What do you mean?"

"I'm not sure yet."

"Maybe your sister ignored your summons," he says. "Her Highness has a reputation for following no one's counsel but her own. It might be a good thing if . . ." Something in my face makes him pause. "What is it?"

I open my mouth, close it, not sure what to say. *It* is the thing I've been forcing myself not to think about. *It* is the fact that I dread seeing Alodia again.

"Elisa?"

"I'm nervous!" I blurt. "I know it's stupid. The world is burning down around us. I have to defeat the most powerful sorcerers in the world, only to dash back home and stop a civil war. Why do I even care about *her*? Why is it so important?" I avoid his gaze, embarrassed. "Hector, I'm afraid you're marrying an idiot."

He chuckles, and I snap my head up to glare at him, only to find his face full of empathy.

"I'm sure it did not escape your notice while we were aboard

Felix's ship," he says, "but I admire my older brother greatly." He leans forward, crossing his arms over the pommel of his horse, and peers at me with a self-deprecating grin. "I followed him around like a puppy until Alejandro brought me into his service. A disapproving word from Felix can still cut me to the quick—but don't you dare tell him I said so."

I gaze off toward the city, as the rightness of his words stick in my gut. I do want Alodia's approval. Hers and Papá's. And I'm disgusted with myself for wanting it. It still bothers me that they married me to a stranger and shipped me off. That they purposely kept me ignorant of essential knowledge pertaining to my Godstone. And when I finally became a queen in my own right, they didn't even bother to attend my coronation.

"Alodia always wanted me to be better," I say softly. "Different. And I spent most of my childhood actively not meeting her expectations."

"I was there during the marriage negotiations between your father and Alejandro. Trust me, she cares for you very much."

I'm not sure what to say to that.

"Alodia assured us you were destined for great things," he adds. "She even quoted the prophecy, 'And God raised up for himself a champion . . .' Why are you shaking your head?"

"I don't think I've fulfilled that prophecy. Not yet. Maybe not ever."

He's about to say something else, but Belén returns, weaving through traffic toward us. "Jacián himself is at the southeast tower," he says breathlessly.

"What did they say? Have the animagi started attacking the city yet? Is my sister here?"

Belén is shaking his head. "I'm a traitor here, remember? That's why Cosmé washed her hands of me and sent me to you. They would kill me on sight. We must take *you* before them."

He can't mask the pain in his voice. How hard must it be for him to return here? To see old friends and family, even an old lover, knowing they despise him for living when he should have died a traitor's death?

Mara's face is stony. She sits stiff and tall on her gray gelding, as if prepared for battle. I expect she won't relax until Belén and Cosmé meet again and she can gauge for herself how things are between them.

"Let's go." And we ride forward, faces set with determination, all of us for different reasons.

The guard tower would hardly be called a tower by Brisadulce's standards. It's only three floors high, with a small eagle's nest at its apex, where a crossbowman stands at the ready. We dismount from our horses and hand the reins to Mara. The rest of us stride right through the door and into a busy armory.

More than a dozen soldiers sit sharpening blades, mending tack, polishing armor. They launch to their feet and surround us with swords in the space of a breath.

We put up our weaponless hands to show we mean no harm. "I require audience with Captain Jacián," I say. "I am Queen Elisa of Joya d'Arena."

They stare in astonishment, weapons half lowered. A few drop to their knees and bow their heads. But one points to Storm and says, "An Invierno!"

"My royal ambassador," I say loud and clear. "And under my protection."

"Is Jacián here?" Belén calls out.

"Fetch the captain," someone calls out, even as whispers of "traitor" and "spy" echo around us. The weight of daggers in my belt begins to feel conspicuous. How fast could I draw them?

An explosion booms, too close, and all the weapons rattle in their racks. The guards shift uneasily, torn between keeping an eye on us and rushing to their stations.

"Trebuchet," Hector says. "I recognize the recoil. One of the guard towers nearby took a shot at the Deciregi."

"They're closing in," I say.

The guards part to make way for someone, and suddenly he's here. Jacián. Sharp featured and dark, with a deep glower that I once found menacing. He elbows his men out of the way and barrels toward me.

"Elisa." He wraps me in a great hug, then he pushes me back to get a better look. "When word reached me that Eduardo is amassing an army in Brisadulce, I worried he had gotten to you."

"It's good to see you, Jacián."

He steps back, collects himself. His eyes darken when he sees Belén, but he lifts his chin in greeting. My heart hurts for them. They used to be best friends.

He hollers instructions at his men, then gestures us forward. "Cosmé is eager to see you."

Jacián escorts us from the guard tower. We collect our horses and quickly follow him through the crooked streets of Basajuan.

This is the second time I've come to this place to stop the Inviernos, and the palace is just as I remember it—small but fine, made of limestone in pastel hues. Tiles trim the windows, painted with the blue four-petaled flower design that gave me the key to unlocking the Godstone's power the very first time I used it.

As we ride under the portcullis, I crane my neck looking to see which banners fly, hoping—possibly dreading—to see the sunburst crest of my native country. And there it is snapping proudly in the breeze, displayed just a little lower than Cosmé's recently adopted crest of a hawk in flight.

Jacián takes us through a barracks of tiny rooms all lined up in a row, through the guards' dining hall, and into the palace. We move fast, almost at a jog, around two corners, up a half flight of stairs.

And suddenly we're there. The door to the audience hall.

32

THE last time I was here, I was placed under house arrest, and the first boy I ever loved was brutally murdered.

A herald stands at the closed door. He starts to inquire how to announce us, but Jacián pushes past him and flings the doors open himself.

Inside is chaos. Pages sprint in and out of the side entrances, no doubt carrying messages to and from the guard towers. Cosmé's personal guards line the walls. A large handful of people—soldiers, attendants, a few nobles—argue loudly over a table strewn with parchment.

I sort through the crowd looking for someone I know, my heart pattering with both anticipation and dread. I find Cosmé first, and when our eyes meet, she elbows people out of the way and dashes toward me, her short curls bouncing wildly.

When at arm's length, she pulls up short. Her mouth works to say something, but nothing comes out. Finally she whispers, "Elisa . . . I'm under attack."

It's the closest she'll ever get to telling me she's terrified. "It looks bad out there," I say gently.

She nods, swallowing hard. "It's so different from . . . from . . ."

"Leading a desert rebellion?"

She raises an eyebrow at me, and just like that, the old Cosmé is back. "We've been through worse, right?"

"Sure we have."

"Liar." She grabs my hands and squeezes. Then she looks me up and down, frowning. "You're disgusting."

"I dressed to commemorate the time you dragged me through the desert."

She snorts, then quickly surveys my companions. Her eyes flicker when she sees Belén, but she says, "Reunions and introductions later. Right now we . . ." Her gaze catches on Storm. She strides over and sticks her nose in his face. "You, I would kill on sight if you weren't in the company of—"

"Queen Cosmé!" I say quickly. "Allow me to introduce He Who Wafts Gently with the Wind Becomes as Mighty as the Thunderstorm. You may call him Ambassador Storm, or Lo Chato. He is a friend and ally, and under my protection."

In a cold voice, she says, "Very well. You are most welcome here, Ambassador Storm." Then she yanks me toward the table. "We have work to do. And there's someone here who wants to see you."

I beckon for my companions to follow, wanting to sense their presence nearby, and I allow myself to be led toward the table. The people surrounding it part to make way.

Alodia stands as tall and stiff as a flagpole, her hands clasped before her. She is as beautiful as always, with golden skin that nearly shimmers and lush black hair pulled back into a loose knot that brings out the perfect lines of cheek and jaw. My sister has always been a study in contrasts, with petite, feminine features that bely her strength of carriage. No one looking at her would think her frail.

She seems older—so much older than the mere year and a half we've been apart should warrant. Her eyes are weary, her lips pressed firm, and she is as cold and unreadable to me as always. A statue of frozen, impenetrable perfection. My hearts sinks. My sister and I might be strangers to each other forever.

But suddenly, I don't care about any of that. My legs run toward her of their own accord, and my arms stretch wide, because no matter what, I am *so glad* to see her. I barely register the moisture brimming in her eyes before our arms are wrapped around each other. She clings fiercely, and I breathe in her familiar jasmine perfume as she whispers into my hair, "Elisa. My sister."

Someone coughs politely, and we disengage. Alodia swipes at her cheek, dons her usual veil of composure, and says, "We have much to discuss."

"Where do we stand?" I say. "What is our plan?"

Cosmé gestures toward the table. She pushes aside several inventory lists to reveal a large map of the city. "The Inviernos circled Brisadulce yesterday, burning out crops and minor holdings. They stopped here"—she jabs the map with a forefinger—"where our fortifications are the weakest. They're staying just out of range of the trebuchets. They haven't begun their major assault yet, and I'm not sure what they're waiting for."

"They need to get their strength back," I mutter as I size up the city's layout. Now that I've destroyed—no, killed—their power source, the *zafira* comes more slowly to them, as it does to me. "How many?"

"Only sixty or so," Alodia says. "But almost every one appears to be an animagus."

"They're keeping a tight formation," says one of Cosmé's advisers, a man I don't recognize. "We've held off attacking, hoping to lure them near enough to do close-quarters damage."

"We hope—believe—the range of our archers to be greater than that of their firebolts," Cosmé adds.

Alodia points to the back wall of the palace. "We have an egress planned through here, just in case," she says. "This alley leads to a secret door in the city wall. We will flee into the hills if necessary."

Cosmé glares at my sister. "I won't give up my city easily."

"Of course not."

An explosion rattles the audience hall, and Cosmé clutches the table.

"Not yet within the wall," Jacián says.

Cosmé gives him a grateful nod, but she gestures to a young page and says, "Find out exactly what that was and where it came from." The page dashes off.

"Your Majesty," someone yells, "we must close the city gates now!"

"Do it," Cosmé says.

"Does anyone know if our mounts are ready yet?" Alodia calls across the room.

Cosmé whirls on her. "Why are you so eager to give up?"

Alodia blinks. "I'm just being cautious. The Inviernos could dispose of all three of us in one blow if we are not quick to flee when the time comes."

"Is that what you'd think if the Inviernos were attacking *your* capital?"

I need to take charge before the situation disintegrates. I catch Hector's eye, and he gives me an encouraging nod.

I take a deep breath. "Cosmé, Alodia," I interrupt, and everyone turns to look at me. "We can't flee. We must stop the Deciregi right now."

"Who?" says Cosmé.

"These animagi are not the usual kind. Eight of them are Invierne's ruling council of priest kings. The most powerful sorcerers in the world."

Cosmé's eyes burn with fierceness. "Deci-something or not, they're close together in a phalanx formation—an easy target. When they get too near the guard towers, my archers will take them out."

I'm shaking my head even before she's done. "You under-estimate them."

Her face darkens. "I've faced the animagi in bat-tle the same as you," she says. "I know full well—

heartbreakingly well—what they're capable of."

I glance at Alodia for support, but my sister just shrugs. "Unless you have a better plan," she says, "I need to get back to strategizing our retreat. Feel free to contribute at any time."

Something snaps inside me. My fists clench at my sides. "I *do* have a better idea."

"Oh?" says Cosmé.

I ignore her. "Storm, this phalanx formation. Is it because of a barrier?"

The Invierno nods. "One of them creates the barrier, allowing the others to attack at will. It also prevents backlash from their own fire, if they're heading into the wind."

"Which means Her Majesty's archers will be completely ineffective."

"Exactly so."

Cosmé and Alodia glance at each other in alarm. The advisers mutter among themselves. I catch the words "trebuchet" and "crossbow"—as if these more powerful weapons stand a chance against magic.

Very loudly, very clearly, I ask Storm, "Could *I* get through the barrier, do you think?"

He nods. "Undoubtedly." He looks around, recognizes that we perform for an audience, and says with a dramatic flair, "You are the *only* person in the world who could."

I promise myself I'll thank him later.

"What do you have in mind?" says Alodia. "Do you think you could walk right up and tap them on the shoulder?"

"Something like that."

Another explosion makes everyone jump. Someone's knee jerks the table; parchment slides off and scatters all over the floor. In the distance, faintly, comes the sound of screaming.

"That was a trebuchet," I tell them. "Such a clumsy, inaccurate weapon. The sorcerers are closing in."

Cosmé rubs at her temples. I hope she's having doubts about her strategy.

"Elisa, just tell us," my sister says, and her tone is so exasperated, so familiar, that I almost smile.

"I'm going to go talk to them," I say. "I'll convince them to turn around and go home."

Lord Zito, Alodia's personal steward, steps toward my voice. A scarf covers his empty eye sockets. "No one has been able to reason with them for generations."

"I'll show them that their magic can't stand against that of my living Godstone. Then I'll convince them that we are united, that even without magic, their armies are no match for all three of our countries working together. And finally I'll offer something they want very badly in exchange for peace."

Cosmé starts to protest, but Alodia says, "Elisa, tell me truly. Have you attained that kind of power? The kind that would frighten an animagus?"

"I have."

Her eyes widen and her lips part. She says to Storm, "You always speak truly, yes?"

"Yes, Your Highness."

"You are also an animagus, are you not?"

"I am."

"And you believe my sister has the kind of power she claims?"

"No," he says. "She is being modest."

Storm is overstating things. Walking up to the Deciregi while under fire could easily get me killed.

But a smile spreads across Alodia's face.

Storm opens his mouth to say something else, but nothing comes out. He seems caught in the mesmerizing beam of my sister's smile. I've seen it happen a dozen times before. My sister's beauty is one of the most powerful weapons in her arsenal, and she always uses it to good effect. I'm a bit surprised, though, that Storm is susceptible. For some reason, I thought him above such things.

"Even if we agree that you should risk yourself," Cosmé says, "which we do not, we would need to give them proof of our unity. There's no way we could come up with a proper accord so quickly. Maybe an abbreviated agreement, to be filled in later? No more than a page long. We could . . ."

I sigh as she drones on. This is why I called us together, after all. As we reach a unique crux in history, when three queens regnant rule the larger part of the world, I wanted us to be in accord. I wanted to bring a treaty back to Joya d'Arena to wave around and say, "See? These monarchs have made an agreement with *me*, your true queen." Such an accord would make it very difficult for anyone challenging my rule to gain leverage.

But we don't have time. The ground shakes, and Alodia clutches her steward's shoulder. A soldier bursts through the door. Breathlessly, he exclaims, "They're in the city. The castle watch is flinging quarry stone at them, but they keep coming. We have not been able to injure even one. They're burning people. . . ."

It's time to make my last play.

"I'll save this city," I say. "And I'll either destroy the Deciregi or send them home." I let my gaze sweep the room, trying to appear composed and regal. No, *imperial*. "But I will do it only if Basajuan and Orovalle swear fealty to Joya d'Arena."

Someone gasps. Cosmé and Alodia gape at me. And suddenly I am facing down a roomful of rage.

One of Cosmé's guards puts a hand to his scabbard. My companions shift around me so that within the space of a breath, I have Hector and Storm to my left and right, with Mara, Belén, and Red at my back.

"I admit, I never guessed you were so ambitious," Alodia says. She bites it off like she would an insult, and I am very careful not to wince.

Of course she would misunderstand me. I've never had ambition to rule the world. Even now, knowing it's my best possible course, the title "empress" tastes like dirt in my mouth.

Cosmé says, "You would hold my own country hostage over me?"

I smile sadly at her. "You know me well enough by now, don't you, Cosmé? You know I would do anything, *anything*, to save us all?"

Another explosion rocks the castle, even more powerful than before. The windowpanes rattle. "That was not a trebuchet,"

Hector says. "That was a Deciregus."

"So what's it to be?" I say. "Your archers have failed. Do I go out there with your written oaths in hand? Or do I go home to defend my own kingdom?"

"This is outrageous!" says one of Cosmé's advisers. "The audacity, the *arrogance* it must take to—"

Cosmé holds up a hand to silence him. "I want full ruling autonomy," she says softly.

I'm careful to keep my surge of triumph from showing on my face. "I make no promises. I require total fealty so I can make very fast decisions in the coming months. I can say that I'll try not to interfere. I've no interest in meddling in daily affairs."

Cosmé plunks into the nearest chair and lets her face fall into her hands. "Everything I've fought for. Everything I've accomplished. All for nothing."

"No," I protest. "Basajuan is still yours. You'll still be its queen. I swear it."

Alodia is stiff in the space beside us, her arms crossed. "I assume Joya would require an annual tithe?" she says.

I nod. "In return, I'll station garrisons along your border at my own expense. I'm willing to reduce the first year's take to five percent, if paid in sheep's hides." There. That ought to mollify the tanners' guild, which has been suffering the shortage ever since Basajuan seceded.

My sister turns her back to me. Such a familiar gesture. A year or so ago, I would have thought myself the object of her contempt, not worthy to be faced. But I see the truth of it now.

She hates looking vulnerable in front of anyone, but especially in front of me.

"They will take Basajuan," I say softly to her back. "They will do it today. Then they will use Basajuan as a base to launch an army at Orovalle. They'll come for me last, when they are strong again. I can't hold off a whole army. I'm only one person, and I can't defend every approach at once. Swear fealty to me, Alodia. This is my one chance, my only chance, to protect us all at the same time. And Invierne will know forever after that attacking any one of us will result in severe retaliation."

"I want an addendum," Cosmé says. "Separate from the document you show the Inviernos, stating that our fealty is contingent upon you being able to keep your word."

Alodia turns back around. Her face is blanched, her eyes dull with weariness. "Yes," she says. "An addendum. Elisa, if you can drive the Inviernos away and ensure peace, you can have your empire."

I almost wilt with relief. I gesture toward the man still feverishly scribbling at the table. "Mr. Secretary," I say. "Write this down."

I dictate a short missive, proclaiming myself empress of the Joyan Empire, vowing to serve and protect our treasured kingdoms of Joya d'Arena, Orovalle, and Basajuan. Then Cosmé and Alodia each dictate a paragraph swearing utter fealty. We sign, seal, and stamp it. The secretary hurriedly scribes two copies, and we sign, seal, and stamp those too.

Cosmé dictates the addendum, declaring my proclamation

null and void should I fail to rid our three nations of the Invierno threat.

It all happens so fast, without trumpets or fanfare; the only thing that accompanies my rise to the highest possible station in the world is a general deflating of spirits.

The secretary shakes sand from one of the copies and blows on the remaining ink. I snap my fingers at him s the earth quakes again. "No time. Give it to me."

He does, and I'm careful not to smear it, holding it out from my body. Alodia's signature catches my eye. She has written "queen" beside her name and stamped the wax not with the seal of the crown princess, but with Papá's own signet ring. Something unpleasant twists in my chest.

For years now, she has had authority to act in his stead, with all the rights and privileges due a fully empowered monarch. I thought it was because Papá favored her so much. Because she was being groomed to reign.

The parchment in my hand trembles. "Papá . . ." I say. "He's . . . he's gone, isn't he?"

A muscle in her cheek twitches. "Last month," she says. "I postponed my official coronation to come here." Her voice is colorless; she might as well be reading a storeroom inventory list.

"He's been sick a long time, hasn't he?" It all makes sense now. How thin he became. Alodia's growing responsibilities. The fact that he declined to attend my coronation.

"He lived longer than we expected." Finally, there is a softening of her features, as her lips part and she casts her eyes downward. "He worked hard—right up until the point when he could no longer hold a quill in his hand."

I want to rage at her. I want to throw a colossal fit, kicking and screaming and pummeling her with my fists. *Why, why, why did you not tell me, Alodia?*

But I already know the answer. They did not tell me *anything.* They didn't tell me why they married me off to King Alejandro. Or that my nurse, Ximena, was a specially ordained guardian, trained to fight and kill. They worked especially hard to keep me ignorant of all matters pertaining to the Godstone. I had to figure everything out for myself. And though they've excused themselves by citing faith or love or "what's best for you, Elisa," I know differently.

They didn't tell me any of these things because they didn't think I could handle the truth.

I'd like to rage at Papá too. But I can't. Now that I know I'll never see him again, I can acknowledge the hope I've harbored, the silly thought that maybe, after defeating the Invierne army and releasing the power of my Godstone, after stopping a civil war and learning to rule in my own right, we'd meet again and he would say, "I'm proud of you, Elisa. Well done." Then he would hug me and tell everyone, "My daughter Elisa is better than two sons!" And I would know that I was just as dear to him as Alodia.

Such silly hopes. Now, even if I save the world, he'll never know.

"Elisa?" My sister starts toward me, one hand half raised.

I turn my back on her. "Storm, Hector, with me. And

Cosmé—I'll need you to order the gates opened. The rest of you stay here." We're halfway to the door when an unbidden prayer for safety and luck springs to my lips, but I tamp it down. The Deciregi may not know that I'm here yet. It should be an interesting surprise.

When I'm in the doorway, I turn around and say to my roomful of new vassals: "Pray for me."

33

HECTOR knows the palace well, for he held it under martial law for several days while we deposed Cosmé's father, Conde Treviño. He rushes us through the corridors, never hesitating, and I follow without question.

We burst into sunshine. The courtyard teems with soldiers carrying buckets of water and quivers of arrows to the wall. There's an order to the chaos, with organized lines and officers stationed at regular intervals barking orders to their men.

The portcullis is lowered, and behind it, the huge wooden double doors are shut and barred. They rattle every few moments with another impact. Smoke curls through the crease.

"Now, Cosmé," I say.

"Oh, God, Elisa, are you sure?"

"I'm sure." *I'm sure I'm going to try.*

She takes a deep breath and yells, "Raise the portcullis and open the gate!"

"Storm, Hector, stay near so I can keep the barrier over us all." They close in at my shoulders. I plant my feet, reach with my awareness into the depths of the earth.

Hector bends and presses a kiss to my temple. He wastes precious moments holding his lips there, and then says, "For just in case."

Cosmé repeats her command, because no one can believe she would want to do such a thing, but she does, and they do, and the doors open wide to reveal a smoke-hazed landscape of rubble and charred buildings.

The Deciregi face me, all eight of them in a phalanx formation. I allow myself a small surge of satisfaction at the surprise on their perfect faces. Arrayed behind them are dozens of lesser animagi. All are surrounded by robed, barefooted acolytes. Other acolytes lie crumpled on the ground, wide-eyed but sightless, blood pooling beneath their slit throats. Willing sacrifices.

I draw more of the *zafira* into me, and it comes eagerly, almost as if I'm near a power source. The lead Deciregus raises his glowing staff and flings a bolt in my direction. I whip up my barrier to counter, and the bolt shatters against it.

I draw even more power inside me, until my limbs tingle and the power is like a thousand flies buzzing beneath my skin, yearning to burst free.

"Walk forward with me," I whisper to Storm and Hector. "When I say 'now,' we attack hard and fast. Storm, take the man on the right, Hector the left. Try for a killing blow, but don't linger. Get back into position immediately, and I'll spring the barrier back up."

Together, we step outside the gate. The Deciregi level their combined power at us, and bolt after bolt ricochets off my barrier. I feel each blow in my bones, as if I'm parrying with my daggers, but I grit my teeth and push us forward.

The lead Deciregus thrusts his staff to the side and reaches for an acolyte—a young Invierno man no older than me, with knobby feet. The young man kneels, his eyes glazed with either fear or mania, and the Deciregus grabs his hair, yanks his head back, and slashes across his throat with a dagger, and oh, God, it's such a familiar, awful sight that bile rises in my throat and my barrier wavers.

The young man twitches as blood gushes from the wound. It seeps down his front to the ground where it puddles—and then the earth begins to absorb it.

The power inside me flares, and suddenly I understand. Their blood sacrifices don't power their Godstones. But somehow they keep the *zafira* renewed, prevent the animagi from tiring too quickly. This is why they only needed a brief rest after razing the fields, how they were able to pound bolt after bolt against my walls during the Battle of Brisadulce.

I ground myself against whatever comes next. The Deciregus smiles slightly as he retrieves his staff, raises it high. Blue-white fire curls into a ball at the tip; the air around it shimmers. He shouts something, and the ball streaks forward, too quickly to track.

The impact is like a thunderclap. My barrier crackles and sparks, but then the fire dissipates and we are left shaken but standing.

The other Deciregi shift uncomfortably in their formation.

"Hold your ground!" their leader yells in the Lengua Classica.

"Keep moving," I say to Hector and Storm. More bolts smash against my shield, and my head begins to pound, but pain is nothing, their bolts are nothing. They have no idea what is coming at them. I have bolstered an entire mountain.

I draw my dagger, let the *zafira*'s strength seep into it. I sense Storm edging back from my burning blade. Almost there. Just a little more power and then . . .

I lower the barrier, sweep my dagger around, and sling-shot a bolt so hot it blazes white. Their shield collapses like shards of glass that evaporate into steam just before hitting the ground. The Deciregus behind the leader staggers to her knees.

The rest are stunned. A split second is all I need. "Now!" I yell.

I leap forward, slashing with my blazing dagger, and flay the Deciregus's throat open. His skin sizzles, and blood pumps out, pours onto the ground. He stares at me, his oily black eyes unreadable, and he tries to speak but can't.

The earth loves his blood, slurps it up like it's spring rain in the cracked desert. I reach for the *zafira*, and it's as though his blood becomes my blood, and power darts like lightning through my veins.

I take the barest moment to assure myself that Storm and Hector have hit their targets. "Back!" I yell, and I slam the barrier into place as a barrage of firebolts rains down around us.

Two Deciregi are slain, toppled across the bodies of their

willing sacrifices. Another bends over, clutching his abdomen, which steams and reeks of liquefied skin.

"I should have hit harder," Storm says in a disgusted voice. "I didn't know how much the blood would renew me."

The remaining Deciregi are backing away. One turns to flee.

"Wait!" I yell, and I thrust out with my barrier and surround them. Instinctively, I draw it tight, tight, tighter, until they are completely frozen. *So that's how they do it.* "I would speak with you."

I give them a moment to fully comprehend their situation before saying, "I will not require your surrender. I intend to let you go. In return, I ask only for a peaceful audience."

Gradually, ready to snap it back in place at the slightest provocation, I loosen my barrier. They glance around at one another, wide-eyed and breathless.

Finally a woman steps forward. She is the only woman among them, and she looks almost exactly like Hawk, with her kohl-black eyes and shimmering white hair. Unlike Hawk, tiny lines spread from her eyes and the edges of her mouth, and though the rest of her skin is stretched as taught as a girl's, I have a feeling she's as old as the stars.

"We trapped you," she spits. "You were captive in the bearer's pit."

"Yes. I was."

When no explanation is forthcoming, she says, "There will be no audience. Kill us now. Without a power source, we're dead anyway."

I shrug. "Eventually. You'll sicken and die over many generations. But it's not necessary. You see, I can take you to the gate that leads to life."

Her eyes widen. "All you Joyans—"

"Are filthy liars, yes, yes." I wave a hand dismissively. "Please, put aside a few thousand years of mindless hatred toward me and my people and *think* for just a moment. How else did I acquire so much power? Why does the *zafira* come to me so easily? Why am I the only bearer in your history to escape from your pit?"

She hesitates.

"You saw the Eyes of God explode, did you not? You know what I'm capable of."

She reaches up to clutch the amulet hanging from her neck. "You've been there," she accuses. "You've tasted the *zafira* directly. There is no other explanation for such power."

"And I'm willing to show it to you."

Her eyes narrow. "Why? Why would you do this?"

"Because I am your champion."

Her eyes flicker, and someone behind her gasps. I hand her the parchment, hoping I haven't smeared it. "I am a bearer and a quee—"

"Empress," Hector whispers in my ear.

Oh, God. I start over. "I am a bearer and . . . an empress. Twice chosen by God." I hate that I'm parroting the zealous words Ximena once spoke to me, but Inviernos respect egregious demonstrations of arrogance. "As you can see from that document, three nations are now united under my rule—against you. Your armies cannot withstand the combined might of the Joyan Empire. And your magic cannot stand against mine. So I suggest you reconsider your willingness to hold audience."

She cocks her head at me, like a cat eyeing potential prey. "I must consult with the other Deciregi."

"Please." I wave her off, and she turns to the others. They huddle like hens, whispering.

Hector bends his head and whispers, "Are you all right?"

"I'm fine."

"But that barrier . . . and your father . . ."

"I said I'm fine," I snap. Sympathy is the last thing I need right now, and I don't dare look at his face. If I read the understanding there, the love, I'm likely to fall apart. But I reach back for his hand and give it a squeeze. "I'm sorry," I say. "Thank you."

The Deciregus turns back around. The others take up formation behind her, only six of them now, and one badly injured. A breeze kicks up, whipping their cloaks around their legs and flinging ash into our faces. "We agree to hold audience," she says, and anger practically drips from her voice. "But I assume this means placing us under house arrest while we have discussions? In that case, only two will stay. We cannot risk losing more of us. The others will return to Invierne."

"Agreed." I was going to suggest it anyway. Two will be much easier for us to keep an eye on.

Without another word, one of the Deciregi steps forward.

He is short for an Invierno, not even Hector's height, and his snow-white hair is tied back in a single braid that reaches almost to his knees. The others peel off and begin walking away. There are no farewells, not even a glance backward.

"Come," I say. "I'll introduce you to the queens of Basajuan and Orovalle."

We sit at the table in the audience hall. Everyone is straight-backed in their chairs, eyes hard and angry, voices sharp. No one wants the Inviernos within the palace walls, but I personally vouch for their good behavior. Alodia demands that the sorcerers be placed in the prison tower under heavy guard, but I refuse. Cosmé demands reparations for the destruction wrought by Inviernos to Basajuan and its surrounding villages. "Years of destruction," she says. "Centuries." But I refuse her too.

For my plan to work, enemies must treat one another as neighbors. And it has to start somewhere.

Beneath the table, Hector sneaks his hand over and grasps mine. I twine my fingers with his.

Our discussion is not going anywhere today. We are too fresh from battle, too exhausted, too frightened. We need time to cool off. To rest. And dear God, I need time to bathe.

I release Hector's hand and rise to my feet. "Let's convene an official parliament tomorrow," I say. "Cosmé, would you mind offering us hospitality for the night?"

"We prepared a whole wing for you when we got your letter, thinking you'd come in state." Her smile is too bright for the circumstances. "There's so much room, we'll just send the Inviernos along with you."

"Of course."

"And guards. Lot of guards. For your own protection in these trying times."

I sigh.

34

THERE are enough rooms for us each to have our own, and at my request, the mayordomo orders baths for everyone. Red is delighted to have a room and bath service of her own, just like a real lady, she says.

The mayordomo ushers us down the hallway. We peel off one by one—first the Inviernos, then Belén, then Red.

Mara sidles up to me. "Are you sure you don't need me tonight?" she whispers.

"Go with Belén," I whisper back.

Her answering grin is shy but wide. She wraps me in a quick hug. "See you in the morning," she says, and then she dashes back down the hall.

"Here we are, Your Majesty," says the mayordomo, indicating a door. "There are fresh linens and hot bathwater inside. Pull the blue cord by the bed if you need anything." He opens the door to a small but lovely suite decorated in ivory and royal blue. "Her Majesty said to put the Lord-Commander in the room next to yours, that you might require his counsel as you prepare for tomorrow's parliament. A door adjoins your suites."

"Oh," I manage, glancing up at Hector's suddenly rigid face. "Thank you." Cosmé misses nothing.

I turn to say good-night to Hector, but as we stare at each other, speech leaves me. Everything that comes to mind seems so formal, so cold, when all I want to do is wrap my arms around his neck and hold him close, tell him how much I appreciate his steady presence, his enduring encouragement, his sure-burning intelligence. Maybe I should just invite him inside, but with everything that has happened today, I'm not sure it's the right time.

The mayordomo clears his throat. We've stood here too long. Hector's gaze on me is open and patient, as though he's waiting for something. I don't know what else to do, so I stretch up on my tiptoes and give him a light kiss on the cheek. "Good night, Hector," I say, and I step inside my room.

The door doesn't slam shut behind me, but I *feel* like it does, the bang too loud and too echoing, leaving me too alone. I should think about tomorrow's parliament and prepare my arguments. I should go over everything I observed today and build my strategy around it.

But all I can do is stare helplessly at the other door to my right, the one that joins Hector's suite to mine, thinking about the slight prick of stubble against my lips when I kissed him, the scents of oiled armor and shaving soap that always tickle my nose whenever he is near.

"When we reach Basajuan," he said, *"maybe I can get you to myself for a while."*

I should knock on the door. This is it. As good a time as any. We might not have another opportunity to be alone for weeks. I raise my fist.

I let my hand drop. Maybe he needs some time to himself. He's probably as exhausted as I am. Maybe he wants to bathe. Or sleep.

Maybe he's changed his mind.

I've just endured another battle. I killed again. I saw friends and family today I haven't seen in more than a year. I learned that my father has died. It's ridiculous that all I can think about is whether or not Hector wants me as much as I want him.

I whirl away from the door, recognizing my own foolishness, my own weakness.

The scent of jasmine draws me toward the tiled bathing area. It's much smaller than my bathing atrium at home, and the tub is a round wooden creature with iron joints that are worn from so many rustings and polishings. But it brims with steaming water and floating rose petals. Two plush towels lie folded beside it, and hanging on a peg nearby is a lovely white dressing gown trimmed in lace.

I will bathe first, I decide, and then I will screw up my courage to knock on the door.

I shuck my boots, pants, and blouse, and step inside. The water is glorious—fragrant and soothing hot. I sink neck deep and scrub days of travel from my skin, from under my fingernails, from my calloused feet. I admire the shape of my legs. Days on the trail have rounded my calves, brought tautness to my thighs. I'll never be elegant and willowy like Cosmé or Alodia, but I'm healthy and strong. I'm glad for what I've become.

I lather my hair and scrub my scalp, then duck underwater to remove the excess soap. Water sluices off me as I get to my feet. I douse myself with the rinse bucket, then towel down. The cotton weave of my dressing gown is so fine that it feels lovely against my skin. Like silk. Like a lover's touch. Or so I imagine.

I sit on the edge of the bed and start working a comb through my hair. My hair is always horribly tangled after a bath. The trick is to get it combed out before it dries enough for the waves to set in, which make combing even more difficult.

Even after my hair is tangle free, I continue combing. Finally I fold my dirty clothes into a neat pile so I can either have them laundered or stashed in my pack in a hurry.

I look around for something else to do. Then I plunk back onto the bed, my face falling into my hands. I'm wasting time with my barely acknowledged hope that Hector will be the one to knock.

Yes, our love is a mutual thing, a thing between equals, but we can't escape the fact that I am his queen. It is up to me whether or not we see each other this night. I must decide.

I walk to the door. I take a deep breath. I knock.

It swings open so fast I recoil a few steps.

Hector's hair is damp and curling from a recent bath. He wears a fresh pair of pants and a white gentleman's blouse, untucked. His feet are bare.

Neither of us moves.

"Good evening," I say, then curse myself for stupidity.

But he answers in kind. "Good evening." He runs a hand through his hair and says, "I wasn't sure . . . that is, I thought with the battle today, and learning about your father, and—"

I blurt, "Are you going to come inside or not?"

His face breaks into a wide grin, and he steps inside, shuts the door behind him, and pulls me into his arms.

We fit together so beautifully, and without my bodice, without his armor, I can *feel* him at last, and I am dizzy with it.

"I'm a little nervous," he admits.

"Me too," I whisper. "We'll probably be awkward and ridiculous."

He reaches for the ties of my nightgown, and I marvel how the slightest touch of his fingertips on my neck can make me shiver so. "Probably. But you and I"—he brushes the collar of the gown aside—"are students of knowledge. We believe in careful practice to attain perfection."

"Yes, practice," I breathe as he leans down to kiss the collarbone he just bared. "I am a very good student," I manage.

He slips my dressing gown off the other shoulder. It drops to the ground, and I am naked before him.

"I never peeked, you know," he says. "I always turned my back."

"I know."

But he's looking now, and looking thoroughly, as I tell my worries and my nervousness to go bury themselves in a snowdrift. His gaze roves the entire length of my body, and it's almost a palpable thing, this caressing with the eyes. I grab his hands and back toward the bed, my skin flushed everywhere, with desire, with fear, maybe a little shame at being so exposed. But the urge to cover myself drains away when he says breathlessly, "You are even more beautiful than I imagined."

I lie back, and he bends over—toward the Godstone. He studies it carefully. Then he lowers his head as if to kiss it, and my heart breaks a little. Because even though everything in my life is about the Godstone, always the Godstone, I want this to be a magical exception. I want this to be just about me. Heartsick, I lift my hands to push his head away.

But his lips brush my skin, and I gasp. I've misread him.

It's not the Godstone that had captured his attention; he doesn't even seem to know it's there. Instead, he's kissing the scar I received from an assassin's dagger, all along its near-deadly length. Tears prick at my eyes.

"This," he says, "won't happen again." He straightens to pull off his shirt and toss it aside. I swallow hard. He is strong and dark and so beautiful my chest aches.

"Don't make promises you can't keep."

"I'll keep this one."

"Well," I say, unable to tear my gaze away from him. "If a scar makes you kiss me like that, I might hire some mercenaries to give me a few more."

"No need to go to such lengths," he says with a half smile. He puts a hand to either side of my head, then he dips to kiss me hard. I wrap my arms around him and pull him tight against me, not wanting even a whisper of air between us.

Hector sighs into my neck. He says, "I love you, Elisa."

We *are* awkward and ridiculous, with knees and elbows and bedsheets in all the wrong places, and even some laughter. But after a while, the awkwardness is subsumed with warmth and light and the tenderest moments I've ever known. It's not perfection yet, but it's perfect.

35

IT is not quite morning. The air is cool but not cold, for winter is gentler here in Basajuan. The open windows of my suite face eastward. A breeze flirts with the wispy ivory curtains, flashing views of jagged mountains that are black in relief against the bright edge of dawn.

Strange to think that I just came out of those mountains. They look so huge and foreboding, yet my companions and I conquered them thoroughly.

Hector stirs beside me but does not wake. I don't know how he's managed it, but the top sheet is twisted inextricably around his leg. He has shifted toward the middle, arms flung wide, and I think, *We are going to need a bigger bed.*

I study everything about him, memorizing each detail— the tiny freckle at the crease of one eye, the morning stubble that contrasts so beautifully with his pale lips, the puckered scar running across his lower back. I want to know the stories behind every one of his scars.

I can't help myself; I reach out and gently trace it.

His eyes flutter open. "Good morning," he says sleepily.

In answer, I kiss him hard. His arms snake around me and he pulls me against him. "I guess this means you have no regrets?" he says, and his hands start exploring my body in very interesting ways.

"None. I'm so glad it was you," I say. "And not—and not . . ."

"Alejandro."

"Yes."

He releases me in order to lift a lock of my hair, which he studies intently. "I admit," he says, rubbing the hair between thumb and forefinger, "there were times I wanted to punch him."

"Oh?" Never, ever have I heard him say such a thing. "Why?"

Hector's eyes grow distant. "The way he treated you. He had the greatest prize of all, and he didn't realize it until it was too late." He leans forward and kisses me soundly, then says, "Can't seem to help myself anymore."

I put a forefinger to his lips to forestall yet another kiss, even though I'm smiling. "Wait. Just how long, exactly, have you been in love with me?"

He winces. "It's highly inappropriate."

My eyes widen. "Hector! Tell me!"

He flops onto his back to stare up at the canopy. "Remember the day I found you here in Basajuan?"

That long ago? "Yes. You saved me from Conde Treviño."

He snorts. "Hardly. As I recall, I walked into his office to find that you had pinned him to his desk, holding his own daggers to his throat."

I grab his hand and bring his fingers to my lips. Never in my life have I been so glad to see someone as I was to see Hector that day. "A few reinforcements would have had me dead in moments. If you hadn't walked in when you did . . ."

"Afterward, one of my men said, 'I'm so glad you recognized the princess. I was about to put a sword through her, for raising a blade to a nobleman of the realm.' And I had to ask myself—how *did* I know it was Elisa?"

I don't remember any of Hector's men being there. Just him.

He turns onto his side to face me. "You had changed so much," he murmurs into my hair. "You were wearing the clothes of a desert warrior, holding weapons. *Your back was turned.* But I knew it was you. Instantly. I had memorized everything about you. The way you stood, the way you moved, the sound of your voice, the sheen of your hair. . . ."

I blink against threatening tears. Hector loved me even then. Before I found my own way. Before I did or became anything.

"Your turn," he says. "When did you know?"

"When I healed you. The thought of you dying . . . it was awful."

His smile is as bright as the sun, and I marvel that I have such power over this man, that a mere declaration of love can affect him so.

"Hector, going back to Brisadulce might be the scariest thing we've faced together. I mean, it's civil war there. And a civil war is a particularly awful sort of war, with friends and family fighting against one another, killing one another."

He nods. "I'm sure General Luz-Manuel has control of the

palace and the city. We'll have to lay siege to our own home. But we can't just wade in, flinging magic and swords at everyone. We can't destroy our own city, murder our own people." One of the reasons I love Hector so much is that he is never patronizing. "We will have to be fast, efficient, and perfectly timed to pull it off."

Exactly what I've been thinking. Bludgeoning my way back into power at the expense of my people would do irreparable damage. But my signed treaty with Cosmé and Alodia will create sentiment in my favor. If I'm lucky, all I have to do to diffuse the war is remove a few key individuals.

Until recently, I have always chosen precision over power, stealth over frontal assault. It's a precarious way of doing battle, even though there are times when it's the only option. But in my own home, surrounded by my own people, it will be more dangerous than ever. "If it doesn't work," I say. "If we fail, and we have a chance to get away, would you consider . . . that is, would you be willing to . . . flee? With me?"

He reaches up to tuck my hair behind my ear. "I'm never leaving you again."

I lean over and kiss him deeply. He pulls me close and returns my kiss, rougher this time, demanding, and I love it. I will never have enough of him.

Someone pounds on the door.

Hector swears, and I stifle a giggle.

I grab my dressing robe and move to answer the door, but Hector jumps out of bed and intercepts me, grabbing my forearm. "Let me," he says. He tugs on his pants, pulls my dagger from my pack, and holds it just out of sight as he cracks open the door.

It's Cosmé's mayordomo. Hector lowers the knife.

He is young for the position, with a roundness to cheek and chin and a slender frame that promises further growth. But then almost everyone in Cosmé's court is young. Basajuan lost an entire generation in the last war with Invierne. "Apologies, Your Majesty," he says. "But the Inviernos are up and awake and making demands, and I have no idea what to do with them. Her Majesty Queen Cosmé said you had claimed responsibility."

I grimace, knowing our guests are probably being as arrogant and difficult as possible. "I'll take care of it," I tell him, and he abases himself with such relieved gratitude that it's hard not to smile.

After the door closes I grab Hector's hands. Someday soon—I hope—I will have days and days alone with him. I'll make it an imperial edict, maybe. Threaten beheading if anyone bothers us.

But not today.

"Let's get dressed and go put some self-important Deciregi in their places, shall we?"

After I tell the Deciregi to shut up and eat the "inedible pig slop" the palace kitchen so painstakingly prepared, and assure them that no, their bathwater is not poisoned, and yes, it is a regular practice here for servants to enter quarters unasked to get a fire going in the early morning, we all convene in the audience hall to discuss terms. Everyone is there: all my companions, Alodia and her advisers, Cosmé and her council, the two Deciregi.

I reveal that the *zafira* lies beneath a mountain of rubble. But I confer total mining and exploring rights on Isla Oscura to the nation of Invierne.

The Deciregi fear—and rightly so—that Joya's citizens will not allow them to travel safely. I promise an edict declaring harsh penalties for any kind of harassment.

I have two stipulations: one, that Invierne must agree to an immediate and total cessation of hostilities. Any hostile act will be met with severe reprisal and the rescinding of all mining rights. And two, that Invierne may never purchase or build its own ships. They must pay Joyan or Orovalleño captains for passage and cargo transport. If there is even a hint that they are building a navy, I will blast their ships out of the water with the fire of my Godstone—and rescind all mining rights.

Cosmé continues to demand reparations, and I don't blame her. Her territory has always suffered the brunt of our conflict. I try to talk her down from it, but her black eyes flash at me, with a desperate, grief-stricken rage that reminds me how much she has lost. Parents, friends, a dear brother.

After a while, something sly flits across the Invierno woman's face, and she suddenly capitulates, saying, "We'll do it. In reparation, we'll pay the first two years' tithes to the Joyan Empire on behalf of Basajuan and Orovalle."

Cosmé gasps. Alodia is too composed to react much, but I know her well enough to recognize the interest sparking in her eyes.

There's a catch. I know there is. "With what currency will you pay?" I ask.

"Glass," she says. "We have the finest glassmakers in all the world, and I'd love to introduce your people to it. Also, we had a surplus of maize this harvest. It's going to rot in the bins when the weather warms, so we might as well send it along. We'll throw in a few tapestry samples too."

I can't help my smile of triumph. I don't imagine there's a huge market for glass baubles in my country—at least not until my people have extra coin for luxuries—but if she thinks she's trapping me into opening a trade opportunity for Invierne, then she truly considers peace as a long-term solution.

One of Alodia's advisers, a man I recognize as one who rules a remote territory along her border, bends forward and whispers something in her ear. She nods.

"Conde Paxón is good to remind me," Alodia says to us. She places her elbows on the table and leans forward. "The Inviernos must agree to stop supplying the Perditos with food and weapons. In fact, they must sever the alliance completely."

Cosmé mutters agreement. The Perditos have been harassing the southern border of Orovalle for years, ever since Joya's prisons overflowed and their inmates were dumped into the jungle-choked Hinder Mountains between our countries. Once Invierne began supporting them, they banded together and became very powerful, making trade by land nearly impossible.

"Agreed," the Deciregus says. "They will be as dead to us."

That's a more dramatic statement than we required, but our secretary adds it to the formal accord.

"One last thing," I say. Everyone regards me expectantly as I take a deep breath. This will be the hardest part. It might also be the most important. "The Deciregus of Crooked Sequoia House has agreed to a marriage alliance between a son of his house and a titled person of my choosing, to further cement goodwill between us."

Cosmé's face blanches. "Out of the question!" says one of Cosmé's advisers, a pudgy man with a thick beard that manages to defy the obvious, oily attempt at grooming. "We will not mingle, we will not *breed*, with those animals."

"We already have."

Everyone stares at me.

"Come here, Red," I say gently, and she pads over, her golden eyes regarding me with perfect trust. I stand and drape an arm down across her slight shoulders. "This is Red Sparkle Stone, my handmaiden. She is diligent and loyal, intelligent and warmhearted." I look down to find her beaming as bright as the stone she named herself for. She doesn't realize I've just made her a national symbol. Poor child. I'll have to make it up to her. "Red is one of my most trusted companions. She is also half Invierno."

"A mule!" says the adviser. "Surely you don't propose that one of our esteemed titled persons produce a mule. Of all the insulting—"

"*You* have Invierno blood inside you," I tell him. "We all do."

I might as well have told everyone in the room that camels can fly, for the way they gape at me.

"It's true, isn't it, Storm?" I say.

"Of course. Your ancestors, the First Families as you call them, used their strange machines to mix some of our blood with yours so that they could survive better on this world. And they mixed some of yours with ours, to limit our power and make us easier to control. We believe they intended for our two races to meld and become one."

"But something went wrong."

He nods. "Records in our archive indicate there was a schism. One of the Families disagreed with the others. They sabotaged the machines and fled east with the remaining Inviernos. They taught us the ways of God. They saved us from the others. If your ancestors had completed their work, we would have been able to interbreed easily and produce fertile children. And all Joyans would be like you today—bearing a living Godstone."

Which means some of us might be a little more Invierno than others. Like me, who can bear a living Godstone. Like Alodia, who—if she were a little taller, a little fairer—could be the sister of this foreign woman we are negotiating with.

This is why God could raise me up as a champion for the Inviernos. Because I am one.

"We have struggled along for millennia," Storm adds. "Growing weaker and more desperate, because of what your people did to ours."

"I don't believe it," says the adviser.

But Alodia does, and she grasps the extent of my plan before anyone else, because her eyes turn as feral and angry as a cornered cat's. "Are *you* the sacrificial offering?" she says to Storm in the most scathing tone possible. "The princeling who must wed the enemy?"

Most people flinch away from my sister's crushing condescension, but not Storm. "Yes, Your Majesty," he says calmly. "And a most willing one."

Cosmé is looking back and forth between them. She bursts out laughing. "You want him to marry Alodia!" she says to me. "She deserves it." And at Alodia's withering glare she adds, "Well, you do. You married her off to that spineless imbecile of a king and then didn't bother aiding her when she had to work around him to save the world." One of her advisers whispers in her ear, and Cosmé says, "I can say whatever I want about him. He'd dead."

Alodia has the grace to look ashamed. "Is it true, Elisa? Is this your revenge?"

"No." Now that I have Hector, I'll never deny someone I care about the same opportunity at love. "You don't have to. I won't make you."

She doesn't bother to disguise her puzzlement, and it saddens me that she still doubts me so much, that her default assumption is always that I'm seeking to hurt her—as if we are still children together in the nursery. How long will it take to convince her otherwise? The Inviernos are in a similar position, I suppose. One horrendous act thousands of years ago, and they have assumed ill intent ever since.

Peace is such hard work. Harder than war. It takes way more effort to forgive than to kill.

"It's an opportunity, Alodia," I say. "Storm will be a

Deciregus someday. The equivalent of a king. Surely you want an alliance with such a man?"

"Impossible!" interjects the Invierno woman, and her oily black eyes shimmer. "He is outcast. Anathema. He—"

"His father reinstated him and consented to this union," I say. "And Storm has been claimed by the *zafira*, which means he is probably more powerful than even you."

Alodia is shaking her head. "How can you ask such a thing of me? It would consign the royal line of Orovalle to extinction."

Not extinction. Hector's and my grandchildren would be eligible for her throne. But now might not be the best time to say so. "You could appoint an heir," I say. "You'd have time to prepare. To groom exactly the right person. I understand how difficult it will be for your people to accept, and no, I won't require it of you. I ask only that you consider it. Think of it, Alodia. A God-ordained alliance with a prince of Invierne. No one in history has achieved so much."

She blinks at me. She's a smart woman. She knows how to make the hard decision.

She straightens, clasping her hands in her lap, and then she says, "In that case, Prince Storm, I invite you to visit my palace in Amalur as soon as it is convenient for you. We should . . . see if we can learn to bear each other's company."

"I accept," he says, with a slight lowering of his head. Just enough deference, I note, to show respect without appearing cowed.

We adjourn for the day, agreeing to hammer out the finer details of our accord tomorrow. Cosmé offers to take the

Deciregi on a tour of the palace and its grounds. They decline, because why would they want to do that? Cosmé takes a calming breath and patiently explains that it is a customary honor extended to visiting dignitaries. They exchange glances, shrug, and grudgingly agree. I smile after them as they depart, proud of my friend for trying.

I'm heading out the door with my companions when Alodia pulls me aside. "Elisa . . ." she begins, but declarations have never come easily to her, and she stalls.

"I've missed you," I say.

She pulls me into her arms. "My little sister is all grown up," she says, her voice wavering. "There were times I didn't think it would happen, but you proved me wrong."

It's a barbed compliment at best, but it will do as a start.

"Thank you for coming," I tell her.

"I'm glad I did." She releases me and regards me appraisingly. "Even though you stole my country out from under me. You've become so powerful. So decisive and conniving, so—"

"So much like you."

She grins, her rare true grin that always has a little naughtiness in it. "Papá and Zito both always said we were more alike than we wanted to admit."

"I'll tell no one if you won't."

"Agreed. And Elisa? I'm sorry for not telling you about Papá."

Her apology bursts something inside me, and tears prick at my eyes. I'll have to find a place to be alone, and soon. It's as though Alodia has given me permission to grieve.

"Thank you for saying so," I manage.

"Forgive me for asking," she says. "But I must. Is all this a ploy to put one of your heirs on my throne?"

Of course that detail would not escape her. "You are free to appoint one of my heirs as your own—except Rosario. He is for Joya, and that is not negotiable. Your children, if you have them, are free to do the same. But Orovalle belongs to you, Alodia, and it is your choice."

She regards me thoughtfully, then her gaze shifts to Hector. "Not a *horrible* choice, maybe," she says to both of us.

My face flushes a little. All this talk of children and heirs, when Hector and I have yet to discuss it ourselves.

Alodia and I say good-bye, and we both retire from the audience hall, my sister with her advisers, me with my friends.

Hector walks on my left, Storm on my right, the others behind me. "I hope you'll give her a chance," I tell Storm. "I know she's difficult. But she's brilliant and honorable and—"

"She's magnificent," he says.

I whip my head up to stare at his profile. He wears a loopy smile, as if someone put a little too much duerma leaf in last night's tea.

Moments later, Hector shuts the door of our suite behind us and turns the full force of his gaze on me. "Everything you did today, everything, has been with the intent of obliging our people and theirs to comingle. To become accustomed to each other."

I plop onto the bed. "Yes."

"I admit I had doubts about your decision to allow them

access to the *zafira*. But like you said, it will take time to mine through to it. And uniting our kingdoms was a masterstroke."

I hope he's right. "My empire can't last, Hector. It wasn't for no reason that I let Basajuan secede. Empires are too large, too unwieldy. Eventually, another rebellion will rise up—another Malficio. But like the mining, it will take a while. Generations, maybe. And by then . . ."

"By then we'll have lived side by side for so long with the Inviernos that we'll have forgotten to be enemies," he says. "You rose up a champion, just like it says in the scriptures. Though not in the way anyone expected. Maybe this was your destiny, your act of service." His face holds such raw hope, and I'm not sure why it never occurred to me before that the egregious survival rate of God's chosen bearers must weigh heavily on him.

"Maybe." But I doubt it. I put my fingertips to my belly, trace the Godstone's familiar solidity. The few bearers who completed acts of service lost their stones. The stones cracked and died, detached from their bodies, a sign that they were no longer needed. But mine still lives inside me, pulsing with the promise of power.

God is not done with me yet.

36

THE morning brings a letter sent via pigeon from Captain Lucio, Hector's second-in-command. Cosmé herself hands it to me with an apologetic shrug, saying it's been waiting for me for some time. "It's addressed to 'Tuciela,'" she says. "It was passed around a lot before one of our former Malficio friends remembered that you used that name as a code."

I take the missive with trembling fingers. I pop open the canister and unroll the tiny bit of parchment. Hector reads over my shoulder.

> *Dearest Tuciela,*
> *You will be glad to know the house is locked*
> *down safe. Each entrance is heavily watched. The*
> *desert rebels you worry about so much are unlikely*
> *to break in here. They would have to be very stealthy*
> *indeed! The boy and his most precious possessions*
> *have been taken away until it is safer. He wallows in*

self-pity and loneliness at your absence. Please come
home soon.

Ever yours,
Lucio

Dread and relief war inside me, turning my stomach to mush. General Luz-Manuel has locked down the palace and barred me from entrance. But my little prince is safe.

Hector tugs the parchment from my hand and rereads while I pace. "Lucio thought to grab Rosario's signet ring and papers, too," he says. "Good man. It's not exactly an unbreakable code, but I appreciate the effort."

"They're hiding Rosario in the Wallows. In the secret village."

Hector forces a smile. "A hideout like that is paradise for a boy his age."

"Conde Eduardo is probably tearing the city apart looking for him."

He nods. "Whoever controls the heir controls the throne."

I crumple the message in my hand. "I'll never forgive myself if something happens to Rosario."

"He is safe with Lucio. Even if Eduardo finds him, he will come to no harm. He's too valuable."

Hector would not say so if it didn't believe it to be true. I nod up at him gratefully.

We take our leave in the afternoon, after concluding our negotiations. I would love to stay longer, reacquaint myself with old friends, with my sister. But the longer I wait to retake my city, the stronger Conde Eduardo's and General Luz-Manuel's foothold becomes.

I stay just long enough to see the Deciregi on their way. Then I turn to my vassal queens. We stand in a circle for a moment, gripping hands. I love these women—my dear friend and my dear sister. But things will never be easy with us. We must always distrust one another a little as we fight for our own interests and the interests of our people. This time, I outmaneuvered everyone. But it won't always be that way. Cosmé and Alodia are both perfectly capable of outmaneuvering me, and our next battle might belong to one of them.

We promise to reconvene next year, and every year after, for an annual parliament. Both promise to come visit earlier if their schedules allow. I hope they do, but I won't count on it.

We depart on horseback when the sun is high. We will travel hard and fast, exchanging our horses for fresh mounts at trading posts along the way. I hate this idea, though I recognize its necessity. After getting to know Horse, it seems wrong that these loyal, hardworking creatures should be so disposable, so at the whim of their human masters.

To our right, the foothills grow greener and more lush as they stretch into the sky. To our left is the great yellow basin of desert. Heavy winds—maybe even a sandstorm—have kicked sand up from the desert floor and onto the road. In some places it piles and drifts, like soft snowbanks. The first night is as arid as the day but bitter cold. We huddle at the fire, gratefully slurping Mara's hot soup, and fall into our bedrolls exhausted.

Hector follows me into my tent. "For warmth," he says with a crooked grin.

My confidence grows with each day. Part of it is the dry, dusty familiarity of the desert. Some comes from the feeling of being surrounded by the warmth and loyalty of trusted companions. But mostly it is because the acknowledgment settles into my bones about how much I have accomplished. I have finally been to the enemy's gate, and survived. I have negotiated for peace. I have moved mountains.

On the fifth day, an itch begins, a strange restlessness that tingles in my bones. After a meal of hot oats and honey, I volunteer to take the first watch, knowing sleep will be impossible. I pace back and forth across the edge of the plateau, gazing at the velvet-soft, blue moon desert, yearning for something, though I'm not sure what. My Godstone's behavior is subtly different, the usual pulse more like a twitch, as if it's yearning for something too.

Eventually Storm comes to relieve me. We stand side by side for a while, gazing out across the desert, not saying a word. I should ask him about Waterfall, see how he is coping with her death. But I don't, because maybe he wants to talk about it as little as I want to talk about Papá.

At last he says, "Your Godstone. It's different. I can feel it."

"I'm restless," I say. "It often responds to my moods."

"I'll never know what's that's like," he muses. "My Godstone fell out so early that I don't remember it at all. I can't imagine it being part of me, alive inside me. I admit, I envy you."

It's as raw and unguarded a declaration as I've ever heard

from him. On impulse, I reach up and hug him. He stiffens, then he hugs back a little, patting my back awkwardly.

"Good night, Storm."

I crawl into the tent where Hector is sleeping soundly, taking up the middle of our bedroll as usual. I shove him aside and slide in front of him. He wraps an arm around me and hitches me close but doesn't really wake. I am wide-eyed in the dark all night, the itch growing.

By morning, it feels like I'm coming out of my skin. I accidentally pour soup down the front of my blouse. When we're packing up, my fingers fumble as I try to attach my saddlebags. When I drop my bedroll the third time, I kick it across the campsite, grunting frustration.

Hector chases after it, grabs it, puts it on the back of his own saddle. "Good memories here, now," he says, patting the bedroll and eyeing me sidelong. "I'll not stand for you abusing the poor thing."

This teases a smile from me, but it's short-lived. We mount up, and my mare dances nervously, reading something in my mood. I snap at her to be calm, but this only makes things worse.

We set off, Hector in the lead, but after a while I pull even with him, and then I discover that I've moved ahead. I don't even remember nudging my horse.

And then I'm too far ahead, and I hear Hector calling to rein in, that it's not safe to separate myself from the group, but I can't help it. Something pulls me forward, something as inexorable as the tides, as unsatiated as thirst in the desert.

Galloping hoofbeats bear down on me. A cloud of dust chokes me, and suddenly large hands are ripping my reins away, pulling back, slowing me down. "What in God's name are you doing, Elisa?" Hector yells.

I read the fear in his face, but I'm helpless to do anything about it or explain. I try to yank the reins back, but his grip is steadfast.

So I lift a leg around and slide from my saddle to the ground. Then I take off running.

Oh, God, I itch, itch, itch. The need to move forward is so powerful I feel like my skin will burst open if I don't. *I must keep going. I must go faster.*

Hector overtakes me. He slides from his horse and grabs me. "What are you doing? Just tell me! I can help! But you can't run off alone—"

I pummel his chest with my fists. "I have to!" I cry, and as the words leave my mouth I realize they don't make any sense. "I have to keep going. Let me go, Hector."

"Where? Why?"

Tears of frustration leak from my eyes, run down my cheeks. I hate not being able to explain, but not as much as I hate not being able to *go*. "I don't know!" I sob out.

The others catch up to us. "Elisa, what's going on?" Mara says.

I try to wrench my arms from Hector's grasp. "God, Elisa, if I hold any tighter, I'll hurt you."

"It's her Godstone," Storm says. "I can sense it."

I don't care what it is. I'm helpless with need, blinded by it, and I kick out at Hector, colliding with his shins. He releases me all at once, and I fall back onto my rear. I scramble to my feet and run.

Vaguely, as if from very far away, I hear, "Follow her!" I pound down the road, pumping my arms for speed, sucking air and dust. I slip in the sand, fall to my knees. Pain shoots up my legs, but I jump to my feet and run on.

The plateau dips slightly, at a place where the cliff is not so steep and the sand has drifted against it, creating an easy path to the desert. I plunge down the side, knee-deep in sand, slipping and sliding my way down the slope.

I edge along the cliff, something tugging me along. I have no idea where I'm going or what I'll do, but something inside me knows, and I push forward, desperate to satisfy the awful tugging, the awful itch.

Eventually the cliff curves over my head, creating a lip of shade during the hottest part of the day. At the base, where the sand drifts are the deepest, I drop to my knees and begin to dig with my hands.

I shovel as fast as I can, but sand is a nebulous, liquid thing, and more pours into the hole I'm making as soon as I remove it.

So I dig faster and harder.

The others come up behind me, but I keep digging. Sand lodges under my fingernails. One of my cuticles bleeds. But I can't stop.

They watch for a while, puzzled. Then Storm drops beside me and starts digging too. Then Hector. Then Red. Mara and Belén work behind us, moving sand that we've displaced out of the way so it doesn't come pouring back.

We dig and dig. The sun is hot on my back, burning my neck. My hands are scraped raw. Grit fills my mouth, crunches between my teeth.

My right forefinger brushes against something cool. Something smooth-textured and alive. My digging slows as I reveal a tiny dark-green leaf.

It is the most precious leaf in the world, and my fingertips, which had so recently clutched at the sand with such raw abandon, trace its outline carefully, rubbing sand away from its gentle curve, loosing it to spring free of the harsh desert soil. With it comes a fragile stem. Two more leaves. Then a tiny offshoot with a budding yellow-green leaf at its tip.

"It's a baby fig tree," Mara exclaims breathlessly.

"It must have been buried in a recent sandstorm," Belén says.

I hear them, but I can't acknowledge them, because I'm not done yet. I keep digging until the sprout is entirely free of its sand prison, then I pat the ground firm around it to give it some strength against the wind.

"I have moisture here," Hector says. "Look! It's wet." He holds up a handful of sticky sand.

"Another tree," Red says.

And then we all renew our digging with fervor, uncovering two more plants I don't recognize and the unmistakable seepage of a desert spring.

We clear a wide area at the base of the overhang, using nothing but our hands, and when finally the last tiny leaf is entirely dust free, I stop. One moment, I'm frantic with *doing*, and in the next, the itch disappears, replaced by bone-deep weariness that makes me feel like I could sleep for a week.

"Elisa, you've found an oasis," Mara says. "A new one. It was covered by a sandstorm, but you—"

A great crack rends the air. Or maybe the crack is only in my mind, but I cover my ears against it, moaning at the ache suddenly zipping up my spine. My vision turns cloudy red, swimming with black spots. Bright pain explodes through my belly.

And the Godstone falls away, catching in the waistband of my pants.

I lurch to my feet. The Godstone slides down my leg like a warm scurrying rodent, lodges in the top of my boot. I shove my hand inside for it. My fingertips just brush it. It's edged, like broken glass. And wet.

I wrap my fingers around it and pull it out slowly, afraid of what I'll see.

I hold it up to the sun. It's blue-black now, a huge crack zagging through the center. The back side is smeared with blood. I put my other hand to my navel, my empty navel. It's monstrously large, sore to the touch, and seeping.

It feels like a camel is standing on my chest, and I can hardly breath. I know this means something, something important. But I can't think what.

Mara slips an arm around my waist. "You've done it, Elisa. This was it. Your act of service."

"And you lived," Hector says, his voice dropped and gruff.

I turn around, survey our handiwork. We cleared an enormous area. One spot grows dark with damp, like a blot of ink in the sand. Beside it are my fig tree and a few smaller sprouts, their living green a stark contrast to dry sand and shale. Off to the side is the mountain of sand we removed to reach it all. I stare in awe. I would have killed myself trying to dig it all out alone.

That's why I didn't die, I realize with a start. Mistress Jacoma obsessively painted herself into an early grave. Lucián drained his youth carving the Hand of God, which now sits in my throne room at home. I would have driven myself to death too, were it not for my friends. They helped shoulder the burden.

"I think we just saw history being made," Belén says.

Mara drops to her knees to study my fig tree close up. "We've watched Elisa make history all year," she says, fingering a fragile leaf. "So why this? God wanted an *oasis*? It's so . . . uninspiring."

Belén shrugs. "'The mind of God is a mystery and none can understand it.' Damián the Shepherd never knew why he was compelled to dig his well. He died long before the well caused an accident that ended a battle. We may never know why Elisa was called to serve in this way."

"You know what else this means?" Hector says. He gazes down at me with an expression that can't be interpreted as anything other than smug. "It means everything else you've done—starting a rebellion, saving Brisadulce, finding the *zafira*, negotiating peace with Invierne—none of it was your act of service. Your Godstone didn't drive you to do all those things. You did them all *yourself.*"

I understand their words but can't absorb them. The only thing that feels real and true to me right now is that the Godstone no longer pulses inside me. I can't sense the *zafira* squirming beneath the crust of the world. I won't be able to call upon its aid to save my home.

I am powerless.

I am ordinary.

PART IV

37

THE urgency of our journey does not abate, but I'm taciturn and reclusive, preferring to take my meals a few strides away, where I can feel a little bit alone. I'm different now. A whole new Elisa. And it seems as though I ought to think it through, learn who I am again, before I'm fit company for everyone else.

One afternoon, when I'm sure no one is watching, I pull my detached Godstone from my pocket. It glimmers dully in my palm, and the fissure through its center snags on my skin. I close my eyes and try to call the *zafira*. Nothing happens. Not even a tickle of power.

I try again in the evening, this time using the pristine jewel I retrieved from Lucero's altar. Maybe I can be like Storm, a sorcerer with a detached stone. But again, nothing happens. No matter how hard I pray, how firmly I ground myself to the earth, I remain an empty, powerless vessel.

Something must have happened when my stone cracked. I gaze out across the expanse of desert, slitting my eyes against the glare as wind whips strands of hair against my cheek. *This place is still part of me*, I tell myself firmly, even though it feels as though I've been severed from the world.

I feel a hand on my shoulder. "No one thinks any less of you," Mara says, and I wonder if she spied on my failed attempts. Then she sighs. "But if you need to be unreasonable for a while, go ahead."

I *am* being unreasonable. But the Godstone has been an inextricable part of me—both my body and my life—and I don't know how else to be.

"You completed your service and *lived*," Hector says to me that night as we lie in our tent. "You might not be glad about that, but I am. I'm hugely relieved, to tell you the truth."

"But I'm powerless," I whisper.

"Yes, powerless," he echoes. "Which is why I have no desire to do this." He kisses my forehead, letting his lips linger. "Which is why I can easily say no to this." He presses his lips to mine, teases them open, and kisses me long and deep. "And why I am not utterly compelled to do this." He yanks my body against his, and his hand slips under the hem of my shirt. "Do you see, Elisa?" he says, his voice dark. "How little power you have over me?"

The next morning I take breakfast with everyone else.

Exhausted and saddle sore, with sand creeping into crevices I didn't realize I had, we reach Brisadulce in a record two weeks. Gloriously high walls blend seamlessly into the desert landscape. Were it not for the steady stream of traffic in either direction, you'd never know you approached a massive city, until all of a sudden it rises from the sand, a huge and ancient monolith of stone guarded by tiny toy soldiers who peer from its regular crenellations. I breathe deep of the warm desert air. It smells of camel dung and ocean salt and hot-baked sand, and I love it.

Hector holds up a fist, and we pause well outside the view of the city guard. The laughing, affectionate, talkative Hector has been replaced by the other one, the coldly calculating commander.

He shields his eyes against the sun's glare and says, "The guard at the main gate is tripled," he says. "I'm sure it's the same at the other gates."

"Could we get in through the harbor?" Belén asks. "We could disguise ourselves as sailors or dockworkers."

From habit, I place my fingertips to my navel to send up a quick prayer for wisdom and luck, only to find concave emptiness. So I send my prayer out into the nebulous mental space of dreams and hopes and imagination—which might be sending it nowhere at all—while I wonder if God hears. This is what it's like to be everyone else, to pray and never have a physical assurance that someone is listening.

"We'd be recognized anyway," Mara says. "We're too well known to the city watch. The general has eyes everywhere; I'd bet my spice satchel on it."

"Not me," Red says. "No one knows me."

"Surely there's a secret way in?" I say. "Every ruler has an egress from his own city."

"There used to be a tunnel," Hector says. "It collapsed in

the war. I kept meaning to tend to it, but it was low on my list of—"

I wave it off, recognizing his I-have-failed-to-protect-you tone. "We'll find another way. What about the sewers? They lead to the cliffs and the sea, right? Are they climbable?"

Mara groans. "Sewers. Caves. Why does it always have to be sewers and caves?"

Hector rubs at his chin. "It's possible. They are slick and dangerous. But our biggest obstacle would be the surf just below. It's hard to get close in a boat without getting pounded to death."

"We need disguises," Belén says.

Hector shakes his head. "They're searching everyone who seems suspicious. We can't risk it. If they search us, we'll be recognized for sure."

"I have an idea," I say. Triumph fills me. *I have an idea.* This is my only lasting power.

They all turn to me. Belén grins.

"The monastery is open to the public," I say. "We'll send Red to Father Nicandro. Ask him to bring us priests' robes and escort us into the city. We'll pose as visiting clergy from . . . Amalur. On a pilgrimage to God's first monastery. No one would dare search priests on a holy pilgrimage."

"It's a good plan," Hector says.

"I prefer it to sewers," Mara says.

"It could be dangerous for the girl," Belén says. "Her Invierno blood is strong."

"I'll do it," Red says with a lift of her tiny chin. "It's just my eyes that make people mean. I have lots of practice hiding them."

"You're certain, Red?" I ask. "Brisadulce is a very big, noisy place."

She shrugs. "I can do it."

"All right, then." I crouch down before her. "I'm not going to write this down, in case it's intercepted, so you must memorize it."

She nods gravely.

I give her specific directions to the monastery and ask her to repeat them back to me. She does, flawlessly, and I silently vow to find the best possible tutor for the girl and her quick mind. "When you get to the monastery, ask for Father Nicandro. Insist that you have a message for him. He is the head priest, and not everybody has access to him. So whoever you speak with will ask you to tell them the message. Don't. Your message is for Father Nicandro only. If pressed, say it's a message from Ambassador Alentín and must be delivered in private."

Alentín's name should get her an audience. He is a priest in his own right, as well as the head of Queen Cosmé's foreign delegation.

"When you are with Father Nicandro, and only then, you will tell him about us and about our need to sneak into the city."

Her eyes are wide with focus. She mutters to herself, committing what she has heard to memory. On the chance that the priests try subterfuge to get information out of the girl, I add, "I want you to ask Father Nicandro a question to verify that it is him. Say this: 'You once met with the queen in the dead of night, in the scribing room, after the watch rang the first hour. How did you make arrangements for this meeting?' Now repeat it back to me."

She does, making only one small mistake, so we go over it once more.

I smile. "I snuck a note to him during the sacrament of pain, right before he pricked my finger. He shoved it into his sleeve." My smile fades. "If the person you speak with does not mention it, he is not Nicandro."

Red shifts, avoiding my gaze. "It will be hard to hide my eyes once I start talking to people," she says, and her tone is so apologetic that I bend down to hug her.

"If they notice, they notice," I say. "Tell them anything you want. Tell them you are island bred and all your brothers have the same eyes, maybe. And I swear to you, Red, after this, if we are successful, you'll never need to hide your eyes again."

She hugs me back fiercely, then disengages, draws herself to full height—which is no height at all—and says, "I'm ready."

Everyone else hugs her next, and no one says it, but we all know it's for just in case.

She shoulders her pack and trudges down the hill toward the road. We watch her tiny form merge with traffic, and then I only catch glimpses here and there as she weaves her way toward the city entrance.

Hector raises his hand to shadow his eyes and says, "She's at the gate."

She is barely a mote in my vision, but Hector has the eyes of a hawk.

"There's a carriage in the way . . . oh, there she is. The guards have stopped her." He puts his other hand to his scabbard, as if he can protect her from a distance. "They're talking to her."

Mara and I exchange an alarmed glance. "She's clever," Mara says. "She'll think of something, right?"

I nod, my heart in my throat. She's just a little girl. A sweet, precious child as ardently innocent as my own little prince. Why did I send her on this dangerous errand?

"Still talking," Hector says. "Lots of back and forth. One just grabbed her pack. He's looking inside."

"If they hurt her . . ." Belén says.

"Her hands are on her hips," Hector says. "I think she's yelling at them."

Oh, God. I can just imagine. *I am Lady Red Sparkle Stone, handmaiden to the queen, and you had better let me pass!* No, she's cleverer than that. She knows better. Doesn't she?

"She's in!" Hector says, and relief floods me. "They let her go. One of the soldiers snagged her food pouch, though. I'll kill him."

We settle down to wait on our hillside overlooking the road and the desert beyond. The sun burns the air until it shimmers, but none of us moves up the hill to take advantage of the shade provided by a few stunted palms there. We stare toward Brisadulce's massive gate, as if we can summon Red back to us with the force of our collective gaze.

But she does not return. The sun sinks huge and orange behind the outline of the Sierra Sangre, and the temperature drops so low that my breath frosts in the air, but there is no sign of her.

Belén traps a few jerboas and deftly fillets them. Mara gets a soup going while Hector climbs a nearby date palm and shakes the ripe fruit to the ground. After a meal of jerboa soup and fresh dates, we sit in silence, watching the road. Storm gets up, yawning, and says, "She will either return, or she won't." He crawls inside his tent and is softly snoring in moments.

I sit shoulder to shoulder with Hector. He puts an arm around me and I lean into him, absorbing his solid strength as comfort. It seems like only a moment passes, and suddenly I'm blinking awake to brilliant sunrise.

"Good morning," he says, pressing his lips to my hair.

I roll my neck to work out the kink. "Did you stay awake all night?" I ask.

"I dozed. Traded watches with Belén."

He gets to his feet and stretches. I stand beside him and wrap my arms around his waist. His fingers tangle in my hair as we gaze across the desert.

"It's Red!" Mara says, pointing up the road. "She's back."

Storm barrels from his tent, then stops short and collects himself until he appears as haughty as ever. "She brought people with her," he observes coolly.

I squint against the rising sun. Red is followed by two others. One leads a camel piled high with lumpy cargo.

"I hope that's Father Nicandro," Hector says. Keeping an

eye on the road, he buckles his gauntlets and checks his blades.

Both wear priests' robes. One is slight, barely taller than a child. The other . . . my heart begins to pound. I know that frame, that heavy but inexorable stride.

"Ximena," I whisper.

Hector looks at me sharply. "Didn't you tell her to go back to Orovalle?"

I nod, unable to speak. I dismissed my nurse months ago for taking important matters pertaining to my life and reign into her own hands. But I love her still. Maybe she found a post with Father Nicandro. It makes sense—she is a student of the holy scriptures and a scribe of some renown.

"Well, this should be interesting," Mara says.

Red's face shines with triumph as they approach. And then she can't contain herself any longer; she runs forward, kicking dust up with her heels, and flings herself at Mara, who hugs her tight. "It was just like Elisa said!" she gasps out. "They tried to trick me. But I didn't say anything. Not a word, until I knew for sure it was Father Nicandro."

The priest in question huffs up the rise, then holds out both hands in greeting, and I grab them. "Dear girl," he says. "It does my heart good to see you well."

"Thank you for coming, Father," I say, squeezing his fingers.

Behind him, my former nurse hangs back, hands clasped before her. She has always appeared innocuous—a rosy-cheeked woman with plump arms and an easy smile. But no longer. She looks fierce, with small black eyes that are sharper than ever, and a puckered scar that now traces the line of her cheekbone. A few months ago she took a glancing arrow to save my decoy. But it didn't work. The next arrow got the poor girl anyway.

"Hello, Ximena," I say.

She inclines her head. "Your Majesty."

"I'm surprised to see you here."

"Father Nicandro made me an unusual offer," she says. "And I could not refuse."

I raise an eyebrow at him.

"And it was lucky she was available," the priest says, releasing my hands. He hurries over to the camel and begins unloading bundles of undyed woolen cloth tied with twine. "Your Royal Guard chose to go into hiding instead of defending the palace," he explains, tossing a bundle to each of us. "They were too far outnumbered. But it left their families exposed. Their children. We brought them into the monastery, hoping the general's men would be less likely to retaliate against them or use them for leverage if they were placed in a house of God." He tosses the last bundle to me. I untie it and shake it out. It's a robe, but much too long for me.

"I've been looking after them," Ximena says. "I'm a nurse, after all."

"A nurse who could kill an intruder with her bare hands," Nicandro adds with a glint in his eye.

"Yes."

Hector and I trade robes—his is much shorter—and we pull them on over our regular clothing.

"So," I say to no one in particular. "Do I look . . . priestly?"

Nicandro's expression is pained. "You and your Invierno friend . . . well, I say we wait until late evening. The general locks down the city at night. We'll have to go at dusk, right before they close the gate."

I did not think it was possible to become angrier at the men who would usurp my throne. A citywide lockdown is a serious matter. The effect on trade, on morale, is immeasurable. I would only consider it in times of plague or siege.

But that's exactly what they're worried about. Siege. And I am the invader.

"You'll take us straight to the monastery?" I ask.

"It would draw attention if we did not," he says. "But in the morning, we'll go out as missionaries to the Wallows, to give coins and bread to the poor along with an encouraging word from God."

"To the Guard," I say.

He nods. "They've been hiding in the underground village for months. There are several people there who will be very, very glad to see you. Conde Tristán is with them."

My joyous smile dies on my face. If Tristán is in hiding, it means the announcement of his ascension to Quorum Lord was met with resistance.

We sell our horses and tack at a huge loss to a passing merchant caravan, keeping only one as a packhorse. We take turns descending into the desert to trudge around in the sand, the hems of our robes dragging, so it will appear we have been on the road for days. A few rare, early winter clouds roll in from the sea, and the sunset coats their underbellies in blazing pink by the time we set off toward the gate.

"Any word of the prince?" I whisper to Father Nicandro as we walk.

"General Luz-Manuel is desperate to find him," the priest says in a low voice. "At even the slightest hint of loyalty to the de Riqueza line, he sends his men into homes without warning to search. They've been seizing property. As part of their investigation, they say, but they've been using it to pay for the war effort."

If I get a chance, I will kill him. "The citizens of Brisadulce cannot be pleased with this turn of events."

"Many are not, and his actions have solidified your base of support. But there are plenty who feel the general's actions are justified. He and the conde have labeled you a traitor and blasphemer, someone who will bring our enemy upon us like a plague. And people are never more atrocious as when they are afraid."

"But the boy." I glance around to make sure no one is within earshot. "Rosario. Is he . . . ?"

Nicandro gives me a reassuring smile. "We cannot hide him forever. But he is well for now."

We continue in solemn formation. Father Nicandro carries an incense brazier that swings back and forth on a chain, curling musky smoke into the air. He chants with each step-swing, and we keep time as best we can. Red takes up the rear. She is dressed in a white acolyte's robe and holds the reins of our camel and packhorse.

The gate looms above our heads as we approach. The

massive doors are open wide. Each has a patched area of lighter wood—the only remaining indication that Invierno sorcerers burned through it only a year past.

Soldiers line the entrance, six on each side, standing at a diagonal so that traffic is funneled to a small, controllable point. Archers and spearman peer down at us from the crenellations above.

We are outnumbered and outweaponed. These are not rough mountain brigands or half-frozen mercenaries exhausted from their trek. These are well trained, well rested, battle-hardened soldiers, and if they do not let us pass, it will be impossible to fight our way out.

I look neither to the right nor the left. I keep my head down in humble supplication but stride unerringly, as if I have every right to be here.

"Halt!" one calls out. "State your business."

Father Nicandro steps forward. He approaches close enough for the incense to snake up toward the guard's face. The guard's nose twitches. "We are about God's holy business," Nicandro says.

A different guard steps forward. "Good evening, *Holy Eminence*," he says with a sidelong glance at his companion. The first guard blanches. "I didn't realize you'd left the city."

"Should I have told you?" I can't see the priest's face, but I imagine him looking charmingly confused.

"These are dangerous times. If you share your travel plans with us ahead of time, we can provide an escort if needed, ease your passage through our checkpoints. It's for your own safety, you see."

Checkpoints? They've set up checkpoints along my highway? My face grows hot beneath my priest's cowl.

"I do see. Next time I'll do exactly that."

No one says anything, and no one moves.

The guard clears his throat. "Would you mind . . . er . . . for our record-keeping, you see, telling us what took you away from the city?"

Father Nicandro gestures toward us. "I received advance word that our guests were arriving, and I left to escort them on the final leg of their journey as a show of hospitality. They are pilgrims, come on behalf of Father Donatzine and Queen Alodia from the Monastery-at-Amalur. They seek spiritual renewal at the site of God's first monastery, and to exchange translation notes with our scribes."

The guard rubs at his jaw. He knows he ought to search us. Our pack animals are heavily laden, and our voluminous robes could conceal anything. He is right to be worried.

He steps closer. Not one of us moves or even twitches. I force myself to breath normally. He peers at the person nearest to Nicandro. "Lady Ximena," he says, with no small amount of surprise. And his voice has an unmistakable note of suspicion when he says, "I would not have expected you to accompany His Eminence on this journey."

"Oh, yes, Sergeant," she says brightly. "As you know, I'm originally from Orovalle. I was anxious to see some old friends."

An awkward moment passes. The guards glance at one

another. The sergeant steps toward Belén, eyes narrowed.

"Good sir!" Nicandro says, a little too loudly. "I do hope you won't detain us much longer. Our guests have experienced an arduous pilgrimage, and I'm anxious to show them the hospitality their rank and purpose deserve."

I'm praying madly—*Please, God, please, please, please let us pass*—even as I eye our surroundings, looking for the best escape route. The road south, I decide. Enough traffic that someone on foot would be difficult to track. I don't stand a chance in a close-quarters fight with so many. I've never practiced with my daggers while wearing such voluminous sleeves.

"Have a nice evening, Your Eminence," the sergeant says, stepping back. Nicandro starts forward, and we follow after. In my peripheral vision, I note the guards staring as we pass. They will remember this unscheduled group of foreign priests. They will certainly send someone to the monastery to inquire after us.

38

THOUGH I itch to take off running, we proceed solemnly up the wide Colonnade toward the palace, within perfect view of the stately townhomes that rise on either side with their hanging gardens and sparkling windows. The light dims with the setting sun, turning the sandstone and adobe buildings a fiery orange. The night bloomer vines that twist through mortar cracks and up the trunks of helpless palms open their glowing hearts to the night. My beautiful, beautiful city.

But I frown at the sight of fortifications along the road—wooden barriers that can be turned to block the road at a moment's notice, canvas bags filled with sand that will be used to shield spearmen and archers.

We enter the palace courtyard, and my heart sings, *Home!* for the briefest moment before we turn away from the main entrance toward an adjacent, lower building made of stucco and wood beams. Red hands off our pack animals to a stable boy, then Father Nicandro leads us through a wide foyer and into the sanctuary.

It's a hushed, sacred place, glowing with candles, swimming with the heady scent of sacrament roses. So Nicandro's voice rings startlingly loud when he says, "You must be ravenous after such a long journey from Amalur! Come, I'll have our kitchen prepare something for you." He ignores the stares of priests, acolytes, and petitioners, and ushers us through a side door into an empty dining hall.

He shuts and bars the door behind us. "You should be safe here for the time being. The dinner hour is long past. Make yourselves as comfortable as you can. I'll bring refreshments."

He and Ximena leave for the kitchens, and we settle on the hard stone floor to wait.

"What do you think Ximena is up to?" Hector says, staring after her.

"I don't know," I say honestly. Ximena has always kept her counsel, made her own plans—even if they were in conflict with my own. "I know she'll do what she thinks is right." But isn't that what we all do? Conde Eduardo believes he's saving the country by plunging it into civil war. A regrettable course but worth it, if that's what it takes to put himself on the throne in my place. The Inviernos thought it was right to invade Basajuan, leaving a wake of fiery wreckage in their path, if it meant avenging the wrong done to them millennia ago.

"I don't trust her to be a true ally," I admit. "Not after what she did to you. I'm going to ask Nicandro to make sure she doesn't interfere."

"But you still love her."

I reach over and squeeze his hand.

Nicandro returns alone with fresh bread, a round of cheese, cold wine, and honey coconut scones. The scones are a day old, but I'm so delighted he remembered my favorite pastry that I don't mind.

I screw up my courage and tell him that Ximena must be kept away. "As you wish, Majesty," he says. "But I think you underestimate her."

He turns to go, but I grab his sleeve. "Father. There is something else."

Something in my face causes him to lead me a few paces away, out of the hearing range of everyone else. "What is it, Elisa?"

"My Godstone. It . . ."

"I have not sensed it since you returned."

"It fell out."

His eyes grow wide as I tell him about rescuing the fledgling oasis. "You did it," he breathes. "You completed your act of service."

"But what does it mean?"

He seems vaguely stunned. "I don't know. We might never know."

"Surely you have a theory? Many of your peers would scour the scriptures looking for something even tangentially related to what has happened to me. They would create an entire doctrine out of whatever they found. Declare it a fulfilled prophecy, maybe. And then they would believe it unto death."

My words are too sharp, too angry, and I'm about to apologize when the priest says, "It is human nature to concoct explanations to fill the great void of the unknown."

I frown. "Isn't that what we do whenever we ascribe something to God?" That's what Ximena always did. *"The mind of God is a mystery and none can understand it,"* she would say. It felt like she was brushing off my questions.

Father Nicandro's face turns thoughtful. "I suppose so. Take, for instance, your Godstone. The animagi are born with theirs. But when did you get yours?"

"On my naming day. It appeared as if by magic."

Nicandro nods. "And so it is with all bearers, once every hundred years. You see, dear girl, the animagi's Godstones are natural. But yours? Yours is divine."

"You have just ascribed that which you do not understand to God."

He grins. "And I will continue to do so. Until I have a better explanation." He gives my shoulder a gentle squeeze. "Never stop asking questions, Majesty. God honors truth seekers."

On impulse, I wrap him in a hug. He and Hector were my first true friends in Brisadulce, and I'll never forget it. "Thank you, Father."

He pats my back, then disengages. "Try to get some rest."

Nicandro lights a few candles for us, then retires for the night. I pace for hours, thinking about prophecy and God and Godstones, wondering how it's possible for me to wish Ximena far, far away—but at the same time wish she were here to soothe my worries with a hug and an *Everything's going to be fine, my sky.*

⊹ ⊹ ⊹

The next morning, our backs and necks ache from lying on the stone floor of the monastery dining room. Nicandro escorts us as we wind our way into the Wallows, the most dangerous district of my city. It's impossible to distinguish one building from another here. They are a continuous, twisting structure of rundown adobe patched with driftwood and palm thatch. The streets are narrow and crooked, the paver stone buckled—or removed completely for building material. Dirty, barefooted children scamper through the crowd, brushing against everyone they pass, making me grateful for my scratchy robe's lack of pockets. Everything smells of sewer.

We make a show of handing out bread and coins and are almost mobbed before Nicandro holds up his hands and yells, "No more left! We'll be back next week!" The crowd melts away.

He hurries us through a warren of merchant stalls—mostly fish and useless sea scavenge—and into a narrow alley. We come to a door that is warped and dry from heat and salt, its hinges and lock mottled with rust. He looks around to make sure we are not being watched; then he pulls out a key and unlocks the door. I wince as it squeals open. We step into cool darkness.

"I must return to the monastery," he says. "Someone needs to answer questions about the strange party from Amalur that arrived here. In the next room, there's a trapdoor. The stair will lead to the underground village."

I reach out and take his hands. "Thank you, Father."

"God be with you, dear girl. When it begins, I'll help however I can."

I search for words to tell him how much it means to have him as a friend and ally, ever since that night, more than a year ago, when he welcomed a frightened princess into his sacred archive and told her the truth. But he is gone before I can bring it to my lips.

For once we have a quick, easy journey. The stair is long and steep, and it dumps us into a small clay hut with an earthen floor. We peer warily through the doorway into cavern gloom, interrupted with the occasional stream of sunlight.

The underground village is just as I remember it—the ceiling crevices filled with sunshine and lush plants, hanging vines that almost brush the tops of the huts, the wide river curving around the far wall before plunging into a tunnel that leads to the sea. But this time, instead of just poor villagers hiding from guild taxes, the cavern is also filled with my own Royal Guard. Some sit sharpening blades and oiling armor. Others practice with wooden swords in a cleared space near the river. Still others nap or cook or help the villagers mend nets.

They do everything quietly. No one speaks above a whisper.

When I left, my Guard was depleted by the war to only thirty-one strong. But I see lots of unfamiliar faces, enough to fill a full garrison of sixty. Maybe more. They practice with everyone else, seemingly fully integrated.

I sent a Godstone to Captain Lucio with orders to trade it on the black market and use the funds to rebuild my Guard, but his achievement has exceeded my expectation, and my chest swells with wondrous, bubbling hope.

Two guards stand at attention outside the clay hut, and they step forward to block our path, swords drawn. Hector is the first to remove his hood, and they gasp.

"It's the commander!" one yells, and the other shushes him. He winces. "Sorry." But his declaration has grabbed the attention of every person in the cavern. And when I remove my own hood, an even deeper silence descends on the place.

Then all of a sudden we are swarmed with soldiers wearing brilliant smiles, whispering exclamations of welcome, patting us on the back and hugging indiscriminately.

The villagers latch on to Storm. They clutch the edge of his robe to their cheeks as if it confers some kind of blessing. Murmurs of "Lo Chato!" and "He has returned!" echo throughout the cavern. Storm takes it in with monstrous indifference, his head high, his gaze full of exquisite boredom. He must be enjoying every second.

"Back," Hector orders when I'm jostled one too many times. "Give Her Majesty some space."

The guards collect themselves, looking around at one another shamefaced, and as one they drop to their knees.

I gaze out over the small sea of bowed heads, breathing deep of the moment, savoring it. My Guard. My people. My power. "It's good to be home," I say. "And I am so very glad to see you all." I open my mouth to say something else, but a small figure darts out from one of the huts.

"Elisa?" Rosario launches at me, wrapping skinny arms around my neck. The guards titter with amusement as I hug my little prince tight. "I told them you would come back," he says. "I *told* them."

I swallow the sudden lump in my throat. "You told them right."

He squirms out of my arms and throws himself at Hector next, who hugs the boy just as fiercely. "I'm in hiding," Rosario tells him gravely.

"And doing a good job of it, I see," Hector answers with equal gravity.

Rosario spots Red and cocks his head. "I'm seven," he announces. "How old are you?"

Red just shrugs, avoiding his gaze.

"You're almost as big as me. Are you six?"

"I don't think so," she says witheringly.

I raise an eyebrow at Mara, who takes my cue and rounds up the prince and the girl. "Let's go inside and get acquainted, shall we?" she says, and I mouth a "Thank you!" at her. When this is all over, I'm going to spend lots of time with the boy. Playing cards, practicing with wooden daggers, maybe even going riding. Whatever he wants.

I return my attention to my Guard, and find Captain Lucio off to the side. "Captain, how do you find the Guard? Are they battle ready?"

"At a moment's notice, Your Majesty."

I expected nothing less. "I see a lot of new faces among you. Know that you are most welcome. If Lord-Commander Hector deems you ready, I would accept your oaths tonight."

This is met by a flurry of excited whispers. Being oath sworn to the queen is a wonderful thing for some; it means three meals a day and a monthly stipend.

I spot Fernando in the crowd and resist the urge to single him out by waving. Beside him is young Benito, a boy I brought back with me from the desert to train with the Royal Guard. He is too young still, but Lucio must have promoted him to full Guard anyway.

And then, to my absolute delight, I notice Conde Tristán, kneeling alongside the rest, surrounded by men in the ivory and sky blue of Selvarica. Our eyes meet, and he smiles broadly. I know that his presence here means things have not gone well for him, but I'm glad to see him still.

I would love to spend time catching up with everyone. I'd love a long nap and days' worth of hot meals. And dear God, I'm desperate for a bath. But it won't be long before the general figures out I'm here; Father Nicandro can't keep the truth of his visiting "pilgrims" a secret for more than a day or two.

We must act now. Tonight.

With a deep breath and a raised chin, I address my Guard. "The fate of Joya d'Arena and the world stands on a knife's edge, so pay attention. Conde Eduardo's adviser Franco, the man who tried to assassinate me and who kidnapped Lord-Commander Hector, is dead at the commander's own hand." A few soft cheers greet this announcement. "We crossed the border into Invierne and learned much about our ancient enemy. Then we journeyed to Basajuan, where I met with Her Majesty Queen Alodia and Her Majesty Queen Cosmé. To make a very long story short, I will just say that they swore fealty to me and to Joya d'Arena. You are now an Imperial Guard."

They gape at me.

"We then leveraged our newfound accord to bargain for peace with Invierne." I have an awkward moment where I pull the robe over my head just so I can reach my pants. I toss the robe aside and retrieve a roll of parchment from my pocket to wave at them. "This is a peace treaty, signed by me and members of Invierne's ruling council."

More gaping.

"I share this with you so you know what is at stake. The treaty can only remain effective if I am in power." I pause to consider my next words carefully. "But this is not about me. Our actions will *not* be remembered because of which blundering, disposable ruler we put on the throne. They will be remembered because they turned the hinge of history and determined whether or not the world would have peace."

I give them a moment to consider, to absorb.

Then: "Are you ready? Will you do battle on behalf of the world tonight?"

We are in hiding, so I do not expect a cheering assent or even an "All hail!" But someone draws his sword, slaps it against his thigh. Others follow. Soon the cavern is filled with the low, steady *slap, slap, slap!* of nearly a hundred soldiers ready to lay down their lives.

We are a small force stacked against incredible odds. I must use them to strike fast, hard, and smart. But this is what I do. This is my power.

I smile wickedly, and when their slapping has faded to silence, I speak.

"I have a plan."

39

I'M sliding daggers into the legs of my boots when I feel a presence looming over me, and I know it's Hector even before I look up.

He stares down at me, his heart in his eyes. "God, Elisa, do you have any idea how dangerous this is?"

I straighten to face him. "Not as dangerous as waiting for Eduardo to strengthen his foothold and then engaging in an all-out war that sets friend against friend, brother against brother."

"I mean dangerous for *you*."

"I know what you mean."

A muscle in his jaw twitches. He opens his mouth but changes his mind. Then he turns and strides away.

I ache to call him back. Instead, I bend back to my daggers, mentally going over the plan to make sure I haven't forgotten something important.

Conde Tristán and the Selvaricans will dress as peasants and attend evening services at the monastery. Afterward, when all the petitioners are exiting the audience hall, they will mill about the courtyard with everyone else, gradually moving into place. Tristán will give the signal, and they will strike fast to take the gate. Then they'll create a distraction, drawing as many city guards as possible, and when approximately half of them have rushed the courtyard, he will drop the gate, dividing their forces. Then Fernando and Mara will pick them apart from the ramparts.

They've exchanged their uniforms for the civilian garb of the villagers, donning ragged pants and patched blouses, rope for belts. They can't hide swords beneath their clothing, but Tristán has assured me that daggers will do at first, that they will be able to arm themselves with the swords of fallen soldiers. I've watched him fight. With the arguable exception of Hector, he's the most terrifying bladesman I've ever seen.

Fernando and Mara will don priests' robes ample enough to hide their bows. Red and a few of the village children are tasked with delivering quivers full of arrows to the palace, ostensibly for the palace garrison that mans the gates. Instead, the children will stash them in prearranged caches around the inner courtyard for Mara and Fernando to grab when they can.

Hector will take his most seasoned warriors through the tunnels that lead to the catacombs and into the palace. The entrance to the catacombs is likely guarded by two men. It will be no easy task to silence them before they can raise the alarm. Then Hector's men must move swiftly to the palace barracks and the prison tower, where General Luz-Manuel and his top aides reside. Hector will take the general alive if possible.

The barracks are among the few palace structures made mostly of wood. Highly flammable wood. So Storm will accompany Hector.

Captain Lucio and I will lead our new recruits through the secret egress tunnel to the king's suite. From there, he'll lock down the palace residential wing, isolating Conde Eduardo and any other nobles in residence. He also has orders to capture rather than kill whenever possible.

All three insurgencies must happen at once for us to be successful. So Father Nicandro has agreed to sound the monastery bells—which can be heard throughout the city—the moment services let out, as the signal to proceed

I could spend all day imagining ways it could go wrong. Instead, I check and recheck my weapons. Then I spend some time mingling throughout the cavern, offering an encouraging word here and there, thanking the men for risking everything for Joya d'Arena.

A hand grabs my upper arm. "Come with me," Hector says urgently. "To the barracks."

I wrench my arm from his grasp.

"I don't want to let you out of my sight," he adds.

"You know I can't," I say, though I know how he feels. The thought of him going off to battle without me makes my heart shiver with terror. "I'm the only person in all of Joya who outranks Conde Eduardo. I must be there to give official orders. Otherwise any hand raised against him is an act of sedition."

He steps closer until we are almost touching. "Then let me come with you."

"I need my best fighters to engage the general's men."

His voice drops low. "If this doesn't work, I'll come find you. We'll go away together, like—"

I wrap my arms around his neck and press my body against his, kissing him as thoroughly as I ever have. He crushes me to him, kissing back with a desperate finality.

Hector's men cheer softly all around us, and we separate, both of us wearing shamefaced grins. "That was for just in case," I say.

"Promise me you'll live," he insists. "Because when this is all over, we must discuss how you sometimes kiss me to shut me up, and how I'll no longer stand for it."

I reach up to trace his jaw with my fingers. "I'll promise to live if you will."

His lips press into a firm line, and he says nothing.

Tristán declares his men ready, and I step over to wish him and Mara luck. "Just one more tunnel, right?" she says as she adjusts her robe. "And then no more. Ever again."

"Just one more," I say, and the tip of her bow jabs me as I hug her tight.

Belén joins us. "Ready?" he says to me, and I nod. "This might be your last chance, Mara," he says. "Say you'll marry me."

"You know I can't."

He smiles sadly. "Worth a try." He leans over and kisses her cheek, then takes my arm and escorts me toward Captain Lucio's group.

I stare across the cavern toward Hector, shoring myself up with the sight of him.

We lock gazes. The rest of the world fades away, and without saying a word, we say good-bye.

Then he and his men turn toward the tunnel leading to the catacombs, and the rest of us climb the stairs toward the Wallows.

If Blacksmith Mandrano, formerly captain of King Nicalao's Royal Guard, is surprised to see us, he does not show it. He ushers us all inside his shop, bars the door, and lifts the trap-door that leads to the tunnel and the king's suite in the residence wing.

"Is there anything I can do, Your Majesty?" he asks in a soft voice that belies his enormous frame.

"Just guard this tunnel as always," I tell him. "If our efforts tonight are unsuccessful, we may need it to make a quick escape."

He knocks his chest with the flat of his fist, indicating a sworn oath. "I'll leave a candle burning at the base of the stair," he says. "If it is a white or ivory candle, the way is clear. If it is any other color, the exit has been compromised."

"Thank you, Mandrano."

"Go with God, Your Majesty."

We file down the stairs one by one—about twenty of us. Captain Lucio takes the lead; Belén and I are somewhere in the middle. The tunnel is dry and dusty and reeks of rodent urine. Last time I was here, a cave scorpion scuttled over my boot, glowing Godstone blue. I try not to think about it.

The tunnel takes us under the palace and winds us through

stone walls in a series of rickety steps. No one speaks, and we wince at every groan and creak of the stair, for beyond the wall are servants' quarters, a busy laundry, storerooms, offices. So many opportunities for the denizens of the palace to hear something odd in the walls and raise the alarm.

We reach a landing that dead-ends in darkness. Lucio holds up his candle, revealing a wood-panel wall. He presses something, and the panel slides noiselessly aside, revealing more dark, empty space. My late husband's wardrobe. All we have to do is walk through the double doors to find ourselves in Alejandro's bedroom.

Lucio puts up a hand, signaling for silence. No one dares to breathe.

We all hear it. Footsteps. Men's voices, pitched low. The clink of glass and decanter.

Someone has taken up residence in the king's suite.

Captain Lucio gestures frantically, mouthing, "Back, back, get back!" and we retreat on tiptoe into the dark. Once we are staggered on the stairs a safe distance from the wardrobe, Lucio says in a low voice, "Majesty, we assumed the suite would be unoccupied."

"It has to be Eduardo," I murmur. "It *has* to be."

"It's a bold move, even for him, to usurp the king's suite," Belén says.

I stick my thumbnail between my teeth and start chewing. If Eduardo has claimed the king's suite for his own, it is undoubtedly filled with attendants, maybe even a few bodyguards. We had hoped to sneak through the hallway and take each suite one by one, blocking them in, saving Eduardo's rooms for last. But we can't pour out of a wardrobe into an occupied suite without raising the alarm.

"Majesty? We don't have long until Nicandro rings the monastery bells," Lucio says.

Which means we can't wait for the palace to sleep. If I had more time, I could arrange for a distraction, anything to reduce the number of people in that room and improve our chances.

"We'll squeeze as many men as we can into that wardrobe," I say. "And wait. When that bells sounds, we still wait. We'll have to be patient. Hector and Tristán will cause a ruckus eventually, and people will leave to find out what's going on."

"What if it *is* the conde in there?" Belén says. "We don't want him to leave. We don't want him to slip from our grasp."

My heart thuds. I just came up with a very bad plan. Of course we can't let Eduardo get away. Everything hinges on capturing or killing him. "Excellent point. Anyone have suggestions?"

The tight stairwell is growing hot and musty with our collective breath. Something scuttles nearby, probably a rat, though I hope to never know.

Finally a gruff voice I don't recognize says, "We just need to storm the place and get it over with."

I gape into the dark, in the general direction of his voice. I'm about to protest, insist we'll find another way, but someone else says, "There's no time for anything else. At least we have the element of surprise."

Murmurs of assent echo around me.

But the strategy feels foreign and clumsy. I've always made decisions based on efficiency, on as little loss of life as possible. Never have I considered a plan that I knew would result in heavy casualties.

"Majesty?" says Lucio. "Do we prepare to charge?"

The word lodges in my throat, and I have to try again. "Yes," I manage.

Back up the stairs we go, toward the wardrobe. Lucio puts a hand up to stop me when I try to follow after Belén. "You'll enter last, Majesty," Lucio whispers in my ear. "*After* we've cleared the room. Otherwise the commander will have my head."

I nod, wishing for the hundredth time that I still had the power of the *zafira* at my call. I could have frozen everyone in that room where they stood. I could have burned them to ash. I could have reached in and stopped their hearts.

Soldiers filter into the wardrobe. It's large, made for a king, and more than half fit inside. The rest stand with me on the dark landing, waiting for the monastery bells to give us the command to charge.

Brassy triplets rend the air. My Imperial Guard bursts from the wardrobe. Swords clash, furniture shatters. Someone yells, and I wince, praying, *Hurry, hurry, hurry.* We must secure this room before the palace garrison comes running with reinforcements.

The second wave of guards follows the first, and I hate hanging back, hate not being able to see. It's agonizing to wait,

wait, wait until the storm of swords has subsided, until the patter of footsteps has stilled.

"All clear!" comes the voice. I move through the wardrobe, glad it's over so quickly, grateful for my brave, fierce Guard. I'll find some way to reward them, something memorable and . . .

My Guard has not been victorious, and it's too late to dart back into the safety of the tunnel, for they have seen me—Conde Eduardo, several frightened attendants, and two white-haired animagi who stand at either shoulder, amulets swinging hot from their hands.

40

HECTOR

ELISA trusts Storm, and I should too—I *know* I should.

Maybe I will, after this.

Forty of my men follow me into the tunnel. They walk in tight formation, two abreast. The Invierno, though, I keep at my shoulder.

The tunnel leads downward, to a sandy bottom ankle-deep in water, and I utter a curse into the dark. I knew the tunnel flooded at high tide, and I didn't think to check on it.

A solution snaps into focus. "Everyone, take off your boots. Hold them above your heads." It will be hazardous; the tunnel is full of molted crab shells, barnacles, and all manner of things that could slice our feet to ribbons. But better that than leaving sodden footprints all over the residential wing of the palace.

The men repeat the order down the line, and they all comply quickly. I set off again, barefoot this time. Chains rattle, a metallic clink that echoes and re-echoes. I whirl.

Storm grimaces. "My manacles," he explains. "My boots keep them muffled."

It's gloomy in the tunnel, with only a few candles to light our way, but the water is crystal clear and I can see—though I wish I could not—the discoloration and bruising around Storm's ankles and raw sores where scar tissue has not yet had a chance to form.

My wrists tingle with phantom pain. I suffered hemp rope for only a few weeks. But we have been to the edge of the world and back together, and never once has Storm complained about them. I had forgotten he bore them.

"Likely no one can hear us down here," I say. "Don't worry about it." And I set off again, determined to ignore the rattling.

Water sloshes against the walls, and wet sand squishes between my toes. The air is sharp with brine. It reminds me of the beach at Ventierra. I spent hours at those tide pools. Days. And when I grew tired, I would bury my feet in the wet sand to stand strong against the tide. I want to take Elisa there someday. I want her to know the place I came from.

The ground rises out of the water, and we wipe sand from our feet and put our boots back on. As we climb the stairs toward the catacombs, I expect to hear the clatter of Storm's chains, but he has muffled them well.

The stair collides with a flat stone ceiling. I gesture everyone to stillness and listen hard. Nothing.

I reach up for the tiny lever, feel around blindly with my fingertips until I snag it. A stone slab lifts, pivots, reveals a gloomy chamber filled with candlelight and the reek of roses gone to rot. I poke my head through slowly, ready to charge out, sword drawn if necessary. The tomb is empty.

I signal that the room is clear and creep through the stone caskets. There are five. I can't help pausing at one, the newest, for the banner covering it is untouched by moth or mold. At its center, a cluster of candles sits in a pool of frozen wax. Alejandro is laid to rest here. Dead less than a year.

I place my palm against the casket. There are a thousand things I'd say to him, if I could. *Rosario is safe. You were supposed to outlive me. Elisa is ten times the ruler you were. I've stolen your wife. I'm not sorry.*

I miss you.

"My Lord-Commander?"

I wrench my hand away. "Let's go," I say, striding toward the archway.

It opens into the Hall of Skulls, a massive cavern lined with ribs, craniums, and yawning jawbones, all lit by votive candles. Elisa loves this place. It brings her peace, somehow. It's something I'll have to think about when I have time, how death doesn't always indicate a failure—of protection, of strategy, of character.

At the end of the hall is a tight stair spiraling up into blackness. It leads to a hallway near the inner courtyard. It will be guarded. Usually by only one man, but occasionally two. Knowing Conde Eduardo—a cautious man who leaves little to chance—I'm counting on two.

This will be the hardest part. We have the disadvantages of low ground and a difficult approach. We must sneak up a stair that's only wide enough for one soldier and take out two guards before they can call an alarm.

It would be handy to have Belén with us now, but Elisa needs someone with her who would take a sword to the chest to save her. I sift through my catalog of men to determine who best to send on an assassin's errand.

I settle on Guzmán, a small, sharp-eyed man with a quick blade. I'm about to call him forward when Storm puts a hand on my shoulder. "Let me," he whispers.

I frown. "Elisa would be displeased if I let something happen to you. She is fond of you, though I can't imagine why."

Storm cracks a rare smile. "I can do it."

"There are two men up there, at least. They'll have the high ground."

"I can do it," he repeats.

We stare at each other. Storm says, "She restored my life to me. She treats me with more honor than my own people, my own family. If you let me do this, I will kill whoever is up there, and I will do it without making a sound. I swear it."

"With magic?"

"Partly."

I rub at my jaw. We're running out of time. "Do it."

Storm's whole demeanor changes. His eyes turn to slits, he crouches low, and he slithers up the stairs like a hunting cat.

He disappears around a curve in the spiral step. I step lightly after him, gesturing for my men to follow. We halt just outside the view of the narrow opening. I draw my daggers and prepare to rush the hallway.

Seconds pass. Then a grunt. A muffled *thunk*.

Storm's head appears. "I need help with the bodies," he whispers.

We pour into the hallway like a tide held too long at bay. Two guards lie on the floor, their throats slit. Blood soaks into the padding of their armor, but it does not reach the floor. Almost as if Storm planned it that way.

"How?" I ask.

"Barrier magic," Storm says. "When they were frozen, I slit their throats."

"Well done," I say, forcing it to sound more respectful and less grudging. Storm has earned it.

I allow a quick moment of regret for the two slain guards. They were my brothers-at-arms once, led into treason by a usurper. "Let's get these men out of the hallway; lay them on the stairs. Then—"

The monastery bells peal.

We toss the dead men down the stairs and rush down the hallway. We pass the kitchens, and I signal for one of my men to peel off. I do the same at the laundry, at the entrance to the servants' quarters, at the branching hallway that leads to the stables. They will all convey the same message to the palace residents: Stay where you are. The hallways and courtyards are dangerous right now. Warning them is a gamble, but it might pay off. Elisa has been a favorite with the servants from the day she arrived. I'm *almost* certain they won't raise an alarm.

We reach the inner courtyard and stop. I peer from the archway into the breezy dark. It's a square with hard-packed ground, large enough that I always conduct our more extensive training exercises here. Torches line all four walls. One wall is made up entirely of the palace garrison. It's a long, flat-roofed building with multiple entry points, designed to allow the garrison to flood the courtyard at a moment's alarm. In the corner is the prison tower, rising like a blight against the night sky.

Four soldiers march in time along the garrison wall. The night watch.

"Storm," I whisper. "Can you . . . ?"

In answer, Storm closes his eyes, mutters something, and the marching soldiers freeze in place.

I tap two men on the shoulder and gesture them forward. They slink out into the courtyard, blades held ready. They glide soundlessly up to the helpless guards and slit their throats.

Four down.

I give the signal, and we pour into the open. I place two men at each entrance to the barracks. They take up positions just in time, for the alarm bells sound from the palace wall. Tristán and Mara have begun their assault on the city watch.

The garrison soldiers stream out of the barracks in response to the commotion, but my men cut them down at the entrances. The night air becomes a cacophony of shouting and pounding boots and ringing steel. Bodies pile up. The garrison has superior numbers, though, and it's only a matter of time before we're overwhelmed.

I spare a quick thought for Elisa and Captain Lucio, because as far as I can tell, none of the chaos comes from the direction of the residence wing. There should be some indication of a struggle by now. *Dear God, please keep her safe.* Running to her side is not an option. At least not until I've accomplished the task at hand.

This time, I choose Storm because I do trust him, and because his magic might provide our only chance to fight through a fully alarmed barracks. "With me," I say to him and five others. "To the general's quarters."

I lead them through the entrance nearest the prison tower. The corridor is filled with panic, almost plugged tight with soldiers. More pour into the hallway from adjoining rooms. Fewer than half wear armor; we caught them sleeping.

They rush us at once, swords raised, and I bring up my shield. I'm not sure how we'll get through the press of bodies, but Storm sends an orange firebolt streaming over their heads. A warning shot only, but several flee in the opposite direction.

It gives us just enough room to maneuver, and we push forward, hacking away at men who used to be our brothers.

Pain sears my upper arm. I spin in time to block a downward blow. The soldier grins. His sword strike was a distraction, and I'm too hemmed in to dodge the dagger near my gut.

The air shimmers. The dagger collides with something invisible, and the soldier stumbles, overbalanced. I heave the edge of my shield into his face and crush his eye socket.

Beside me, Storm sways, his eyes glazed. A dagger flies toward him. I bring up my shield just in time, and it bounces away.

"Thank you," he mutters in a voice barely audible over the clash of steel.

"You all right?" I shout, even as I block another blow.

In answer, he straightens, then jabs the nearest soldier in the upper abdomen, just below his ribs. The soldier crumples, and we step over him. "Until the *zafira* refills me . . ." he begins shouting, but then, with a grunt and heave, he grabs the next soldier's arm, pins it to the man's back, and slams him face-first into the stone wall. "I must fight like an *ordinary* man," he finishes as the man puddles at his feet. Then he grins. "Like you."

Together we fight our way down the hall, the other guards at our backs. My shoulder grows numb to absorbing repeated blows against my shield. Blood drips down my arm, but the pain is gone. There is only the next swing, the next strike, the next dodge. We step over bodies as soon as we fell them. The hallway grows humid with blood and offal.

At last we reach the general's quarters. We burst inside to find him surrounded by attendants who rush to get him into his armor. Six bodyguards stand between him and us. We are vastly outnumbered.

"How dare you?" Luz-Manuel says. I've always known him to be a slight man, but with his armor only partly donned, his breastplate hanging from one slender shoulder, he's even smaller than I thought. "I'll have you beheaded for raising a weapon to a superior officer."

"You're under arrest for treason."

Luz-Manuel signals to his guards. "Kill him."

They spring forward.

Storm freezes them in their tracks.

The general stands as tall as his meager height will allow,

but fear flashes in his eyes. "You've always resented me, haven't you? The only man who outranks you. Alejandro made the biggest mistake of his life when he appointed you commander of—"

I dart between the frozen guards, pull back my fist, and send it crashing into the general's face.

He buckles to his knees, head swaying.

"Drag him outside," I order, shaking out my hand. I may have broken my middle finger. It was worth it. "We'll display him publicly and call for surrender."

As soon as the soldiers outside see their general—half dressed, heels dragging in the dirt, a sword leveled at his neck—they lay down their arms. I'm certain I don't imagine the relief on many faces.

Victory fills me, and I close my eyes a moment, breathing deep. *Your turn, Elisa.*

I look up toward the king's suite. One of its windows faces the courtyard, three stories high. Light flashes—the queer blue-white of an animagus' fire.

I start sprinting.

41

"WELCOME, queenling," Eduardo says, his close-cropped beard twitching with amusement. Or maybe triumph.

I step backward. I must make a run for it. They'll probably catch me, but I have to try.

My rear collides with a solid wall, and I gasp. Barrier magic.

"Please, come in," he says, as if inviting me for tea and pastries.

There is nowhere else for me to go. Reluctantly I step forward into the relative brightness of my dead husband's bedchamber.

Captain Lucio lies collapsed and bleeding out on the floor. Others slump against the wall, their armor smoking, their flesh melted from the animagi's fire. Still others stand frozen. The standing ones are alive, I note with relief, with eyes wide open, but they are unable to move against the sorcerer's magic.

I scan the room for Belén, and when I spot him a sob bursts from somewhere deep inside me. He lies on his side, half hidden by the edge of a divan. His eye patch is askew, revealing his ruined socket. Half his hair has been singed away. Blood pools beneath his shoulder.

Oh, Belén.

"Surrender," Conde Eduardo says. "If you sign and seal a proclamation that cedes the throne of Joya d'Arena to me, I'll let everyone else go."

"Why, Eduardo? Why have you done this?" I ask, stalling.

He looks genuinely surprised that I would ask. "Because our nation suffers. After generations of weak rule, we are at the brink of ruin. Now we are ruled by a seventeen-year-old for-eigner. I knew the moment Alejandro died that I had to wrest the throne away from you in order to save it."

"You just admitted treason."

He shrugs. "I am only treasonous if I fail. But I won't. History will judge me a brave visionary for having suc-ceeded." I stare at Belén's tortured body. Whether traitor or visionary, the desire to kill Eduardo is so powerful I almost choke on it.

"So?" he prods. "Do you surrender?"

Maybe I should. Maybe he'll imprison me instead of kill me right out. Maybe it would save the other guards, the ones who are merely frozen.

But his eyes glint keenly, wide with passion or mania or insanity. I've seen that look before, and I know I can't trust it. I can't trust him. If I surrender, we die anyway. "We Joyans are such filthy liars," I mutter.

"What?"

"I said I can't surrender. I've bargained for peace with Invierne, you see. And for the treaty to proceed, I must sit the throne."

Eduardo looks at me like I've just molted and turned into an iguana. He turns to the animagus on his right. "Is that the most ridiculous thing you've ever heard?" To me, he says, "I am the one who has bargained for peace. Several Inviernos are currently in my employ. They agreed to a cessation of hostilities if it meant ridding the world of you."

What an idiot. "You have no idea, do you? Who did you bargain with? Franco? He's dead, you know. You were a pawn in their bid to weaken Joya. But I journeyed to Umbra de Deus and spoke with the Deciregi themselves. My agreement is with them."

"You speak falsehood," hisses one of the animagi.

"I do not." I step forward, hands raised to show I mean no harm. "I journeyed—"

My body clenches up, and suddenly I can't move, can't even blink. The sorcerer's barrier tightens around me until it feels as though my ribs will splinter into my gut.

"Kill her," Eduardo says.

Instinctively, I fling my awareness into the earth, seeking the *zafira*. But there is nothing.

The other sorcerer swings his amulet toward me, and his Godstone begins to spark blue fire from within its tiny iron cage.

I'm frozen, hands raised, one foot in front of the other. How did Hector struggle through this? I can't even flex a muscle. I can only watch, horrified, as the animagus' Godstone grows brighter and brighter.

"Some say you are immune to magic," says the Invierno. "Let us see, shall we?"

I am not immune, not without the Godstone living inside me. I will burn like everyone else. And I will die young after all, like most of the bearers before me.

Oh, Hector, I hope you live. I hope you flee this place, find someone else to grow happily old with. I hope—

The door to the suite bursts open.

The animagus looses a firebolt.

A warrior's cry, a blur of gray in front of me, a large body crashing at my feet.

I can't turn my head to look, to figure out what has happened, but the smell of burned flesh fills my nose, and bile creeps up my throat.

"My sky," someone whispers from the floor.

My heart caves in on itself, as if the firebolt did hit me. Tears flood my eyes, blind me, for the barrier is so tight against me they've nowhere to go.

The animagus who loosed the firebolt swears loudly. He put too much into the blast, thinking it would impact the bearer. Now he must wait to fill up again.

I can't sense him calling on the *zafira*. But I recognize his grounded stance. It does not flood his stone with power the way it did before, in spite of the blood everywhere. He needs more time.

And in the slight relief that comes with knowing I have a

few moments more, the realization hits: If I can't sense him, he can't sense me either. I no longer have my living stone.

I take a shallow breath, for that is all the barrier will allow, and I say, "I am not the queen."

Conde Eduardo's head snaps toward me. But the shock leaves his face as soon as it comes. "Of course you are."

"I'm her decoy. Her Majesty has been using decoys for months." Like the one Franco killed.

Both animagi are studying me carefully now, and I press my case. "I can prove it. Look at my belly. You'll find no Godstone there."

One of the animagi steps close, peers into my face. I try to lurch backward, but the barrier holds me tight. "She speaks truth," he hisses. "I sense no power in her."

Eduardo glares at me. "The resemblance is preternatural."

"The queen is hiding in a secret passage," I insist. "I can take you to her." Maybe I can draw them away from this room and save my remaining men.

Breath fills my lungs in a whoosh of air. The tears trapped in my eyes stream down my cheeks. The animagus indicates the doorway. "Show us," he says.

But Conde Eduardo is out of patience. "Fine. I'll kill her myself." He pulls a knife from a sheath at his belt.

I try to dart away, but his arm hooks my neck, and he spins me around so that my back is pressed against him. He's going to slit my throat, but he doesn't want to be splashed with my blood.

"Good-bye, queenling," he says, and raises his knife.

I lift my heel and slam it into his instep. He bellows, and I grab his arm, shove my shoulder into his, and flip him over onto his back. Just like Hector taught me.

The animagi raise their amulets toward me as they draw on the *zafira*. But they struggle, for both have recently used too much power. Their dependence on magic makes them vulnerable.

I am not dependent on magic.

I draw my own daggers, launch over the conde's sprawled form and Ximena's burned body, and plunge the blade into the stomach of one, right where his Godstone used to be. I gut him hard, twisting with my knife until he crumples to the ground, sliding from the blade.

The other looses a firebolt, but it's weak, and I lift my forearm to block. Pain explodes on my skin and I'm knocked back a few steps. He flings another bolt, but I'm already diving for his knees.

We crash to the ground in a tangle of bodies. His amulet sizzles against my shoulder and I jerk away, rolling off him. I jump to my feet, dropping my right dagger. He crab crawls backward until he collides with the massive bed; then he reaches for his amulet again.

I leap forward, palm flat, and I smash his nose into his brain. He goes limp as a rag doll and puddles onto the ground.

I sense movement behind me and whirl to face Conde Eduardo, who struggles to his feet. But the guards who stood frozen moments ago now ring him with swords.

Relief and sadness and exhaustion all battle so fiercely

inside me that I fear I might vomit. Covering my mouth with one hand, I stumble toward the crumpled body of my former nurse and drop to my knees beside her.

"Oh, Ximena."

Breath still gurgles in her throat. Her eyes flutter open, and she reaches weakly for me with one hand. I grab it before it can drop. It's ice cold.

"My sky," she whispers.

"Why? How . . ." I'm not sure what I'm asking. I can hardly force the words from my throat anyway, for it has become so thick and hot that it chokes me.

"Something was wrong," she says. "Nicandro's informants said the others were in place, but we heard nothing . . . from the residence . . . so he sent me. . . . Oh, it hurts."

And I know it must, for never once in my life have I heard her complain of pain.

"You shouldn't have, Ximena. You should have gone home to Alodia like I asked." I'm gripping her hand so tight it must surely hurt her as well, but I can't help myself. I'm afraid of what will happen if I let go.

"No," she says, and her voice has a smidge of its usual firmness. "I was meant to die for you. I was ordained for it."

And she does. Just like that. The spark of her life winks out, and she seems to cave in on herself. I release her hand finally, feeling like I'm letting go of a huge chunk of myself. Strange how I can be so angry at someone I loved so much.

"He is alive," someone says.

My heart latches onto the word "alive," and I let it pull me to my feet. I cradle my burned forearm and look in the direction of the voice.

A guard bends over Belén's prostrate form. I can't see his face, but his leg twitches. I rush forward, elbowing people out of my way.

Belén is helped to a sitting position. His head lolls, and his good eye blinks rapidly.

"He's lost a lot of blood, Majesty," my guard says. "Hit his head after the animagus burned him. But I think he'll live."

I don't have time to savor my relief. "Take Eduardo to the prison tower. And you, I need a report on the situation in the courtyard immediately. And you—"

The door bursts open and I whirl, but it's my own Imperial Guard, Hector leading the way. I launch myself at him. Our arms wrap around each other. "You're all right," he murmurs. "I can't believe it worked."

42

GUARDS carry the wounded away to be tended. Hector and I reunite with Conde Tristán and Mara near the palace gate. They are covered in dust and sweat and smiles. A large scratch on Mara's arm oozes blood.

"Went exactly as planned," Tristán says. "We waited until half the city watch was in the yard, then slammed the gate down. They surrendered in moments."

I clasp him on the shoulder. "Nicely done, Lord-Conde."

His smile fades as the full import hits him. He is about to become a Quorum Lord, per our bargain. "Iladro can come out of hiding," he says as if he can hardly believe it. "And my mother. Selvarica is *safe*."

Mara is craning her neck, looking everywhere, panic blooming in her face. "Where's Belén?"

"He was injured."

Her face drains of color.

"It's serious, but he should live. I'll take you to him."

We dash across the courtyard and jog down the hallway

to the sick ward. It's full of injured soldiers—Imperial Guard, palace garrison, and city watch. Doctor Enzo scurries around cots with his attendants, barking orders. It already smells of old blood and dying flesh.

I pull her toward Belén's cot. The bald patch on his head has blistered, and someone has covered it in sticky salve.

"Belén," Mara whispers. She takes his hand and kneels beside him.

I would heal him if I could.

He stirs, sees Mara, smiles. "If I promise to live, will you marry me?"

She strokes his cheek. "No."

I leave them alone.

In the following days, I pardon every soldier who followed Eduardo and Luz-Manuel so long as they swear fealty to me and to the Joyan Empire. Not a single one refuses.

When this is done, I announce that I will hold court in the audience hall, inviting all Joyans to witness "an act of judgment and an act of mercy." Every nobleman and woman within a day's journey comes, and the hall is packed tight with bodies. I sit on my hard-backed throne, wearing my crown of shattered Godstones, and formally announce my betrothal to Lord-Commander Hector de Ventierra, and I read aloud both the accord that formed the Joyan Empire and the peace treaty with Invierne.

When the ensuing buzz has died down, I call for the prison guards to present Conde Eduardo and General

Luz-Manuel to the court.

They shuffle in, manacles clanking around their ankles. A guard forces them to their knees at sword point.

My herald unrolls a parchment and reads their list of transgressions. When he is finished, the hall remains silent, save for the shuffle of a skirt, the clearing of a throat. The general looks off into the distance as if bored. The conde glares at me as though he might summon my death by the force of his gaze.

An act of judgment and an act of mercy. I've been pondering it for days. And though Eduardo is the mastermind behind their insurgence, it is General Luz-Manuel who still holds the respect of too many armed men.

"General Luz-Manuel," I say. "For the crimes of treason, murder, and collusion with enemy spies, I sentence you to death. Your beheading will take place tonight, when the monastery bells call the sixth hour."

The audience hall murmurs, feet shifting. This is not unexpected. The general's face betrays nothing.

"Conde Eduardo," I say. "For the crimes of treason, murder, and collusion with enemy spies, your title and lands are stripped and given over immediately to your heir." I lean forward as the audience holds its collective breath. "But you will live."

Everyone gasps.

"Our neighbors the Inviernos will be undertaking a mining project on Isla Oscura. You will aid them. You will live out your days as a laborer in their employ."

And finally the rage in his eyes dims and is replaced by

horror, for there is nothing worse for Eduardo than being subject to someone he hates.

I do not attend the general's beheading. I know I should. But I'm so sick of death. I'm in my suite, curled up on my bed, when the cry goes up and I know the deed is done.

Queen Alodia surprises me by accepting the invitation to attend my wedding as an honored bridesmaid. I'm vaguely aware that I had bridesmaids in my first wedding, but I paid them no mind. They were handpicked by Papá and Alodia from among Orovalle's golden horde. They were political choices, not personal ones.

The day of my wedding dawns bright and cold, with a desert winter sun. Mara, Alodia, and Red help me prepare in my atrium. It might be the last time I prepare here, for Hector and I will take the newly renovated king's suite. It's much larger, more practical for two people. I suppose we might someday prefer adjoining chambers, but I can't imagine it.

I have chosen my own gown this time. I am dark-skinned with a tendency toward plumpness, and I selected a gown that, instead of being in a raucous battle with these features, reveals them. Accentuates them. The fabric is made of dusky cream silk that makes my skin shimmer. The neckline dips low on my chest. Maybe too low. But Ximena was right—I did learn to enjoy my breasts. My rounded arms are shamelessly bared. My black hair falls in artful cascades down my back.

"You look beautiful," Alodia says.

I startle at the compliment. Then I smile. "I'm beautiful to the one person who matters."

She nods. "Hector's mouth will drop open when he sees you."

"I hope so. But I meant me. I'm beautiful to me."

Mara weaves a string of pearls through my hair while Alodia laces up the back of my gown. Red studies the process keenly. She is especially fascinated when Mara rims my eyes with kohl and spreads a bit of rouge on my lips.

"Are you interested in becoming a queen's attendant, Lady Red?" Alodia asks.

She wrinkles her nose. "No, I want to be a spy. Like Belén."

Mara laughs as she places the Godstone crown with its shattered gems on my head. It was Alodia's idea that I wear it instead of a veil. "Let's remind the people, shall we?" she said with that familiar calculating tone. "Of what you have done and who you are."

What I am is a former bearer with an empty navel, but almost no one knows it. And I haven't decided whether or not to tell anyone else.

The monastery bells ring the hour, and it's time to go. I say a quick prayer of gratitude as we exit the suite and are surrounded by my Imperial Guard in their shimmering ceremonial armor. We march solemnly through the palace toward the monastery hall, but I feel anything but solemn. I want to skip like a little girl and shout for joy.

When we reach the entrance, a hush falls over the enormous crowd inside. They rise to their feet as musicians begin strumming the marriage blessing on their vihuelas. Red steps ahead of me with her basket and drops rose petals along my bridal walkway.

At the end of the aisle stands Hector, so straight and strong. My friend, my lover, my chosen life anchor. I was surprised when he picked Storm for one of his attendants, along with Belén; his brother, Captain Felix; and Prince Rosario. They all stand proud beside the groom, and Storm makes no effort to disguise the fact that he is both an Invierno and an animagus. His amulet dangles sharp and stark against his white robe. I hope that in generations to come, many more Inviernos will be included in royal weddings.

Belén is nearly healed. His hair is growing out as white as the animagus' who burned him.

Hector wears a crown for the first time in his life, as befits the imperial prince consort. His eyes shimmer.

My father is dead. I have no brother, no doting uncle or distant conde with whom I fostered. So Father Nicandro volunteered to walk me down the aisle. I declined. Then Belén offered, but I declined him too. This time, I said, I will give myself away.

So I step out alone. But my sister and my best friend step out behind me, and I feel their presence like a comforting blanket, a hot mug of wine, a cool breeze on a sunny day. We reach the altar, and Hector grabs my hands before Father Nicandro indicates that he should. He stares at me, unable to smile for trying so hard not to cry.

Nicandro waxes on about marriage in the Lengua Classica,

but I don't hear a word he says because I'm too busy basking. We made it, Hector and I. We lived. And though our joining merges two regions and saves a nation, this is what I would have chosen for *me*.

"I love you," I mouth at him. He just swallows hard and nods.

The night is beautiful, washed with the warm glow of lanterns, the air moist and cool against my bare skin. I allow myself the luxury of listening to Hector breathe softly beside me, feeling sleepily content.

But sleep does not come.

I've accomplished everything I set out to do. I stopped a civil war, established peace for our generation, fulfilled a prophecy. And I lived to share the next day with the most amazing man I've ever known.

So why am I restless?

I rise from the bed, slowly so as not to wake my husband, grab my dressing gown from its peg, and wrap it around my shoulders. I step into the adjoining sitting room and settle at the small writing table. From the drawer I pull parchment, quill, and ink.

I consider where I ought to start, and once I have it figured out, I dip my quill and begin to write, at first furiously, then with abandon, until my hand cramps and daylight filters through the linen curtains.

My cracked Godstone winks up at me from the writing table where I carelessly tossed it days—or was it weeks?—ago.

I grasp it between thumb and forefinger and hold it up to the dawning light. The center is opaque now, as black as night. It is irrevocably dead.

"What are you doing?" Hector asks.

I almost drop the stone. "I've been writing. Everything I can remember."

He pads in on bare feet and leans down to kiss my forehead. "You have ink on your nose," he says, and he kisses that too. Then he leans a hip against the table and says, "Tell me about it."

I set down the Godstone and rub my tired eyes. "One hundred years from now . . . no, closer to eighty, I guess . . . another bearer will come along. And I don't want her—or him—to have to figure everything out like I did. I was so unprepared, Hector. No, *the world* was unprepared. Everyone had a small piece of the puzzle. I had to learn bits of it from Ximena, from the priests, even Storm and the Deciregi. No one knew everything. Because we were busy being at war or arguing over doctrine or . . ."

I take a deep breath. "I won't let that happen again. I'm an empress now. Right or wrong, my writings will be considered sacred. If I scribe it, it won't be forgotten."

He considers, and I know he's turning it over in his mind, considering all possible angles. "It's a good idea," he says. "But you might want to keep it private, order it released upon your death. It might be a good tool for Rosario too. He'll know that other rulers have struggled before him, that he is not alone."

"Yes, for Rosario." I dip my quill and add his name to a different sheet of parchment.

"And what's that?" he asks.

I blow on the ink, then hold it up. "It's a list. There's so much I want to get done. I want to map the catacombs, find out if that inscription in the tunnel leads to another place of power—maybe there are undiscovered gates of power all over the world. The Wallows are desperately poor, but full of good people—maybe I'll establish a school there, or at least a library."

"If they could read, we could hire some of them to—"

"And how exactly did our ancestors mix our blood with that of the Inviernos? Why are some Inviernos born with Godstones, when mine appeared on my naming day as if by magic? Was it God? If so, where do the machinations of our ancestors end and those of God begin . . ." My voice breaks off at the sound of chuckling.

"You will accomplish everything you set out to," he says. "Of that I have no doubt."

I regard him smugly. "I know."

He indicates the Godstone with a chin lift. "What are you going to do with that?"

I stare at it. There is nothing beautiful or potent about it now. "Maybe I'll make a necklace out of it to match my crown. If I get around to it."

Gently, he asks, "Do you miss it?"

"No," I say honestly. "My true power was never in my Godstone." I grab it from the table, open the parchment drawer, and toss it inside. It glides to the back, out of sight, and I slide the drawer home.

"Speaking of power . . ." I rise from my seat and wrap my

arms around his neck, kissing his cheek, his throat, running my hands over his broad shoulders. He buries his face in my hair.

"It would destroy me to have you just a little," he once said to me. I push him back, regard him thoughtfully. At the time, he was worried I had too much power over him, that I wouldn't be able to give him my whole self.

"Hector, I have to ask. Do you want to be an emperor? Because I could make you one. You could be my equal in rank, with just as much authority. Tristán still owes me votes on the Quorum. We could ram an edict through—"

"No need," he says, reaching up to brush my bottom lip with his thumb. "I'm a good leader, but you're a great ruler. I am strong enough—*man* enough—to be subject to you."

"Are you?" I arch an eyebrow at him.

He scoops me up and carries me to the bed, where he lays me gently down, grinning enormously. "I am."

"Show me," I command.

He shows me.

Acknowledgments

Writing a trilogy is one of the most fulfilling things I've ever done. It's also one of the hardest. Fortunately, I had a trusty band of friends who embarked on this epic, magical quest along with me.

Thank you to:

Martha Mihalick, for her enthusiasm, for her keen editorial eye, and for being generally hilarious and fun to work with.

The Greenwillow and HarperCollins team, for their steadfast belief in this series and their hard work on its behalf.

My agent Holly Root, for detail-wrangling and relentless cheerleading.

Veronica Roth and Tessa Gratton, for reading an early draft of *The Bitter Kingdom* in spite of their own writing deadlines, and for giving pivotal (and eerily similar) advice.

Librarians, bloggers, and independent booksellers, for championing this series from the beginning and getting the word out.

My husband, C.C. Finlay, for long, romantic story-plotting walks and even more romantic eleventh-hour editing. *swoon*

And Rebekah, who liked even my earliest stories, and who believed with her whole heart that her big sister would be a published author one day.